FANGBONE!

THIRD-GRADE BARBARIAN

THE EGG OF MISERY

MICHAEL REX

G. P. PUTNAM'S SONS AN IMPRINT OF PENGUIN GROUP (USA) INC.

G. P. PUTNAM'S SONS

A DIVISION OF PENGUIN YOUNG READERS GROUP.

PUBLISHED BY THE PENGUIN GROUP.

PENGUIN GROUP (USA) INC., 375 HUDSON STREET, NEW YORK, NY 10014, U.S.A.

PENGUIN GROUP (CANADA), 90 EGLINTON AVENUE EAST, SUITE 700,

TORONTO, ONTARIO M4P 2Y3, CANADA (A DIVISION OF PEARSON PENGUIN CANADA INC.).

PENGUIN BOOKS LTD, 80 STRAND, LONDON WC2R ORL, ENGLAND.

PENGUIN IRELAND, 25 ST. STEPHEN'S GREEN, DUBLIN 2, IRELAND (A DIVISION OF PENGUIN BOOKS LTD).

PENGUIN GROUP (AUSTRALIA), 250 CAMBERWELL ROAD, CAMBERWELL, VICTORIA 3124, AUSTRALIA

(A DIVISION OF PEARSON AUSTRALIA GROUP PTY LTD).

PENGUIN BOOKS INDIA PVT LTD, 11 COMMUNITY CENTRE, PANCHSHEEL PARK, NEW DELHI - 110 017, INDIA.

PENGUIN GROUP (NZ), 67 APOLLO DRIVE, ROSEDALE, AUCKLAND 0632, NEW ZEALAND

(A DIVISION OF PEARSON NEW ZEALAND LTD).

PENGUIN BOOKS (SOUTH AFRICA) (PTY) LTD, 24 STURDEE AVENUE, ROSEBANK,

JOHANNESBURG 2196, SOUTH AFRICA.

PENGUIN BOOKS LTD, REGISTERED OFFICES: 80 STRAND, LONDON WC2R ORL, ENGLAND.

PUBLISHED SIMULTANEOUSLY IN CANADA. PRINTED IN THE UNITED STATES OF AMERICA.

DESIGN BY RYAN THOMANN. TEXT SET IN CC WILD WORDS.

THE ART WAS CREATED IN INK AND COLORED DIGITALLY.

LIBRARY OF CONGRESS CATALOGING-IN-PUBLICATION DATA IS AVAILABLE UPON REQUEST.

ISBN 978-0-399-25522-9

1 3 5 7 9 10 8 6 4 2

TO MARK,
WHO HAD LONG BLACK HAIR AND
CAME FROM A DIFFERENT LAND . . .

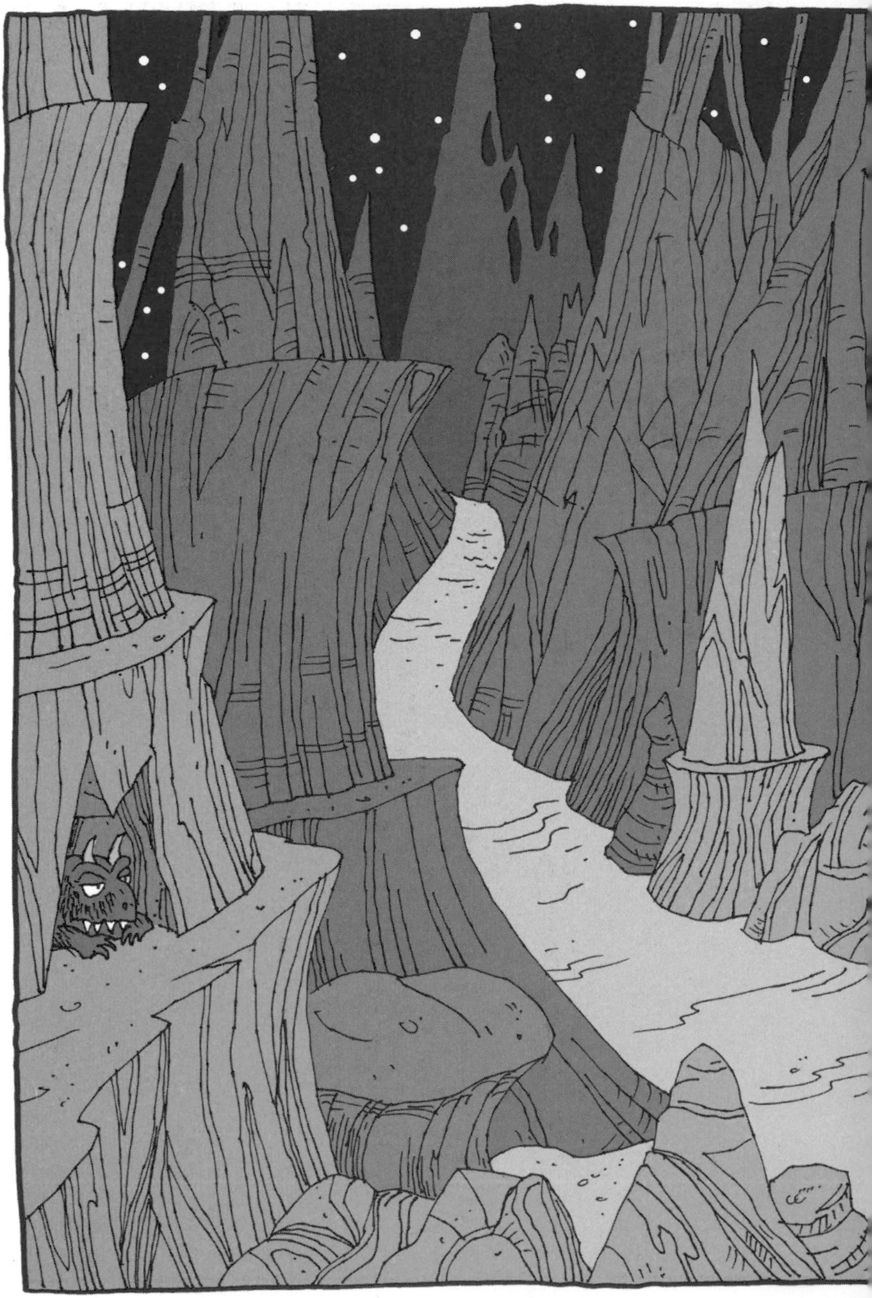

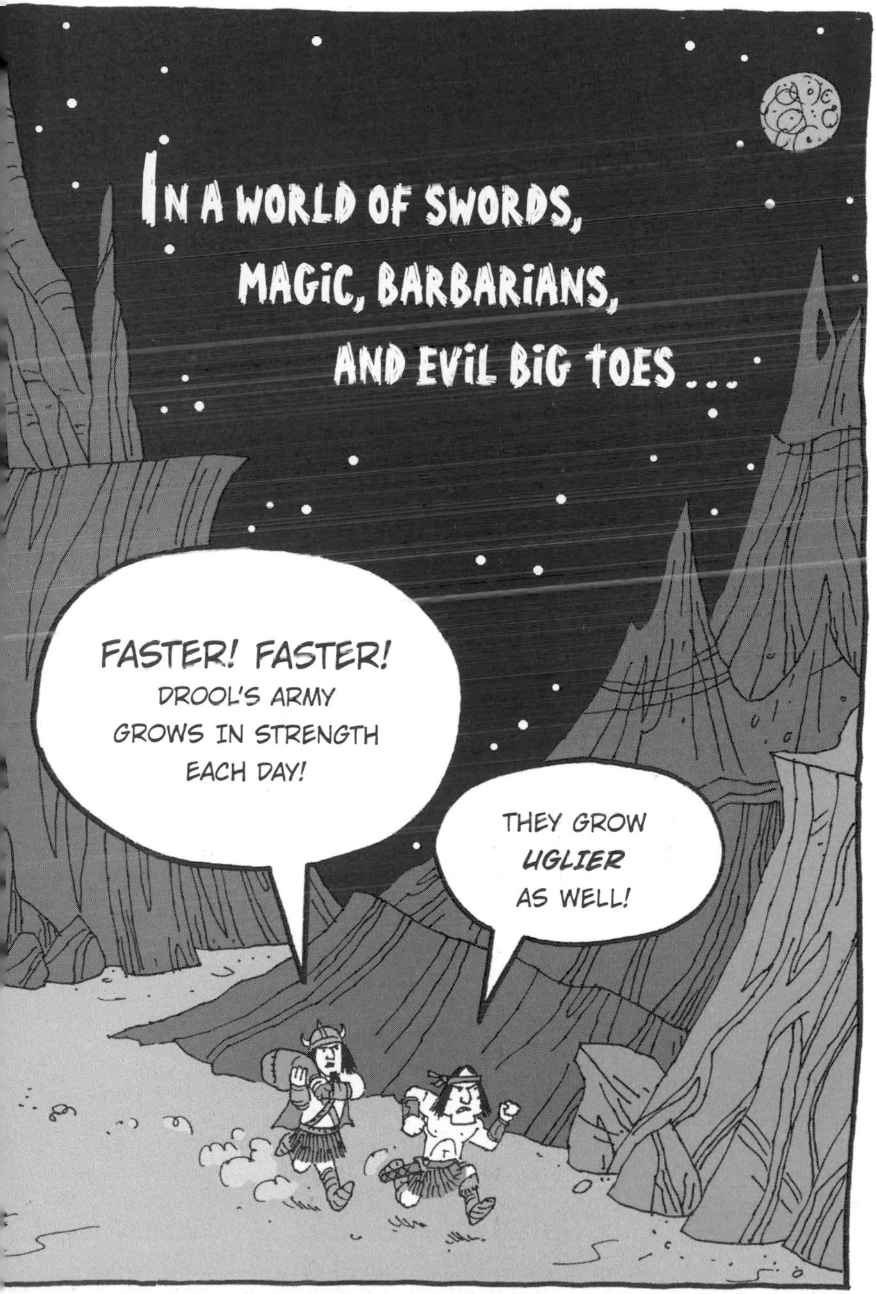
IN A WORLD OF SWORDS, MAGIC, BARBARIANS, AND EVIL BIG TOES . . .
FASTER! FASTER! DROOL'S ARMY GROWS IN STRENGTH EACH DAY!
THEY GROW UGLIER AS WELL!

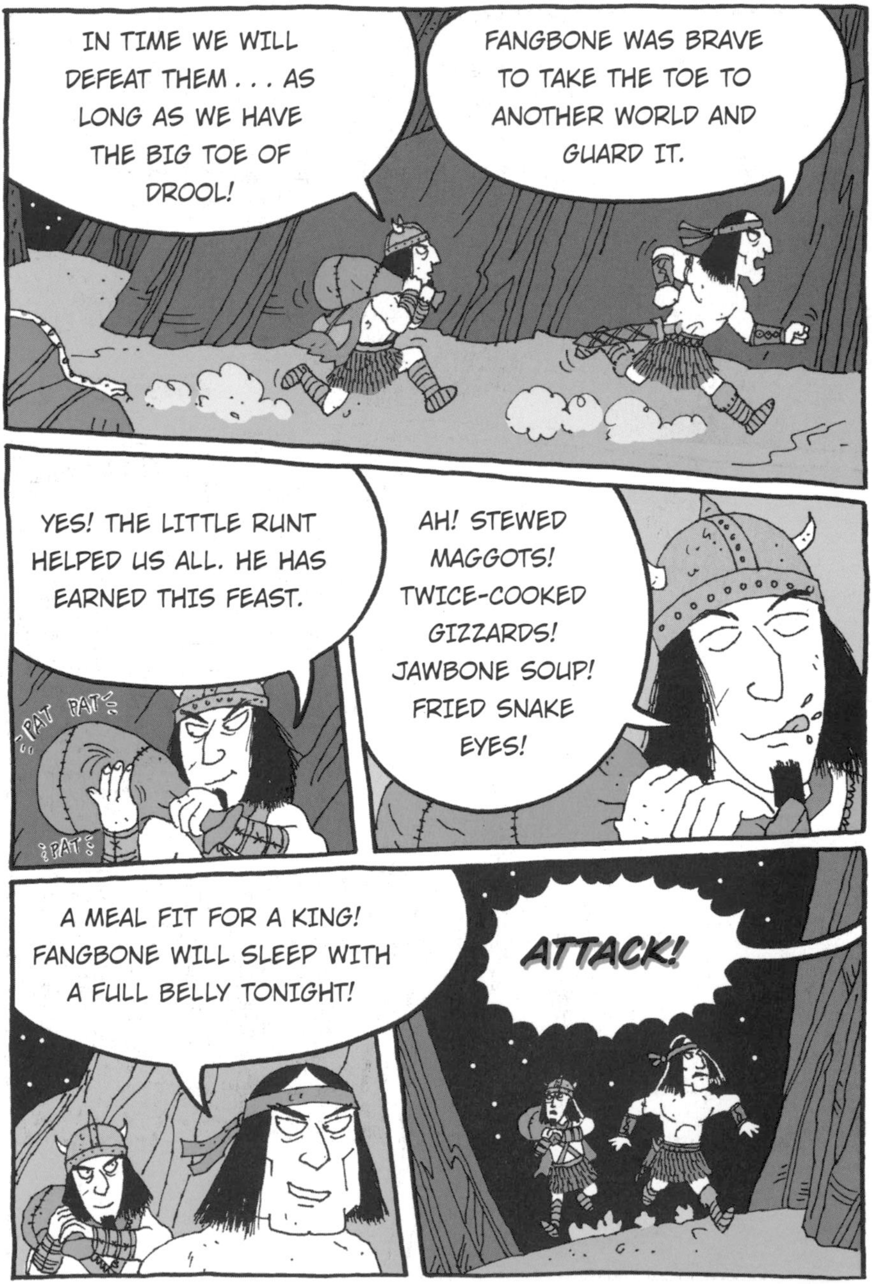
IN TIME WE WILL DEFEAT THEM . . . AS LONG AS WE HAVE THE BIG TOE OF DROOL!
FANGBONE WAS BRAVE TO TAKE THE TOE TO ANOTHER WORLD AND GUARD IT.
YES! THE LITTLE RUNT HELPED US ALL. HE HAS EARNED THIS FEAST.
PAT PAT
PAT
AH! STEWED MAGGOTS! TWICE-COOKED GIZZARDS! JAWBONE SOUP! FRIED SNAKE EYES!
A MEAL FIT FOR A KING! FANGBONE WILL SLEEP WITH A FULL BELLY TONIGHT!
ATTACK!

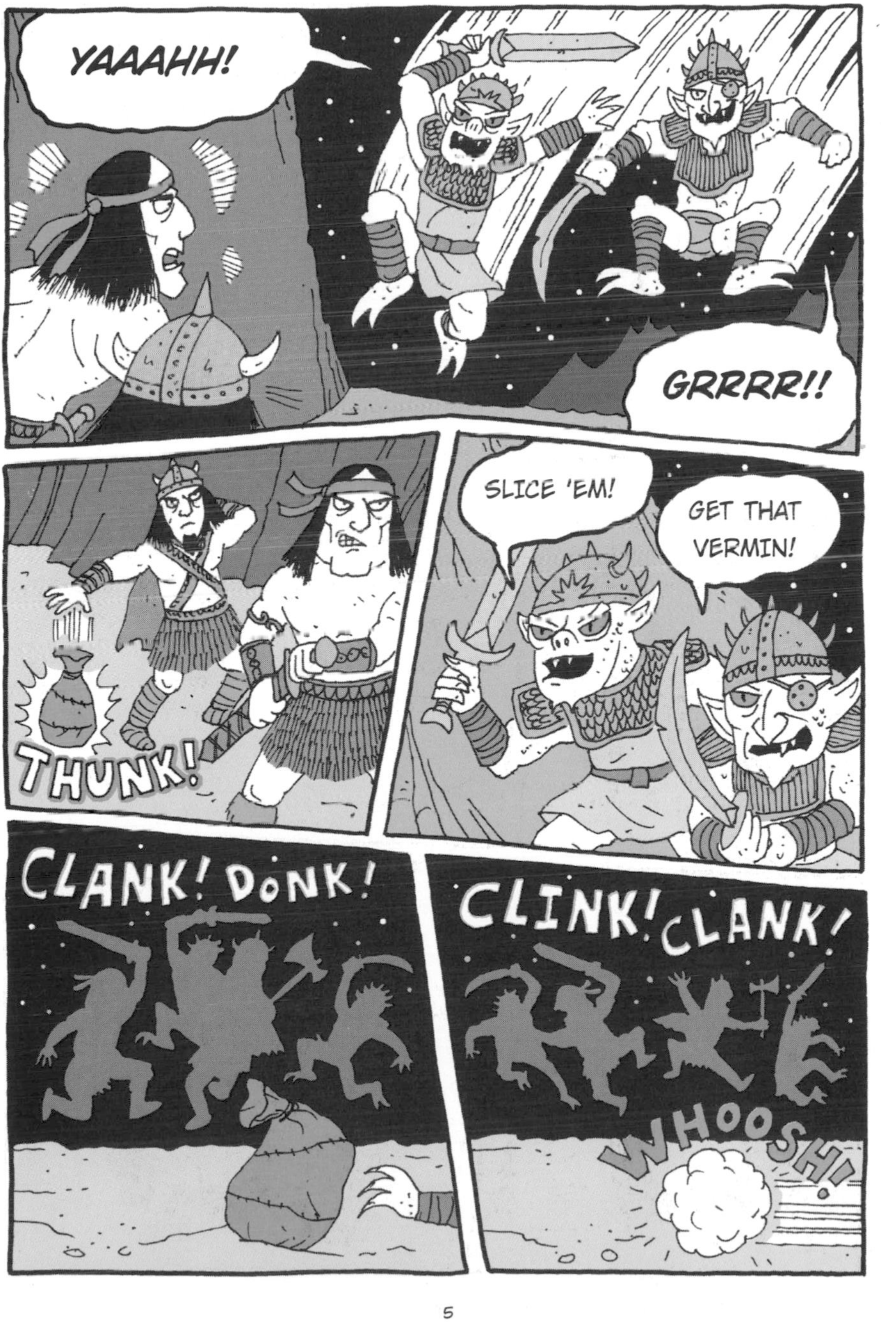
YAAAHH!
GRRRR!!
THUNK!
SLICE 'EM!
GET THAT VERMIN!
CLANK! DONK!
CLINK! CLANK!
WHOOSH!

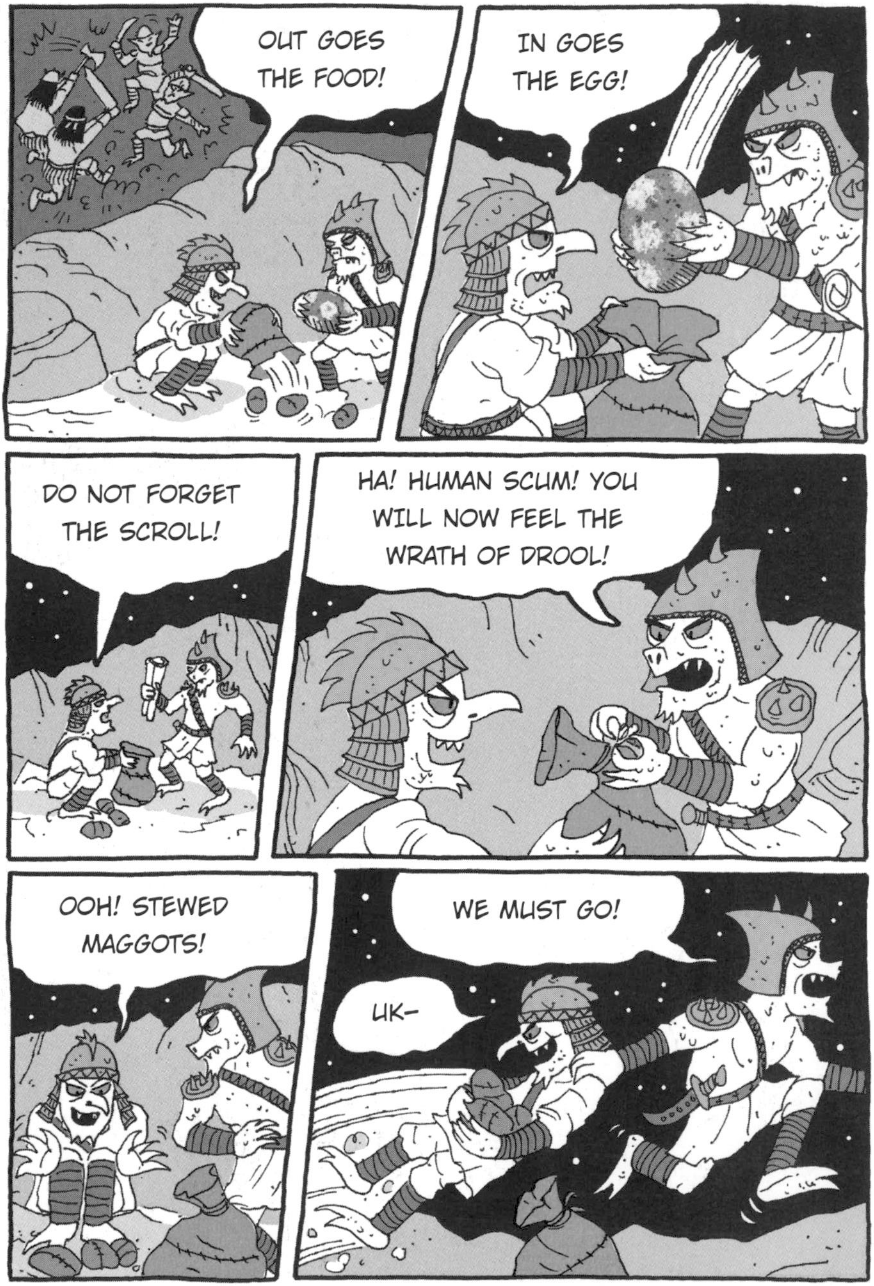
OUT GOES THE FOOD!
IN GOES THE EGG!
DO NOT FORGET THE SCROLL!
HA! HUMAN SCUM! YOU WILL NOW FEEL THE WRATH OF DROOL!
OOH! STEWED MAGGOTS!
WE MUST GO!
UK-

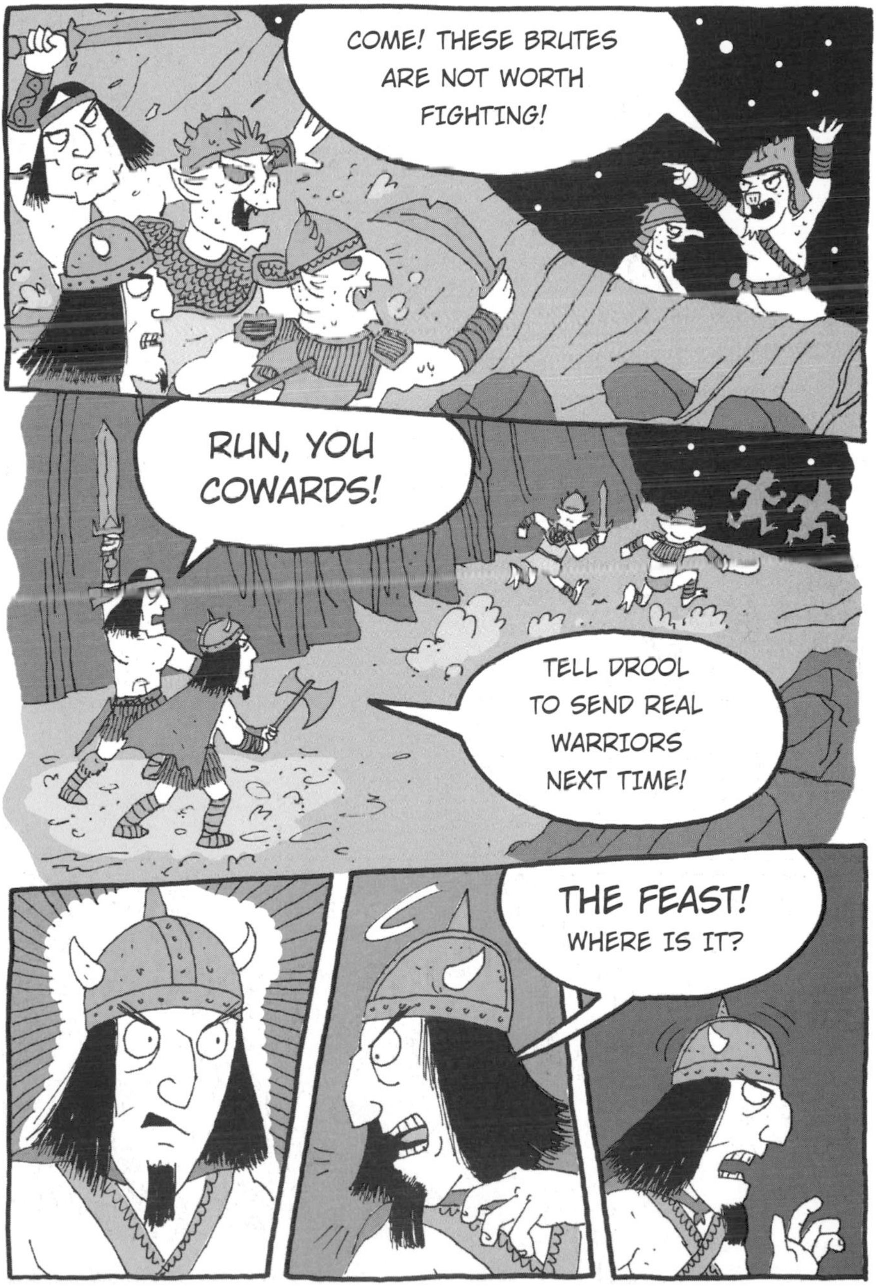
COME! THESE BRUTES ARE NOT WORTH FIGHTING!
RUN, YOU COWARDS!
TELL DROOL TO SEND REAL WARRIORS NEXT TIME!
THE FEAST! WHERE IS IT?

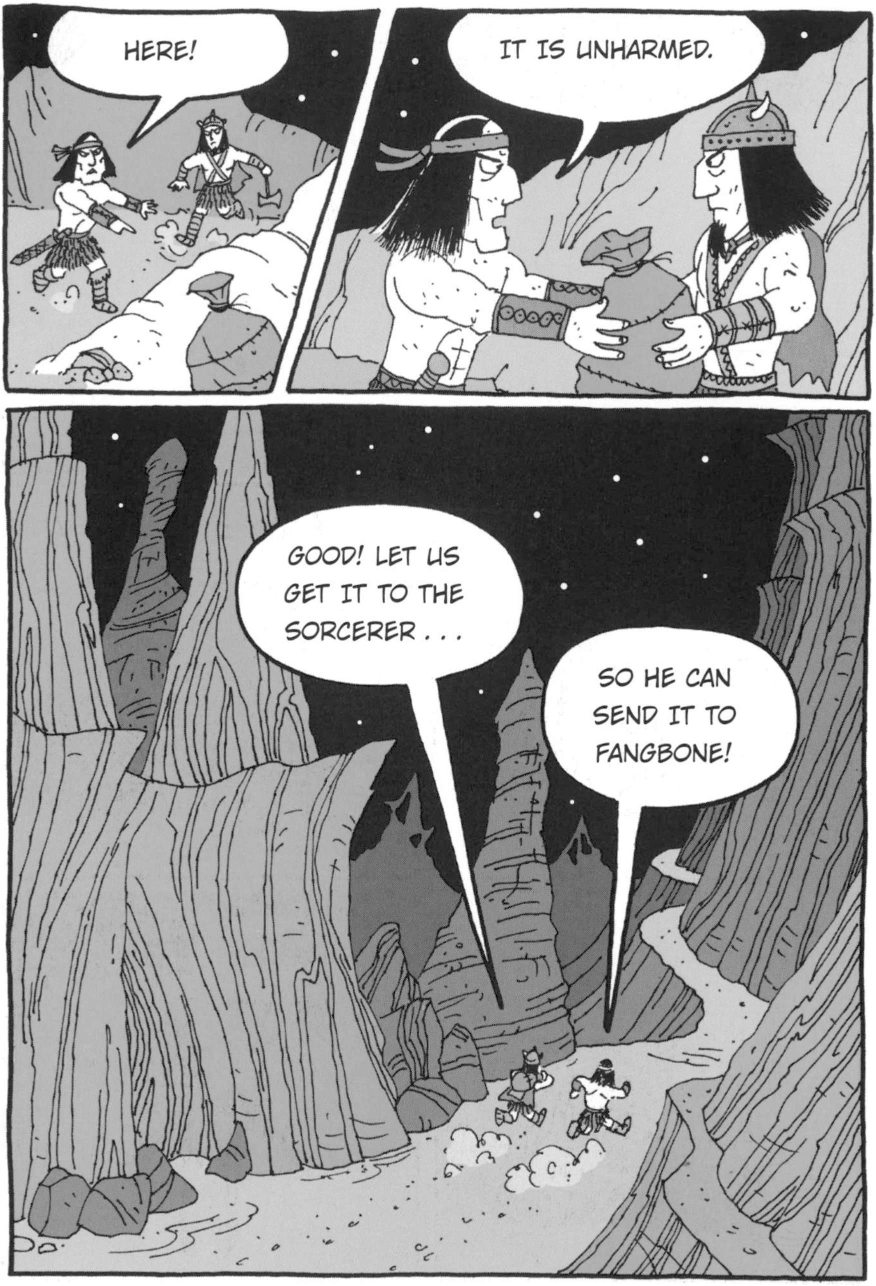
HERE!
IT IS UNHARMED.
GOOD! LET US GET IT TO THE SORCERER . . .
SO HE CAN SEND IT TO FANGBONE!

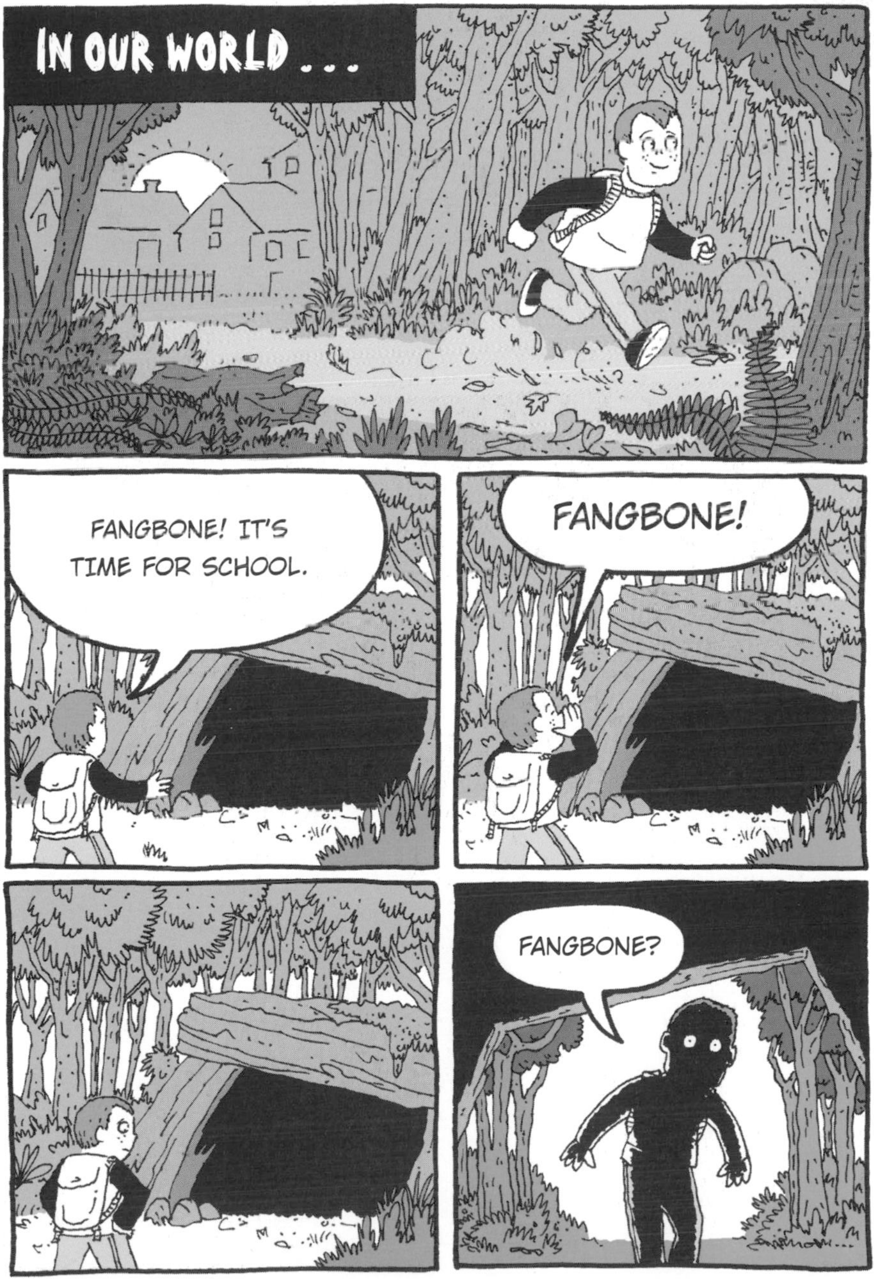
IN OUR WORLD . . .
FANGBONE! IT'S TIME FOR SCHOOL.
FANGBONE!
FANGBONE?

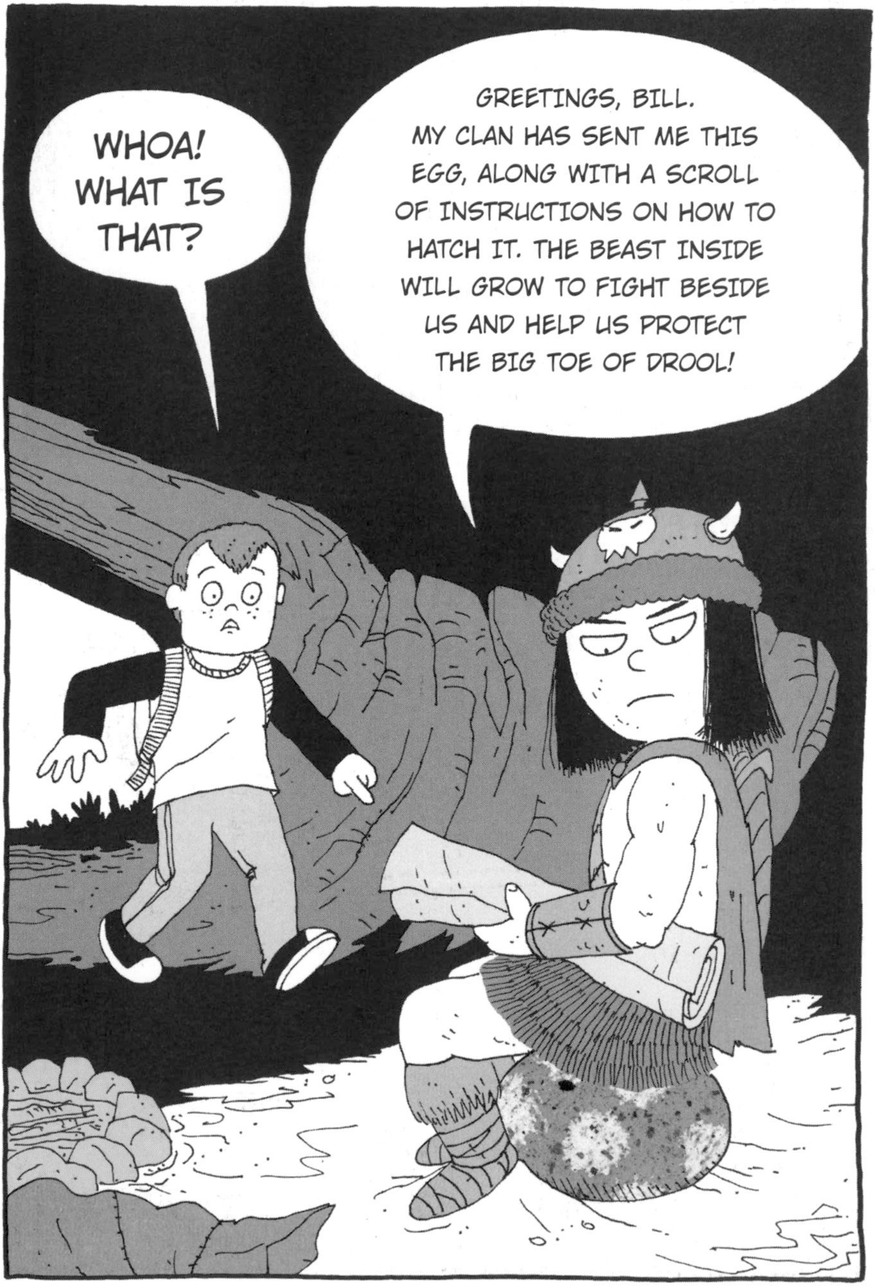
WHOA! WHAT IS THAT?
GREETINGS, BILL. MY CLAN HAS SENT ME THIS EGG, ALONG WITH A SCROLL OF INSTRUCTIONS ON HOW TO HATCH IT. THE BEAST INSIDE WILL GROW TO FIGHT BESIDE US AND HELP US PROTECT THE BIG TOE OF DROOL!

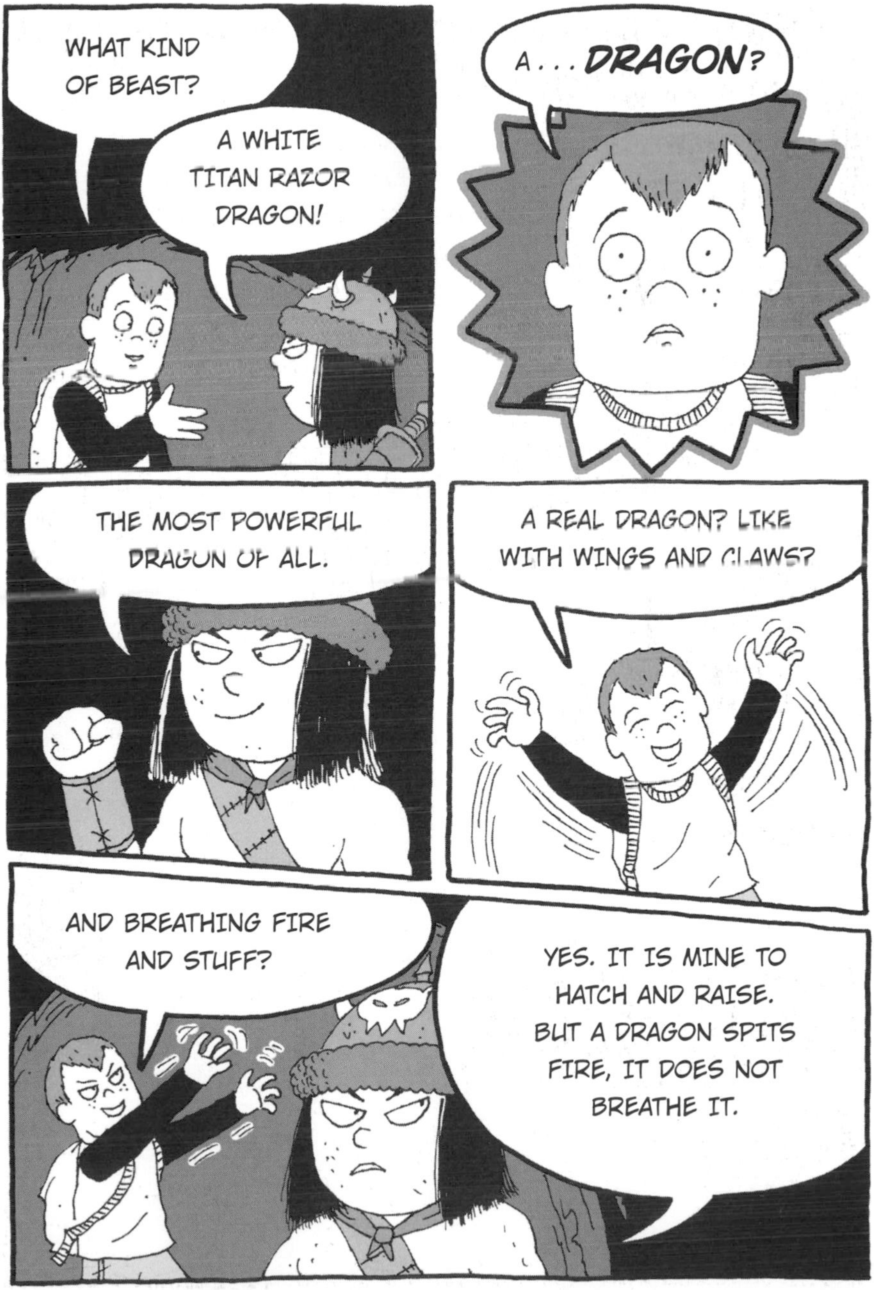
WHAT KIND OF BEAST?
A WHITE TITAN RAZOR DRAGON!
A . . . DRAGON?
THE MOST POWERFUL DRAGON OF ALL.
A REAL DRAGON? LIKE WITH WINGS AND CLAWS?
AND BREATHING FIRE AND STUFF?
YES. IT IS MINE TO HATCH AND RAISE. BUT A DRAGON SPITS FIRE, IT DOES NOT BREATHE IT.

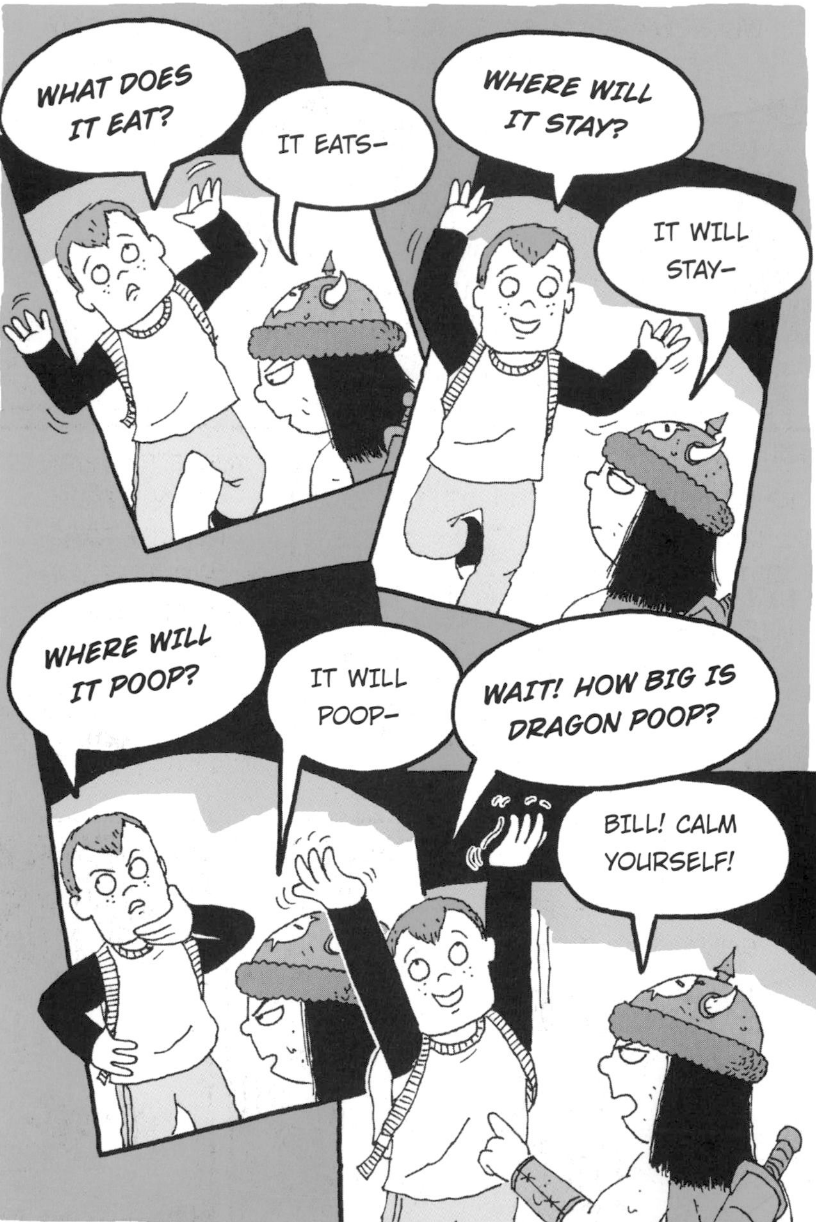
WHAT DOES IT EAT?
IT EATS-
WHERE WILL IT STAY?
IT WILL STAY-
WHERE WILL IT POOP?
IT WILL POOP-
WAIT! HOW BIG IS DRAGON POOP?
BILL! CALM YOURSELF!

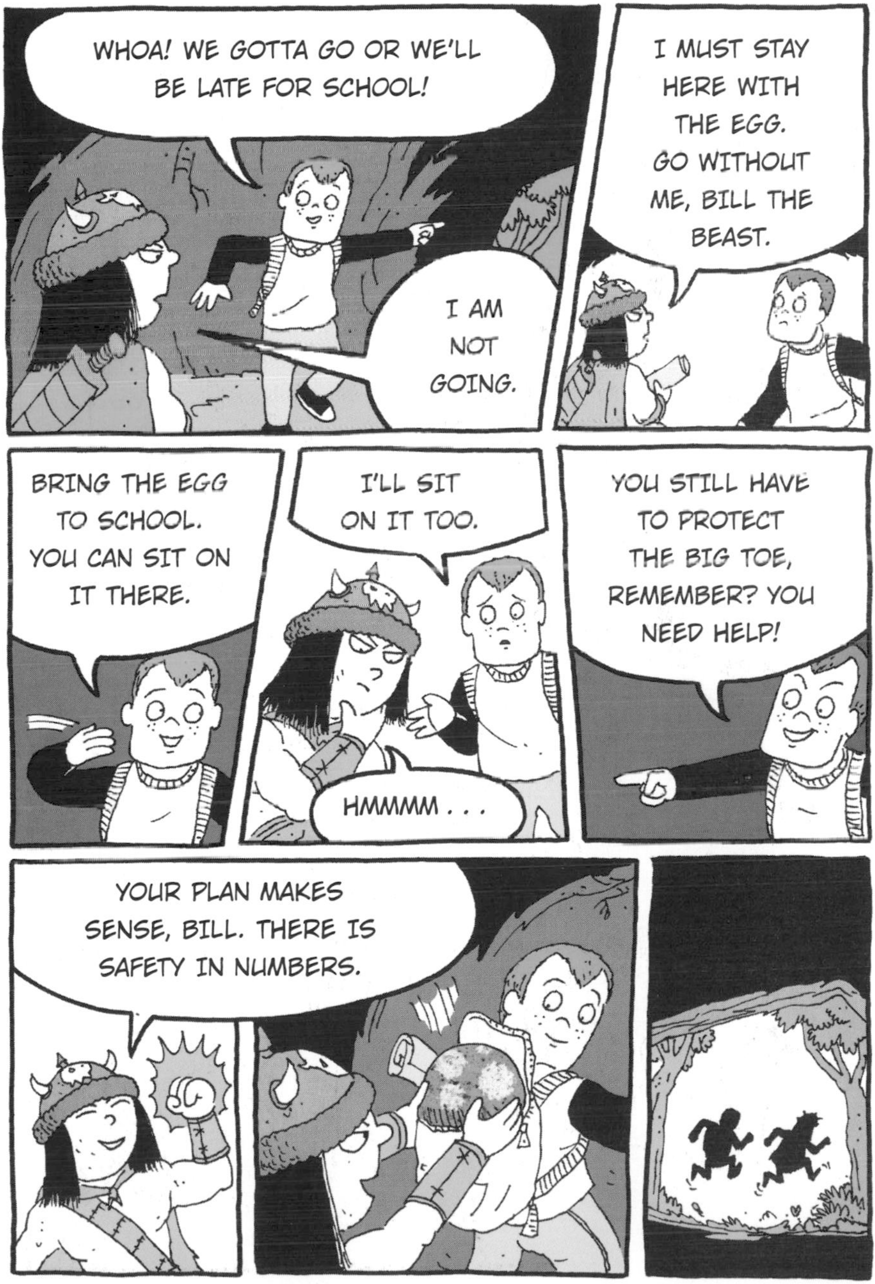
WHOA! WE GOTTA GO OR WE'LL BE LATE FOR SCHOOL!
I AM NOT GOING.
I MUST STAY HERE WITH THE EGG. GO WITHOUT ME, BILL THE BEAST.
BRING THE EGG TO SCHOOL. YOU CAN SIT ON IT THERE.
I'LL SIT ON IT TOO.
HMMMM . . .
YOU STILL HAVE TO PROTECT THE BIG TOE, REMEMBER? YOU NEED HELP!
YOUR PLAN MAKES SENSE, BILL. THERE IS SAFETY IN NUMBERS.

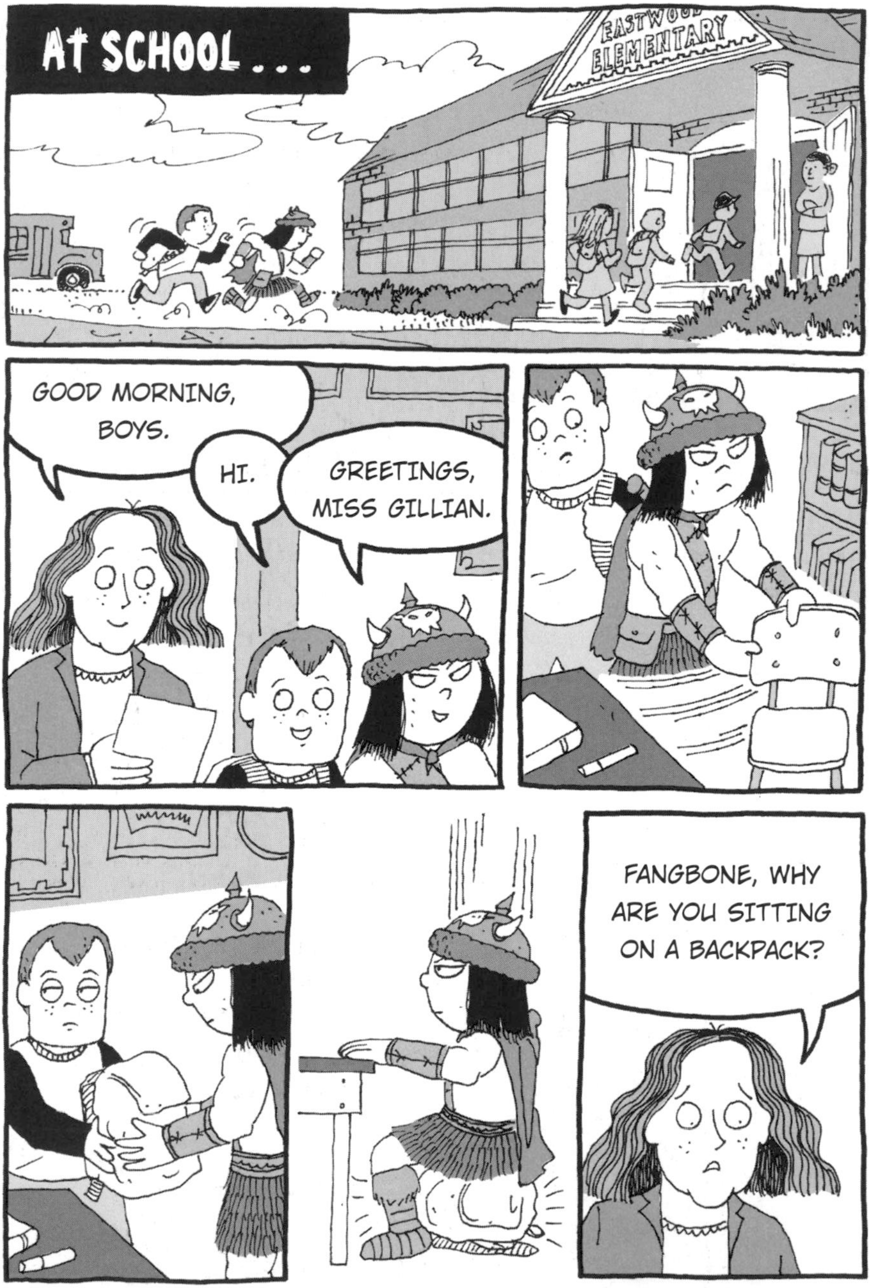
At SCHOOL . . .
EASTWOOD ELEMENTARY
GOOD MORNING, BOYS.
HI.
GREETINGS, MISS GILLIAN.
FANGBONE, WHY ARE YOU SITTING ON A BACKPACK?

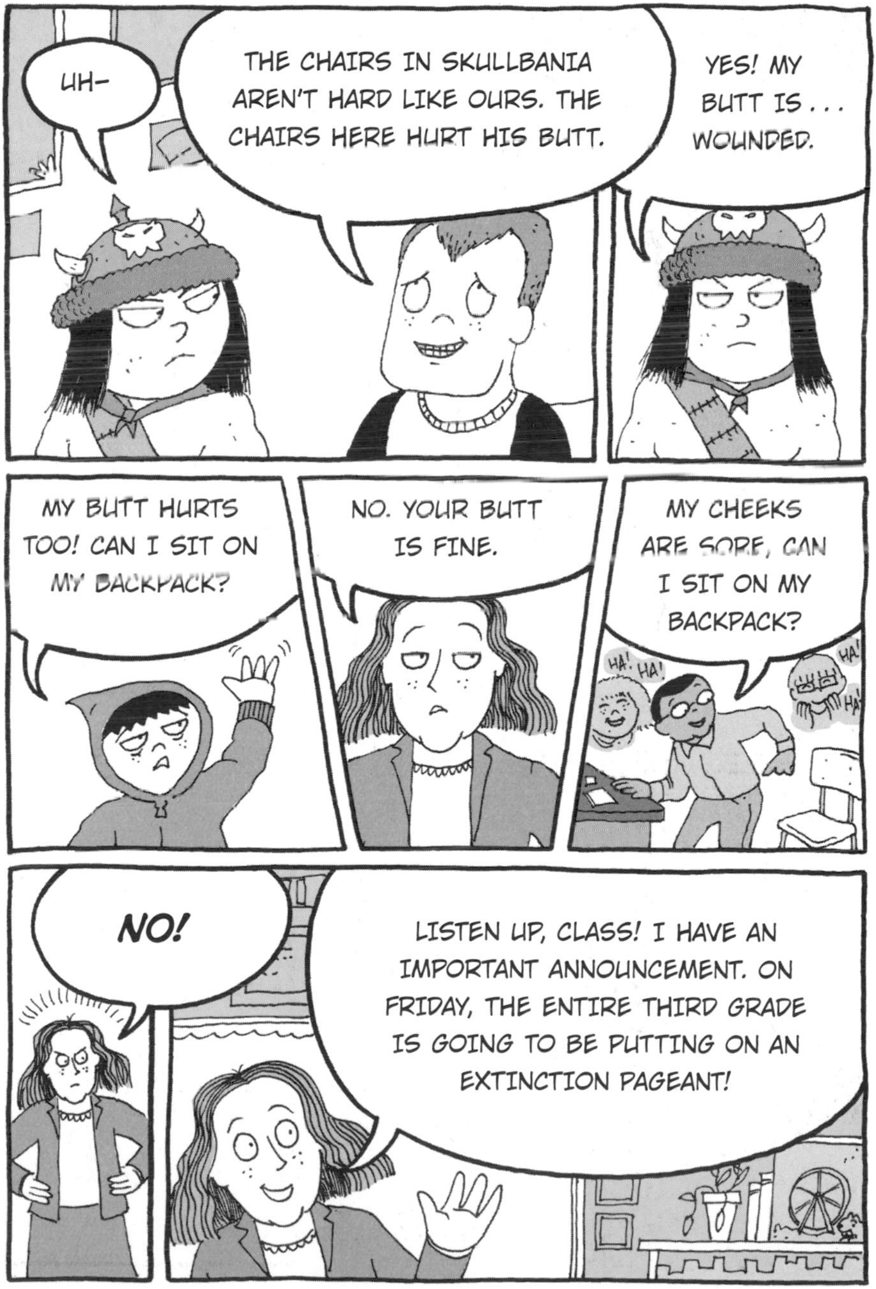
UH-
THE CHAIRS IN SKULLBANIA AREN'T HARD LIKE OURS. THE CHAIRS HERE HURT HIS BUTT.
YES! MY BUTT IS . . . WOUNDED.
MY BUTT HURTS TOO! CAN I SIT ON MY BACKPACK?
NO. YOUR BUTT IS FINE.
MY CHEEKS ARE SORE, CAN I SIT ON MY BACKPACK?
HA! HA!
HA! HA!
NO!
LISTEN UP, CLASS! I HAVE AN IMPORTANT ANNOUNCEMENT. ON FRIDAY, THE ENTIRE THIRD GRADE IS GOING TO BE PUTTING ON AN EXTINCTION PAGEANT!

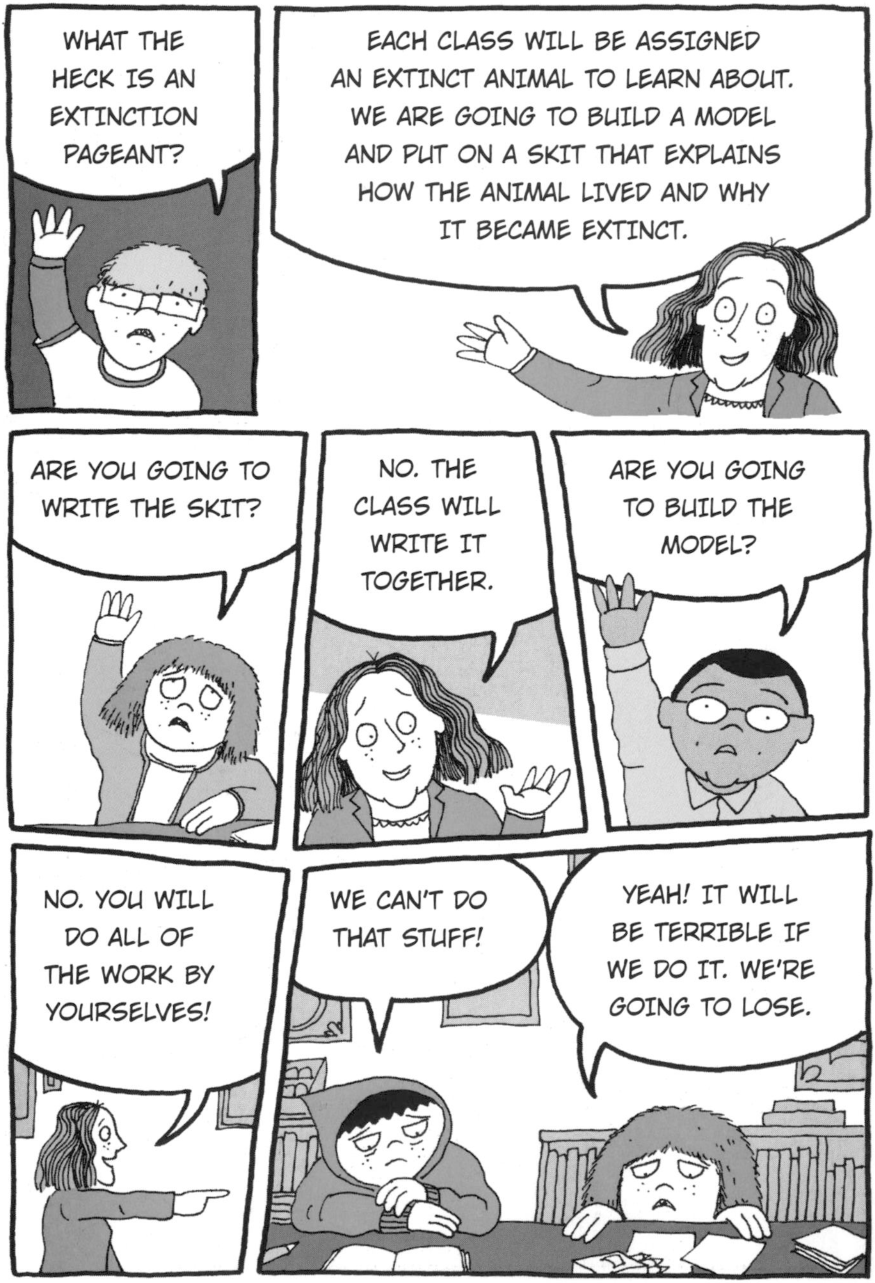
WHAT THE HECK IS AN EXTINCTION PAGEANT?
EACH CLASS WILL BE ASSIGNED AN EXTINCT ANIMAL TO LEARN ABOUT. WE ARE GOING TO BUILD A MODEL AND PUT ON A SKIT THAT EXPLAINS HOW THE ANIMAL LIVED AND WHY IT BECAME EXTINCT.
ARE YOU GOING TO WRITE THE SKIT?
NO. THE CLASS WILL WRITE IT TOGETHER.
ARE YOU GOING TO BUILD THE MODEL?
NO. YOU WILL DO ALL OF THE WORK BY YOURSELVES!
WE CAN'T DO THAT STUFF!
YEAH! IT WILL BE TERRIBLE IF WE DO IT. WE'RE GOING TO LOSE.

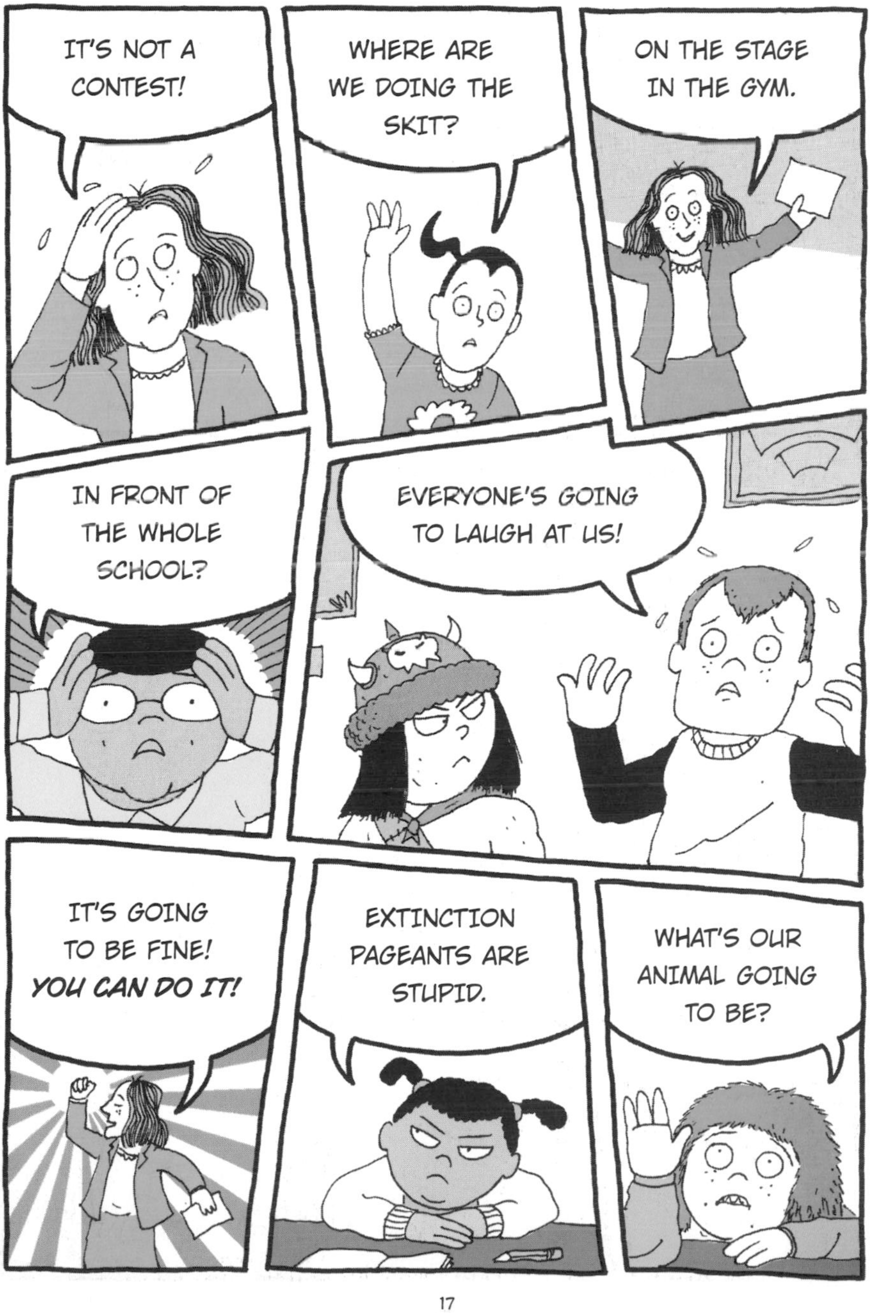
IT'S NOT A CONTEST!
WHERE ARE WE DOING THE SKIT?
ON THE STAGE IN THE GYM.
IN FRONT OF THE WHOLE SCHOOL?
EVERYONE'S GOING TO LAUGH AT US!
IT'S GOING TO BE FINE! YOU CAN DO IT!
EXTINCTION PAGEANTS ARE STUPID.
WHAT'S OUR ANIMAL GOING TO BE?

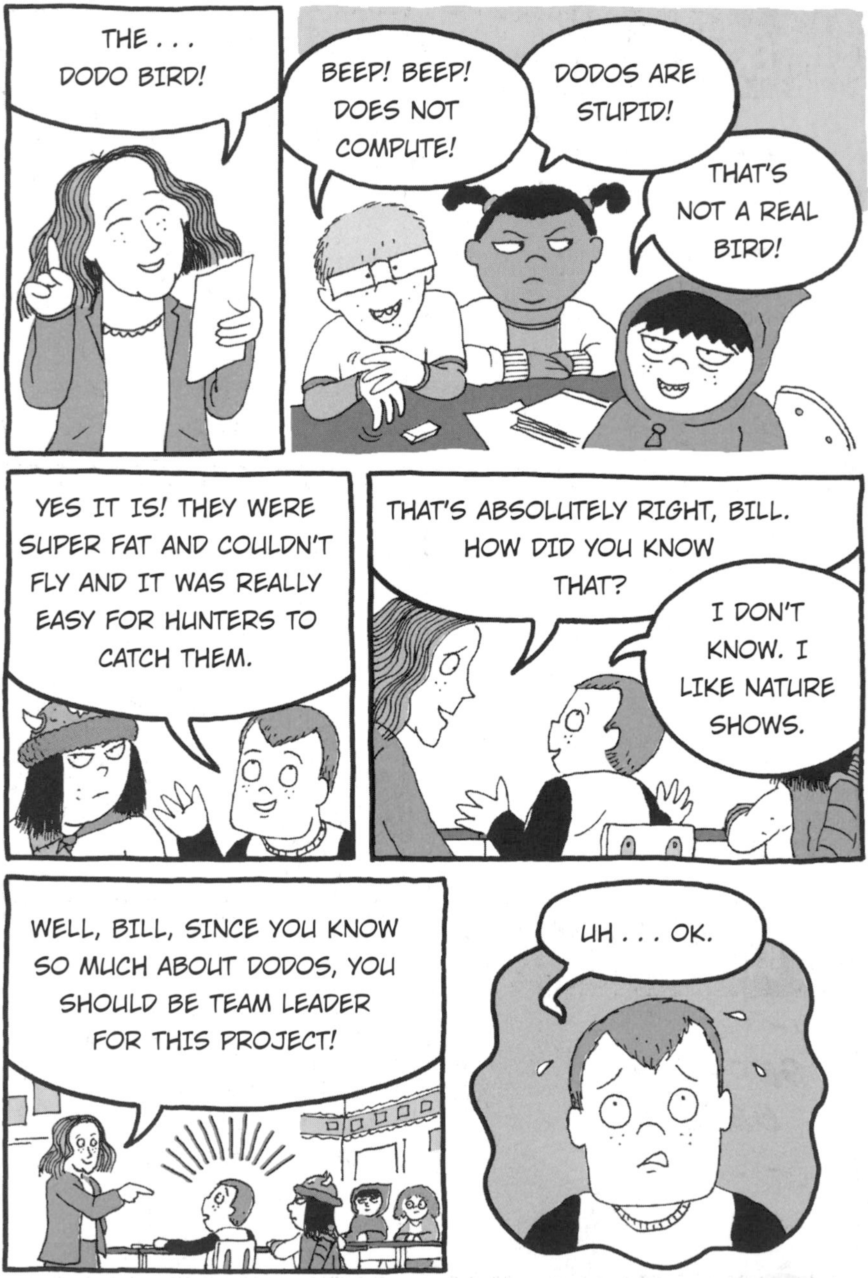
THE . . . DODO BIRD!
BEEP! BEEP! DOES NOT COMPUTE!
DODOS ARE STUPID!
THAT'S NOT A REAL BIRD!
YES IT IS! THEY WERE SUPER FAT AND COULDN'T FLY AND IT WAS REALLY EASY FOR HUNTERS TO CATCH THEM.
THAT'S ABSOLUTELY RIGHT, BILL. HOW DID YOU KNOW THAT?
I DON'T KNOW. I LIKE NATURE SHOWS.
WELL, BILL, SINCE YOU KNOW SO MUCH ABOUT DODOS, YOU SHOULD BE TEAM LEADER FOR THIS PROJECT!
UH . . . OK.

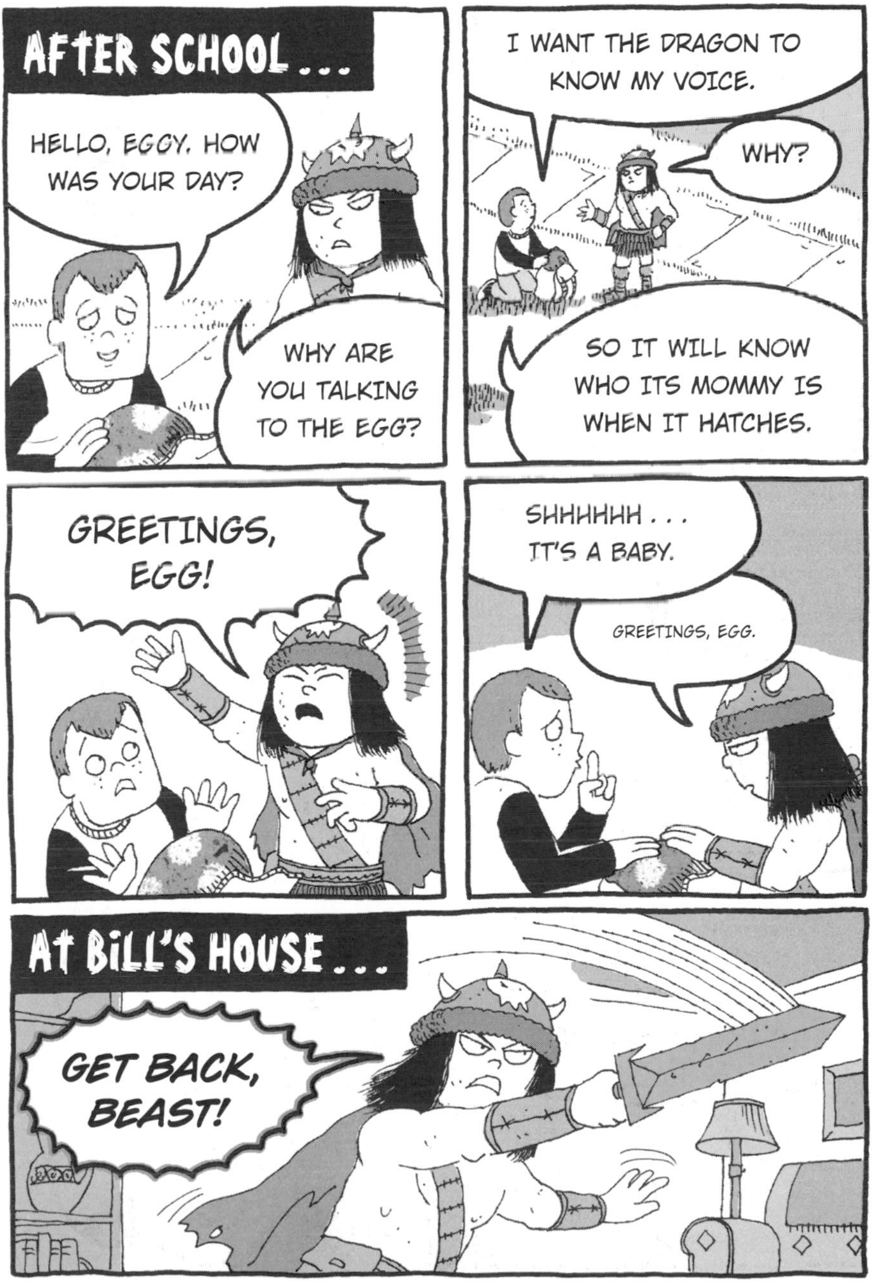
AFTER SCHOOL . . .
HELLO, EGGY. HOW WAS YOUR DAY?
WHY ARE YOU TALKING TO THE EGG?
I WANT THE DRAGON TO KNOW MY VOICE.
WHY?
SO IT WILL KNOW WHO ITS MOMMY IS WHEN IT HATCHES.
GREETINGS, EGG!
SHHHHHH . . . IT'S A BABY.
GREETINGS, EGG.
AT BILL'S HOUSE . . .
GET BACK, BEAST!

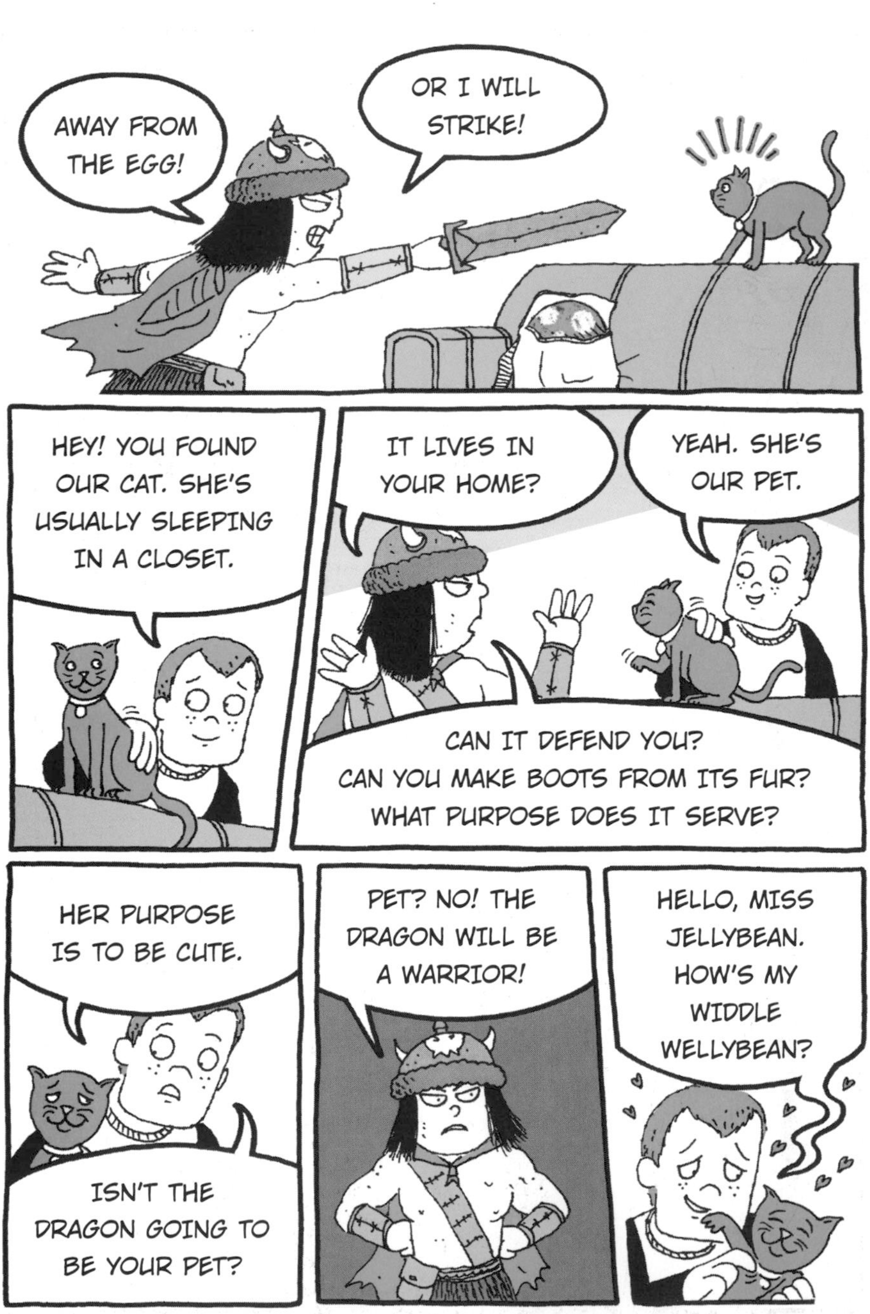
AWAY FROM THE EGG!
OR I WILL STRIKE!
HEY! YOU FOUND OUR CAT. SHE'S USUALLY SLEEPING IN A CLOSET.
IT LIVES IN YOUR HOME?
YEAH. SHE'S OUR PET.
CAN IT DEFEND YOU? CAN YOU MAKE BOOTS FROM ITS FUR? WHAT PURPOSE DOES IT SERVE?
HER PURPOSE IS TO BE CUTE.
ISN'T THE DRAGON GOING TO BE YOUR PET?
PET? NO! THE DRAGON WILL BE A WARRIOR!
HELLO, MISS JELLYBEAN. HOW'S MY WIDDLE WELLYBEAN?

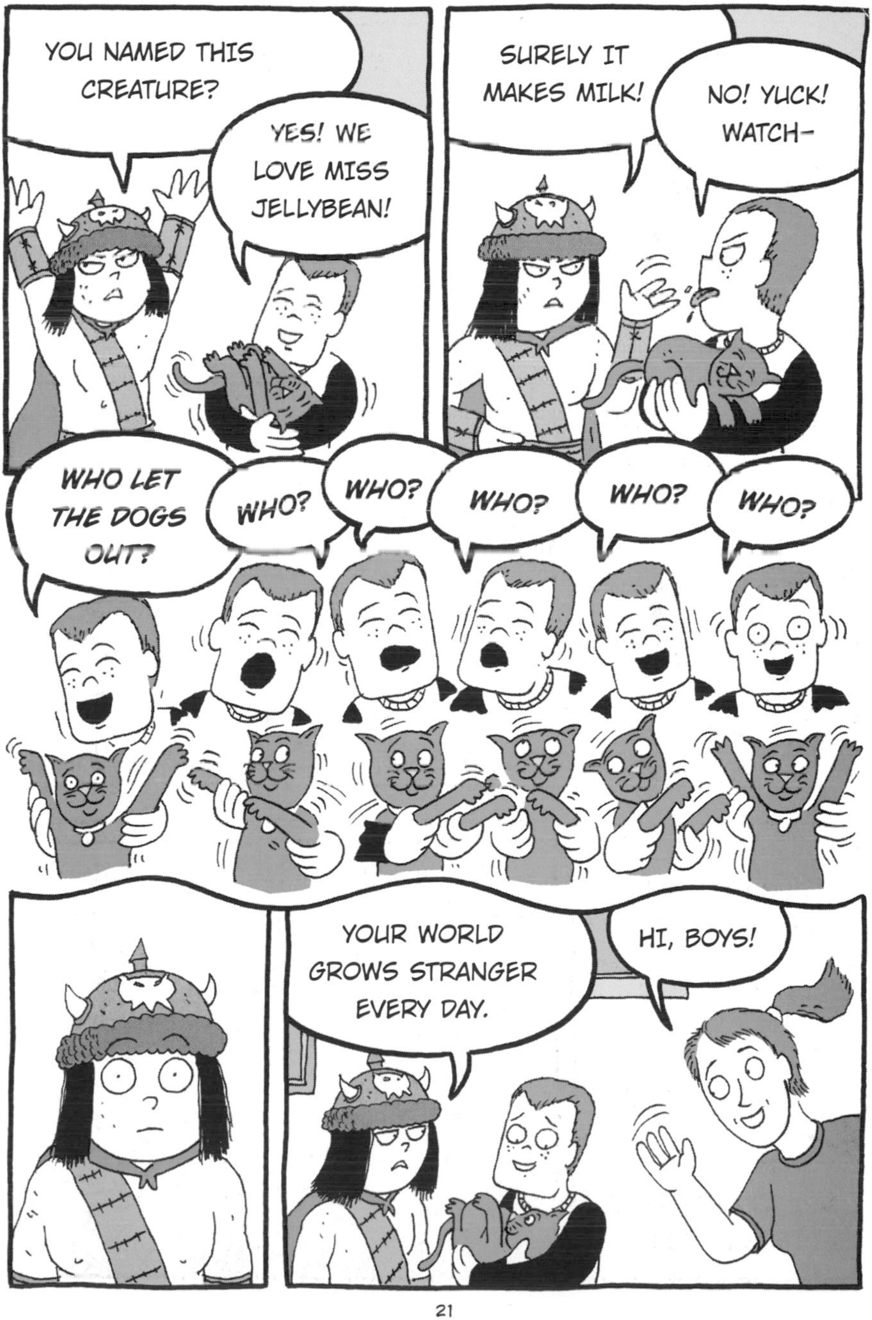
YOU NAMED THIS CREATURE?
YES! WE LOVE MISS JELLYBEAN!
SURELY IT MAKES MILK!
NO! YUCK! WATCH–
WHO LET THE DOGS OUT?
WHO?
WHO?
WHO?
WHO?
WHO?
YOUR WORLD GROWS STRANGER EVERY DAY.
HI, BOYS!

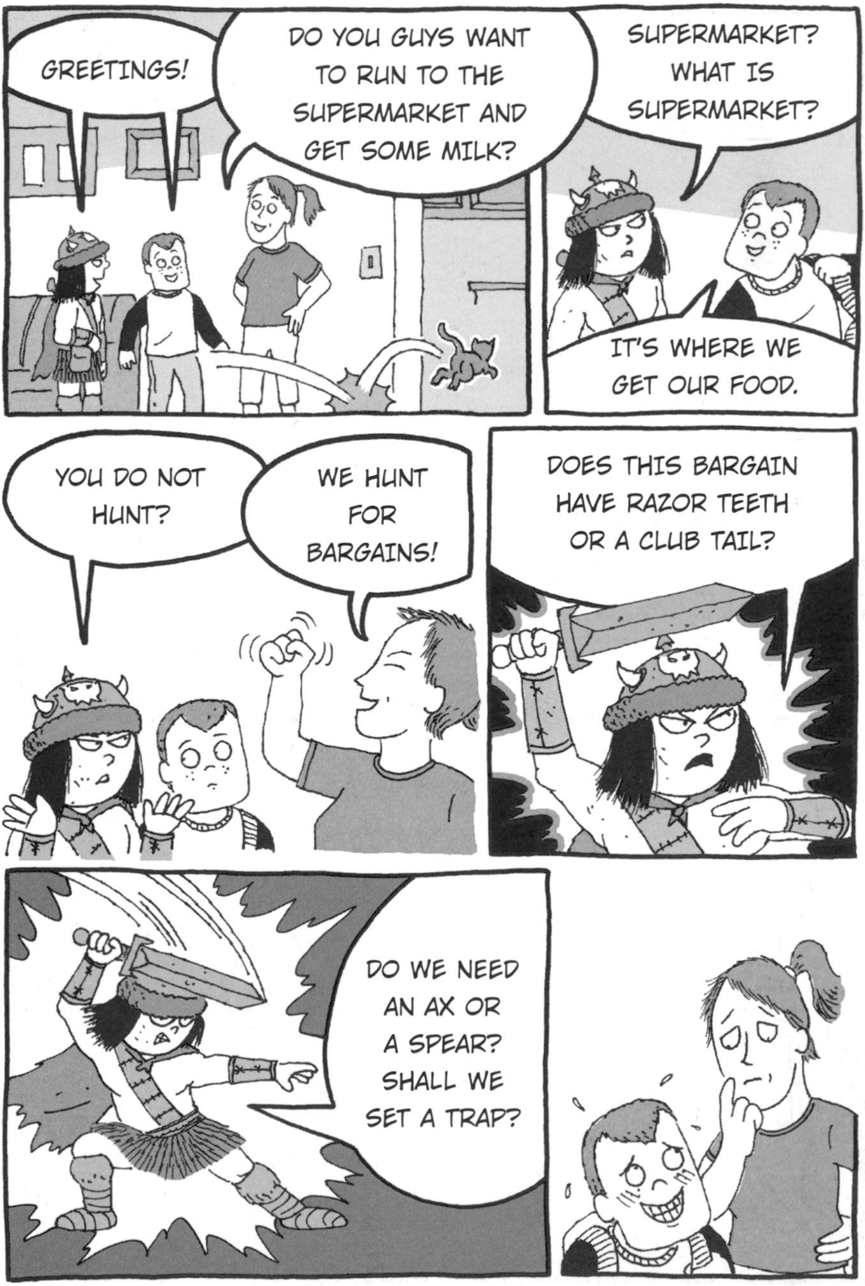
GREETINGS!
DO YOU GUYS WANT TO RUN TO THE SUPERMARKET AND GET SOME MILK?
SUPERMARKET? WHAT IS SUPERMARKET?
IT'S WHERE WE GET OUR FOOD.
YOU DO NOT HUNT?
WE HUNT FOR BARGAINS!
DOES THIS BARGAIN HAVE RAZOR TEETH OR A CLUB TAIL?
DO WE NEED AN AX OR A SPEAR? SHALL WE SET A TRAP?

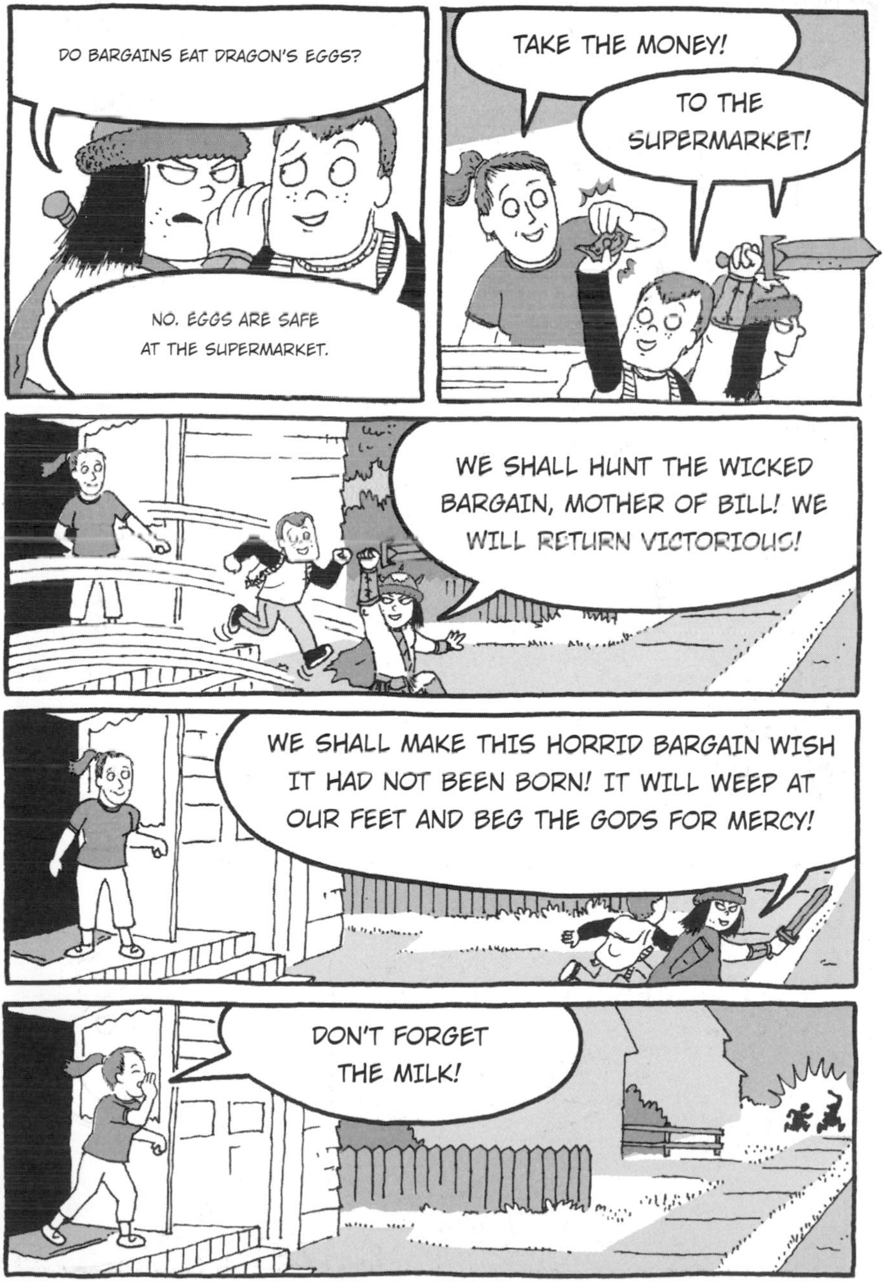
DO BARGAINS EAT DRAGON'S EGGS?
NO. EGGS ARE SAFE AT THE SUPERMARKET.
TAKE THE MONEY!
TO THE SUPERMARKET!
WE SHALL HUNT THE WICKED BARGAIN, MOTHER OF BILL! WE WILL RETURN VICTORIOUS!
WE SHALL MAKE THIS HORRID BARGAIN WISH IT HAD NOT BEEN BORN! IT WILL WEEP AT OUR FEET AND BEG THE GODS FOR MERCY!
DON'T FORGET THE MILK!

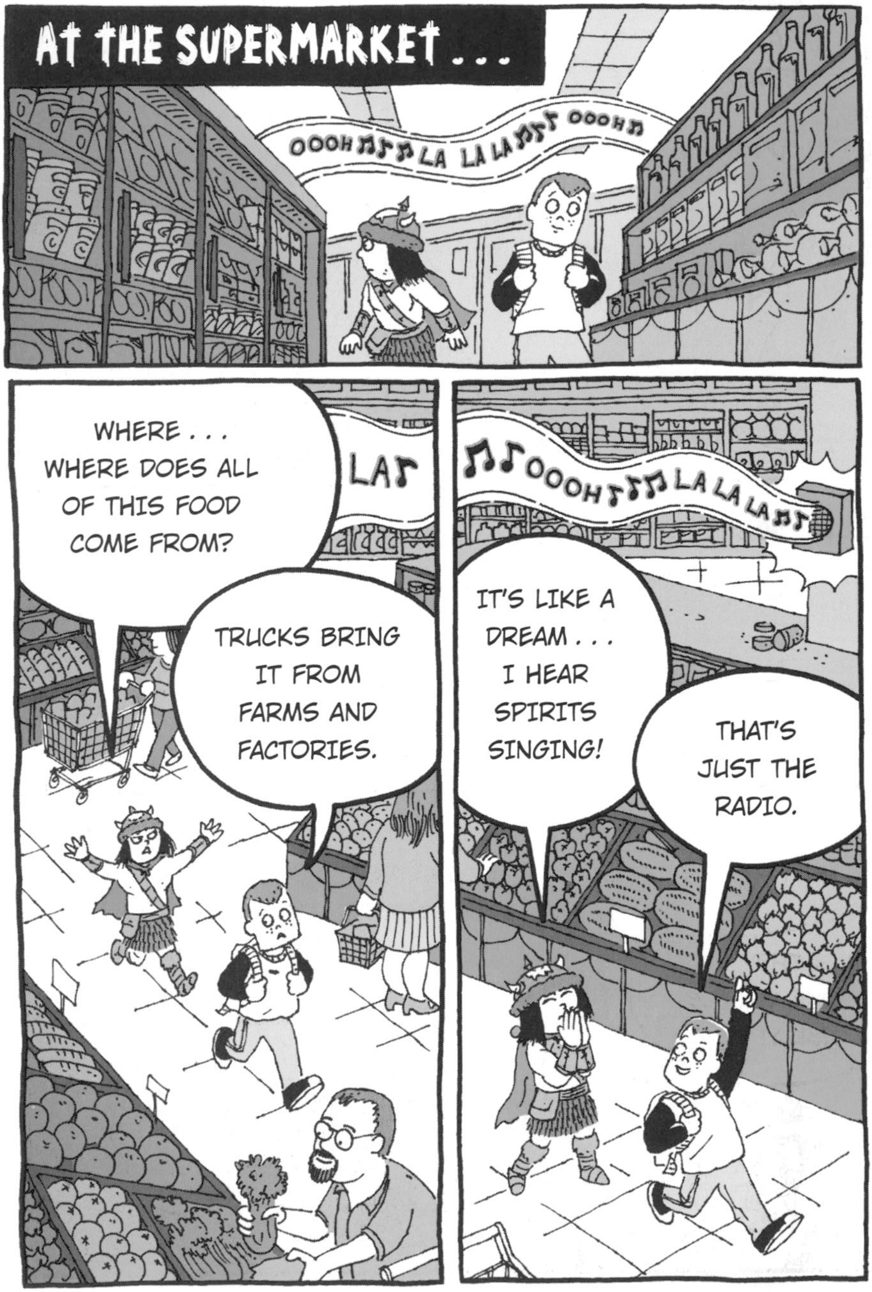
AT THE SUPERMARKET . . .
OOOH LA LA LA OOOH
WHERE . . . WHERE DOES ALL OF THIS FOOD COME FROM?
TRUCKS BRING IT FROM FARMS AND FACTORIES.
LA
OOOH LA LA LA
IT'S LIKE A DREAM . . . I HEAR SPIRITS SINGING!
THAT'S JUST THE RADIO.

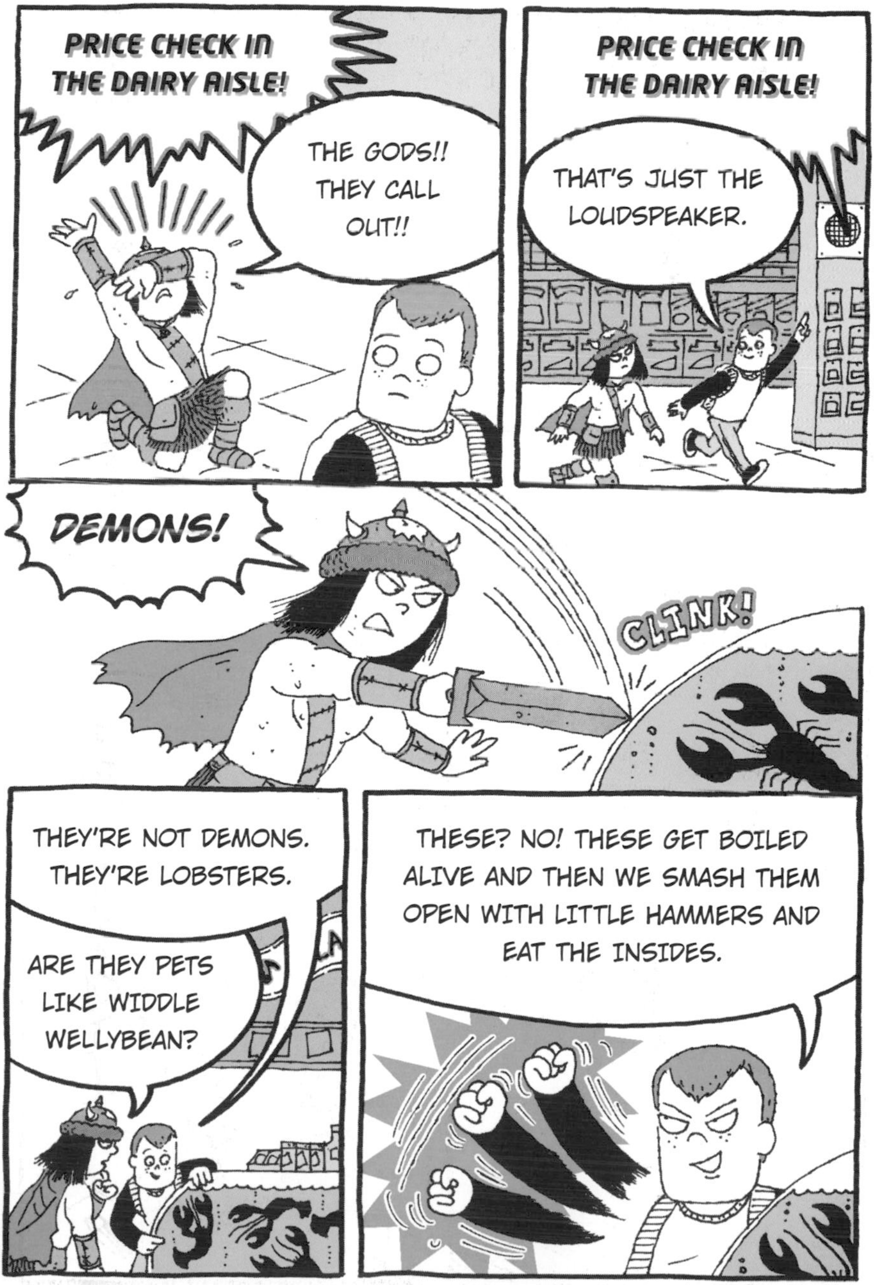
PRICE CHECK IN THE DAIRY AISLE!
THE GODS!! THEY CALL OUT!!
PRICE CHECK IN THE DAIRY AISLE!
THAT'S JUST THE LOUDSPEAKER.
DEMONS!
CLINK!
THEY'RE NOT DEMONS. THEY'RE LOBSTERS.
ARE THEY PETS LIKE WIDDLE WELLYBEAN?
THESE? NO! THESE GET BOILED ALIVE AND THEN WE SMASH THEM OPEN WITH LITTLE HAMMERS AND EAT THE INSIDES.

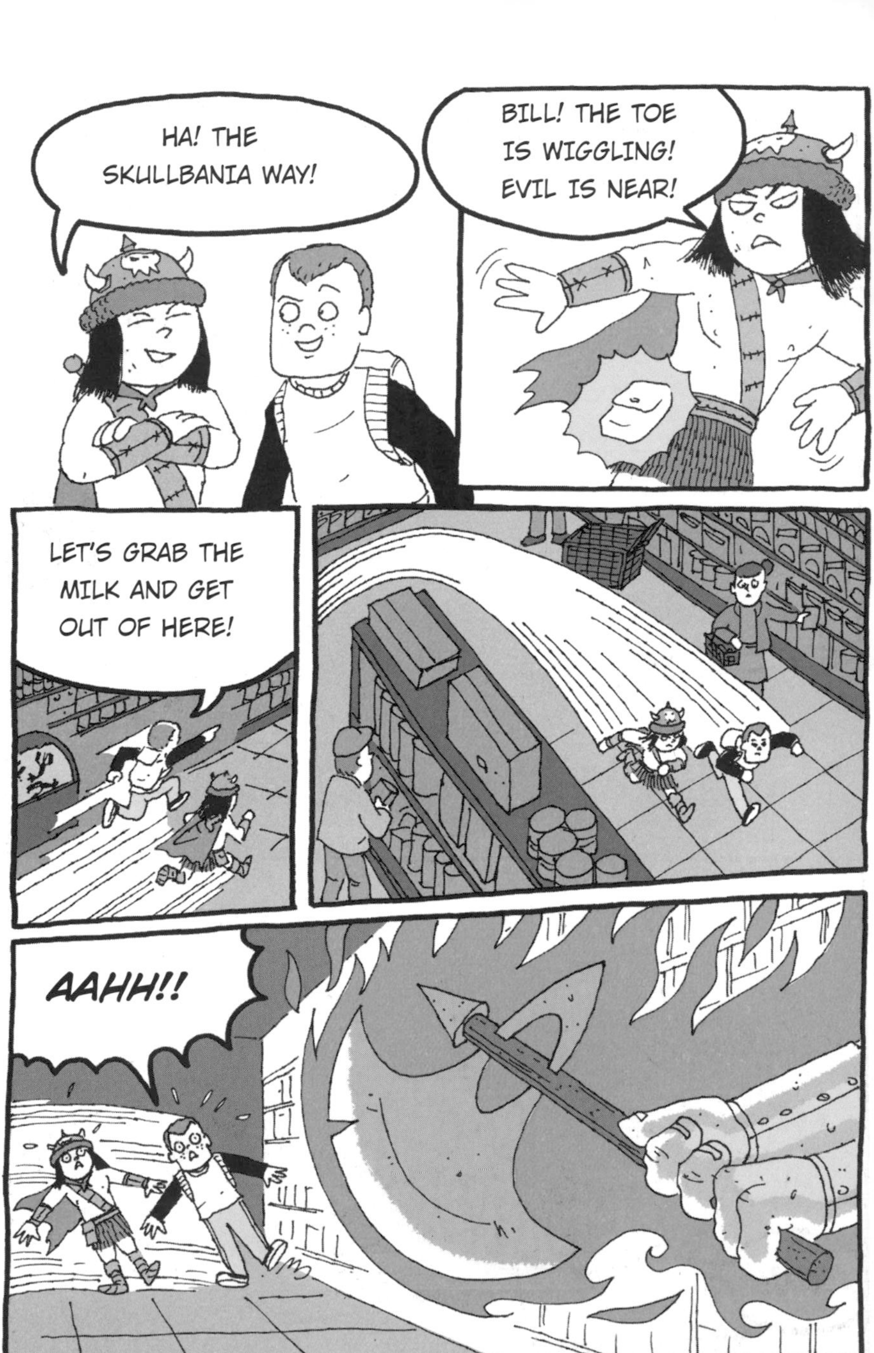
HA! THE SKULLBANIA WAY!
BILL! THE TOE IS WIGGLING! EVIL IS NEAR!
LET'S GRAB THE MILK AND GET OUT OF HERE!
AAHH!!

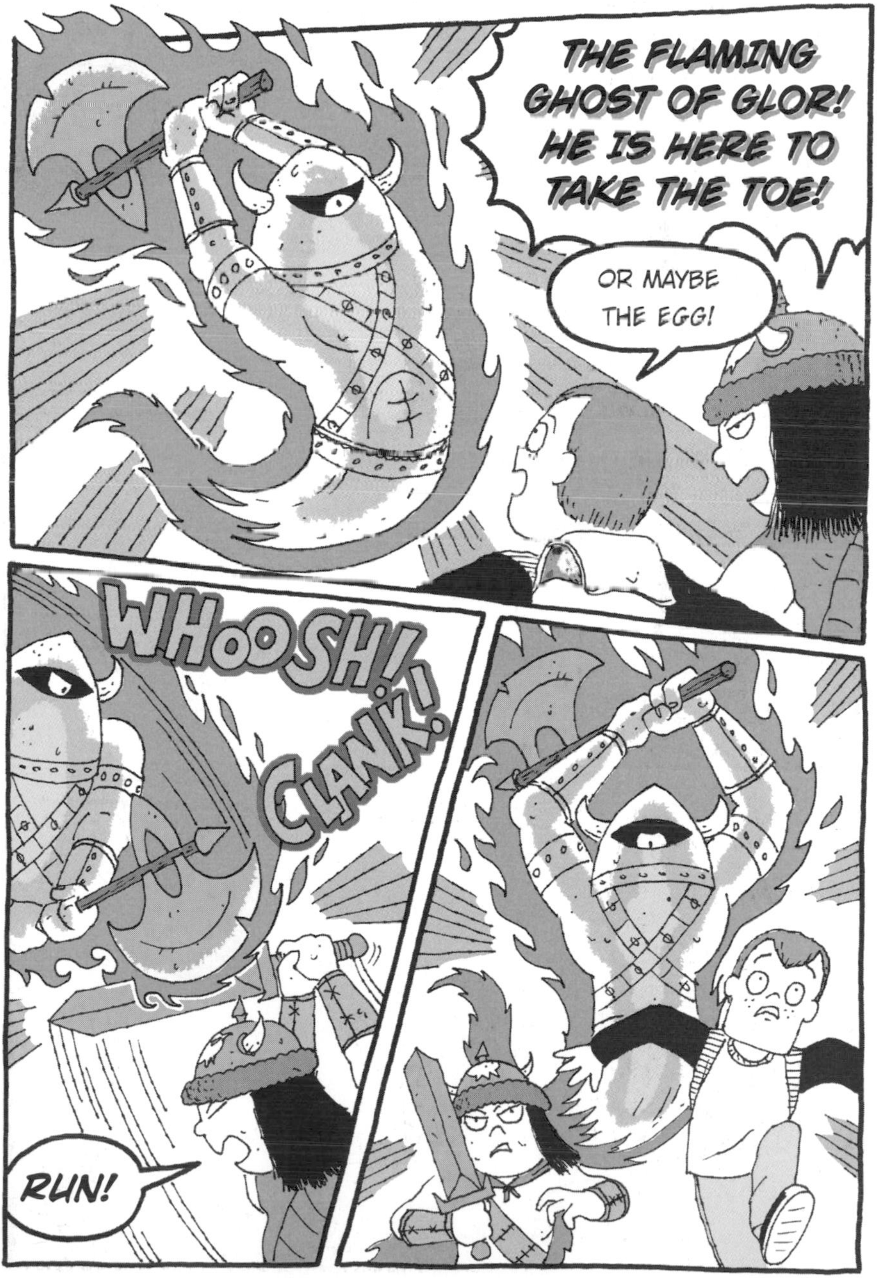
THE FLAMING GHOST OF GLOR! HE IS HERE TO TAKE THE TOE!
OR MAYBE THE EGG!
WHOOSH!
CLANK!
RUN!

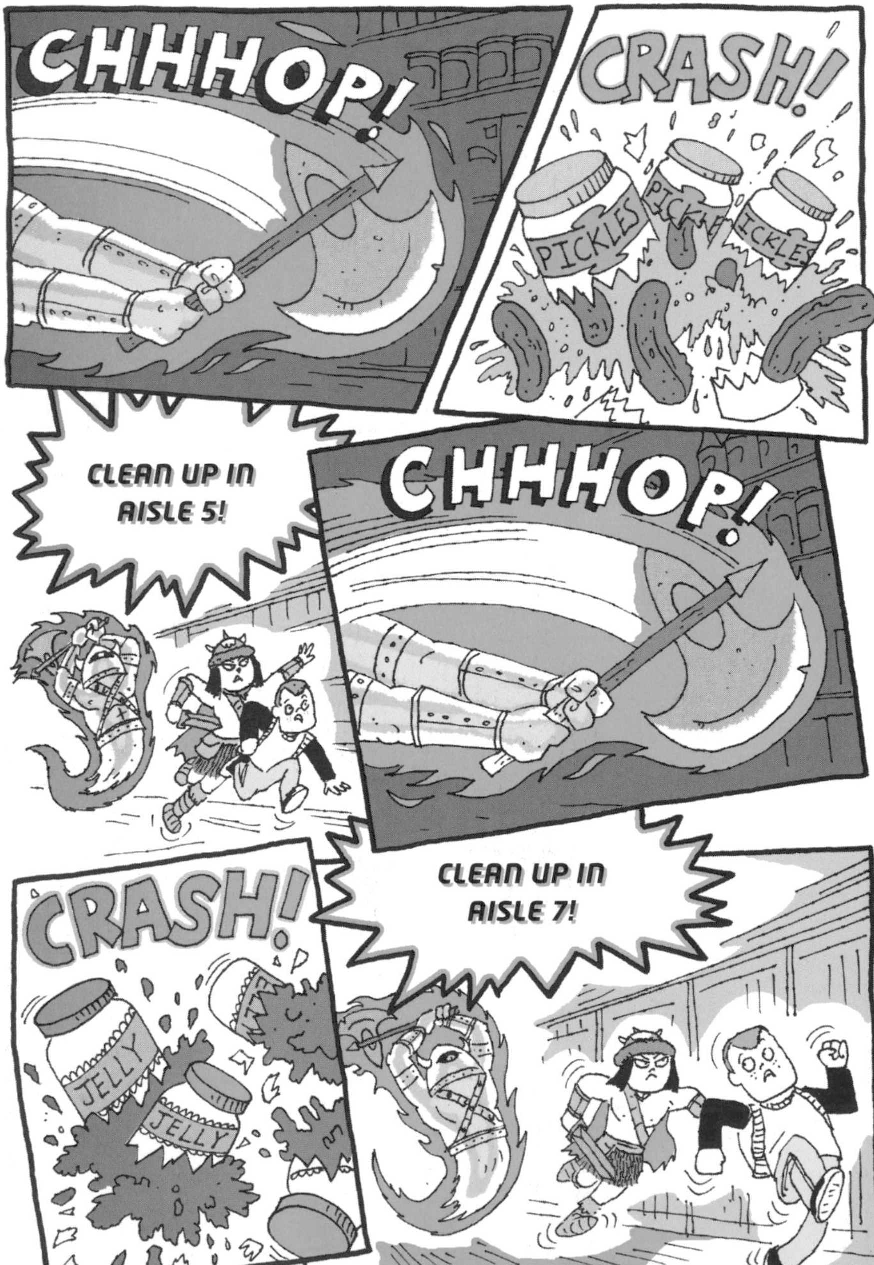
CHHHOP!
CRASH!
PICKLES
PICK
PICKLES
CLEAN UP IN AISLE 5!
CHHHOP!
CRASH!
JELLY
JELLY
CLEAN UP IN AISLE 7!

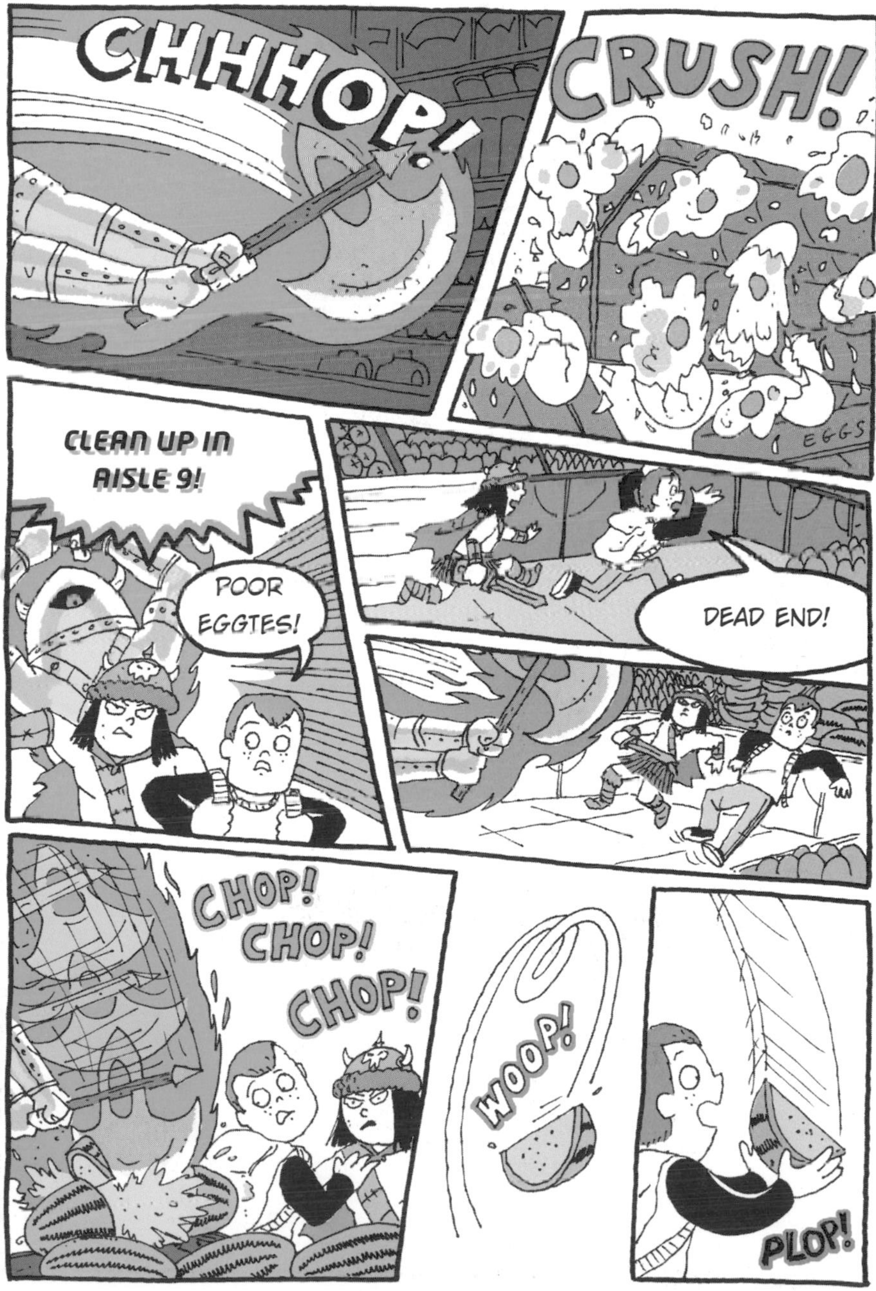
CHHHOP!
CRUSH!
EGGS
CLEAN UP IN AISLE 9!
POOR EGGTES!
DEAD END!
CHOP! CHOP! CHOP!
WOOP!
PLOP!

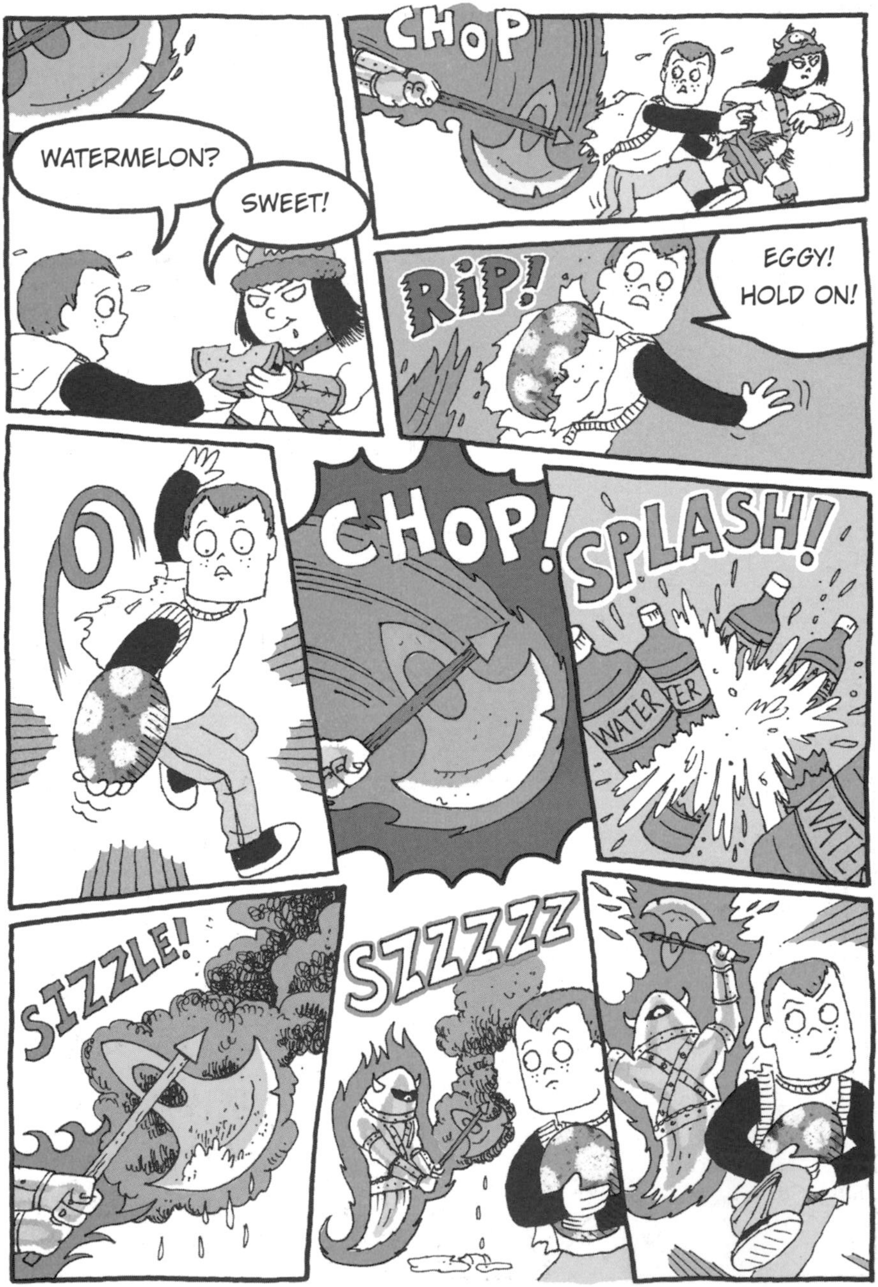
WATERMELON?
SWEET!
CHOP
RIP!
EGGY! HOLD ON!
CHOP!
SPLASH!
WATER
TER
WATE
SIZZLE!
SZZZZZ

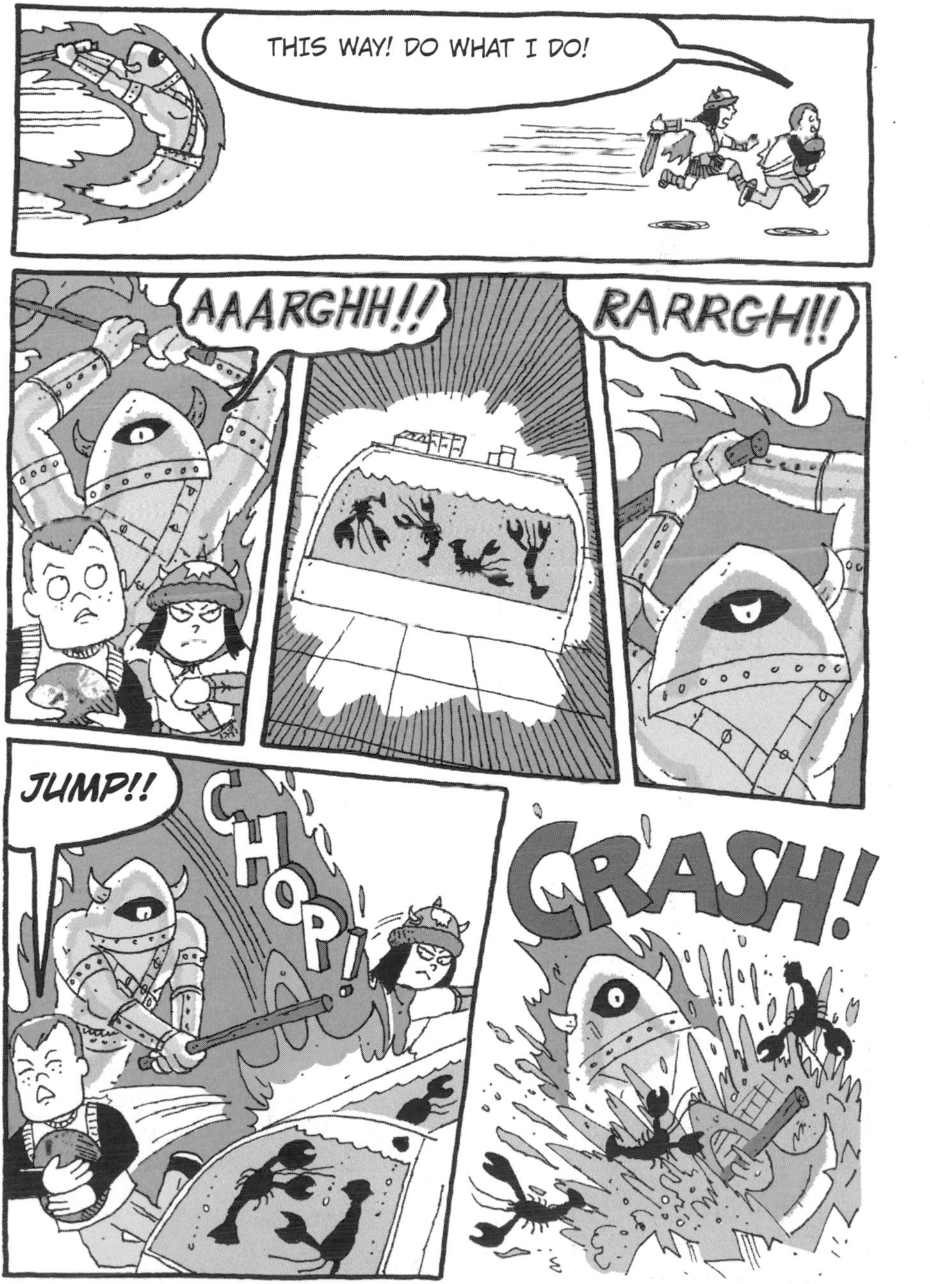
THIS WAY! DO WHAT I DO!
AAARGHH!!
RARRGH!!
JUMP!!
CHOP!
CRASH!

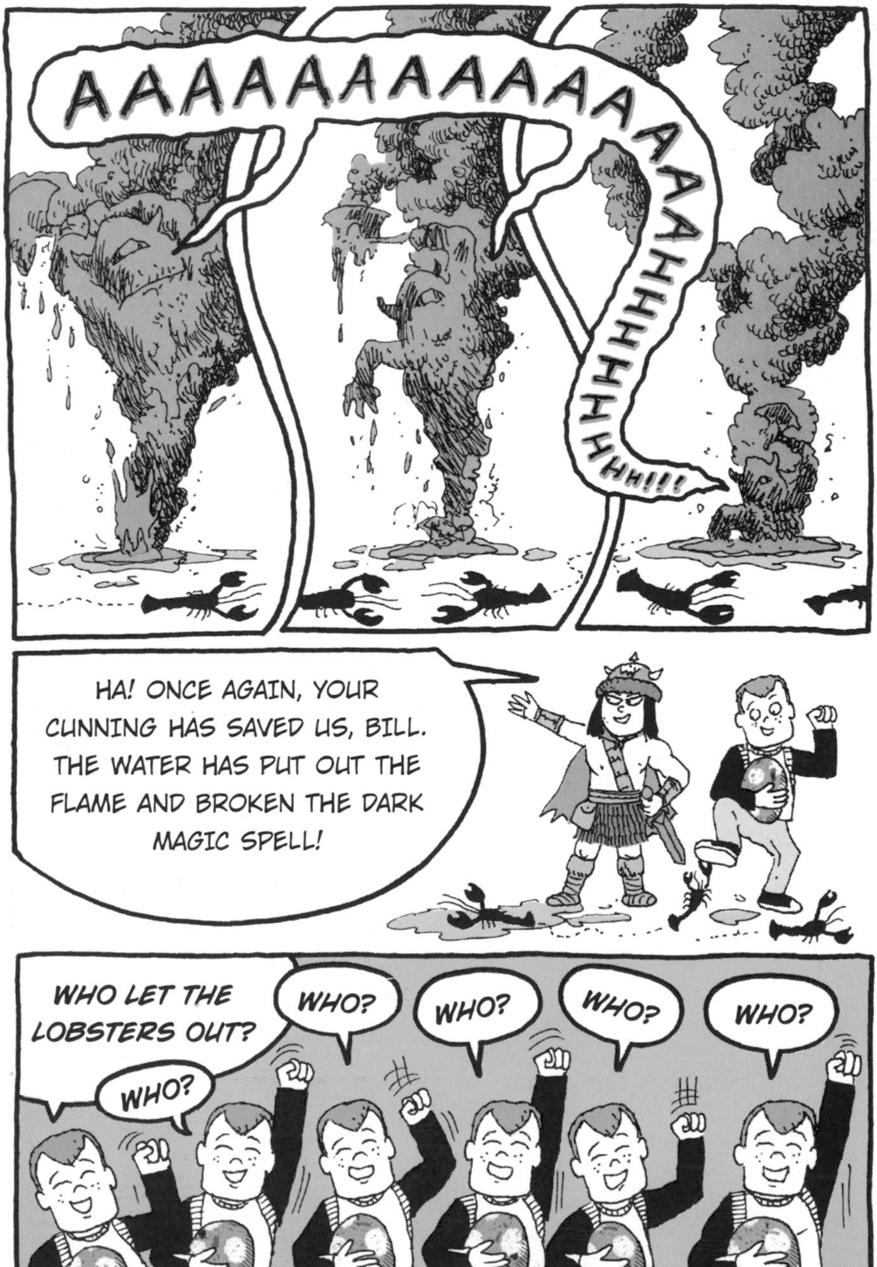
AAAAAAAAAAAAAAAHHHHHHHHH!!!
HA! ONCE AGAIN, YOUR CUNNING HAS SAVED US, BILL. THE WATER HAS PUT OUT THE FLAME AND BROKEN THE DARK MAGIC SPELL!
WHO LET THE LOBSTERS OUT?
WHO?
WHO?
WHO?
WHO?
WHO?

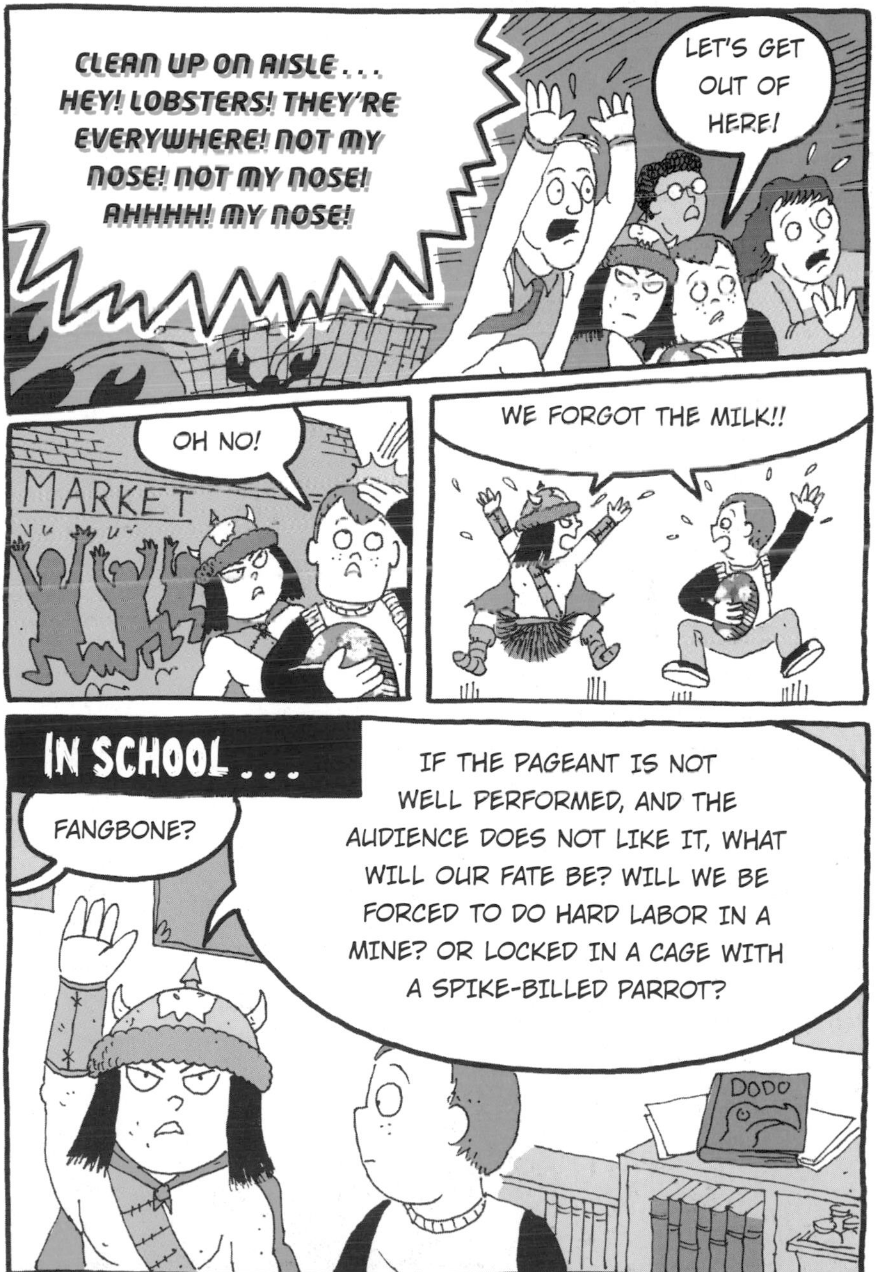
CLEAN UP ON AISLE . . . HEY! LOBSTERS! THEY'RE EVERYWHERE! NOT MY NOSE! NOT MY NOSE! AHHHH! MY NOSE!
LET'S GET OUT OF HERE!
OH NO!
MARKET
WE FORGOT THE MILK!!
IN SCHOOL . . .
FANGBONE?
IF THE PAGEANT IS NOT WELL PERFORMED, AND THE AUDIENCE DOES NOT LIKE IT, WHAT WILL OUR FATE BE? WILL WE BE FORCED TO DO HARD LABOR IN A MINE? OR LOCKED IN A CAGE WITH A SPIKE-BILLED PARROT?
DODO

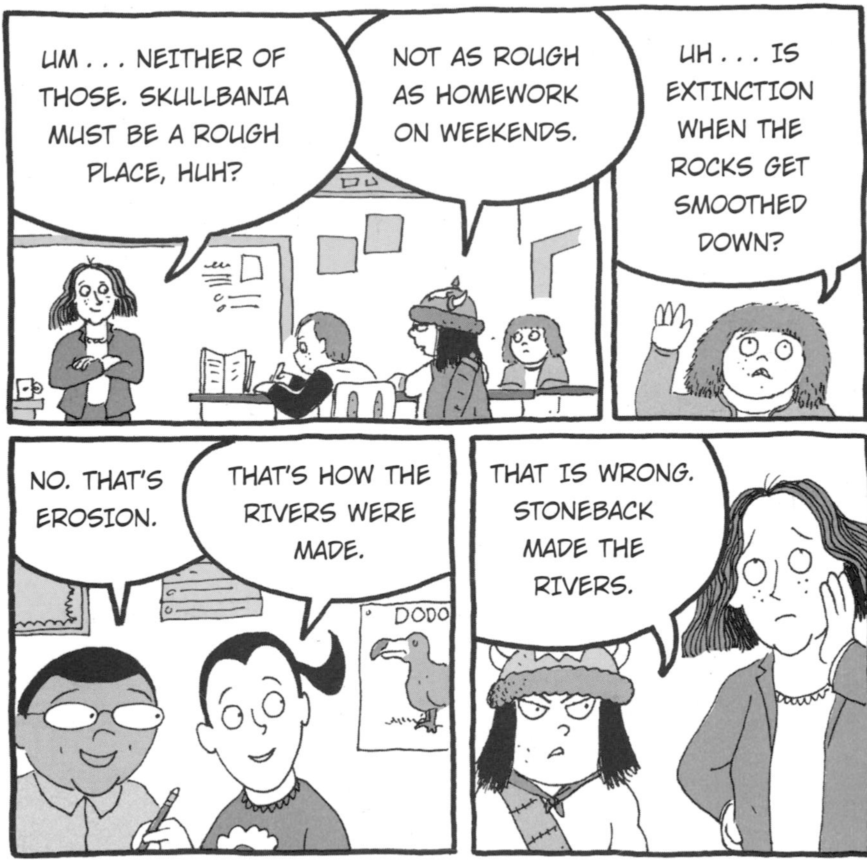
UM . . . NEITHER OF THOSE. SKULLBANIA MUST BE A ROUGH PLACE, HUH?
NOT AS ROUGH AS HOMEWORK ON WEEKENDS.
UH . . . IS EXTINCTION WHEN THE ROCKS GET SMOOTHED DOWN?
NO. THAT'S EROSION.
THAT'S HOW THE RIVERS WERE MADE.
DODO
THAT IS WRONG. STONEBACK MADE THE RIVERS.

WHILE SEARCHING FOR HIS BRIDE-TO-BE, STONEBACK MET THE QUEEN OF SNAKES. SHE TOLD STONEBACK THAT ZIZELLA WAS BEING HELD IN THE DUNGEON OF CASTLE SCALPHEAD.

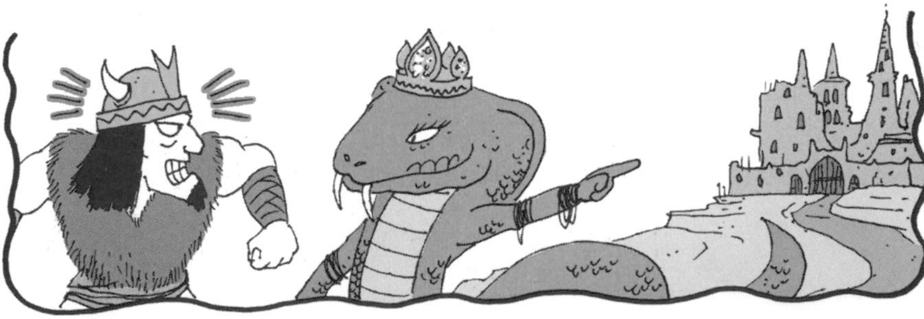

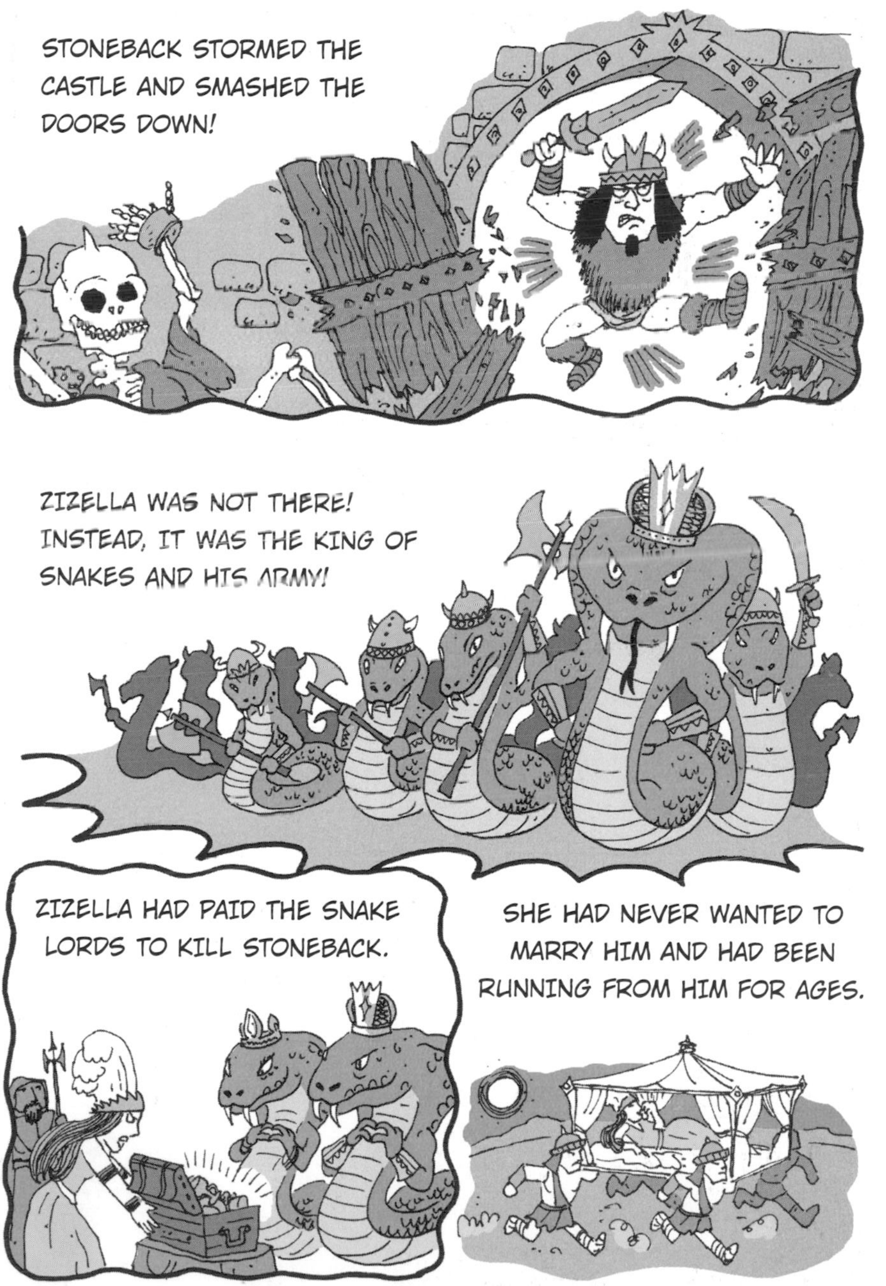
STONEBACK STORMED THE CASTLE AND SMASHED THE DOORS DOWN!
ZIZELLA WAS NOT THERE! INSTEAD, IT WAS THE KING OF SNAKES AND HIS ARMY!
ZIZELLA HAD PAID THE SNAKE LORDS TO KILL STONEBACK.
SHE HAD NEVER WANTED TO MARRY HIM AND HAD BEEN RUNNING FROM HIM FOR AGES.

STONEBACK FOUGHT LIKE A DEMON!

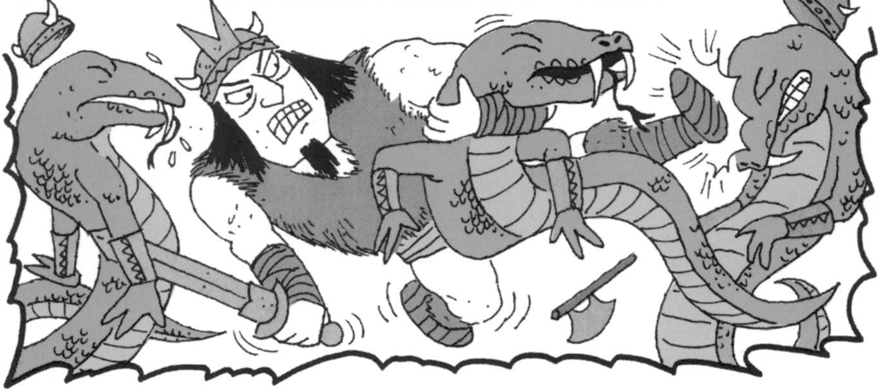

HE BEGAN TO JUMP UP AND DOWN, SMASHING THE SNAKES AND CRACKING THE GROUND!

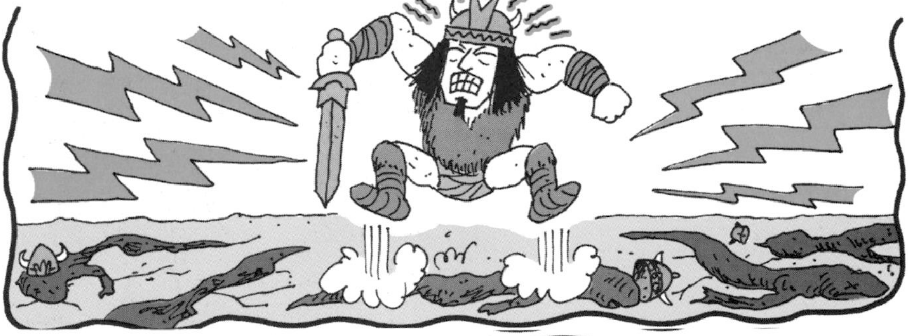

THE QUEEN OF SNAKES WAS SO SAD TO SEE HER ARMY CRUSHED, SHE BEGAN TO CRY . . .

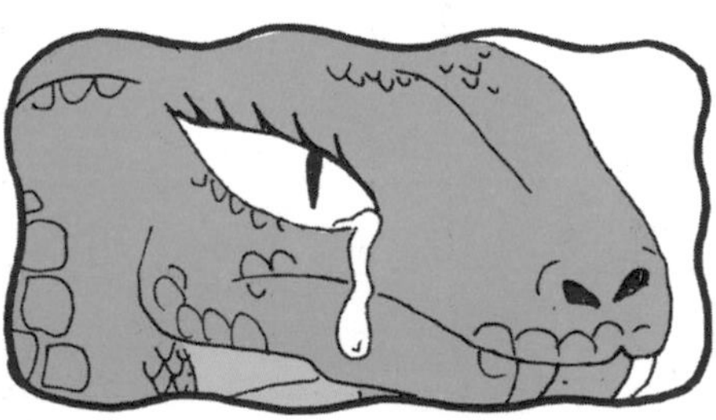

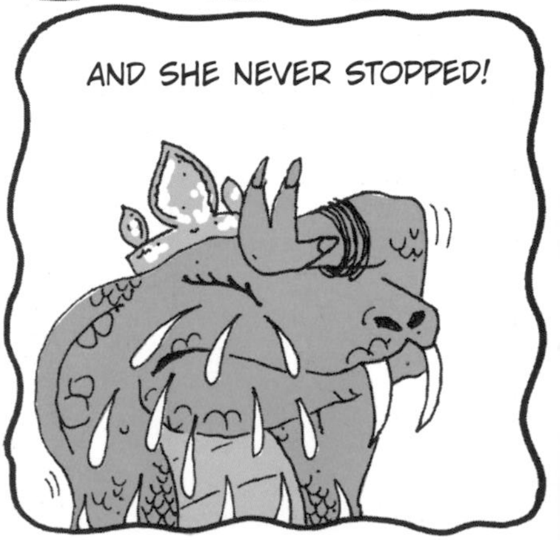
AND SHE NEVER STOPPED!

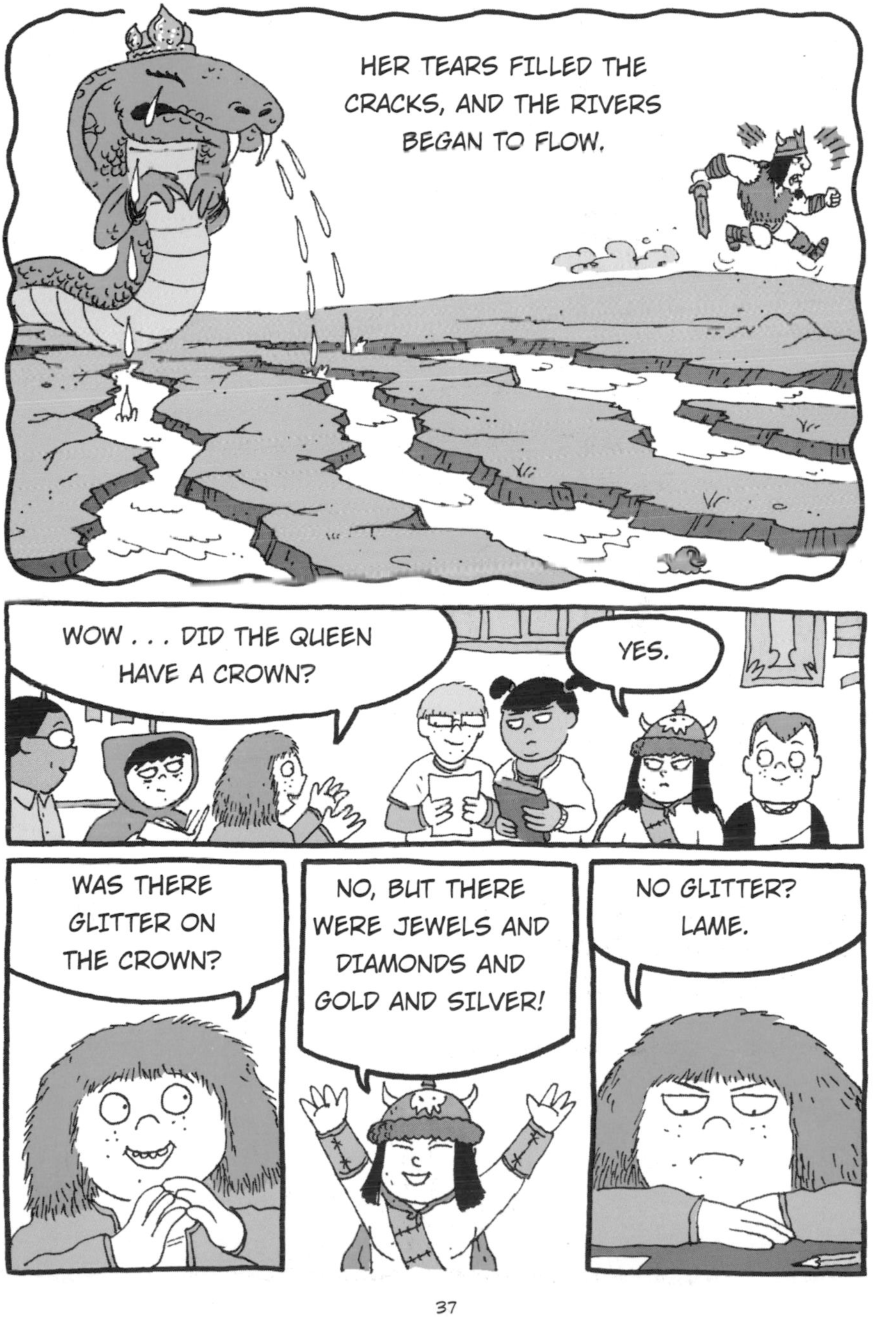
HER TEARS FILLED THE CRACKS, AND THE RIVERS BEGAN TO FLOW.
WOW . . . DID THE QUEEN HAVE A CROWN?
YES.
WAS THERE GLITTER ON THE CROWN?
NO, BUT THERE WERE JEWELS AND DIAMONDS AND GOLD AND SILVER!
NO GLITTER? LAME.

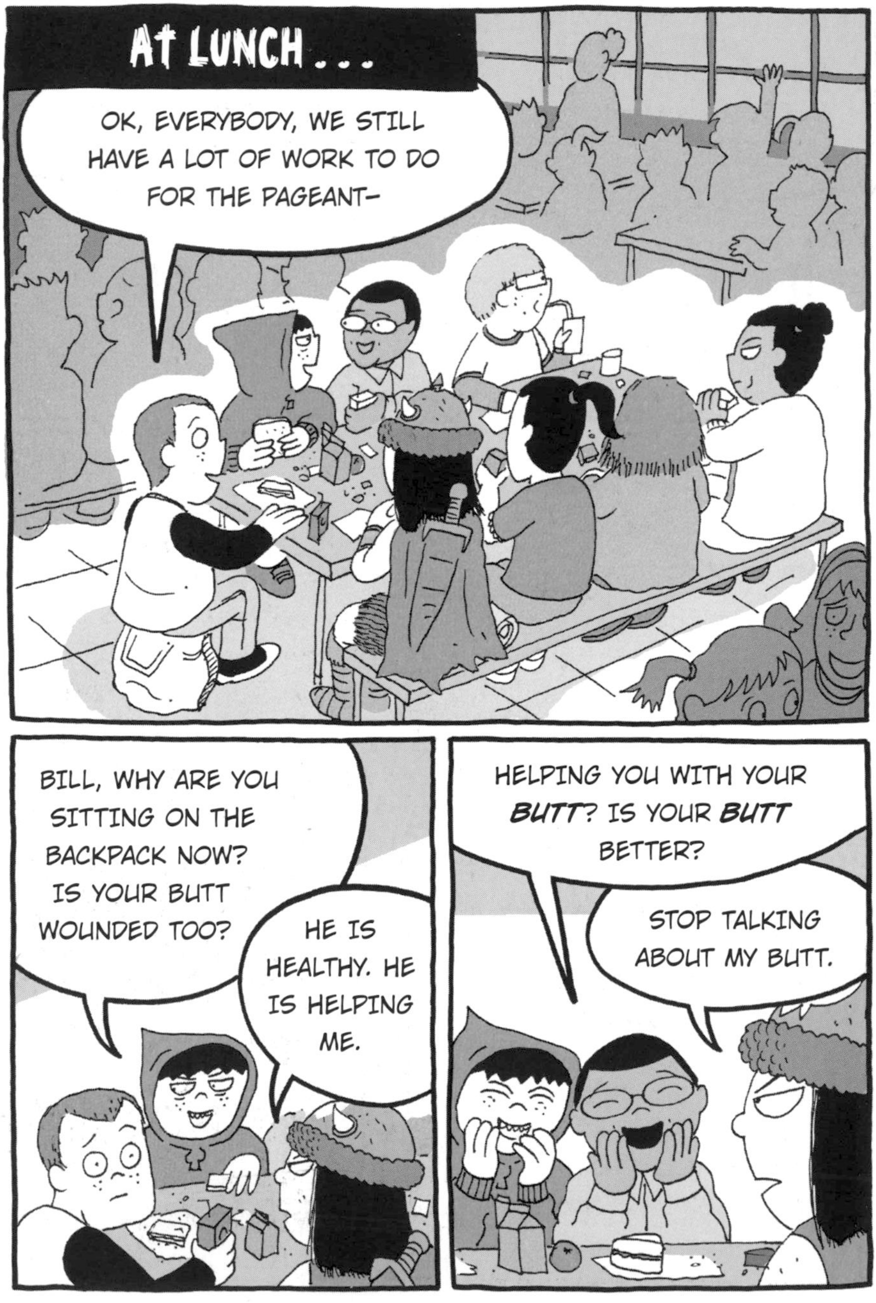

AT LUNCH . . .
OK, EVERYBODY, WE STILL HAVE A LOT OF WORK TO DO FOR THE PAGEANT–
BILL, WHY ARE YOU SITTING ON THE BACKPACK NOW? IS YOUR BUTT WOUNDED TOO?
HE IS HEALTHY. HE IS HELPING ME.
HELPING YOU WITH YOUR *BUTT*? IS YOUR *BUTT* BETTER?
STOP TALKING ABOUT MY BUTT.

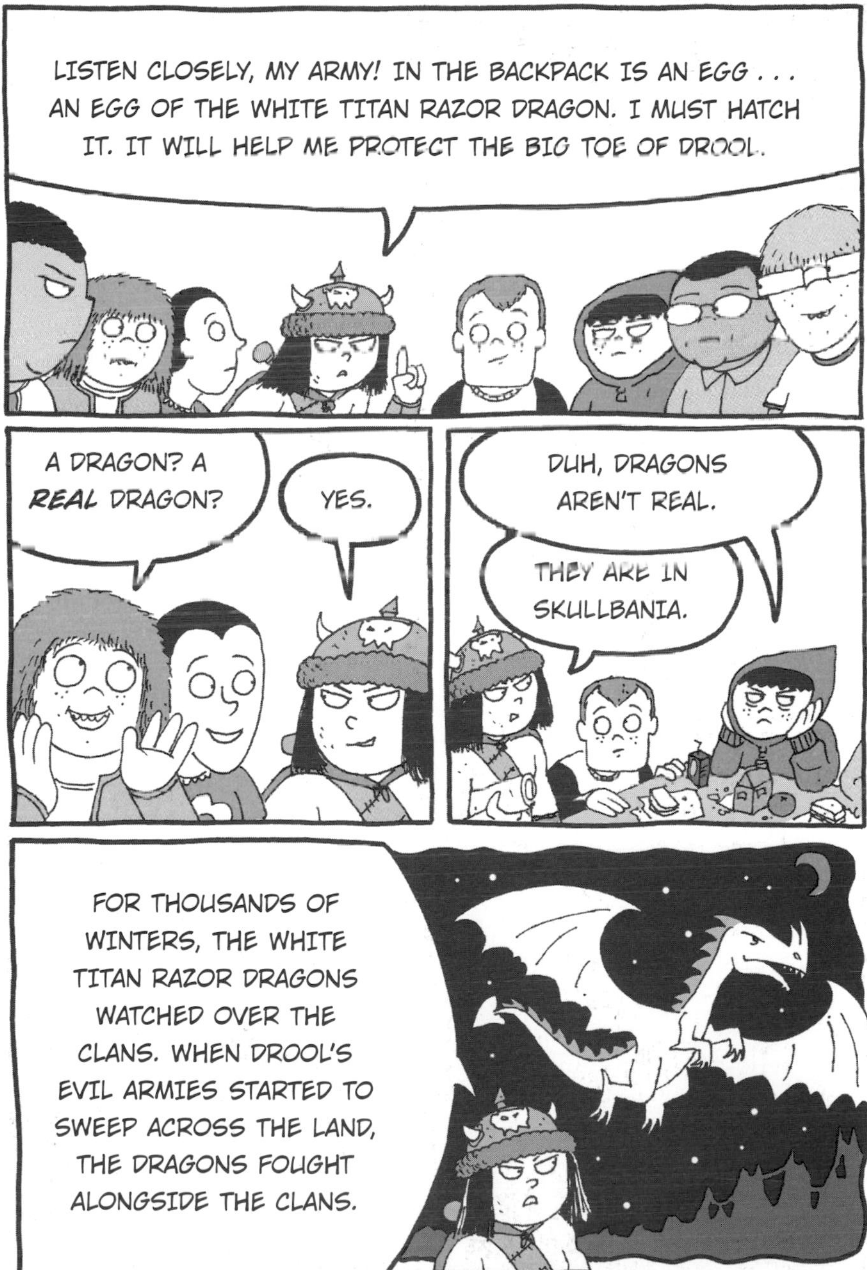
LISTEN CLOSELY, MY ARMY! IN THE BACKPACK IS AN EGG . . . AN EGG OF THE WHITE TITAN RAZOR DRAGON. I MUST HATCH IT. IT WILL HELP ME PROTECT THE BIG TOE OF DROOL.
A DRAGON? A *REAL* DRAGON?
YES.
DUH, DRAGONS AREN'T REAL.
THEY ARE IN SKULLBANIA.
FOR THOUSANDS OF WINTERS, THE WHITE TITAN RAZOR DRAGONS WATCHED OVER THE CLANS. WHEN DROOL'S EVIL ARMIES STARTED TO SWEEP ACROSS THE LAND, THE DRAGONS FOUGHT ALONGSIDE THE CLANS.

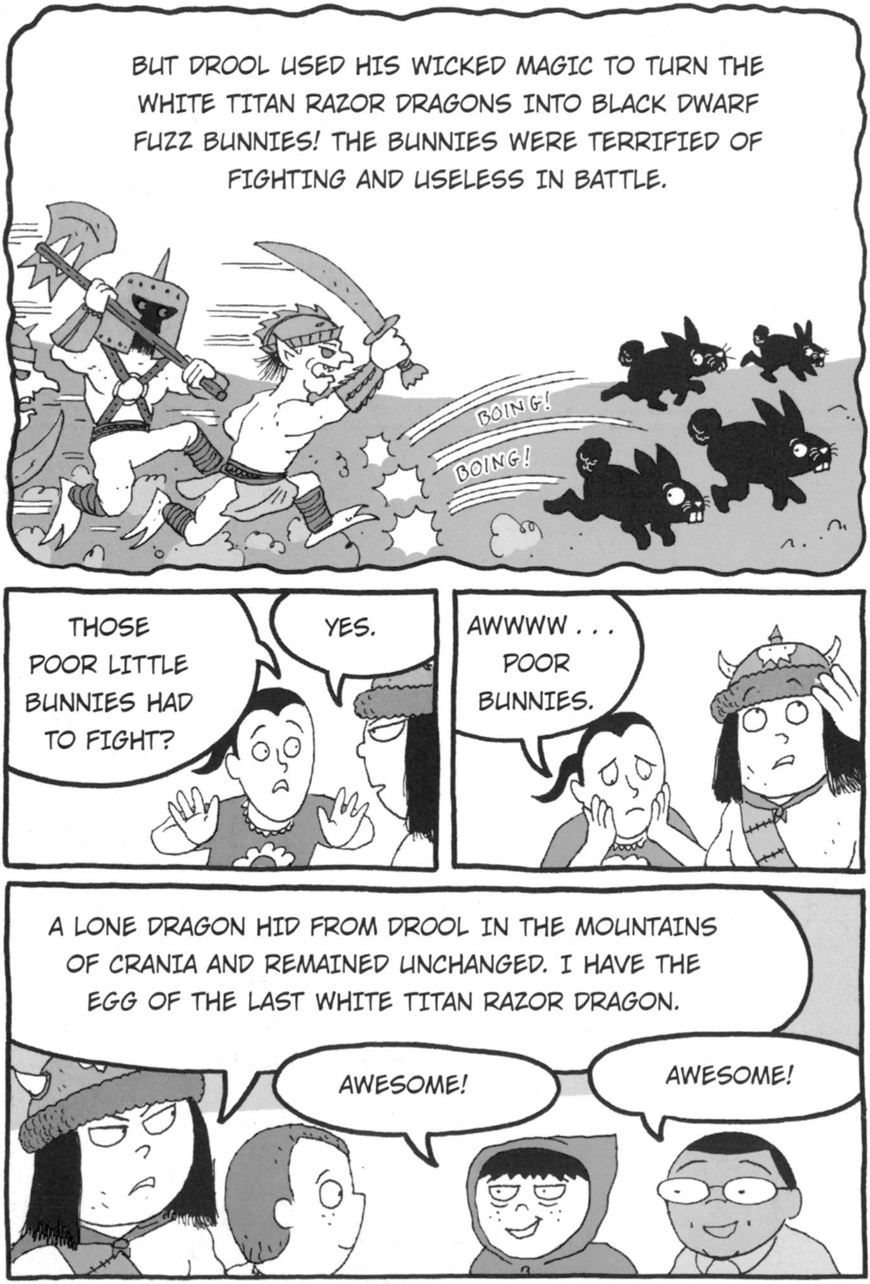

BUT DROOL USED HIS WICKED MAGIC TO TURN THE WHITE TITAN RAZOR DRAGONS INTO BLACK DWARF FUZZ BUNNIES! THE BUNNIES WERE TERRIFIED OF FIGHTING AND USELESS IN BATTLE.
BOING!
BOING!
THOSE POOR LITTLE BUNNIES HAD TO FIGHT?
YES.
AWWWW . . . POOR BUNNIES.
A LONE DRAGON HID FROM DROOL IN THE MOUNTAINS OF CRANIA AND REMAINED UNCHANGED. I HAVE THE EGG OF THE LAST WHITE TITAN RAZOR DRAGON.
AWESOME!
AWESOME!

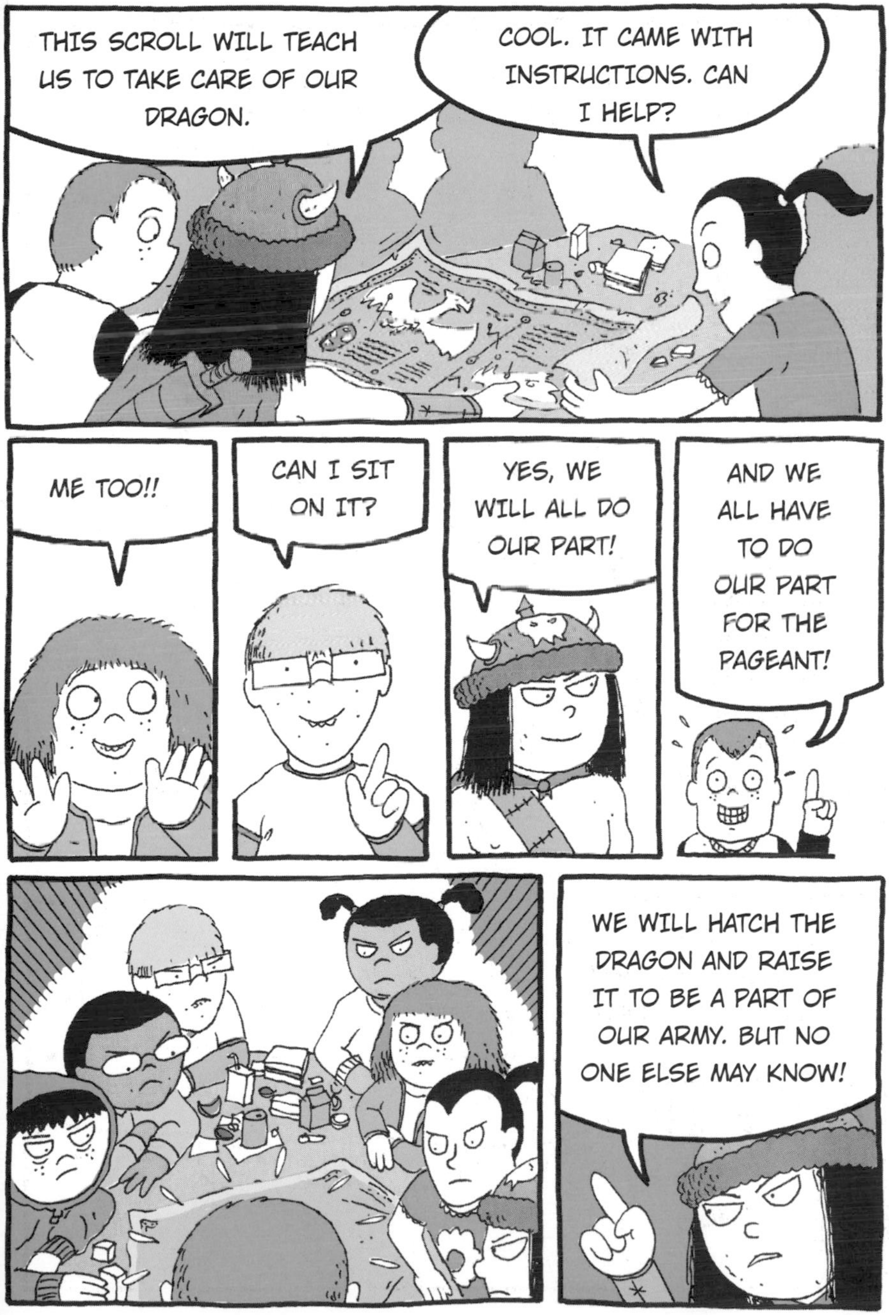
THIS SCROLL WILL TEACH US TO TAKE CARE OF OUR DRAGON.
COOL. IT CAME WITH INSTRUCTIONS. CAN I HELP?
ME TOO!!
CAN I SIT ON IT?
YES, WE WILL ALL DO OUR PART!
AND WE ALL HAVE TO DO OUR PART FOR THE PAGEANT!
WE WILL HATCH THE DRAGON AND RAISE IT TO BE A PART OF OUR ARMY. BUT NO ONE ELSE MAY KNOW!

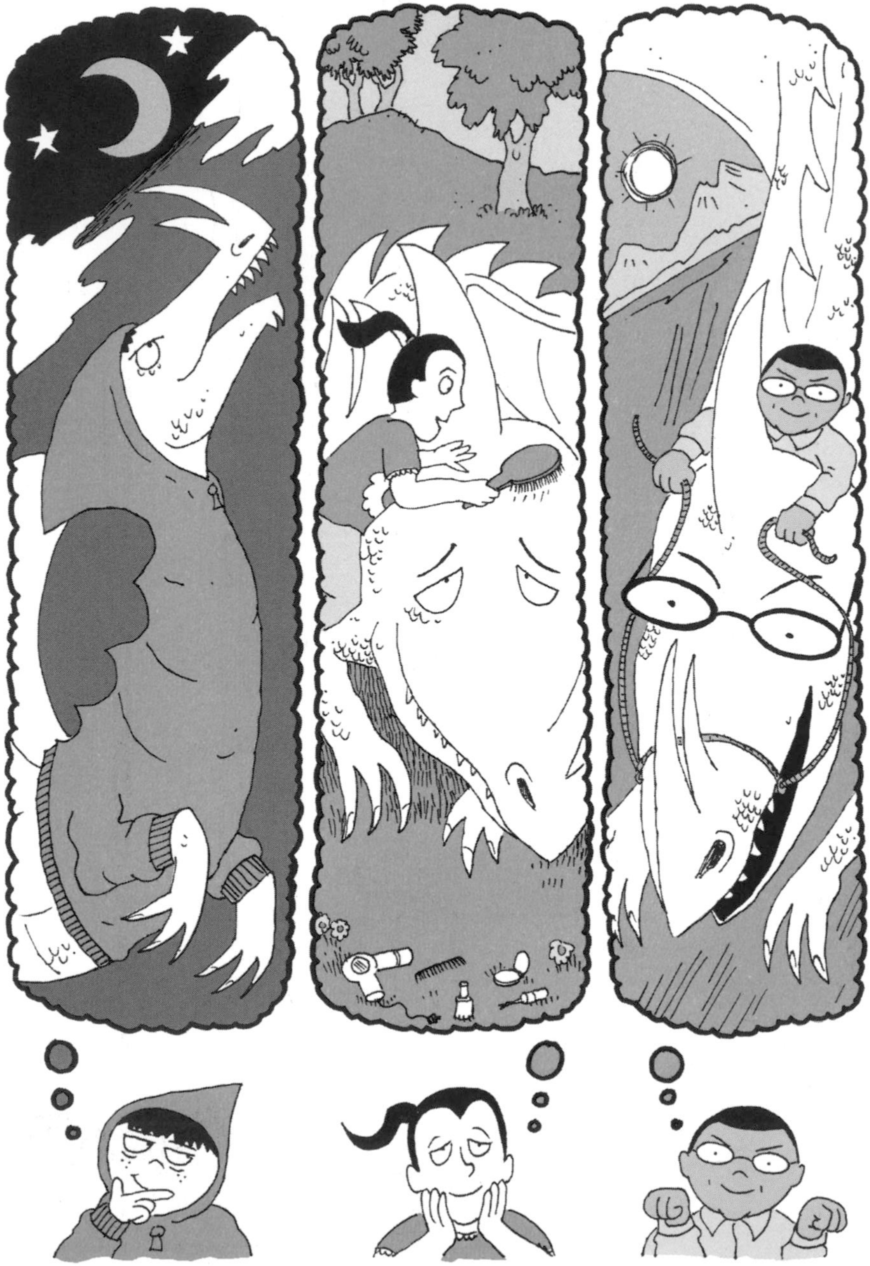

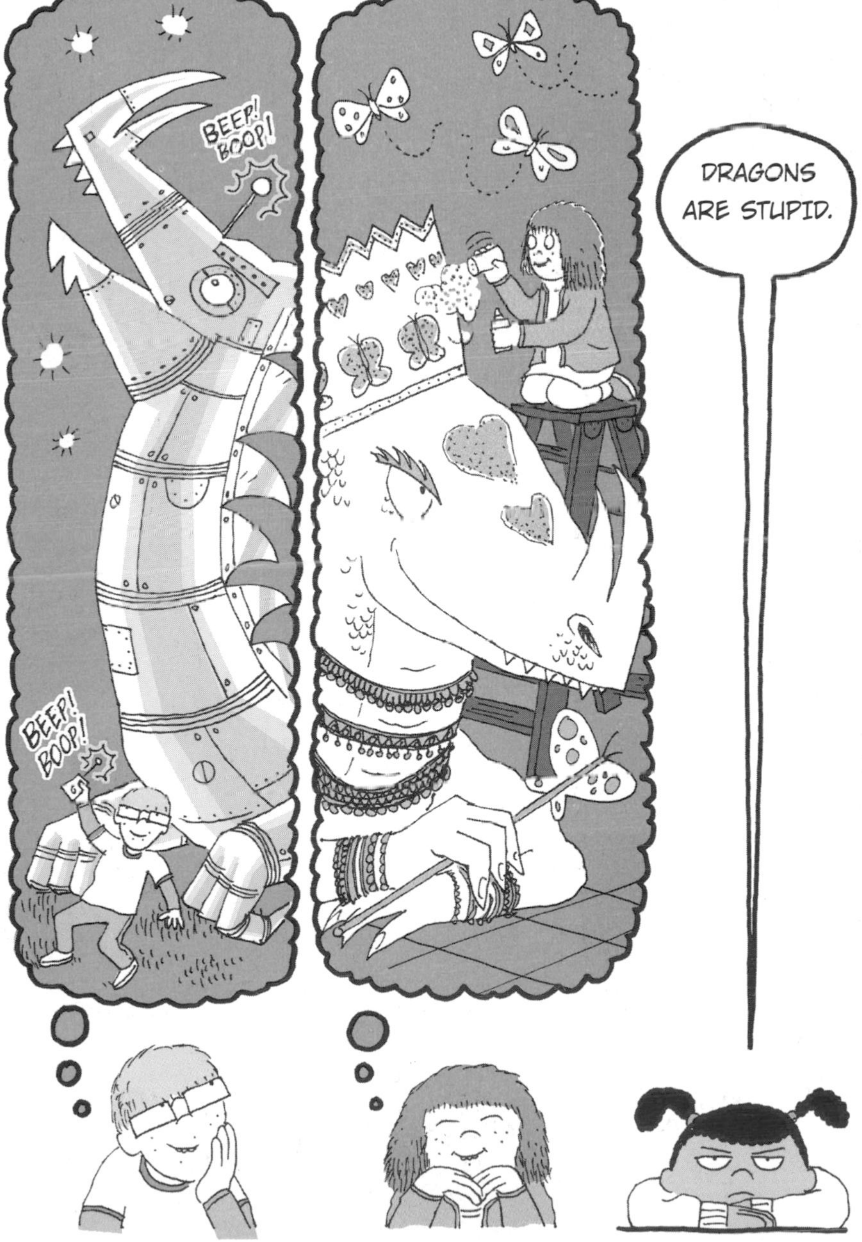
BEEP! BOOP!
BEEP! BOOP!
DRAGONS ARE STUPID.

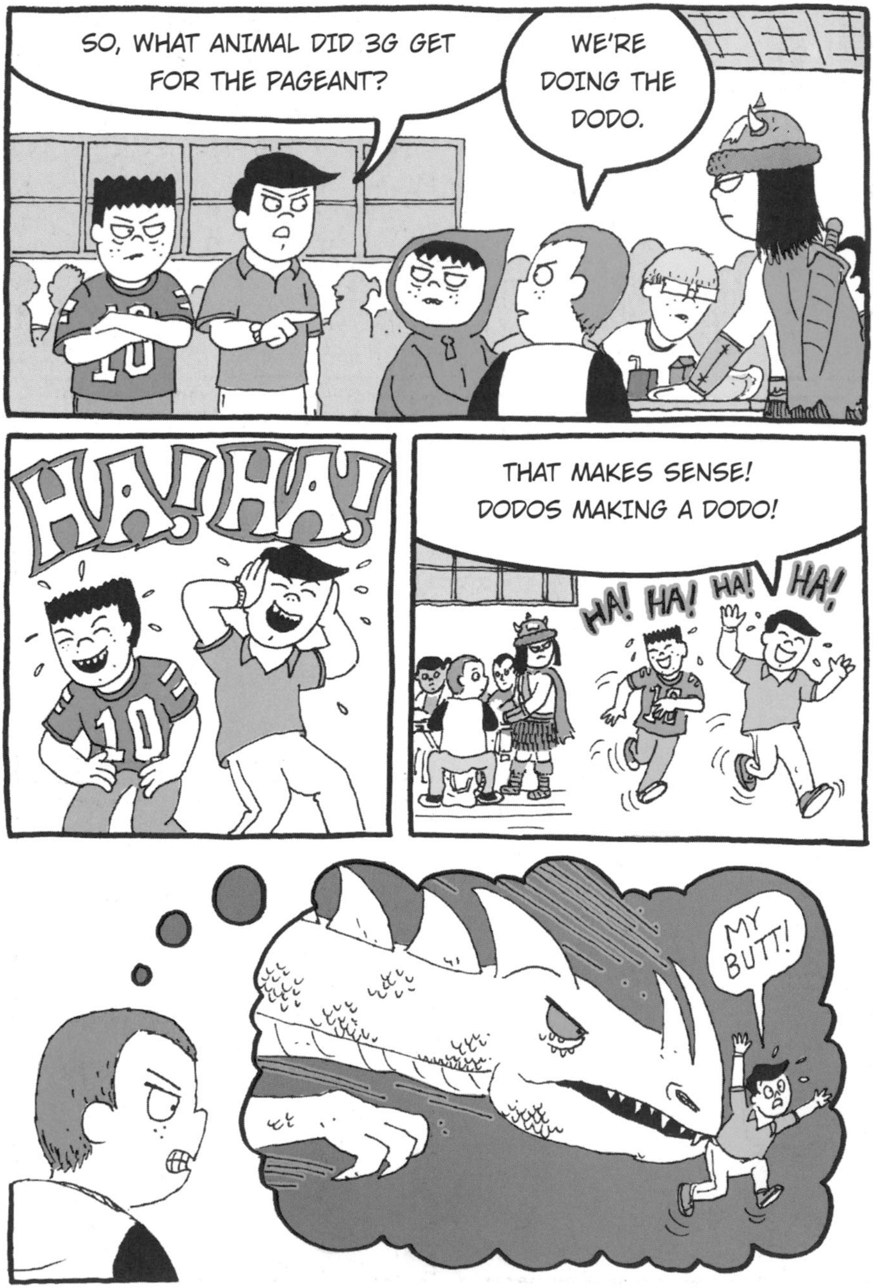
SO, WHAT ANIMAL DID 3G GET FOR THE PAGEANT?
WE'RE DOING THE DODO.
HA! HA!
THAT MAKES SENSE! DODOS MAKING A DODO!
HA! HA! HA! HA!
MY BUTT!

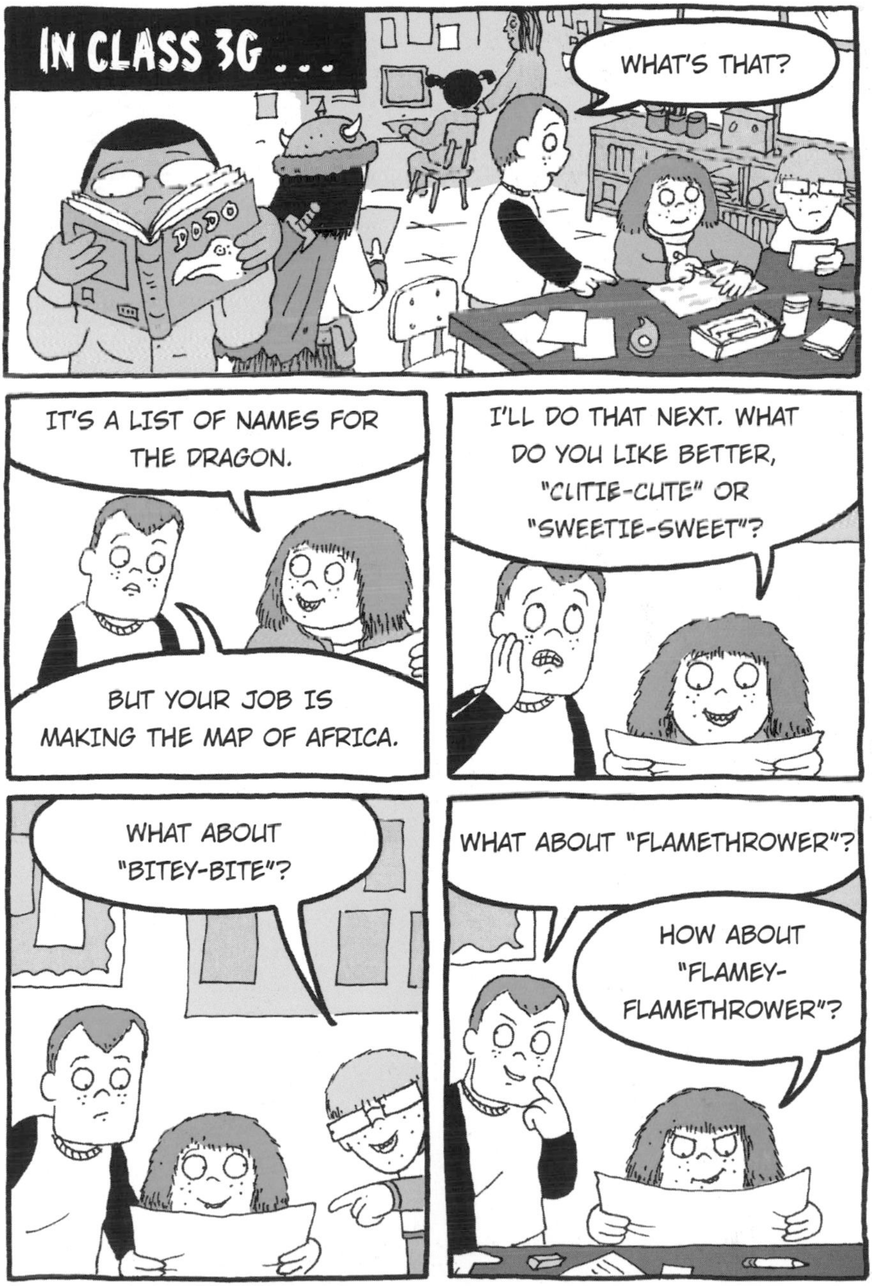
IN CLASS 3G . . .
WHAT'S THAT?
DODO
IT'S A LIST OF NAMES FOR THE DRAGON.
BUT YOUR JOB IS MAKING THE MAP OF AFRICA.
I'LL DO THAT NEXT. WHAT DO YOU LIKE BETTER, "CUTIE-CUTE" OR "SWEETIE-SWEET"?
WHAT ABOUT "BITEY-BITE"?
WHAT ABOUT "FLAMETHROWER"?
HOW ABOUT "FLAMEY-FLAMETHROWER"?

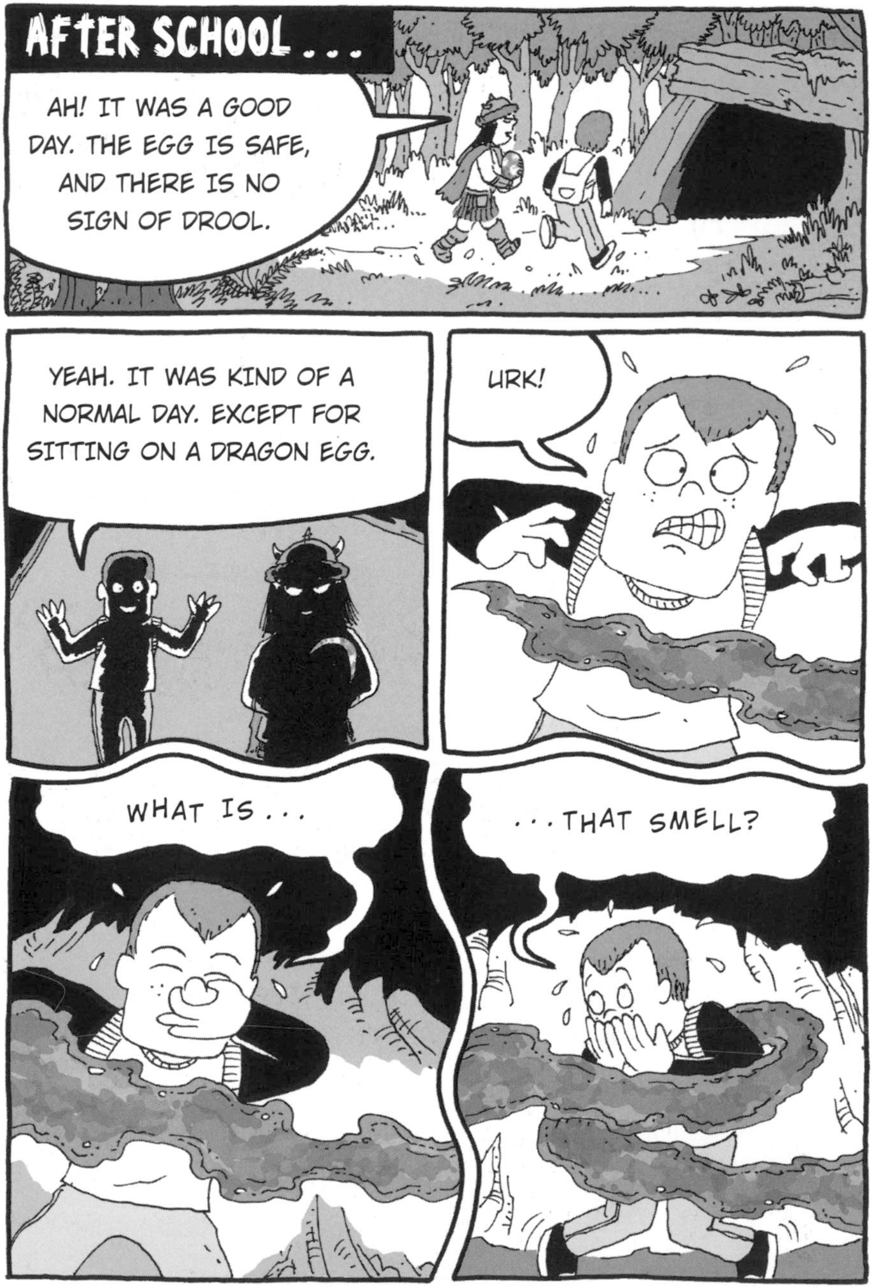

AFTER SCHOOL . . .
AH! IT WAS A GOOD DAY. THE EGG IS SAFE, AND THERE IS NO SIGN OF DROOL.
YEAH. IT WAS KIND OF A NORMAL DAY. EXCEPT FOR SITTING ON A DRAGON EGG.
URK!
WHAT IS . . .
. . . THAT SMELL?

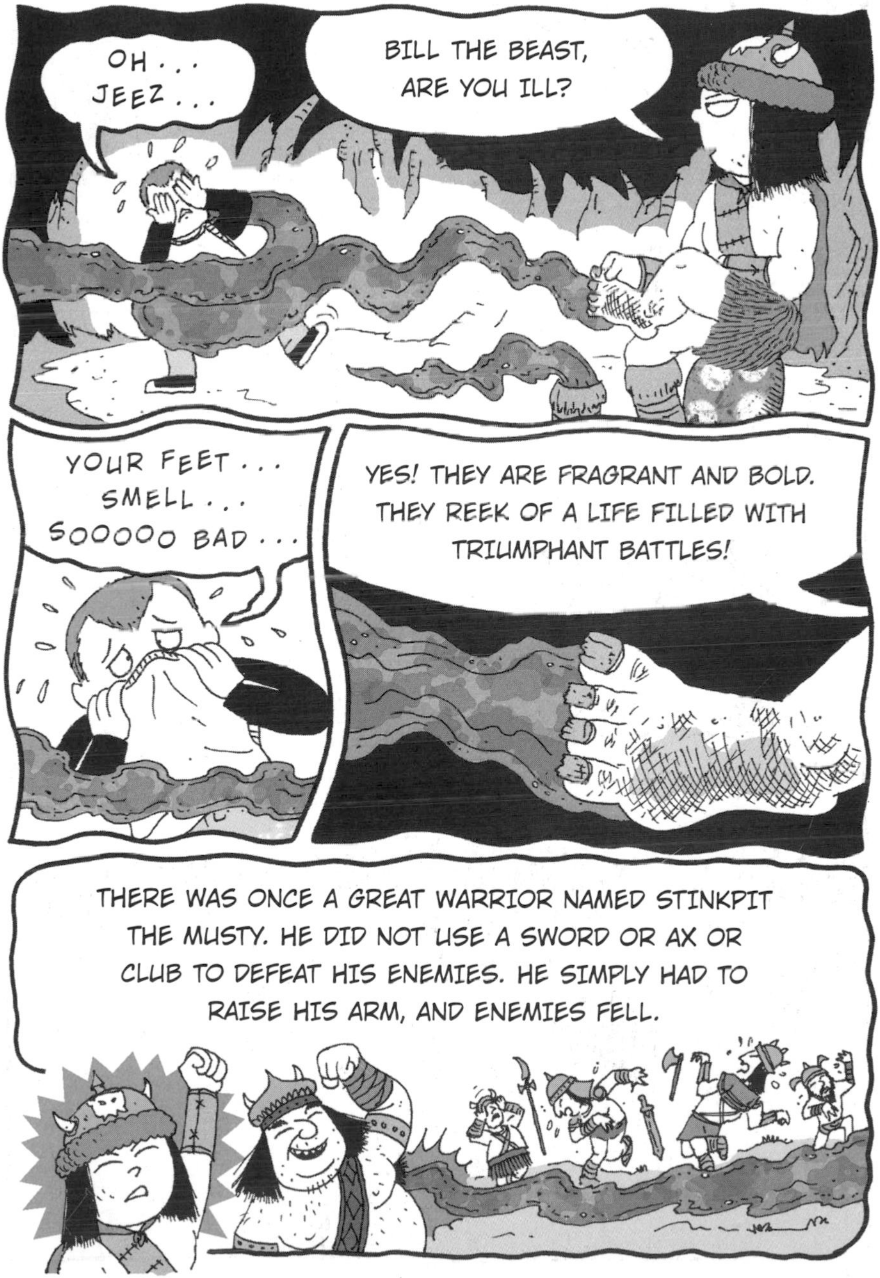
OH . . . JEEZ . . .
BILL THE BEAST, ARE YOU ILL?
YOUR FEET . . . SMELL . . . SOOOOO BAD . . .
YES! THEY ARE FRAGRANT AND BOLD. THEY REEK OF A LIFE FILLED WITH TRIUMPHANT BATTLES!
THERE WAS ONCE A GREAT WARRIOR NAMED STINKPIT THE MUSTY. HE DID NOT USE A SWORD OR AX OR CLUB TO DEFEAT HIS ENEMIES. HE SIMPLY HAD TO RAISE HIS ARM, AND ENEMIES FELL.

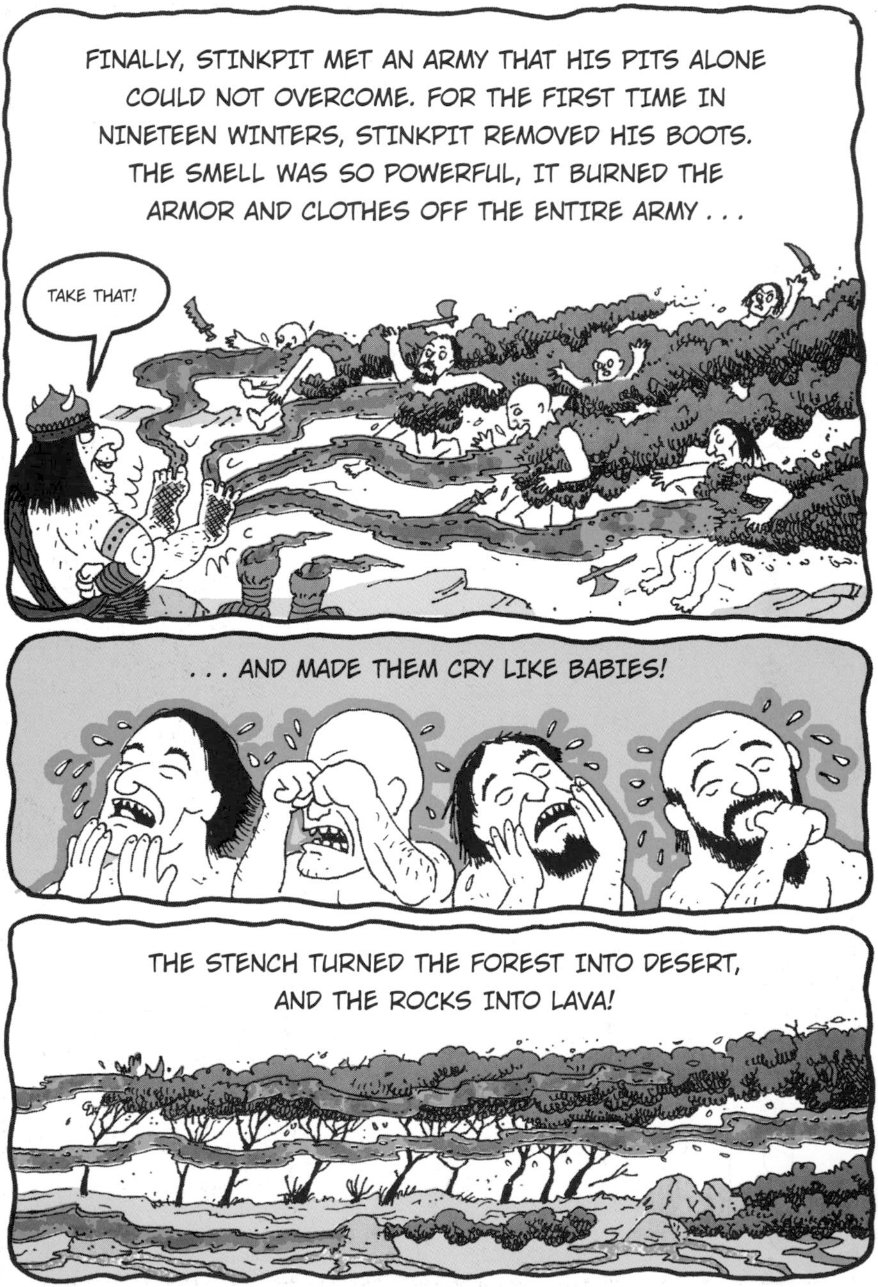
FINALLY, STINKPIT MET AN ARMY THAT HIS PITS ALONE COULD NOT OVERCOME. FOR THE FIRST TIME IN NINETEEN WINTERS, STINKPIT REMOVED HIS BOOTS. THE SMELL WAS SO POWERFUL, IT BURNED THE ARMOR AND CLOTHES OFF THE ENTIRE ARMY . . .
TAKE THAT!
. . . AND MADE THEM CRY LIKE BABIES!
THE STENCH TURNED THE FOREST INTO DESERT, AND THE ROCKS INTO LAVA!

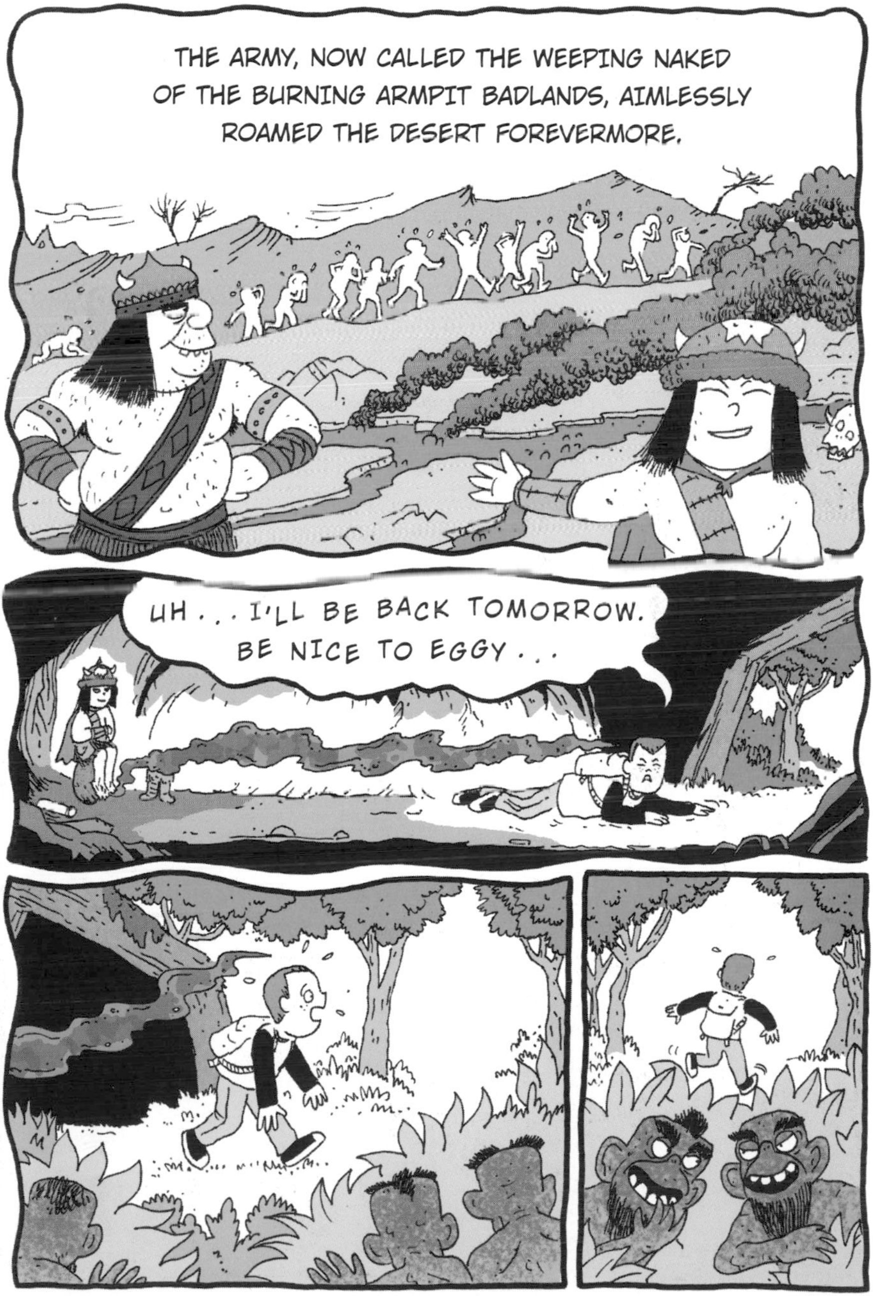
THE ARMY, NOW CALLED THE WEEPING NAKED OF THE BURNING ARMPIT BADLANDS, AIMLESSLY ROAMED THE DESERT FOREVERMORE.
UH . . . I'LL BE BACK TOMORROW. BE NICE TO EGGY . . .

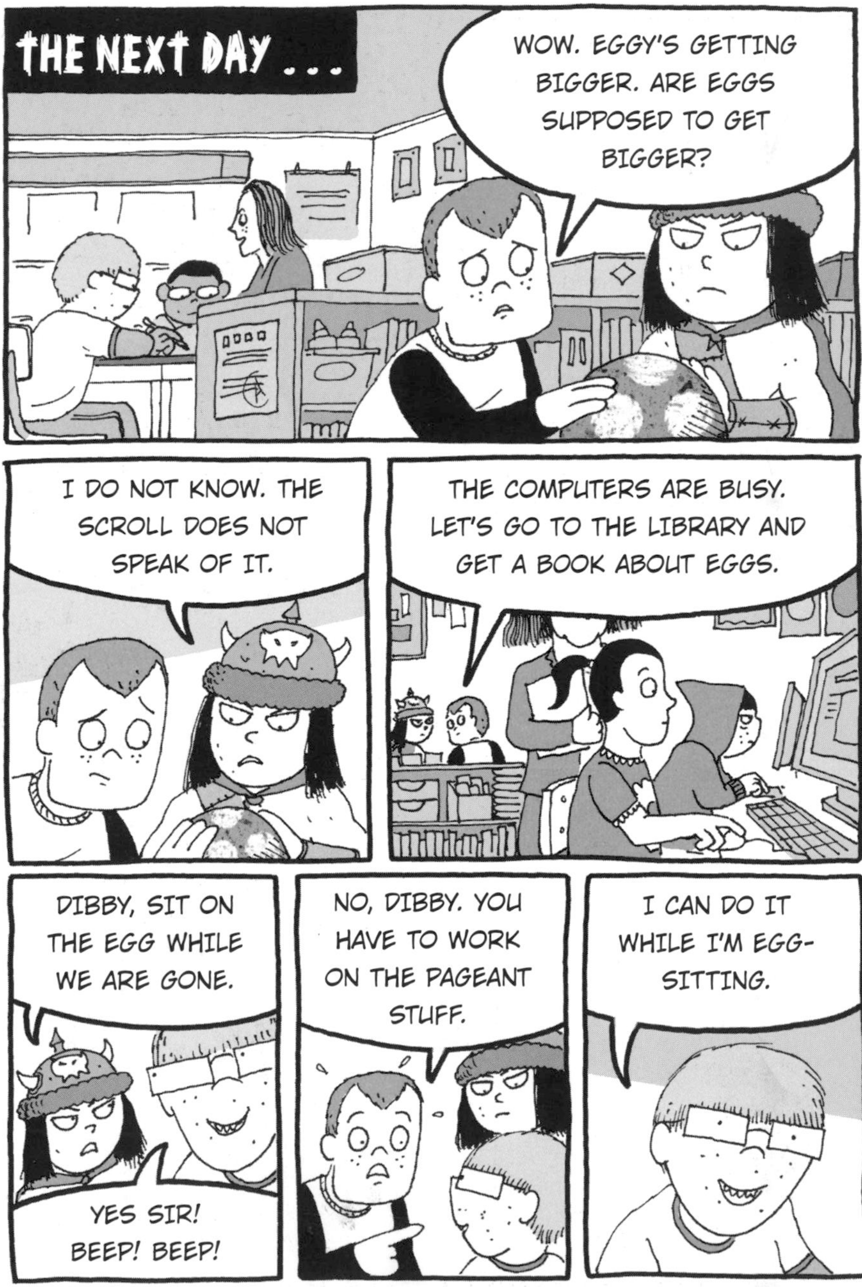
THE NEXT DAY . . .
WOW. EGGY'S GETTING BIGGER. ARE EGGS SUPPOSED TO GET BIGGER?
I DO NOT KNOW. THE SCROLL DOES NOT SPEAK OF IT.
THE COMPUTERS ARE BUSY. LET'S GO TO THE LIBRARY AND GET A BOOK ABOUT EGGS.
DIBBY, SIT ON THE EGG WHILE WE ARE GONE.
YES SIR! BEEP! BEEP!
NO, DIBBY. YOU HAVE TO WORK ON THE PAGEANT STUFF.
I CAN DO IT WHILE I'M EGG-SITTING.

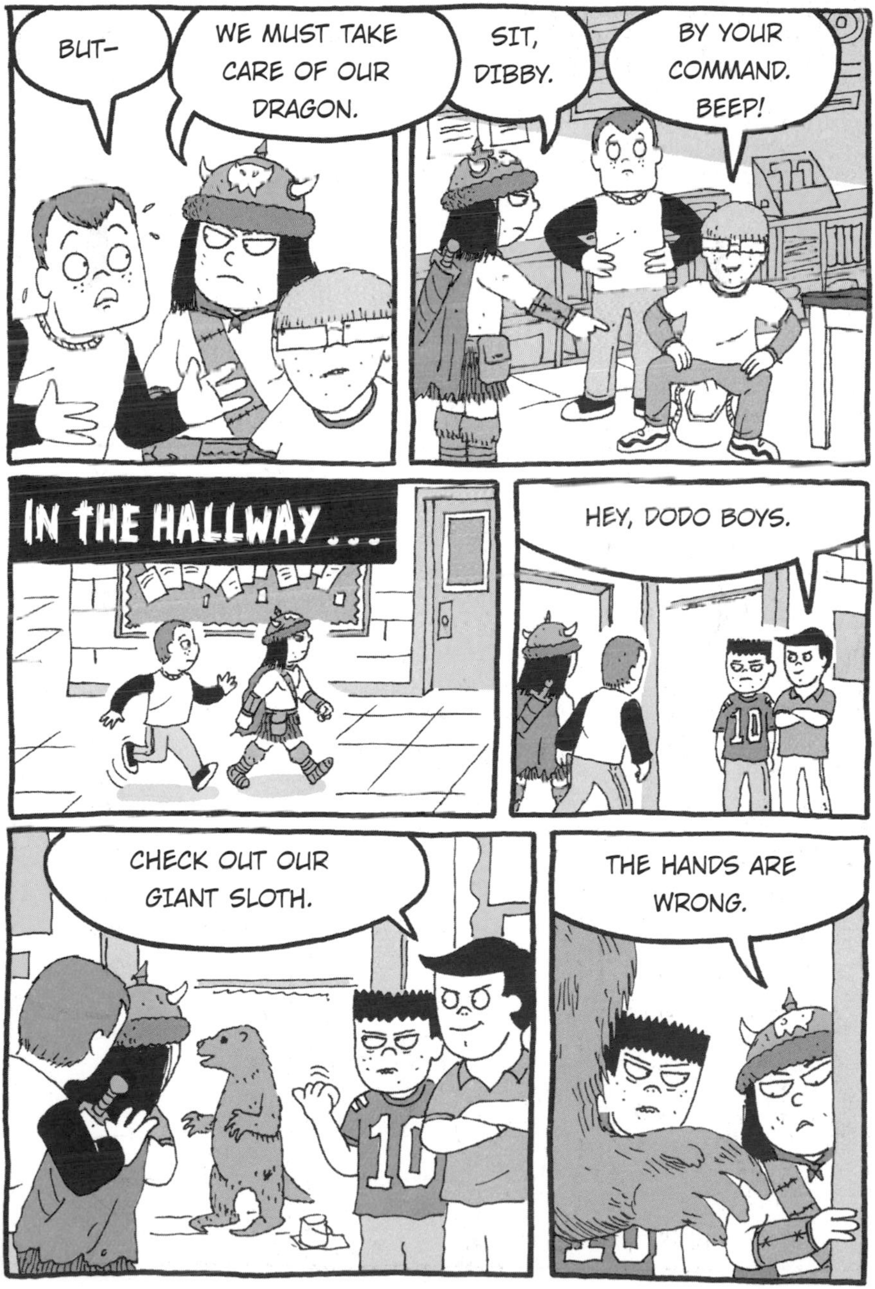
BUT-
WE MUST TAKE CARE OF OUR DRAGON.
SIT, DIBBY.
BY YOUR COMMAND. BEEP!
IN THE HALLWAY . . .
HEY, DODO BOYS.
10
CHECK OUT OUR GIANT SLOTH.
10
THE HANDS ARE WRONG.

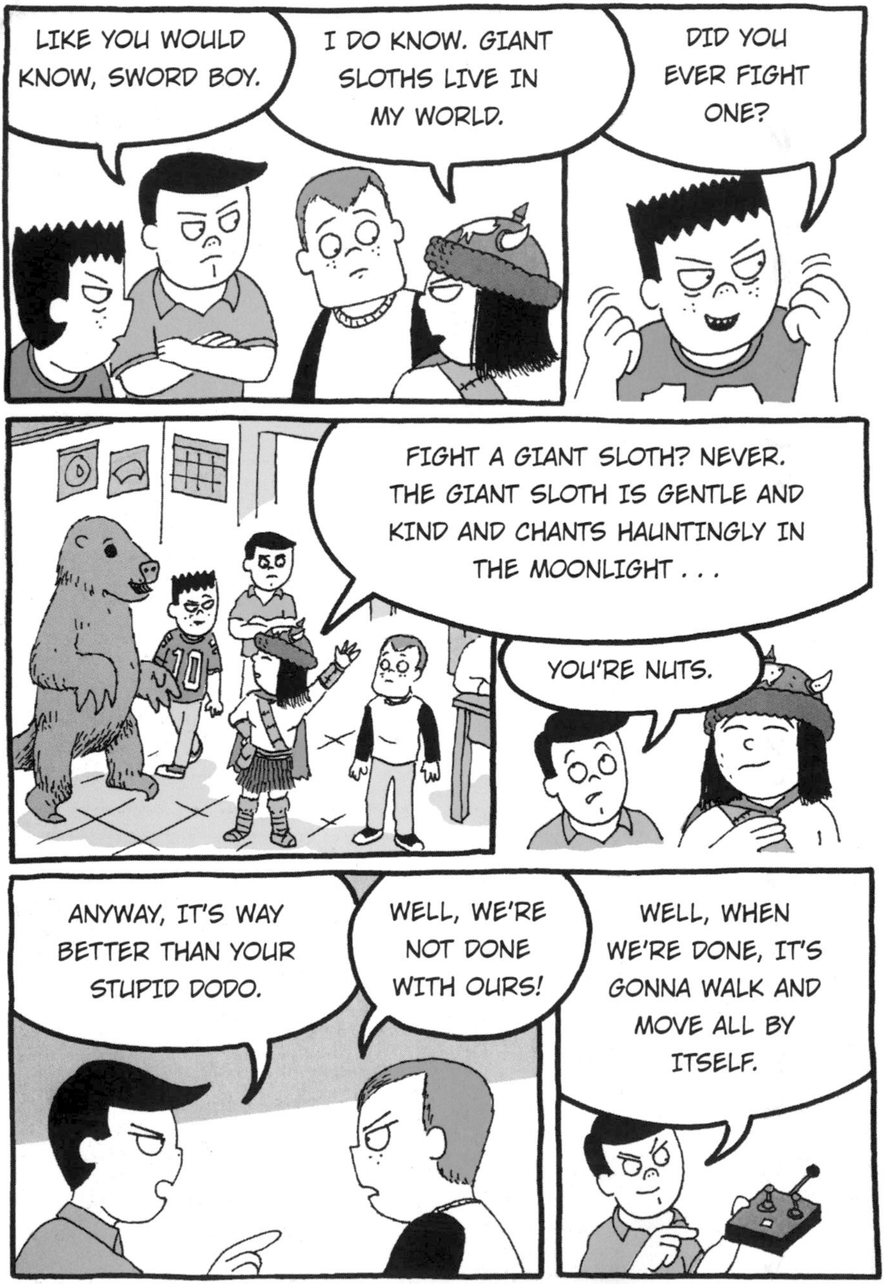
LIKE YOU WOULD KNOW, SWORD BOY.
I DO KNOW. GIANT SLOTHS LIVE IN MY WORLD.
DID YOU EVER FIGHT ONE?
10
FIGHT A GIANT SLOTH? NEVER. THE GIANT SLOTH IS GENTLE AND KIND AND CHANTS HAUNTINGLY IN THE MOONLIGHT . . .
YOU'RE NUTS.
ANYWAY, IT'S WAY BETTER THAN YOUR STUPID DODO.
WELL, WE'RE NOT DONE WITH OURS!
WELL, WHEN WE'RE DONE, IT'S GONNA WALK AND MOVE ALL BY ITSELF.

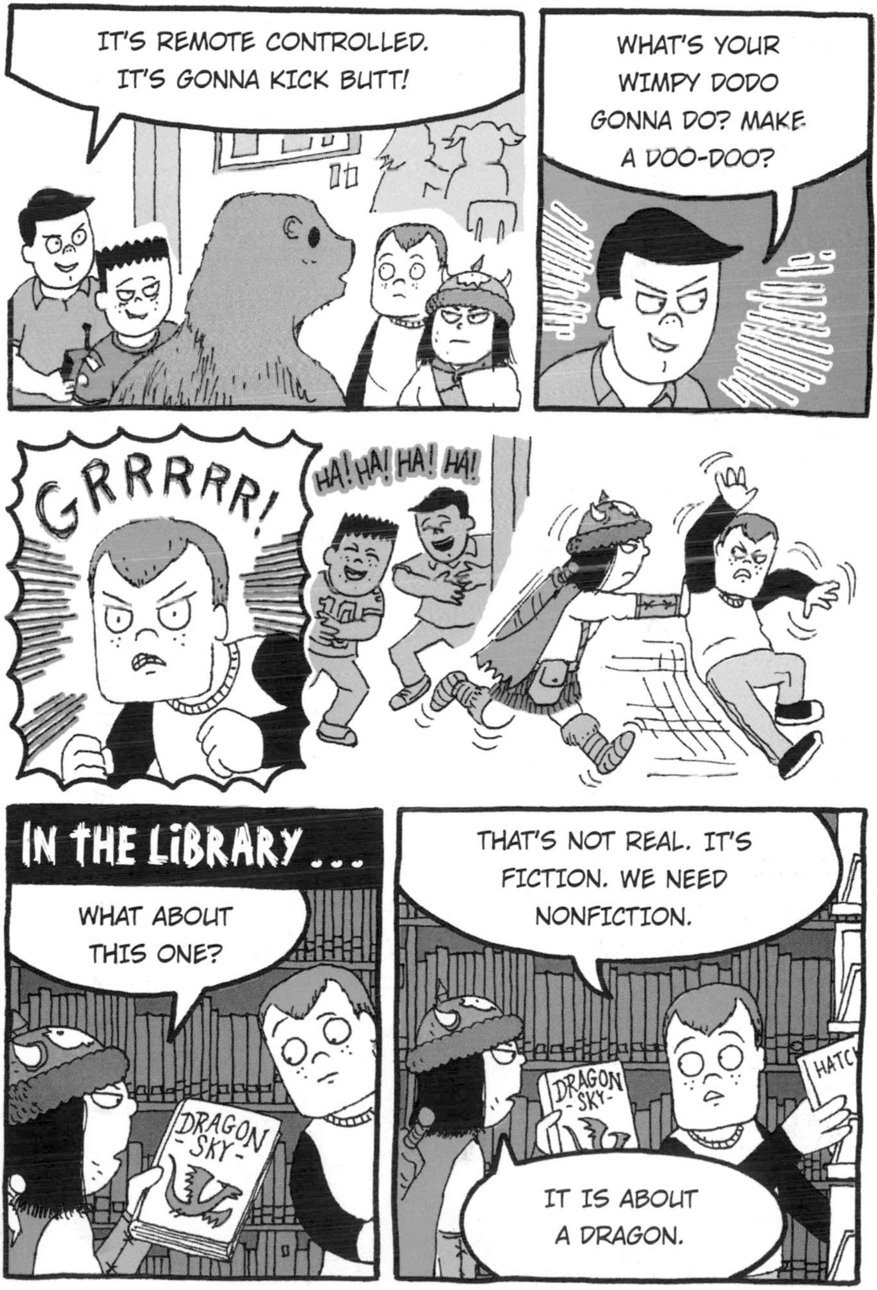
IT'S REMOTE CONTROLLED. IT'S GONNA KICK BUTT!
WHAT'S YOUR WIMPY DODO GONNA DO? MAKE A DOO-DOO?
GRRRRRR!
HA! HA! HA! HA!
IN THE LIBRARY . . .
WHAT ABOUT THIS ONE?
DRAGON -SKY-
THAT'S NOT REAL. IT'S FICTION. WE NEED NONFICTION.
DRAGON -SKY-
IT IS ABOUT A DRAGON.

BUT IT'S FANTASY. WE NEED THESE, SEE? "REPTILES," "BIRDS," FARMS."

REPTILES BIRDS FARMS

ROCKED ART GOOF

DRAGONS DO NOT LIVE ON FARMS.

I KNOW, BUT . . .

DRAGON -SKY-

THIS IS ABOUT A DRAGON.

REPTILES

DO YOU SEE THE DRAGON?

YES, BUT . . .

DRAGON -SKY-

REPTILES

. . . OK.

DRAGON -SKY-

YOU HAVE MADE A WISE CHOICE, BILL.

BACK IN CLASS . . .

HEY, AREN'T YOU SUPPOSED TO BE PAINTING THE DODO?

UM . . . YEAH, BUT . . .

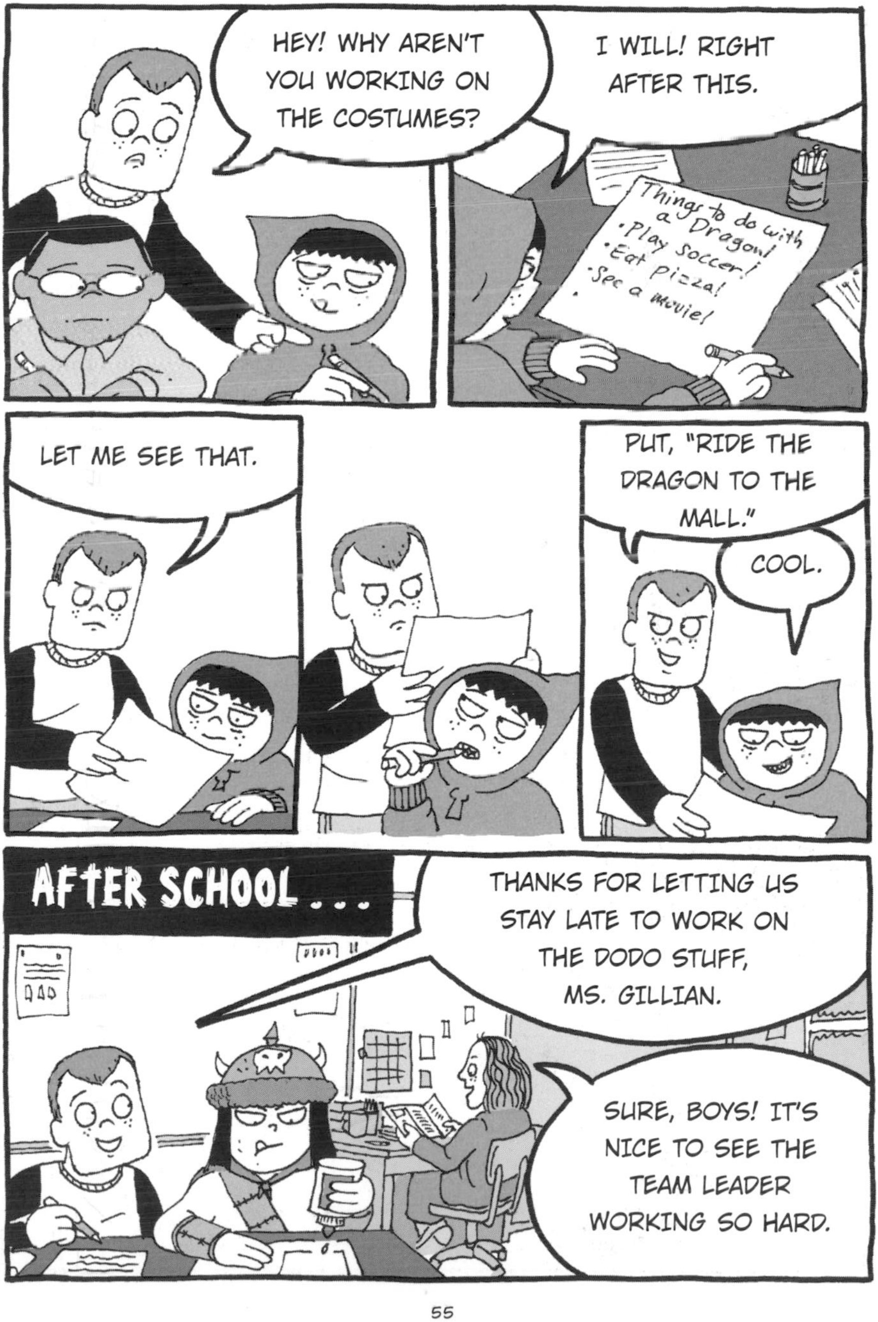
HEY! WHY AREN'T YOU WORKING ON THE COSTUMES?
I WILL! RIGHT AFTER THIS.
Things to do with a Dragon!
•Play Soccer!
•Eat pizza!
•See a movie!
LET ME SEE THAT.
PUT, "RIDE THE DRAGON TO THE MALL."
COOL.
AFTER SCHOOL . . .
THANKS FOR LETTING US STAY LATE TO WORK ON THE DODO STUFF, MS. GILLIAN.
SURE, BOYS! IT'S NICE TO SEE THE TEAM LEADER WORKING SO HARD.

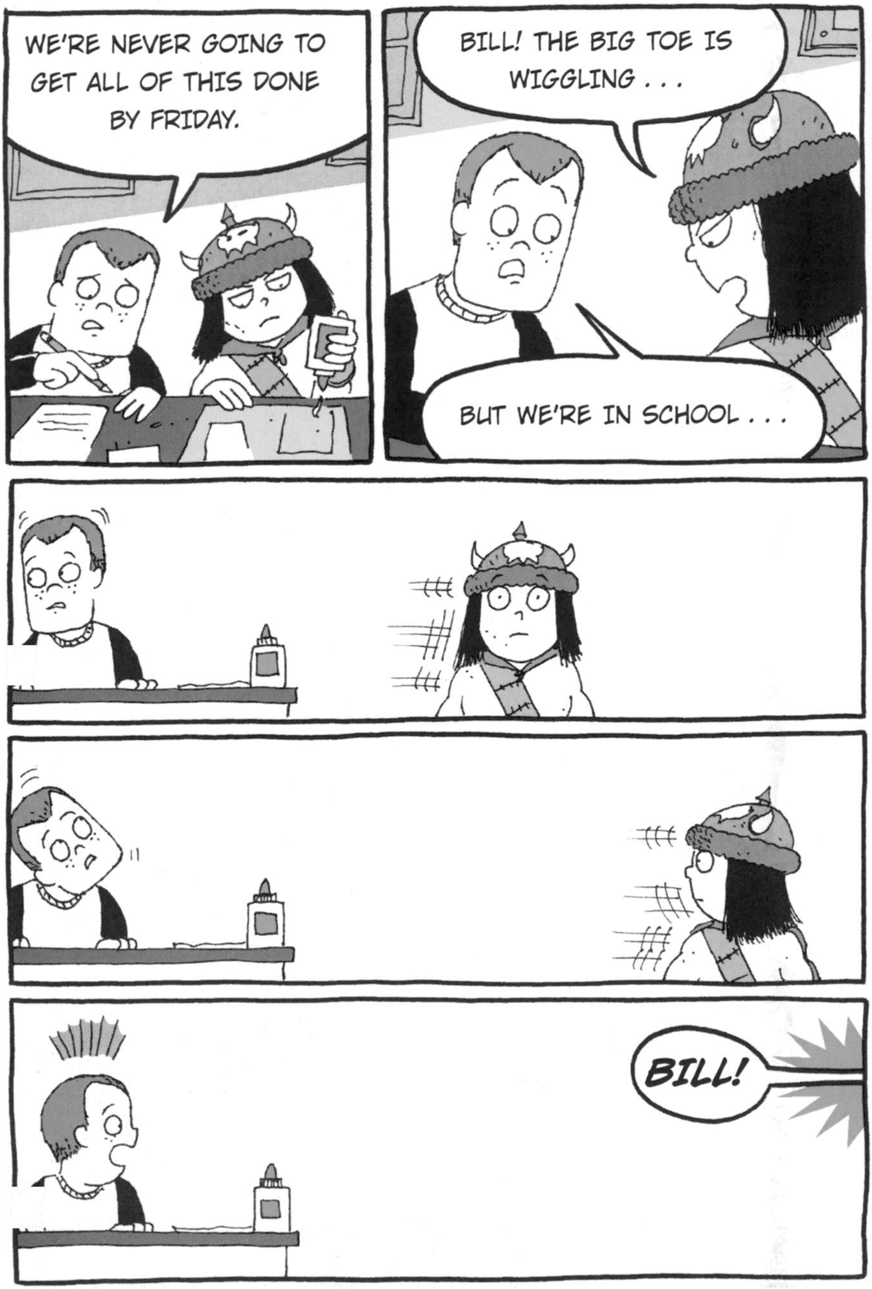
WE'RE NEVER GOING TO GET ALL OF THIS DONE BY FRIDAY.
BILL! THE BIG TOE IS WIGGLING . . .
BUT WE'RE IN SCHOOL . . .
BILL!

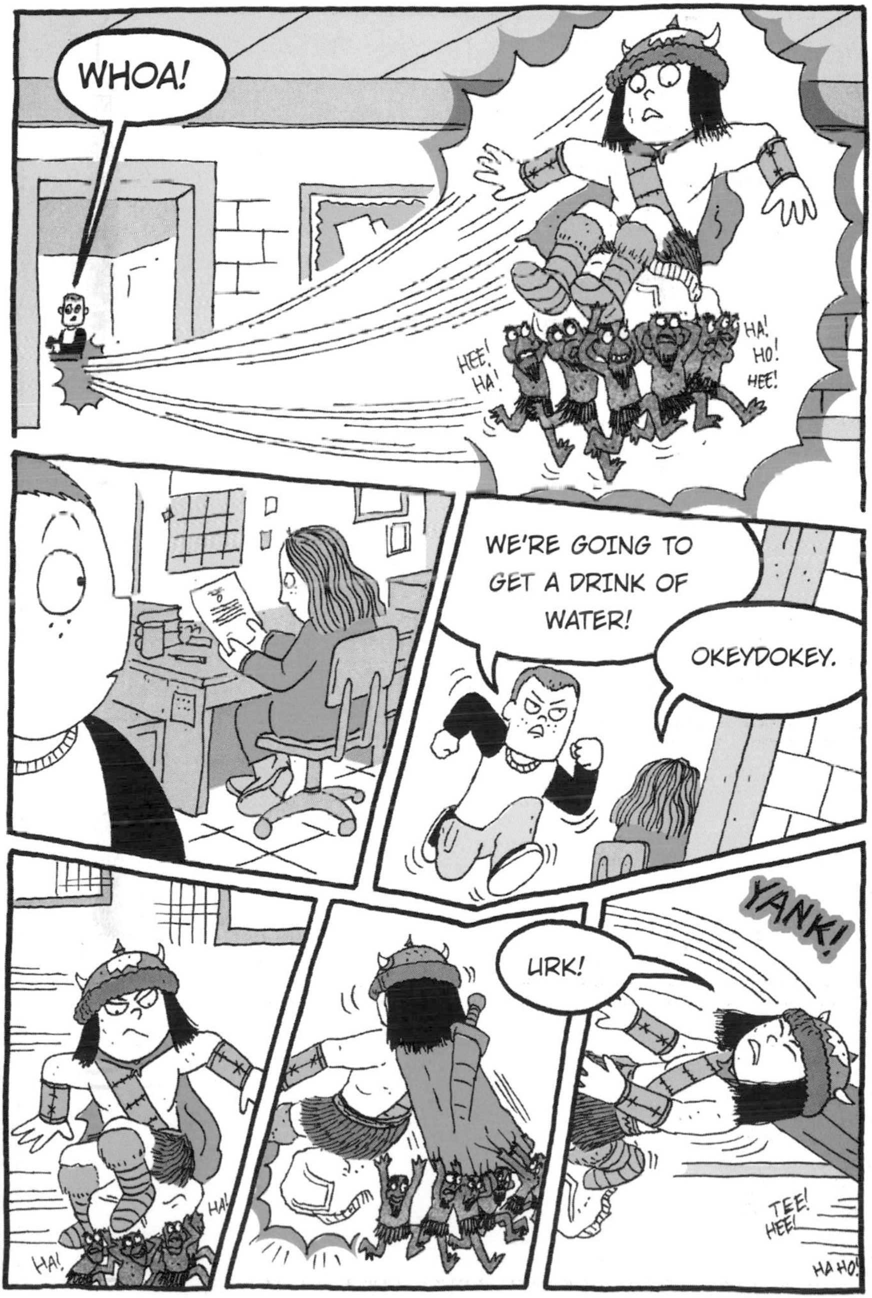
WHOA!
HEE! HA!
HA! HO! HEE!
WE'RE GOING TO GET A DRINK OF WATER!
OKEYDOKEY.
HA!
HA!
URK!
YANK!
TEE! HEE!
HA HO!

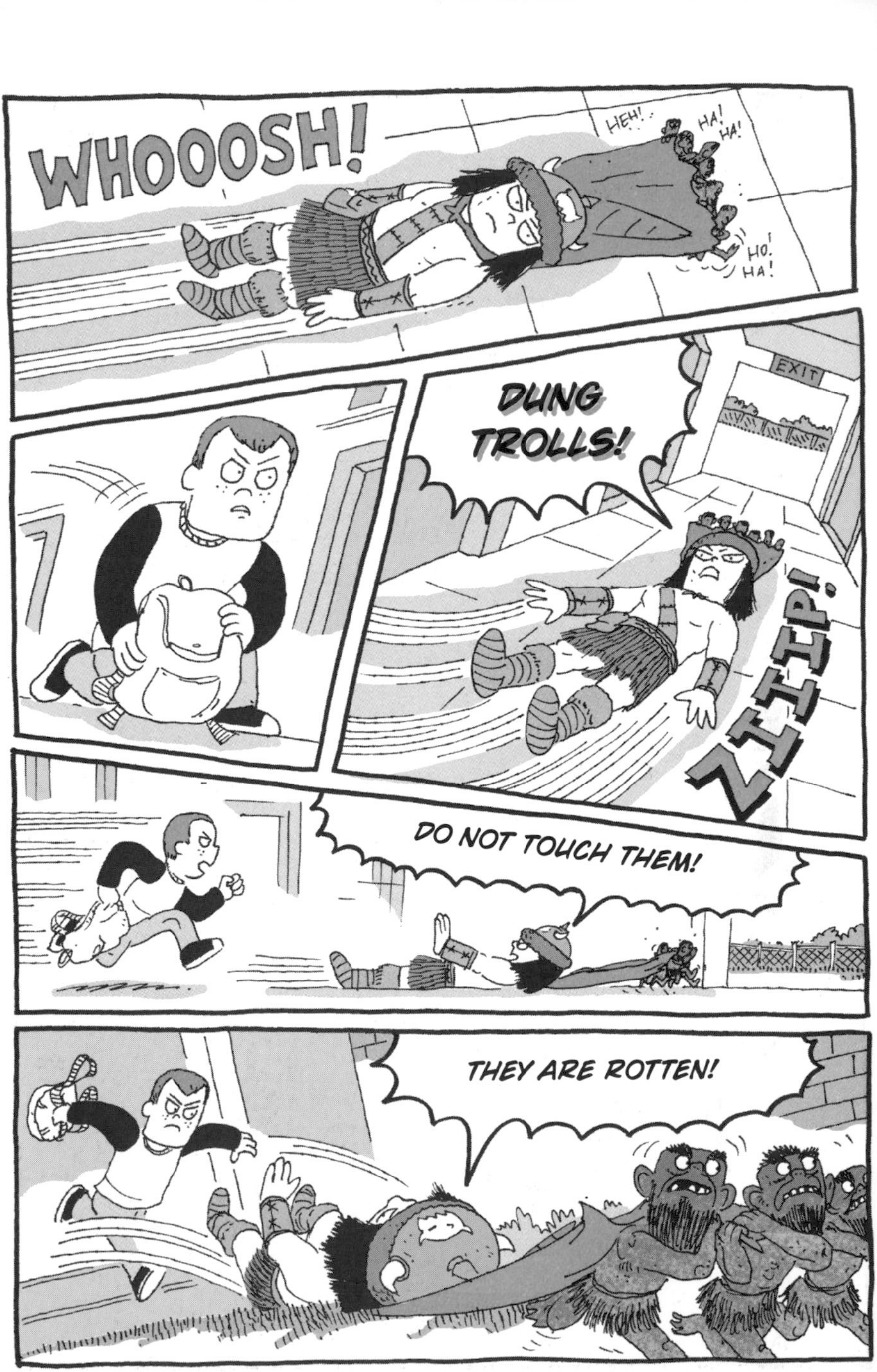
WHOOOSH!
HEH!
HA! HA!
HO! HA!
EXIT
DUNG TROLLS!
ZIIIIP!
DO NOT TOUCH THEM!
THEY ARE ROTTEN!

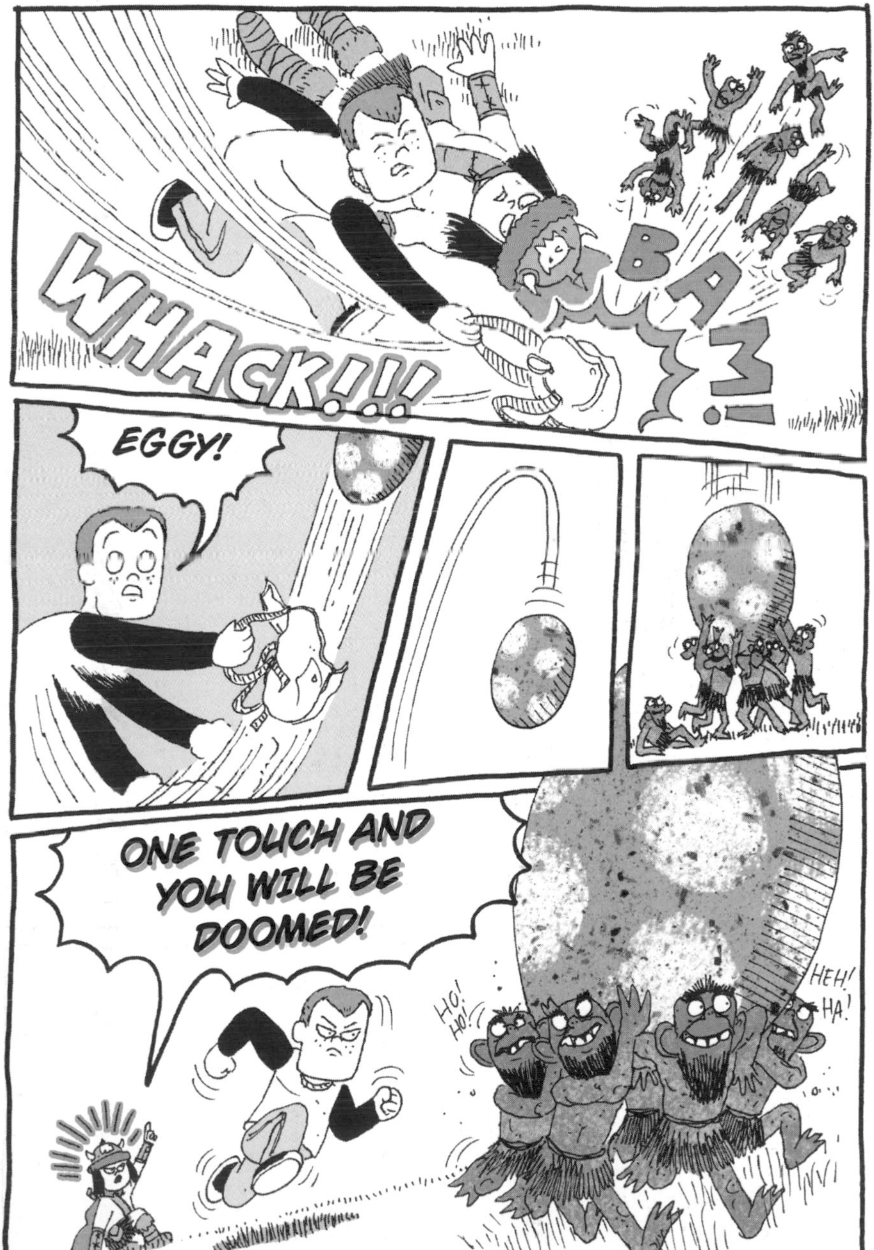
WHACK!!!
BAM!
EGGY!
ONE TOUCH AND YOU WILL BE DOOMED!
HO! HO!
HEH! HA!

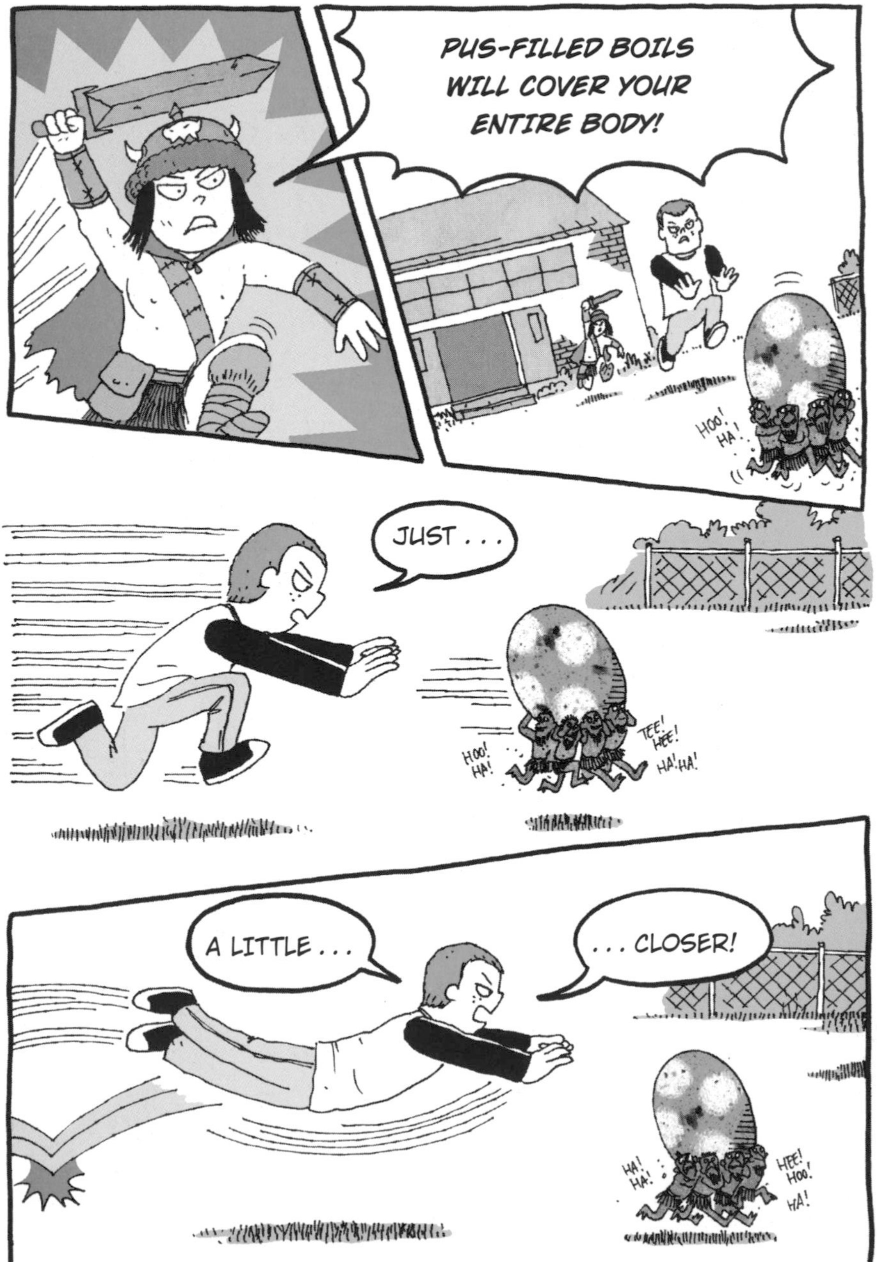
PUS-FILLED BOILS WILL COVER YOUR ENTIRE BODY!
HOO! HA!
JUST . . .
HOO! HA!
TEE! HEE!
HA! HA!
A LITTLE . . .
. . . CLOSER!
HA! HA!
HEE! HOO!
HA!

WHUMP!
EEEEEEE!
AHHHH!
OOOOH
GOTCHA!
HUH?
HEE! HEE!
HA! HA!
FANGBOOOOOOOOOOOOOONE!

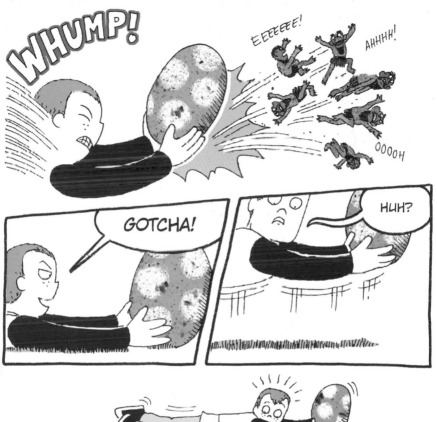

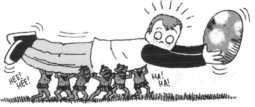

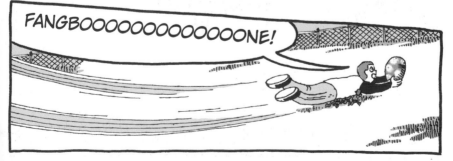

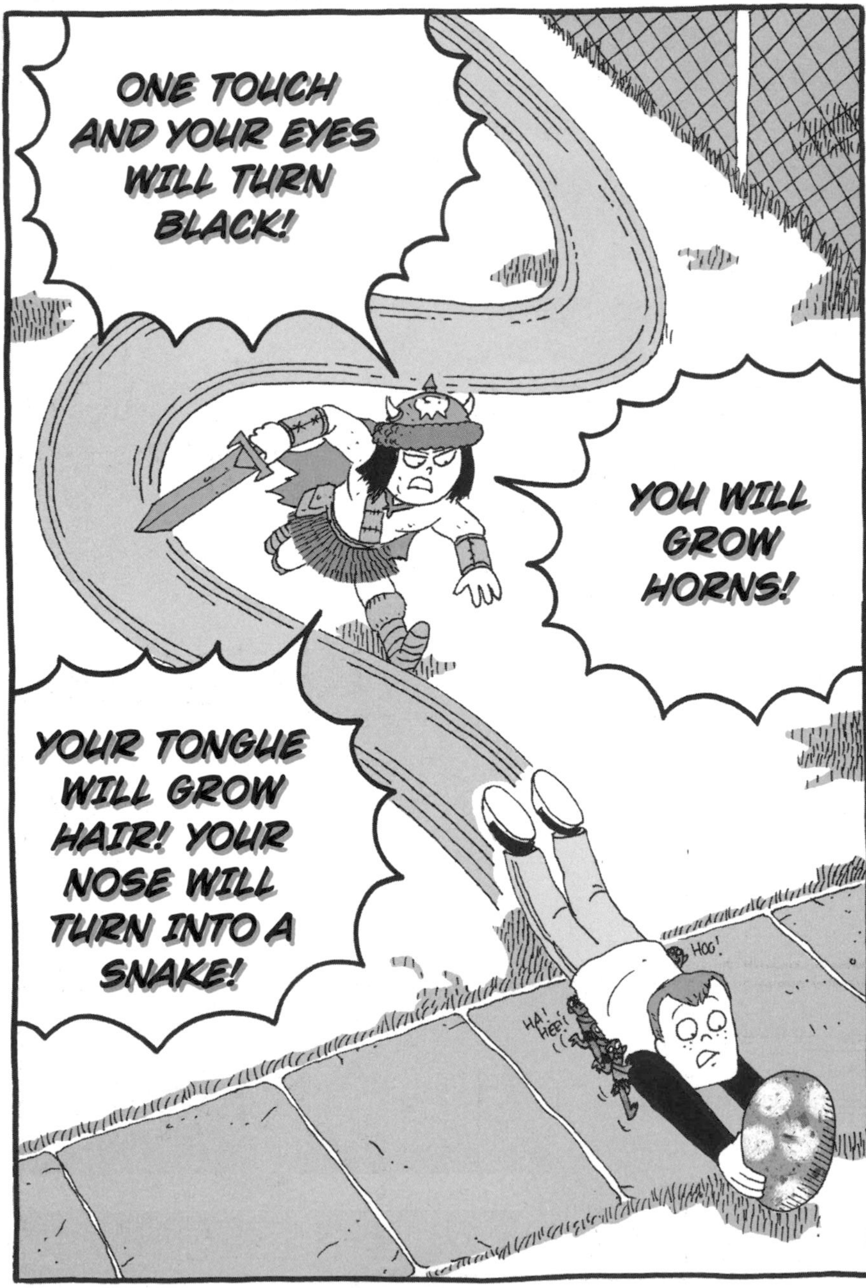
ONE TOUCH AND YOUR EYES WILL TURN BLACK!
YOU WILL GROW HORNS!
YOUR TONGUE WILL GROW HAIR! YOUR NOSE WILL TURN INTO A SNAKE!
HOG!
HA! HEE!

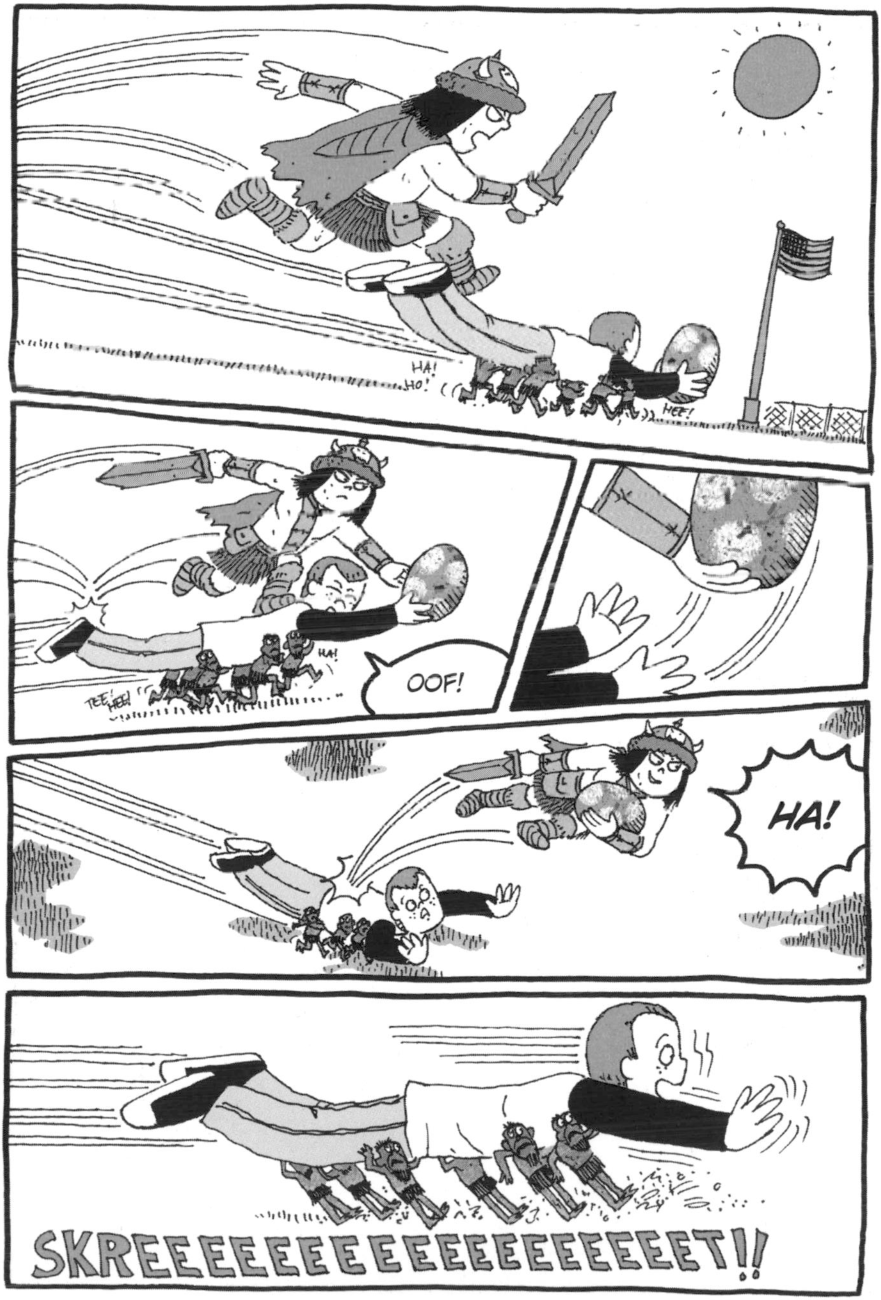
HA!
HO!
HEE!
TEE!
HEE!
HA!
OOF!
HA!
SKREEEEEEEEEEEEEEEEEET!!

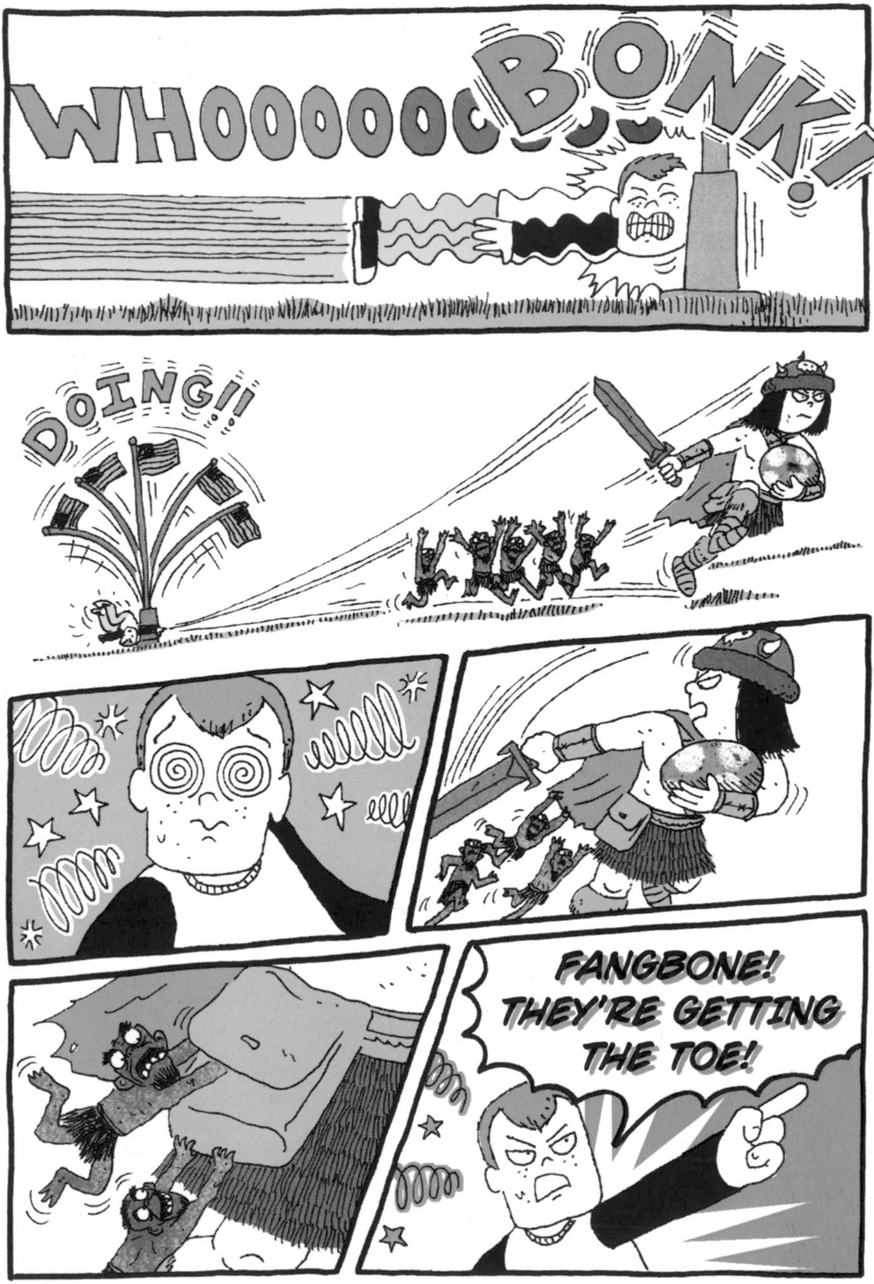
WHOOOOOO
BONK!
DOING!!
FANGBONE! THEY'RE GETTING THE TOE!

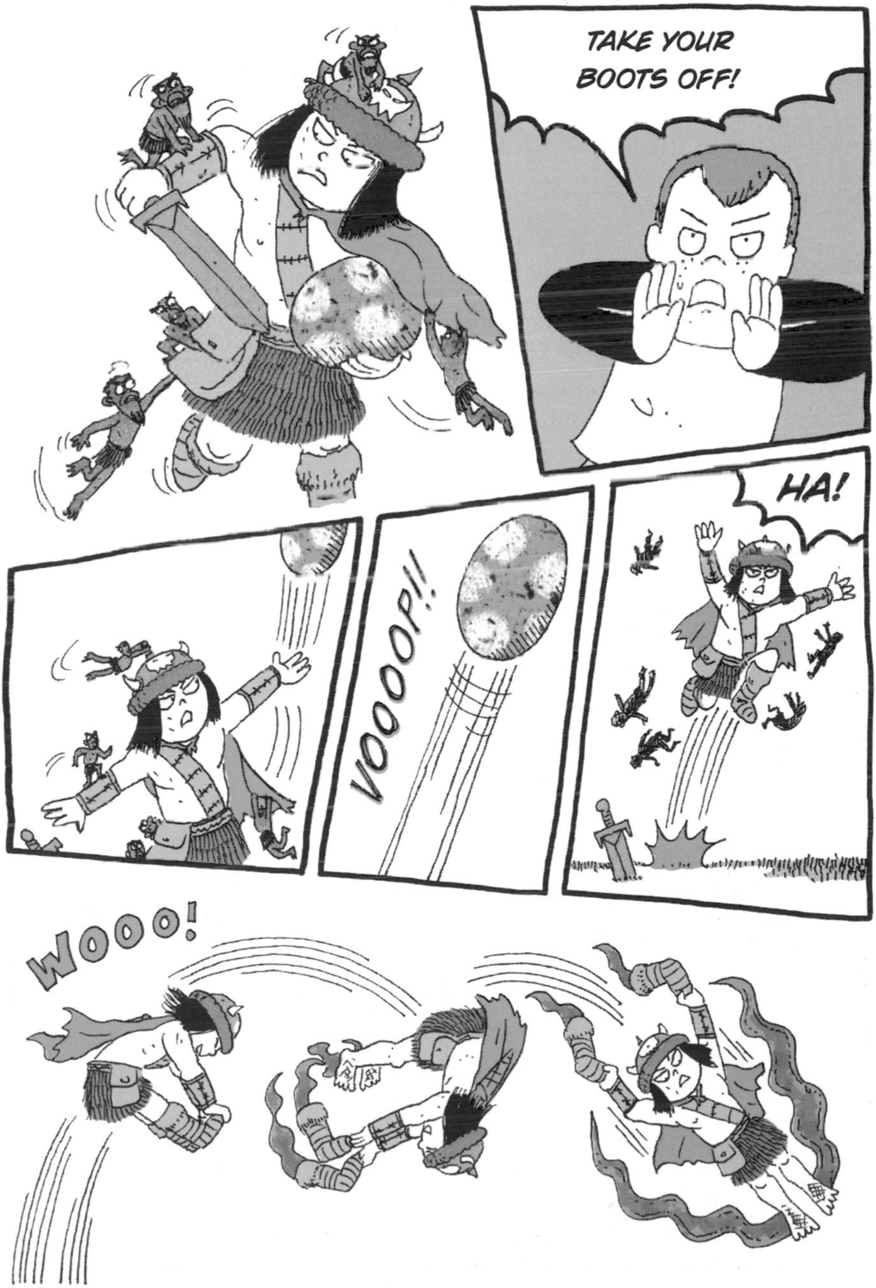
TAKE YOUR BOOTS OFF!
VOOOOP!!
HA!
WOOO!

TOEJAM!

YOU
DID IT!

SPLAT!

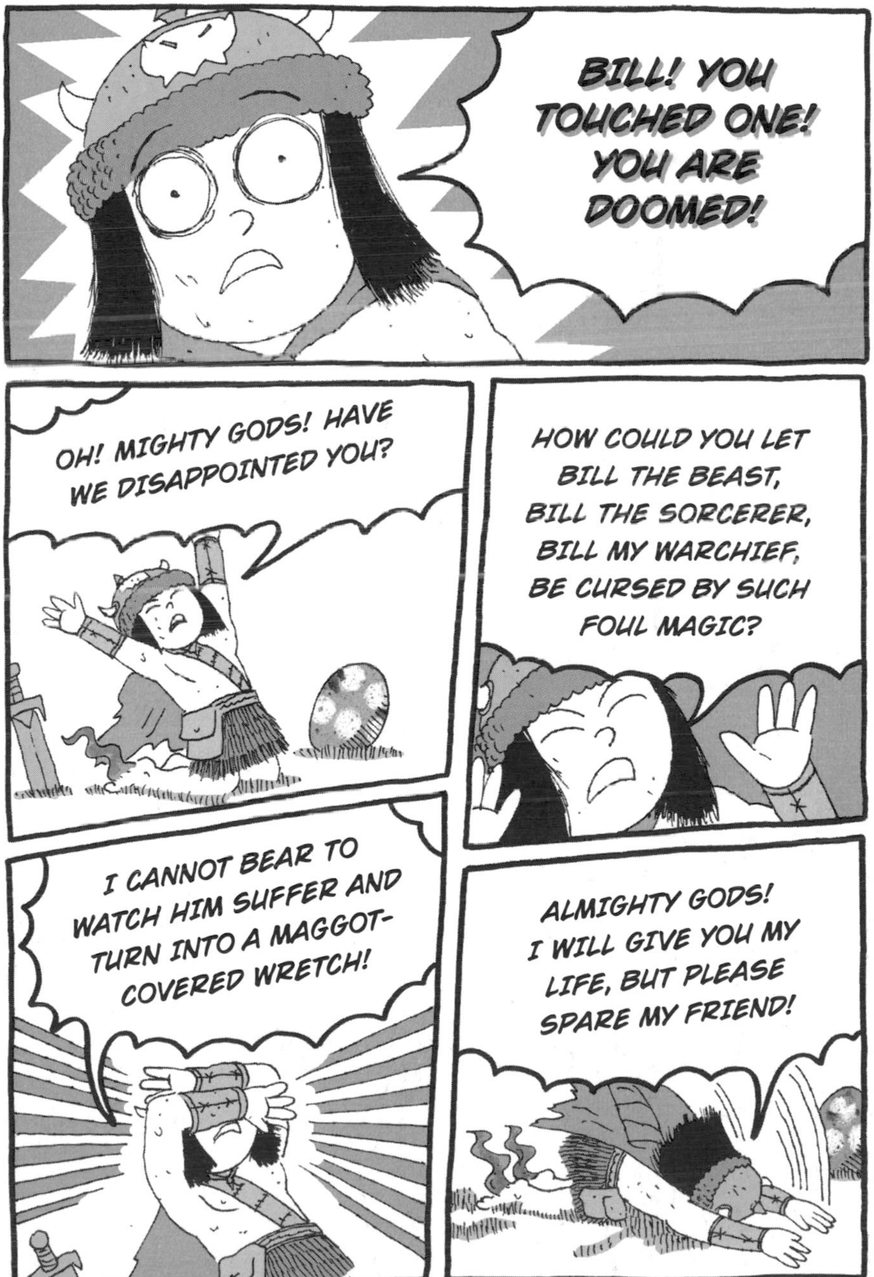
BILL! YOU TOUCHED ONE! YOU ARE DOOMED!
OH! MIGHTY GODS! HAVE WE DISAPPOINTED YOU?
HOW COULD YOU LET BILL THE BEAST, BILL THE SORCERER, BILL MY WARCHIEF, BE CURSED BY SUCH FOUL MAGIC?
I CANNOT BEAR TO WATCH HIM SUFFER AND TURN INTO A MAGGOT-COVERED WRETCH!
ALMIGHTY GODS! I WILL GIVE YOU MY LIFE, BUT PLEASE SPARE MY FRIEND!

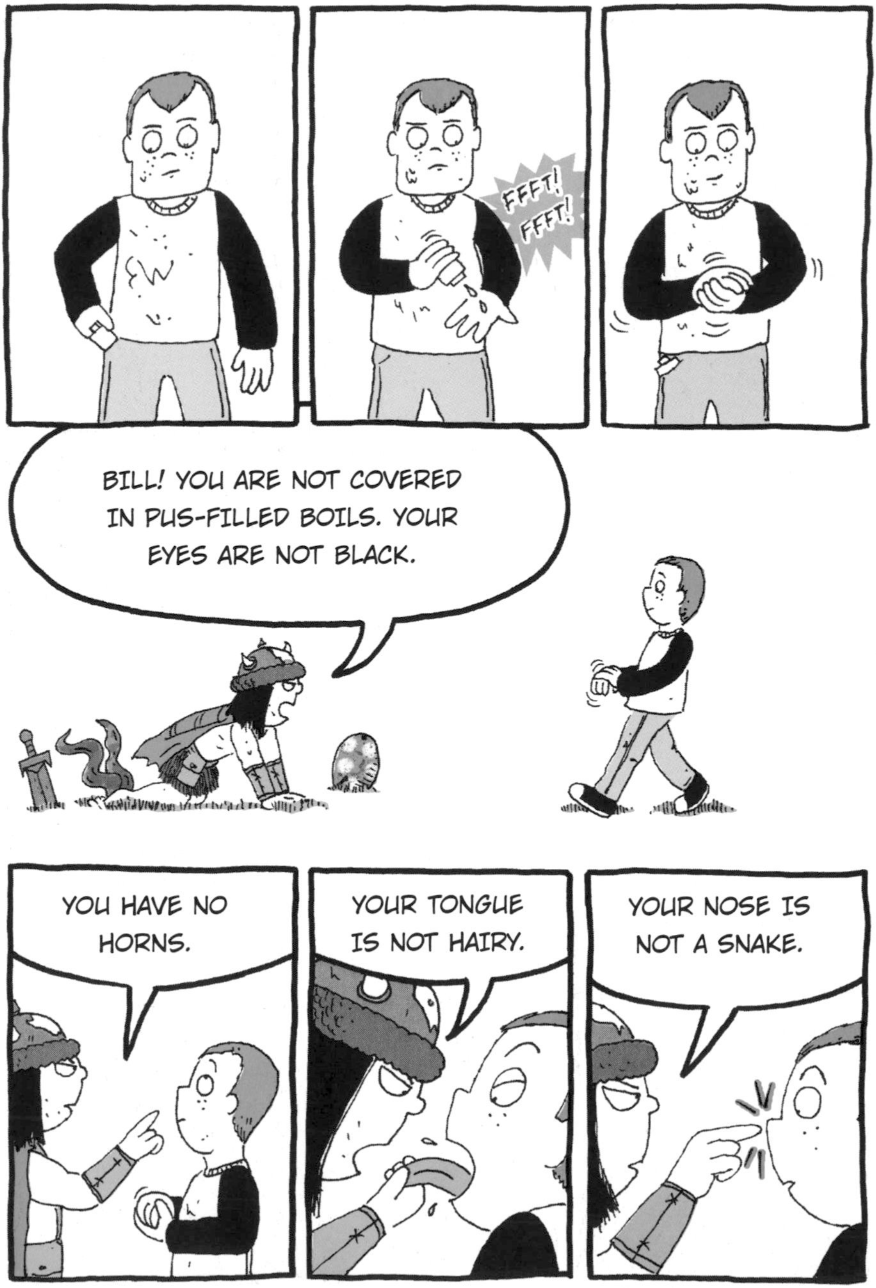
FFFT!
FFFT!
BILL! YOU ARE NOT COVERED IN PUS-FILLED BOILS. YOUR EYES ARE NOT BLACK.
YOU HAVE NO HORNS.
YOUR TONGUE IS NOT HAIRY.
YOUR NOSE IS NOT A SNAKE.

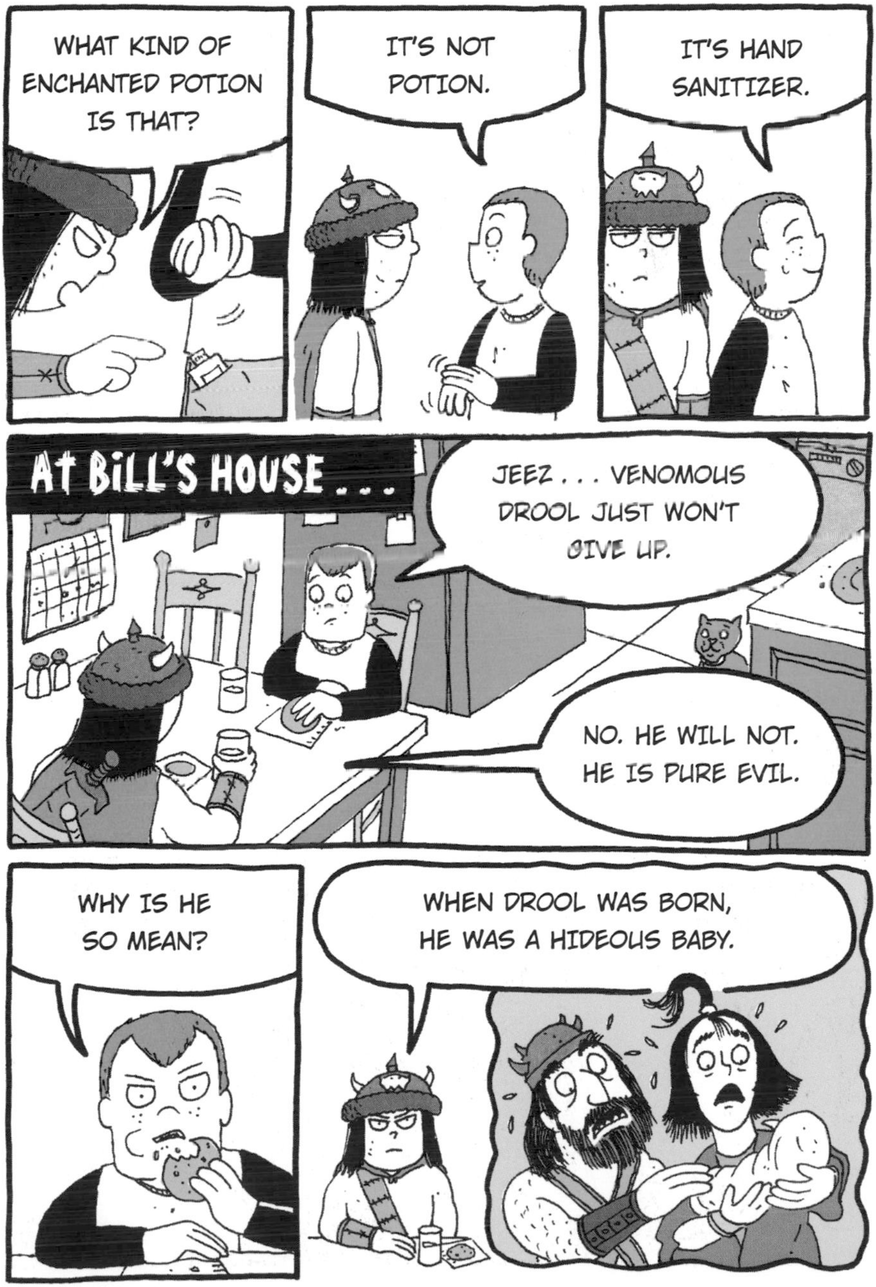
WHAT KIND OF ENCHANTED POTION IS THAT?
IT'S NOT POTION.
IT'S HAND SANITIZER.
AT BiLL'S HOUSE . . .
JEEZ . . . VENOMOUS DROOL JUST WON'T GIVE UP.
NO. HE WILL NOT. HE IS PURE EVIL.
WHY IS HE SO MEAN?
WHEN DROOL WAS BORN, HE WAS A HIDEOUS BABY.

HIS PARENTS DROPPED HIM DOWN A HOLE FILLED WITH BULL-SLUGS. BUT THE SLUGS DID NOT EAT HIM. THEY RAISED HIM AS THEIR OWN. HE BECAME PART SLUG.

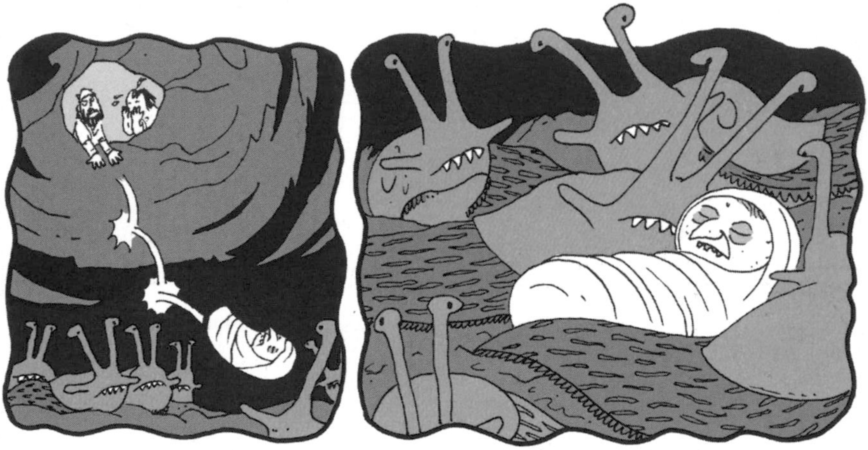

HE CAN STRETCH HIS BODY OUT LONG AND THIN, AND HE LEAVES A SLIME TRAIL WHEREVER HE GOES. HE HATES HUMANS. HE WANTS TO TURN THEM ALL INTO WICKED CREATURES. THAT IS WHY HE WAGES WAR ON THE CLANS.

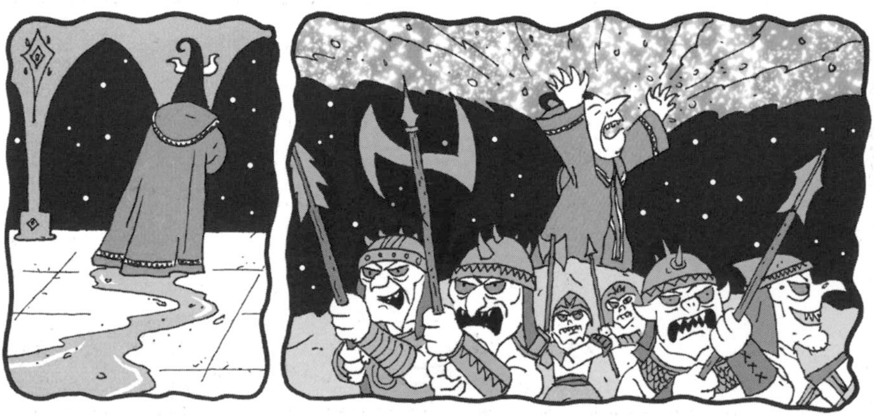

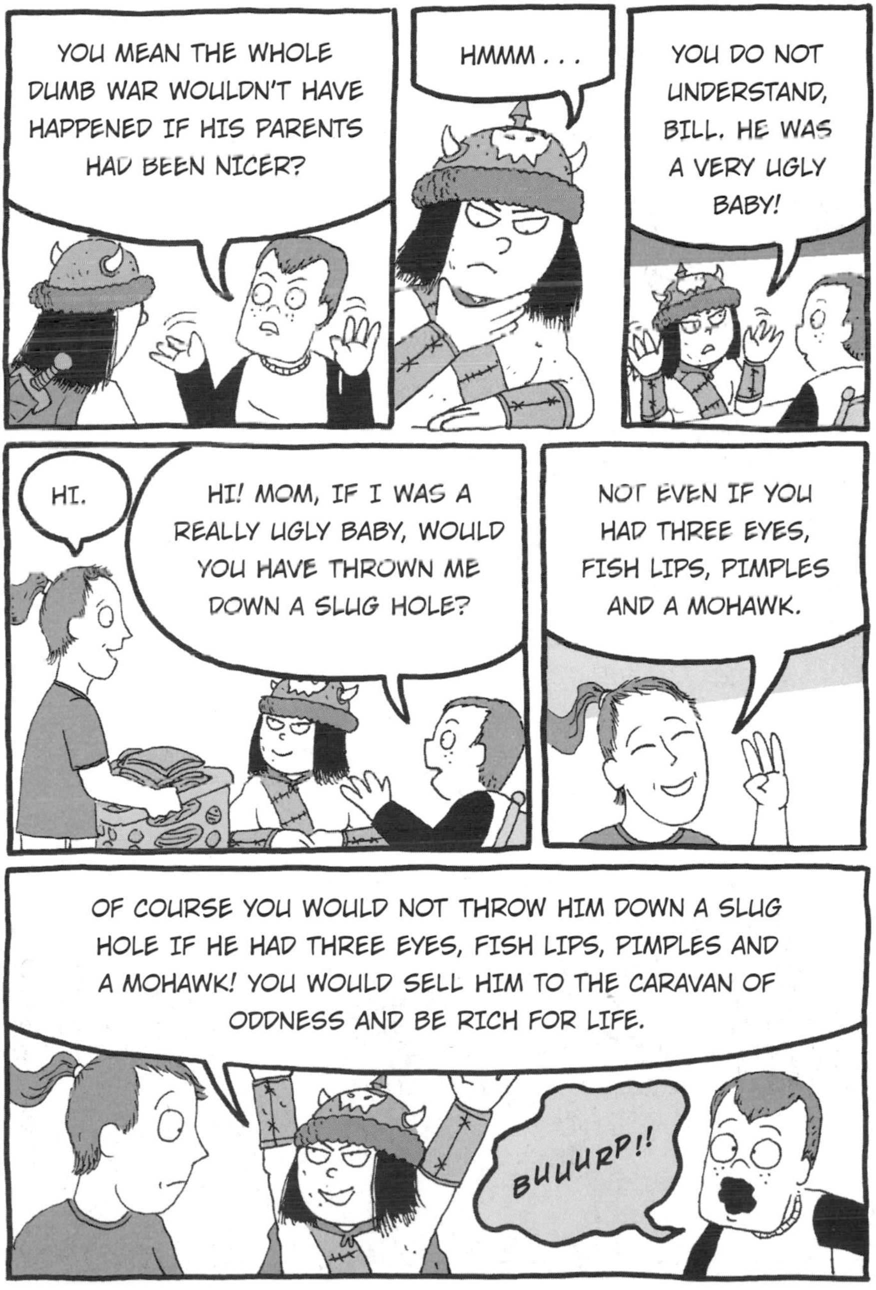
YOU MEAN THE WHOLE DUMB WAR WOULDN'T HAVE HAPPENED IF HIS PARENTS HAD BEEN NICER?
HMMM . . .
YOU DO NOT UNDERSTAND, BILL. HE WAS A VERY UGLY BABY!
HI.
HI! MOM, IF I WAS A REALLY UGLY BABY, WOULD YOU HAVE THROWN ME DOWN A SLUG HOLE?
NOT EVEN IF YOU HAD THREE EYES, FISH LIPS, PIMPLES AND A MOHAWK.
OF COURSE YOU WOULD NOT THROW HIM DOWN A SLUG HOLE IF HE HAD THREE EYES, FISH LIPS, PIMPLES AND A MOHAWK! YOU WOULD SELL HIM TO THE CARAVAN OF ODDNESS AND BE RICH FOR LIFE.
BUUURP!!

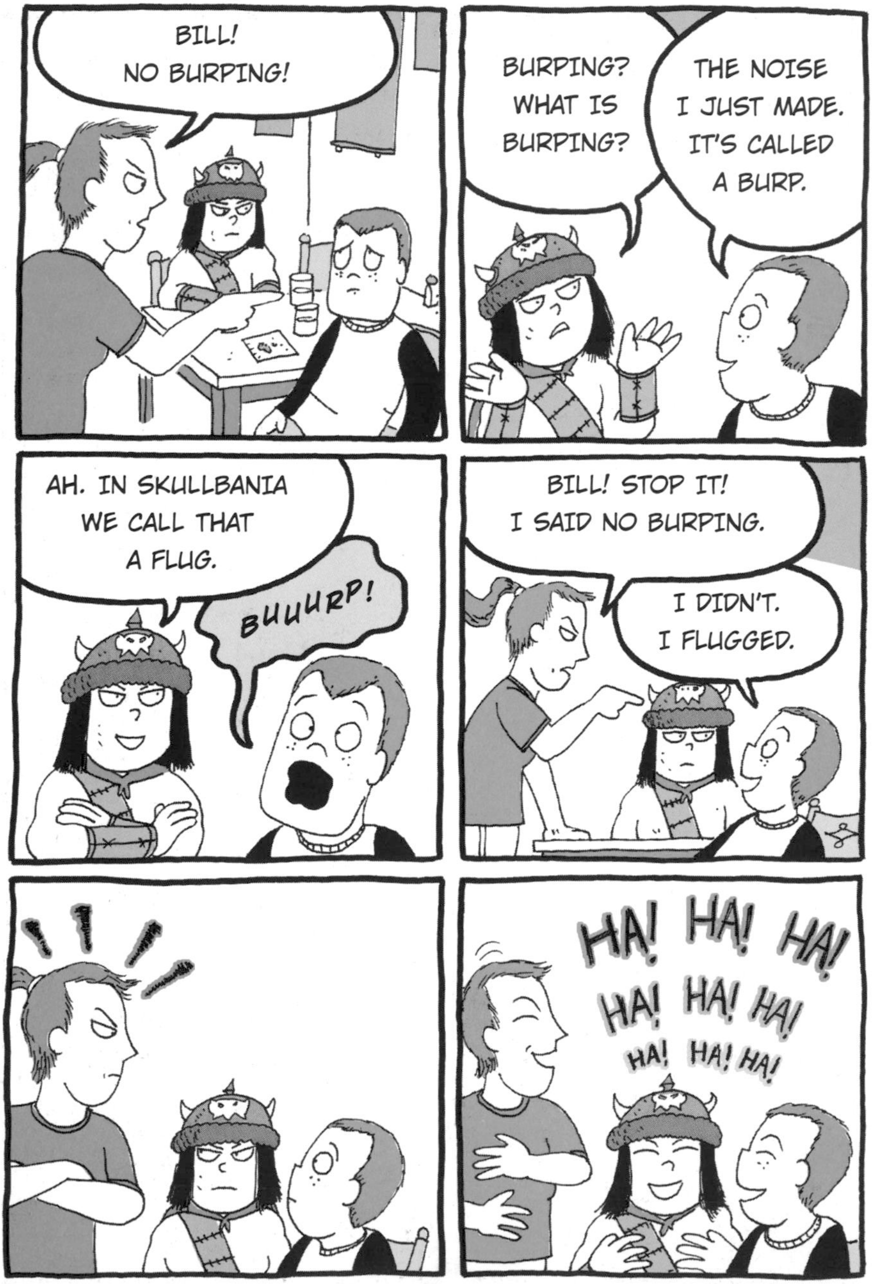
BILL!
NO BURPING!
BURPING? WHAT IS BURPING?
THE NOISE I JUST MADE. IT'S CALLED A BURP.
AH. IN SKULLBANIA WE CALL THAT A FLUG.
BUUURP!
BILL! STOP IT! I SAID NO BURPING.
I DIDN'T. I FLUGGED.
HA! HA! HA!
HA! HA! HA!
HA! HA! HA!

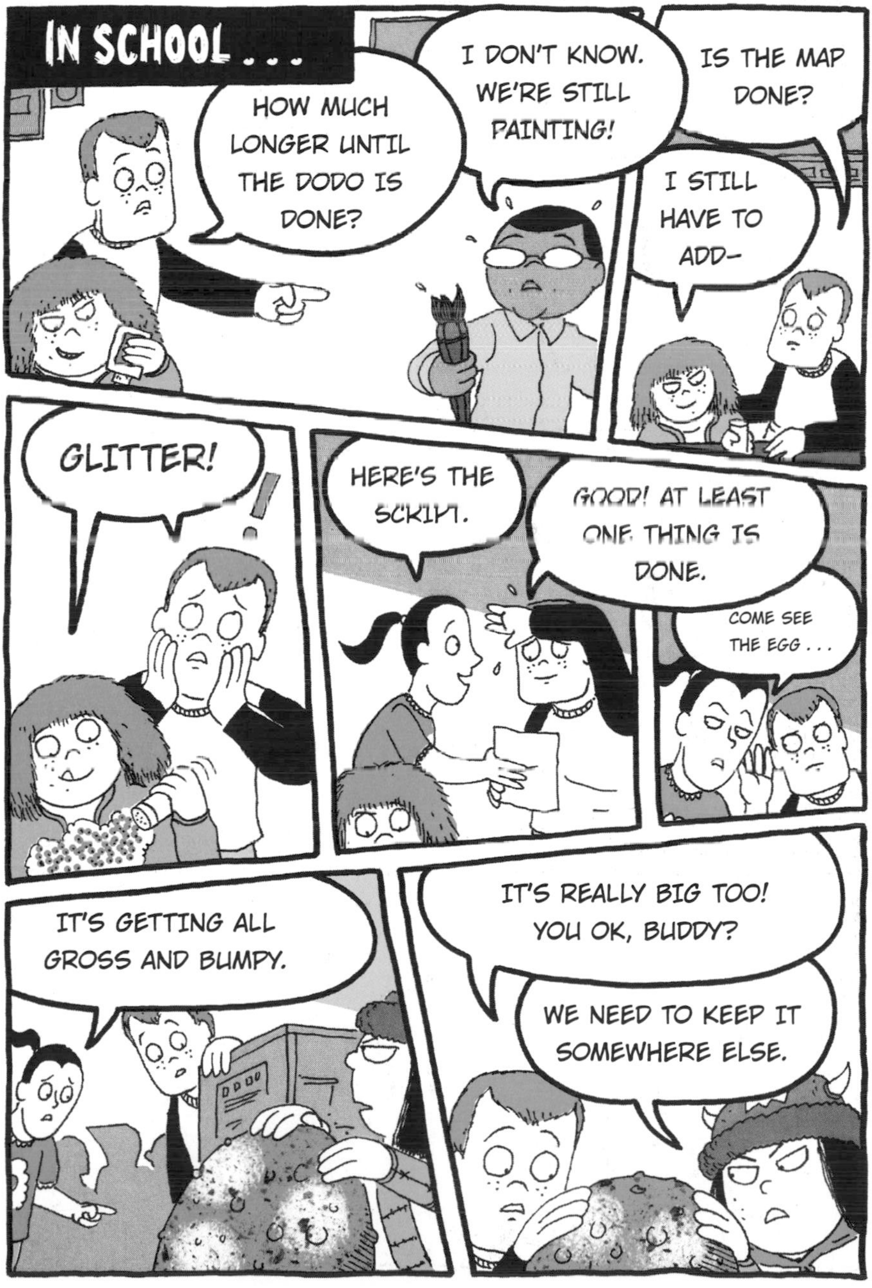

IN SCHOOL . . .
HOW MUCH LONGER UNTIL THE DODO IS DONE?
I DON'T KNOW. WE'RE STILL PAINTING!
IS THE MAP DONE?
I STILL HAVE TO ADD-
GLITTER!
HERE'S THE SCRIPT.
GOOD! AT LEAST ONE THING IS DONE.
COME SEE THE EGG . . .
IT'S GETTING ALL GROSS AND BUMPY.
IT'S REALLY BIG TOO! YOU OK, BUDDY?
WE NEED TO KEEP IT SOMEWHERE ELSE.

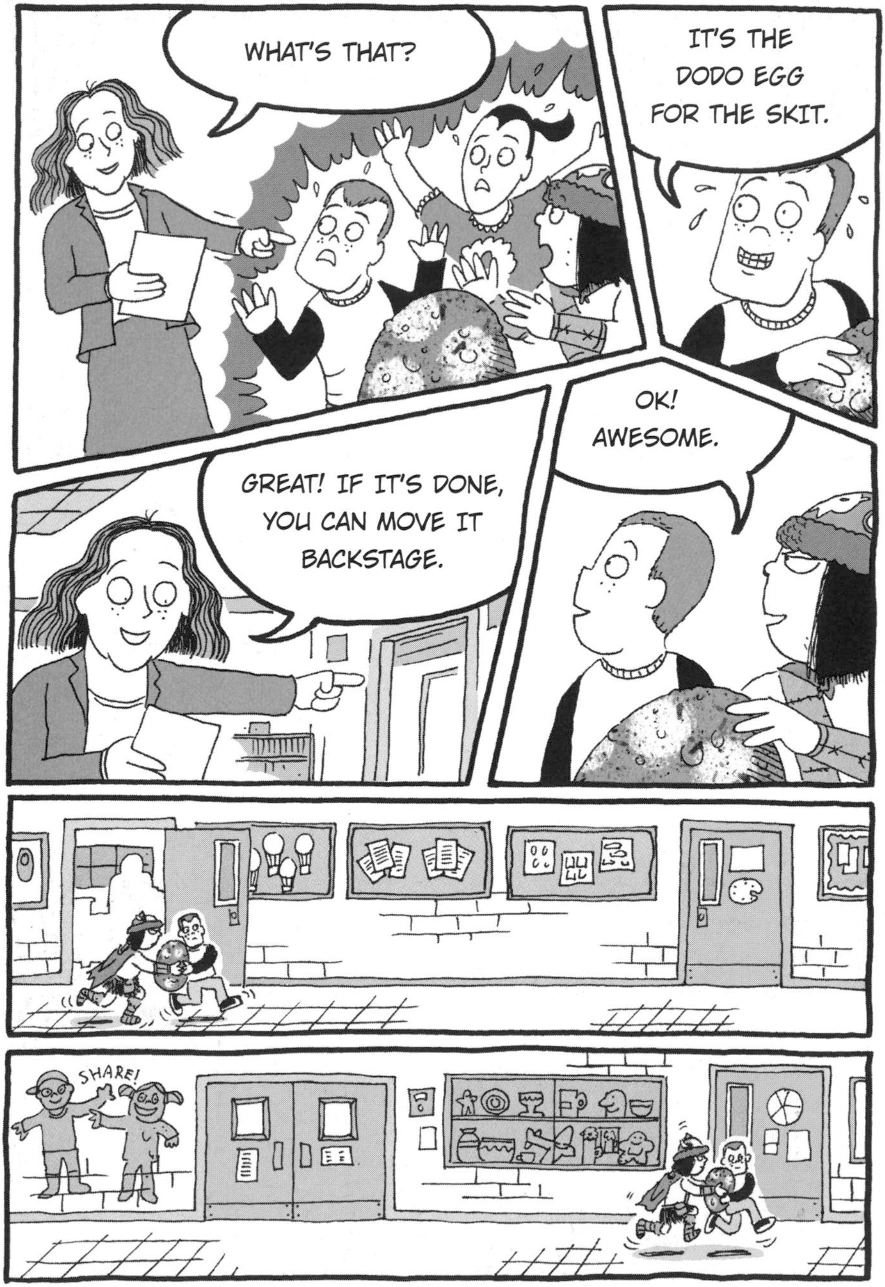
WHAT'S THAT?
IT'S THE DODO EGG FOR THE SKIT.
GREAT! IF IT'S DONE, YOU CAN MOVE IT BACKSTAGE.
OK! AWESOME.
SHARE!

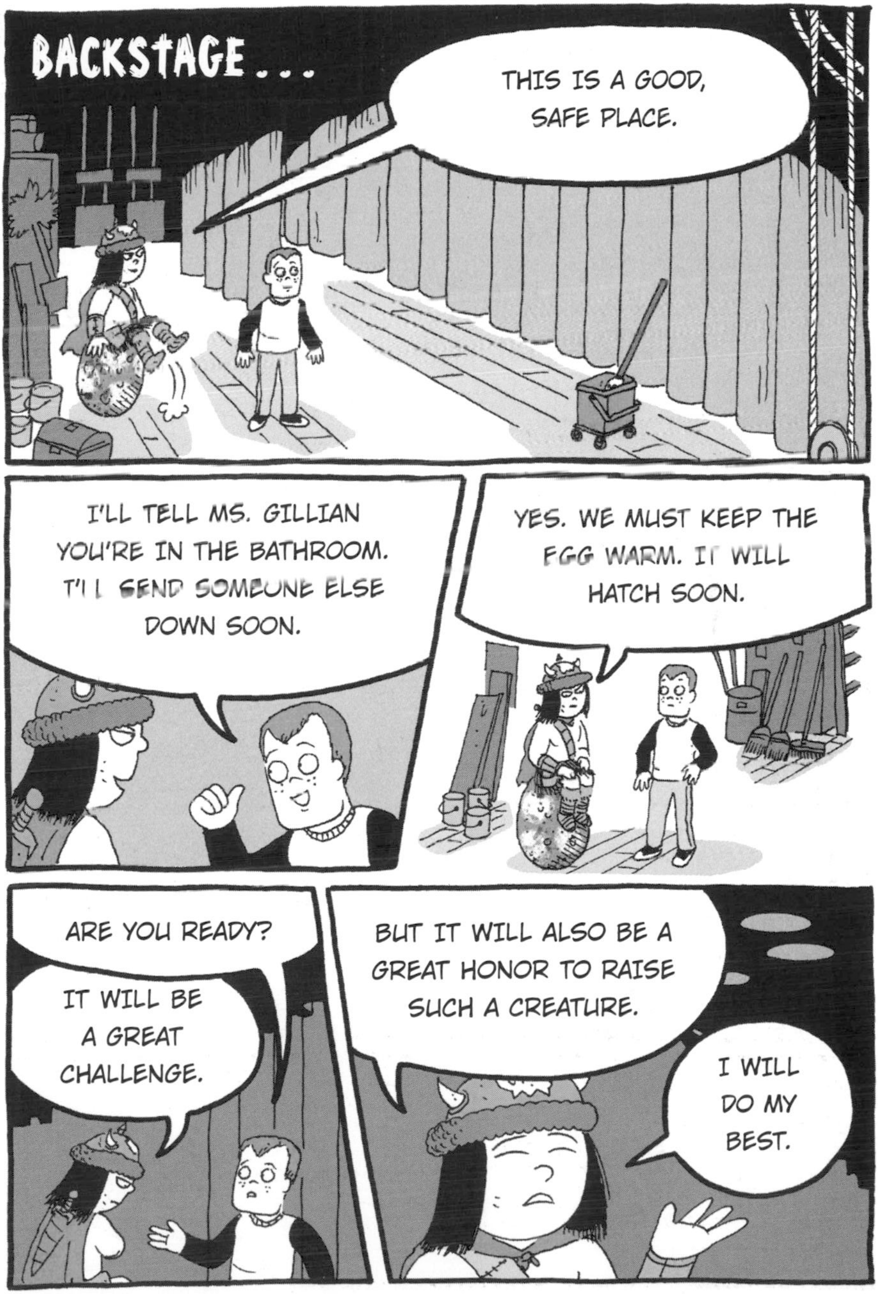
BACKSTAGE...
THIS IS A GOOD, SAFE PLACE.
I'LL TELL MS. GILLIAN YOU'RE IN THE BATHROOM. I'LL SEND SOMEONE ELSE DOWN SOON.
YES. WE MUST KEEP THE EGG WARM. IT WILL HATCH SOON.
ARE YOU READY?
IT WILL BE A GREAT CHALLENGE.
BUT IT WILL ALSO BE A GREAT HONOR TO RAISE SUCH A CREATURE.
I WILL DO MY BEST.

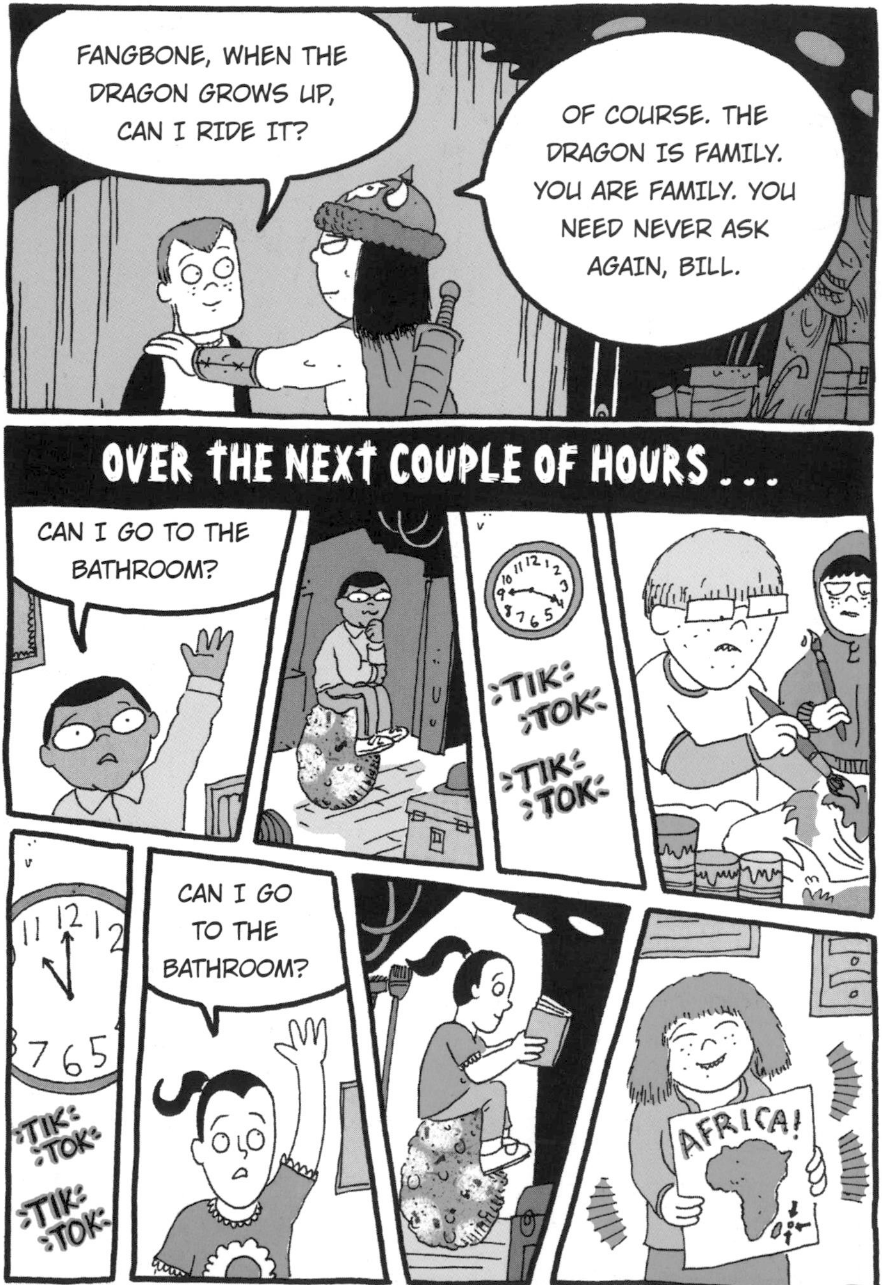
FANGBONE, WHEN THE DRAGON GROWS UP, CAN I RIDE IT?
OF COURSE. THE DRAGON IS FAMILY. YOU ARE FAMILY. YOU NEED NEVER ASK AGAIN, BILL.
OVER THE NEXT COUPLE OF HOURS . . .
CAN I GO TO THE BATHROOM?
TIK TOK
TIK TOK
TIK TOK
TIK TOK
CAN I GO TO THE BATHROOM?
AFRICA!

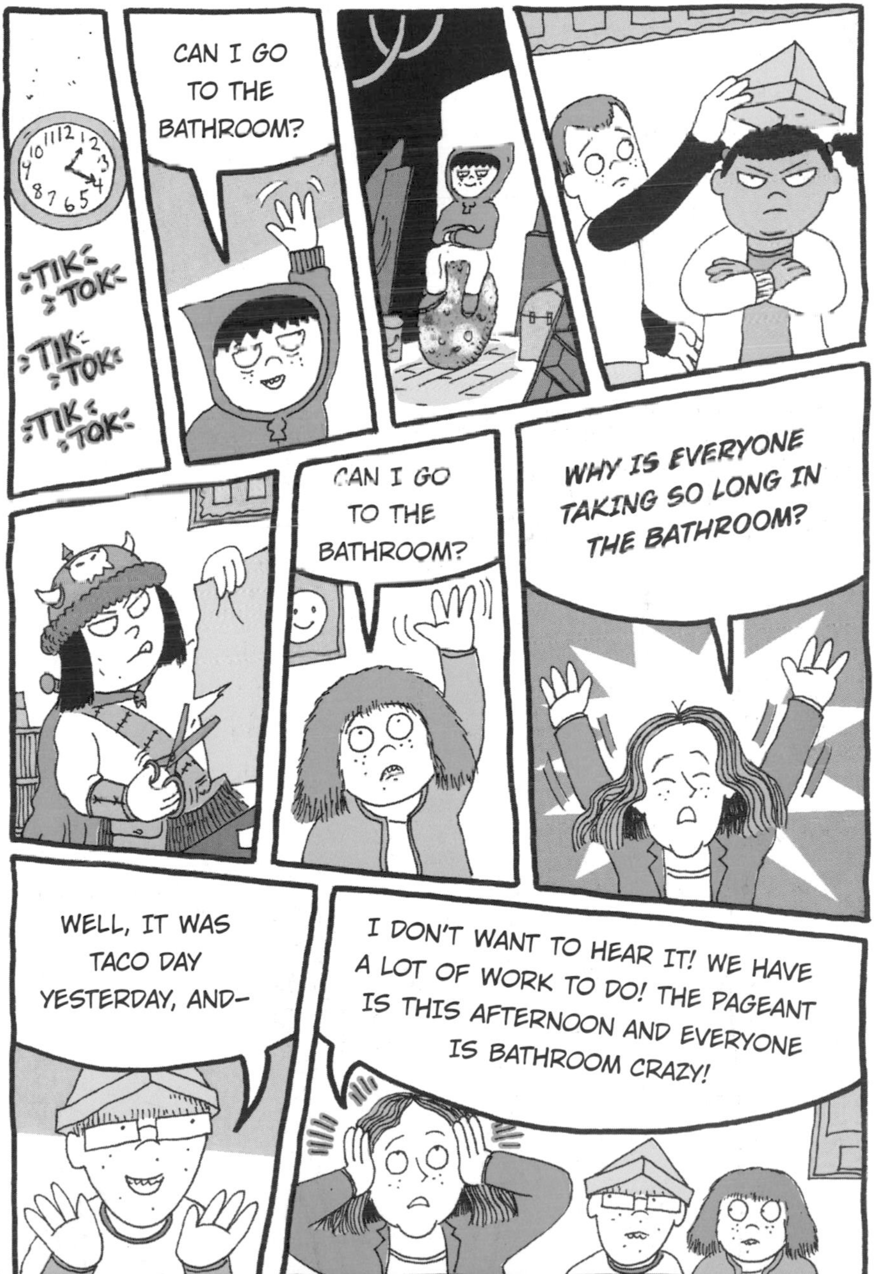
TIK TOK
TIK TOK
TIK TOK
CAN I GO TO THE BATHROOM?
CAN I GO TO THE BATHROOM?
WHY IS EVERYONE TAKING SO LONG IN THE BATHROOM?
WELL, IT WAS TACO DAY YESTERDAY, AND–
I DON'T WANT TO HEAR IT! WE HAVE A LOT OF WORK TO DO! THE PAGEANT IS THIS AFTERNOON AND EVERYONE IS BATHROOM CRAZY!

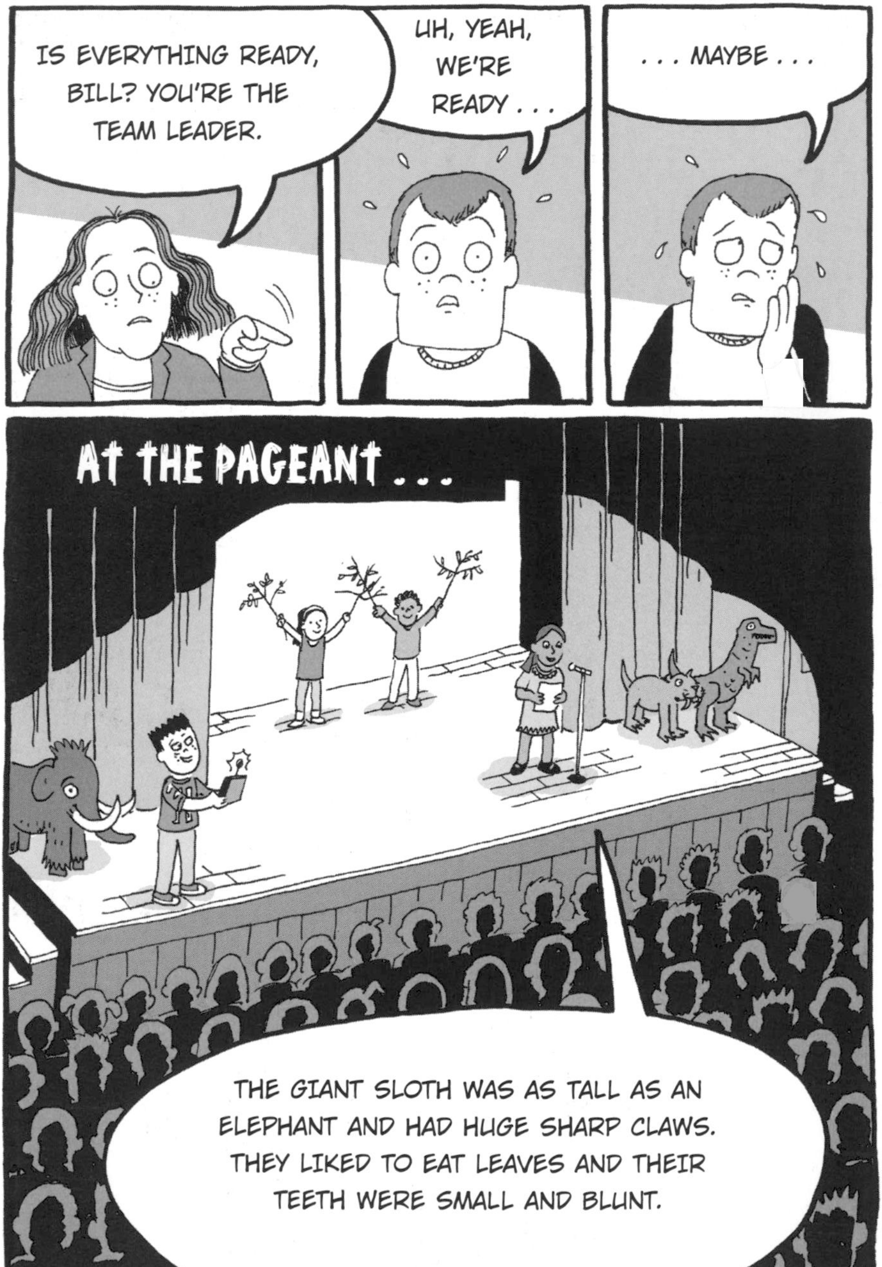
IS EVERYTHING READY, BILL? YOU'RE THE TEAM LEADER.
UH, YEAH, WE'RE READY . . .
. . . MAYBE . . .
AT THE PAGEANT . . .
THE GIANT SLOTH WAS AS TALL AS AN ELEPHANT AND HAD HUGE SHARP CLAWS. THEY LIKED TO EAT LEAVES AND THEIR TEETH WERE SMALL AND BLUNT.

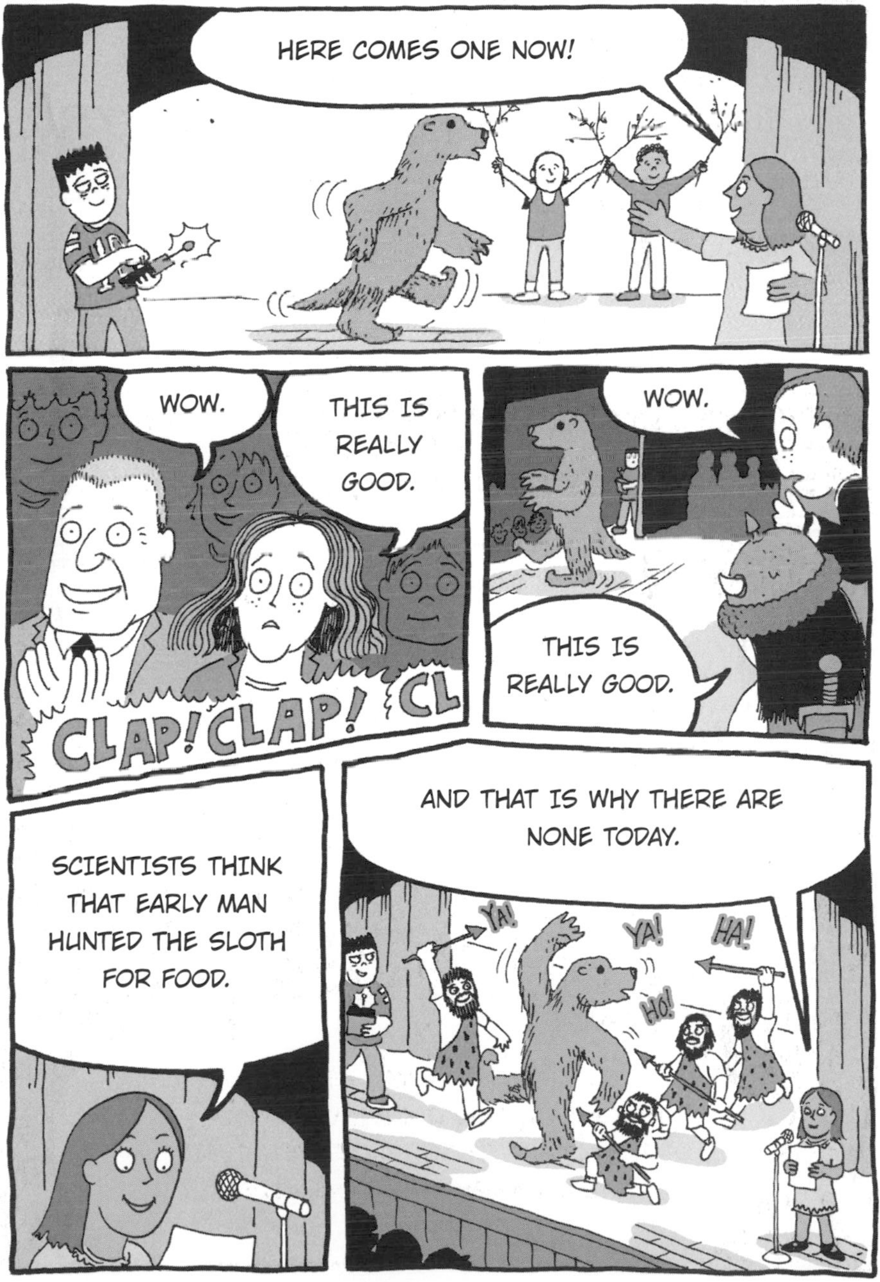
HERE COMES ONE NOW!
WOW.
THIS IS REALLY GOOD.
CLAP! CLAP! CL
WOW.
THIS IS REALLY GOOD.
SCIENTISTS THINK THAT EARLY MAN HUNTED THE SLOTH FOR FOOD.
AND THAT IS WHY THERE ARE NONE TODAY.
YA!
YA!
HA!
HO!

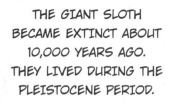

THE GIANT SLOTH BECAME EXTINCT ABOUT 10,000 YEARS AGO. THEY LIVED DURING THE PLEISTOCENE PERIOD.

THE END.

CLAP! CLAP!

CLAP! CLAP! CLAP!

THAT WAS GREAT! I CAN'T WAIT TO SEE 3G'S SKIT.

CLAP! CLAP!

CLAP! CLAP

ALL RIGHT, GUYS! THIS IS IT. WE'RE NEXT. STAND THE DODO UP.

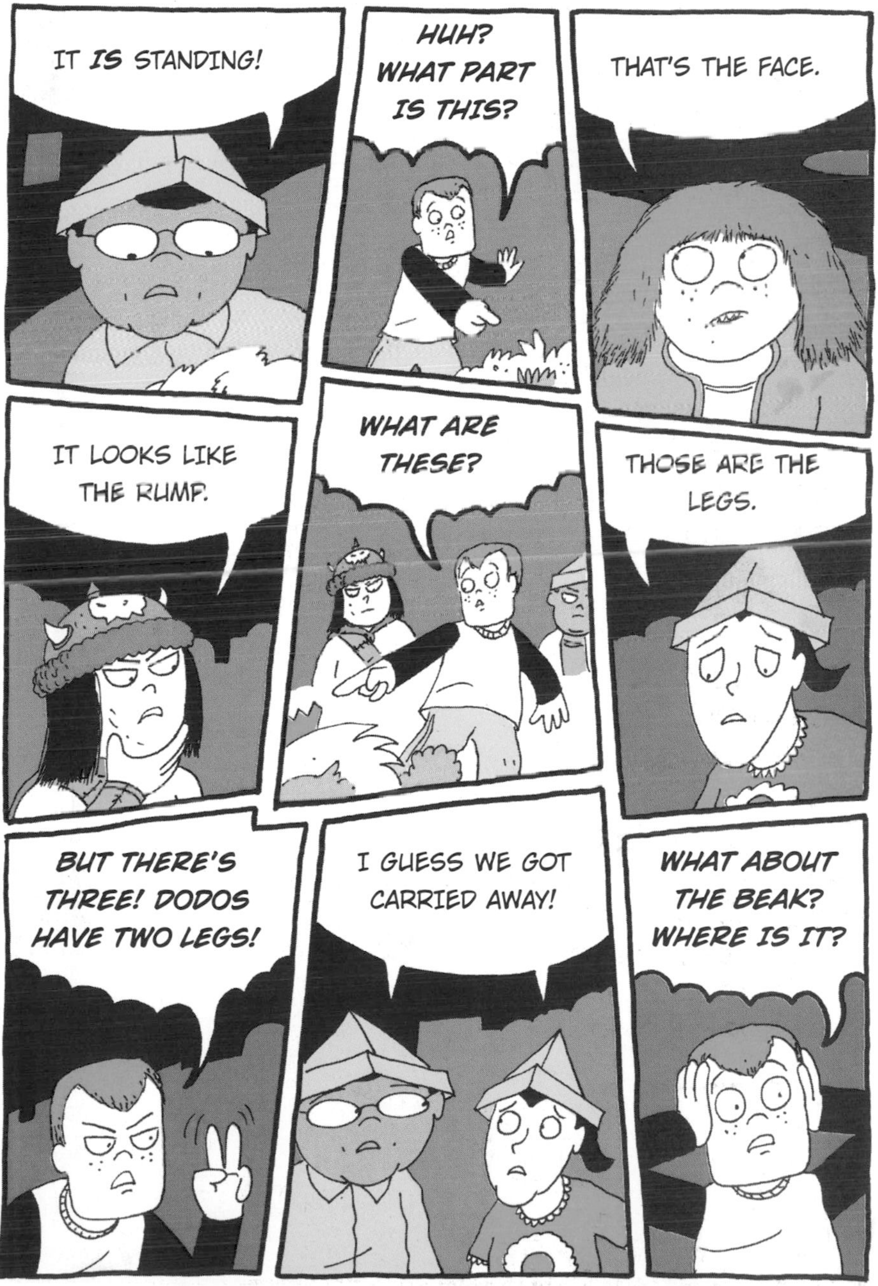
IT IS STANDING!
HUH? WHAT PART IS THIS?
THAT'S THE FACE.
IT LOOKS LIKE THE RUMP.
WHAT ARE THESE?
THOSE ARE THE LEGS.
BUT THERE'S THREE! DODOS HAVE TWO LEGS!
I GUESS WE GOT CARRIED AWAY!
WHAT ABOUT THE BEAK? WHERE IS IT?

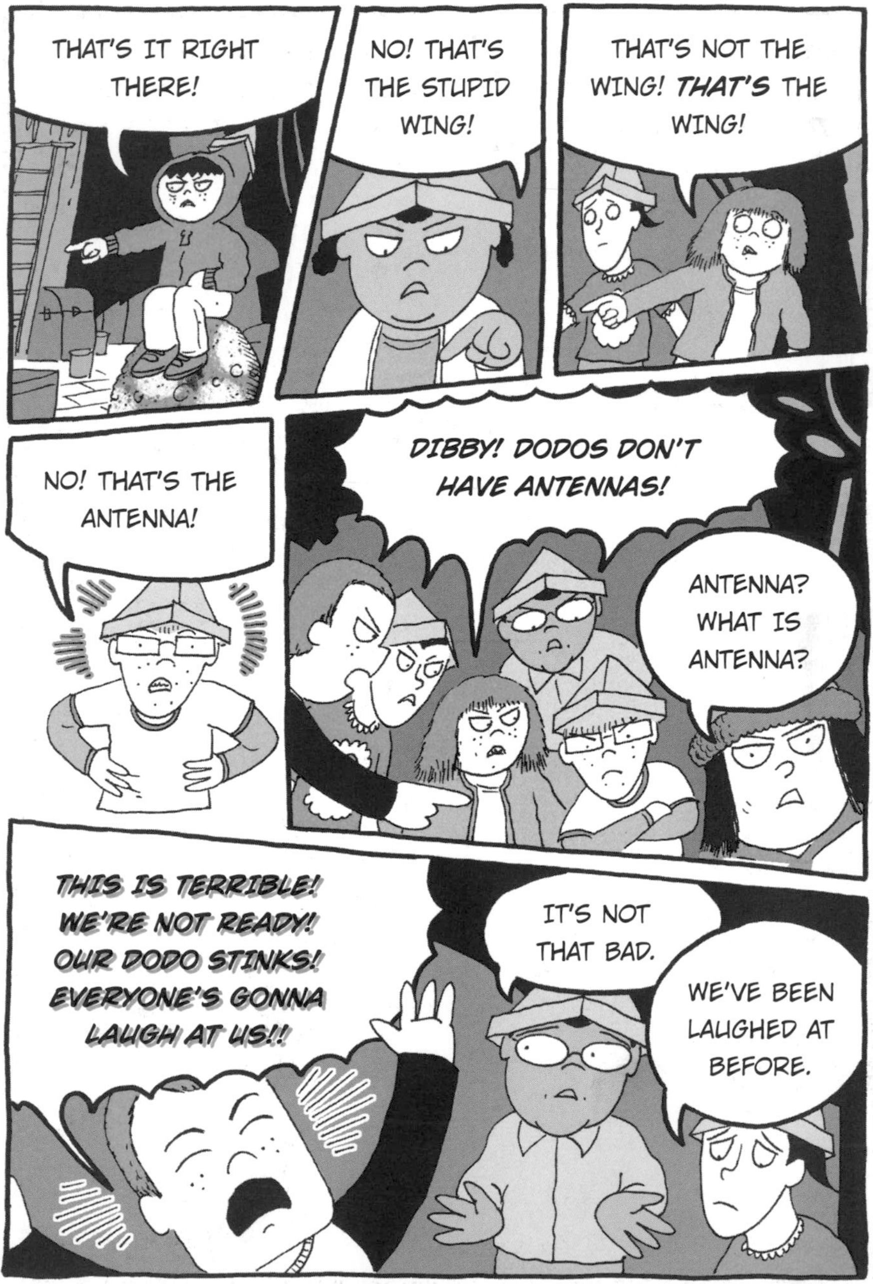
THAT'S IT RIGHT THERE!
NO! THAT'S THE STUPID WING!
THAT'S NOT THE WING! *THAT'S* THE WING!
NO! THAT'S THE ANTENNA!
DIBBY! DODOS DON'T HAVE ANTENNAS!
ANTENNA? WHAT IS ANTENNA?
THIS IS TERRIBLE! WE'RE NOT READY! OUR DODO STINKS! EVERYONE'S GONNA LAUGH AT US!!
IT'S NOT THAT BAD.
WE'VE BEEN LAUGHED AT BEFORE.

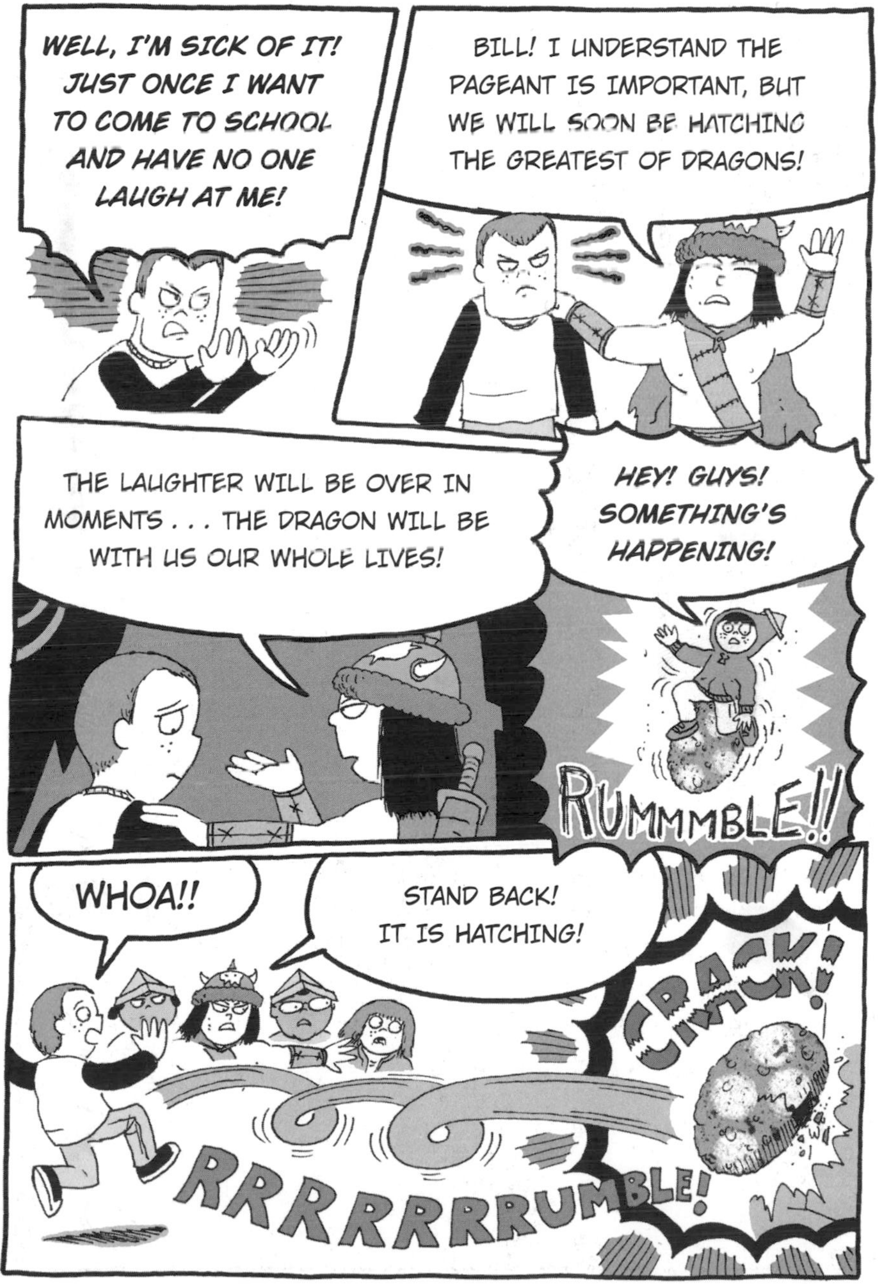
WELL, I'M SICK OF IT! JUST ONCE I WANT TO COME TO SCHOOL AND HAVE NO ONE LAUGH AT ME!
BILL! I UNDERSTAND THE PAGEANT IS IMPORTANT, BUT WE WILL SOON BE HATCHING THE GREATEST OF DRAGONS!
THE LAUGHTER WILL BE OVER IN MOMENTS . . . THE DRAGON WILL BE WITH US OUR WHOLE LIVES!
HEY! GUYS! SOMETHING'S HAPPENING!
RUMMMBLE!!
WHOA!!
STAND BACK! IT IS HATCHING!
CRACK!
RRRRRRRRUMBLE!

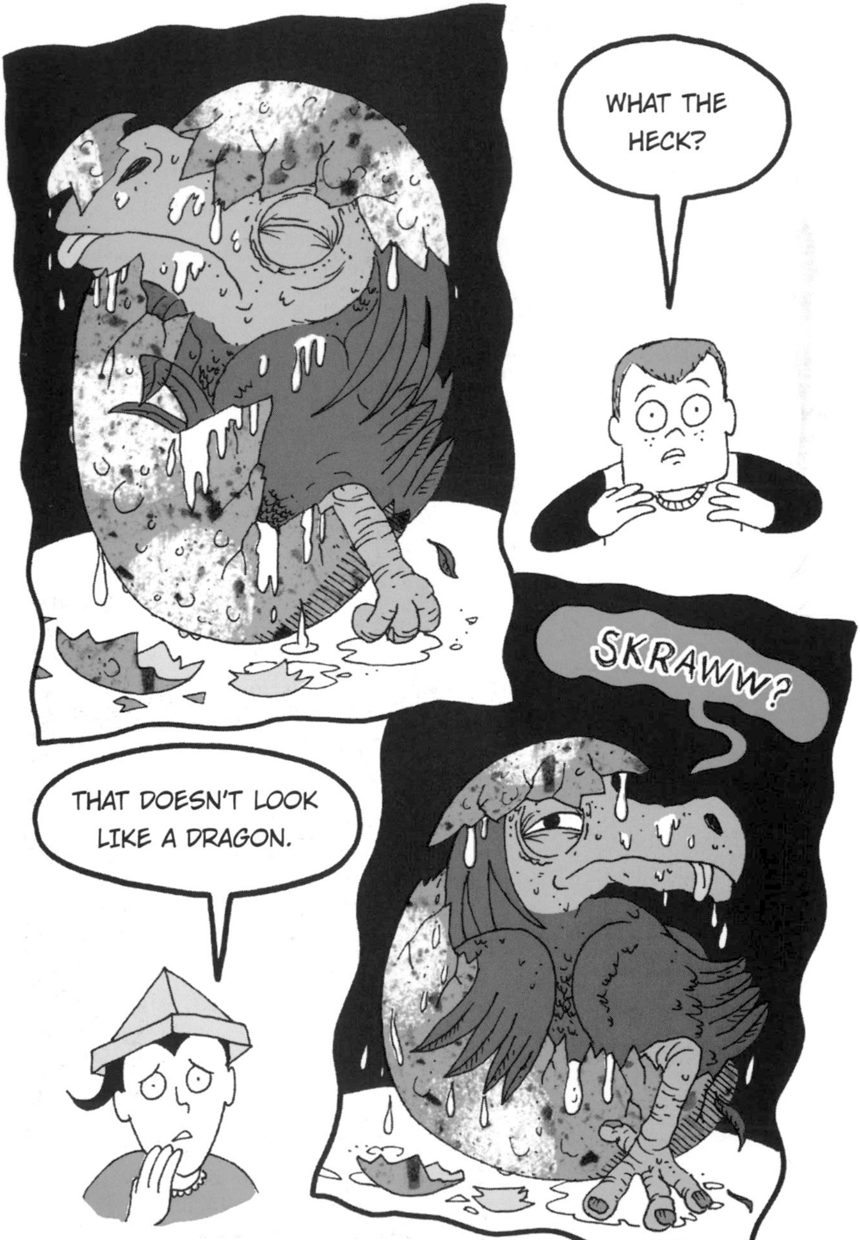
WHAT THE HECK?
SKRAWW?
THAT DOESN'T LOOK LIKE A DRAGON.

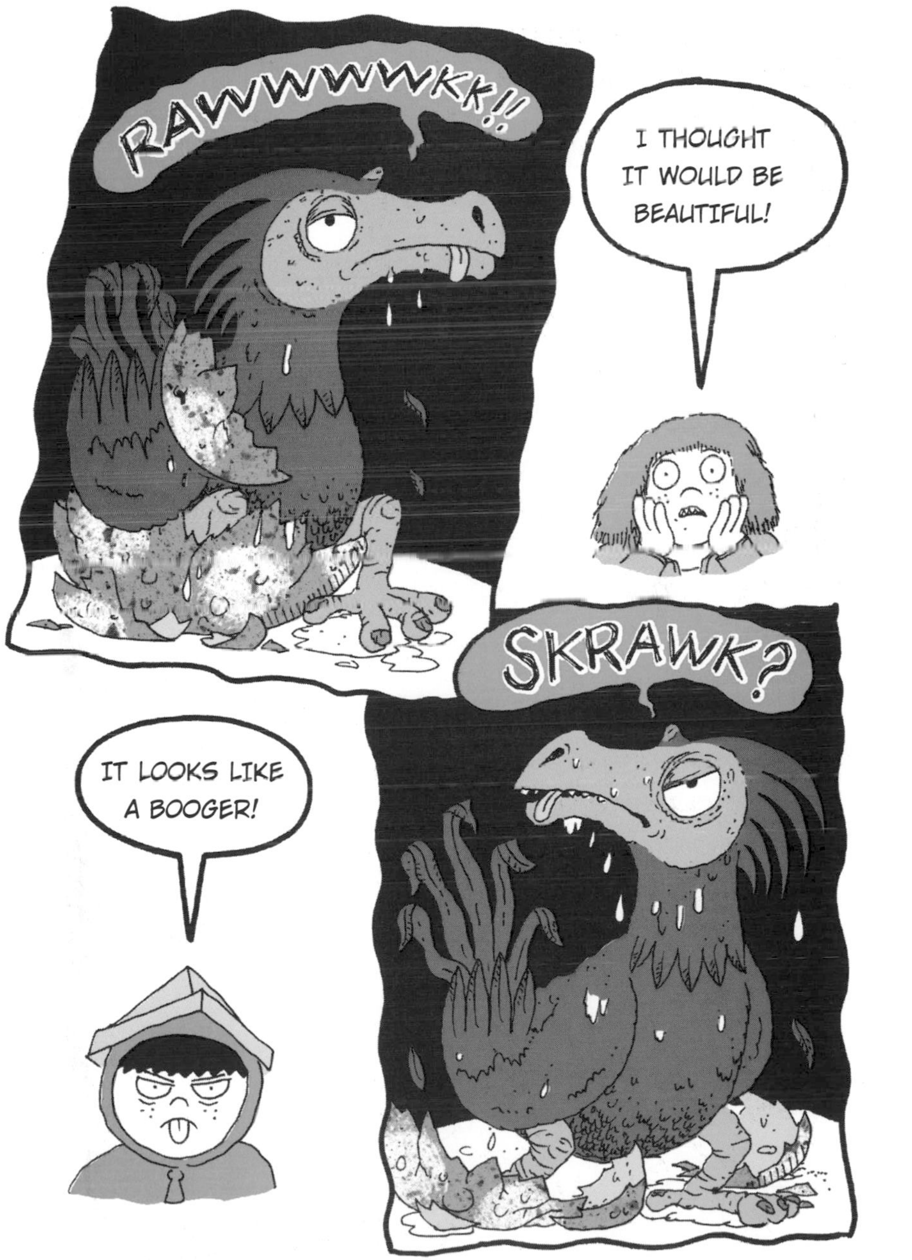
RAWWWWKK!!
I THOUGHT IT WOULD BE BEAUTIFUL!
SKRAWK?
IT LOOKS LIKE A BOOGER!

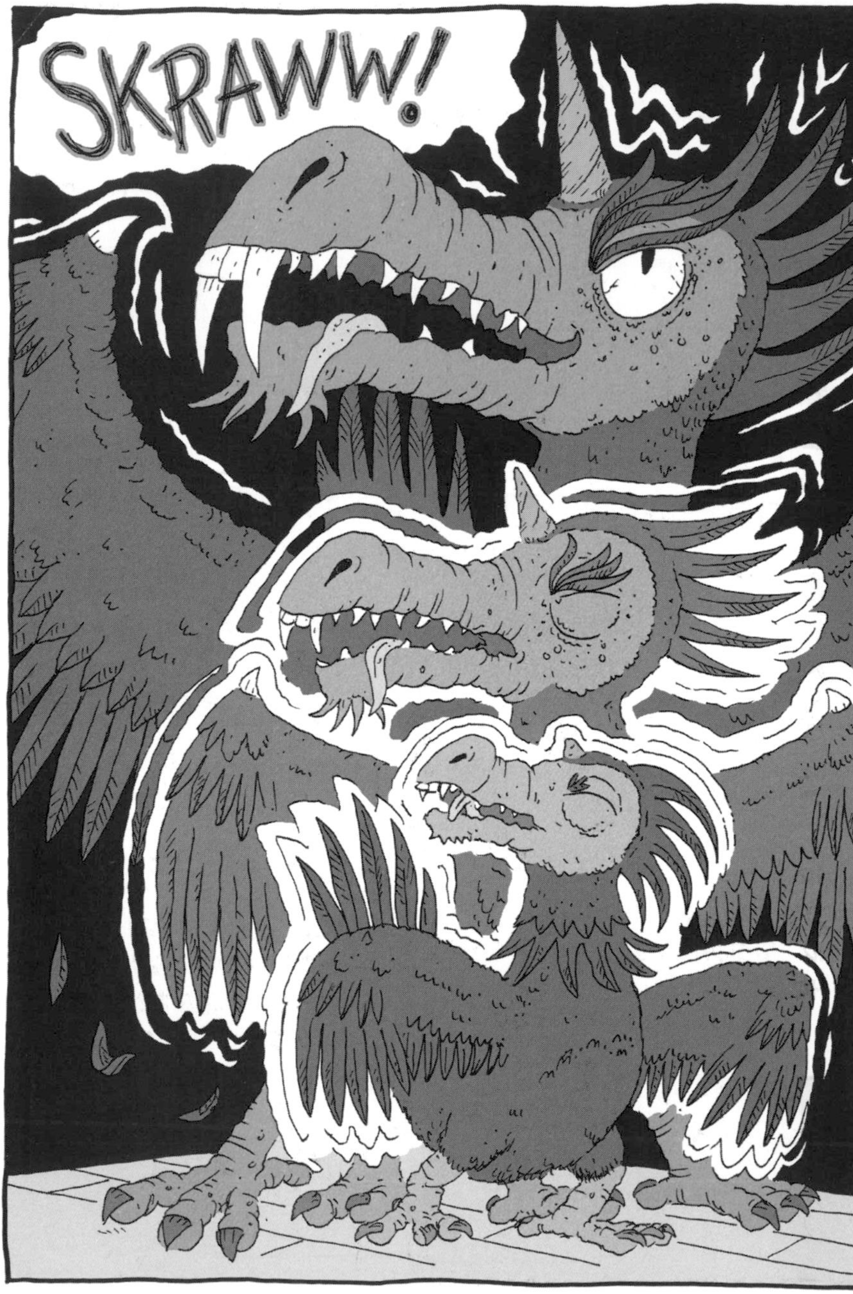
SKRAWW!

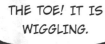
THE TOE! IT IS WIGGLING.

MAGGOT TEETH! WE HAVE BEEN TRICKED! THIS IS NOT A WHITE TITAN RAZOR DRAGON! IT IS A FEATHERED SKEEVE!

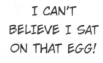

WHAT? NO DRAGON?

THIS BEAST WAS SENT BY DROOL TO STEAL THE TOE!

I CAN'T BELIEVE I SAT ON THAT EGG!

I CAN'T BELIEVE I CALLED IT "EGGY"!

GREAT! NOW OUR SKIT'S GONNA STINK, AND WE DON'T EVEN HAVE A DRAGON!

FEATHERED SKEEVES ARE STUPID!

YOU ARE AN ARMY! STOP GRUMBLING AND PREPARE FOR BATTLE!

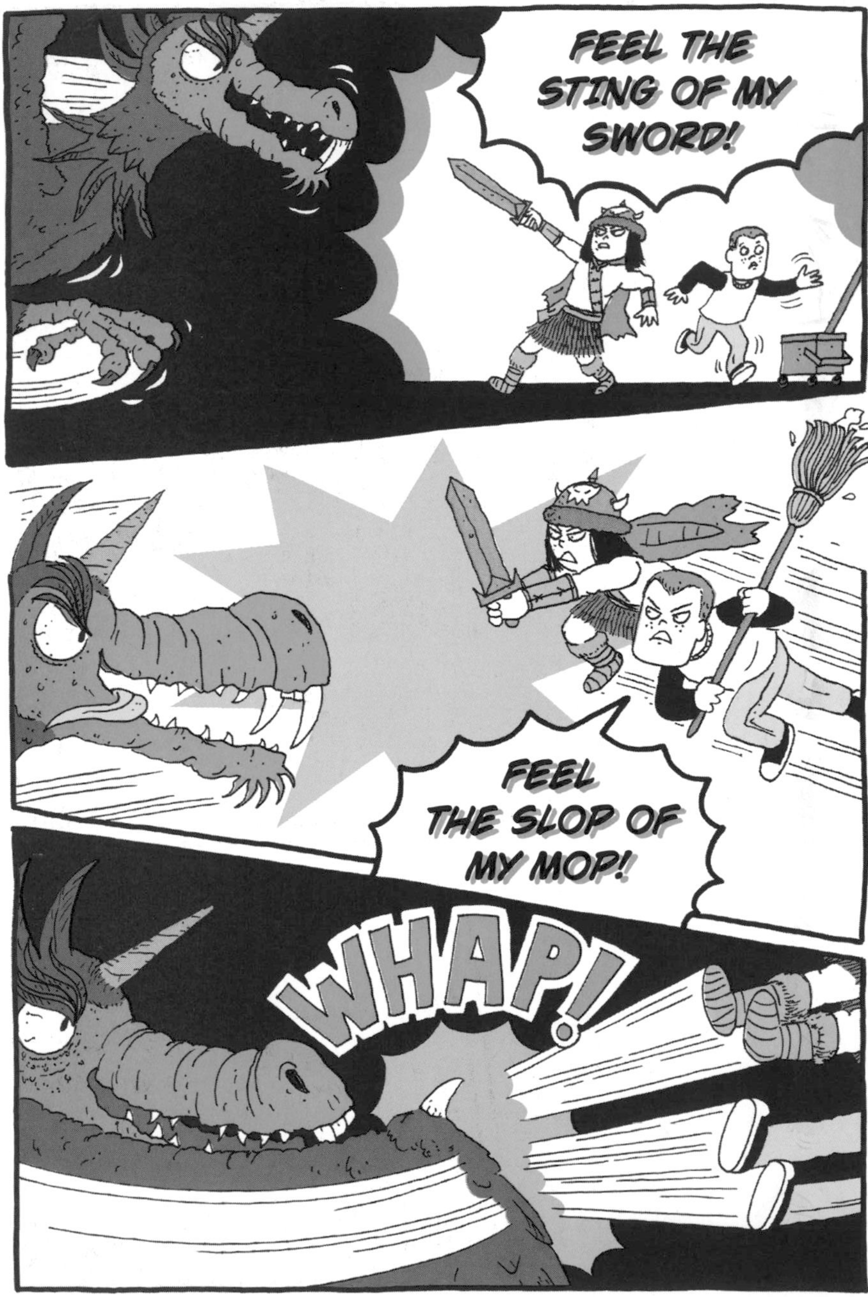
FEEL THE STING OF MY SWORD!
FEEL THE SLOP OF MY MOP!
WHAP!

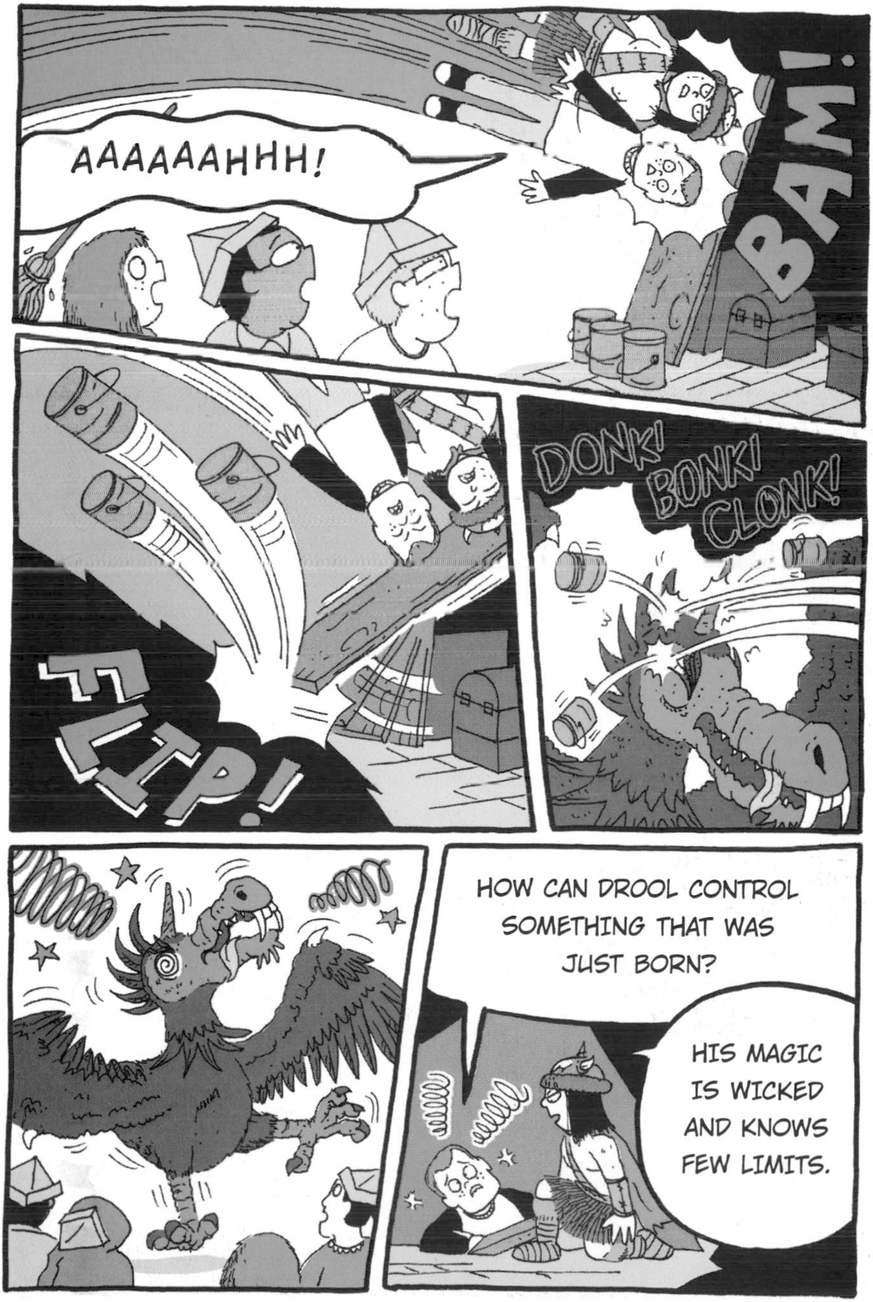
AAAAAAHHH!
BAM!
FLIP!
DONK!
BONK!
CLONK!
HOW CAN DROOL CONTROL SOMETHING THAT WAS JUST BORN?
HIS MAGIC IS WICKED AND KNOWS FEW LIMITS.

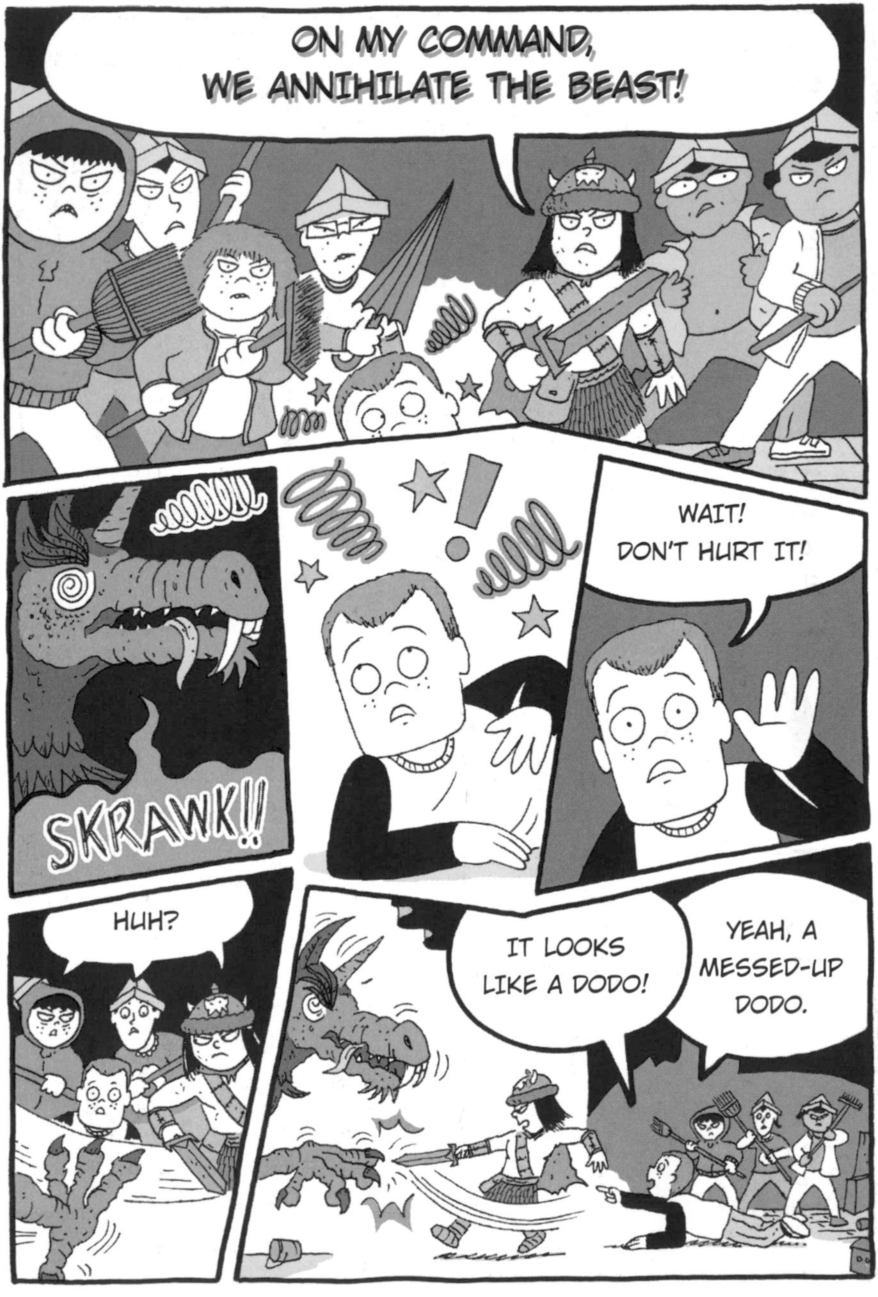
ON MY COMMAND, WE ANNIHILATE THE BEAST!
SKRAWK!!
WAIT! DON'T HURT IT!
HUH?
IT LOOKS LIKE A DODO!
YEAH, A MESSED-UP DODO.

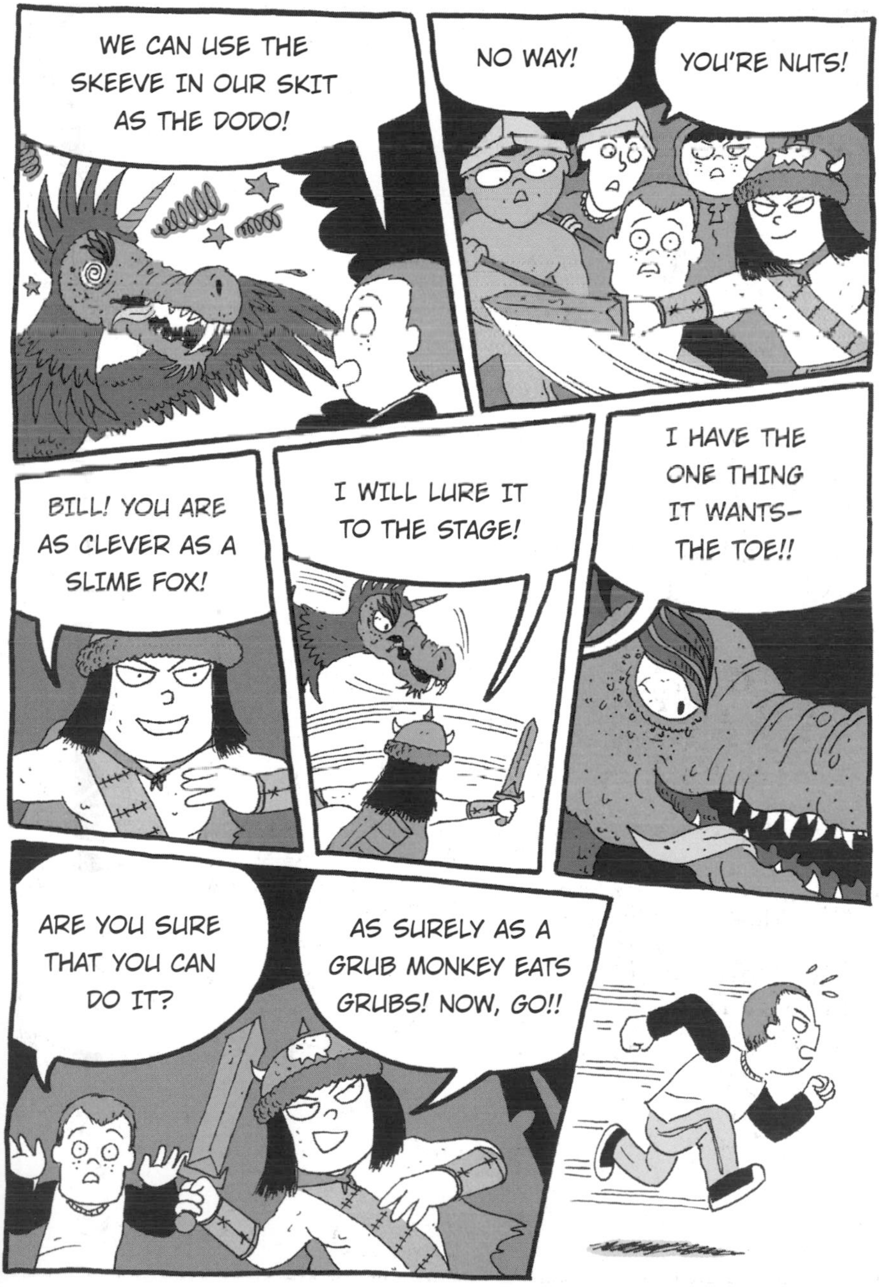
WE CAN USE THE SKEEVE IN OUR SKIT AS THE DODO!
NO WAY!
YOU'RE NUTS!
BILL! YOU ARE AS CLEVER AS A SLIME FOX!
I WILL LURE IT TO THE STAGE!
I HAVE THE ONE THING IT WANTS– THE TOE!!
ARE YOU SURE THAT YOU CAN DO IT?
AS SURELY AS A GRUB MONKEY EATS GRUBS! NOW, GO!!

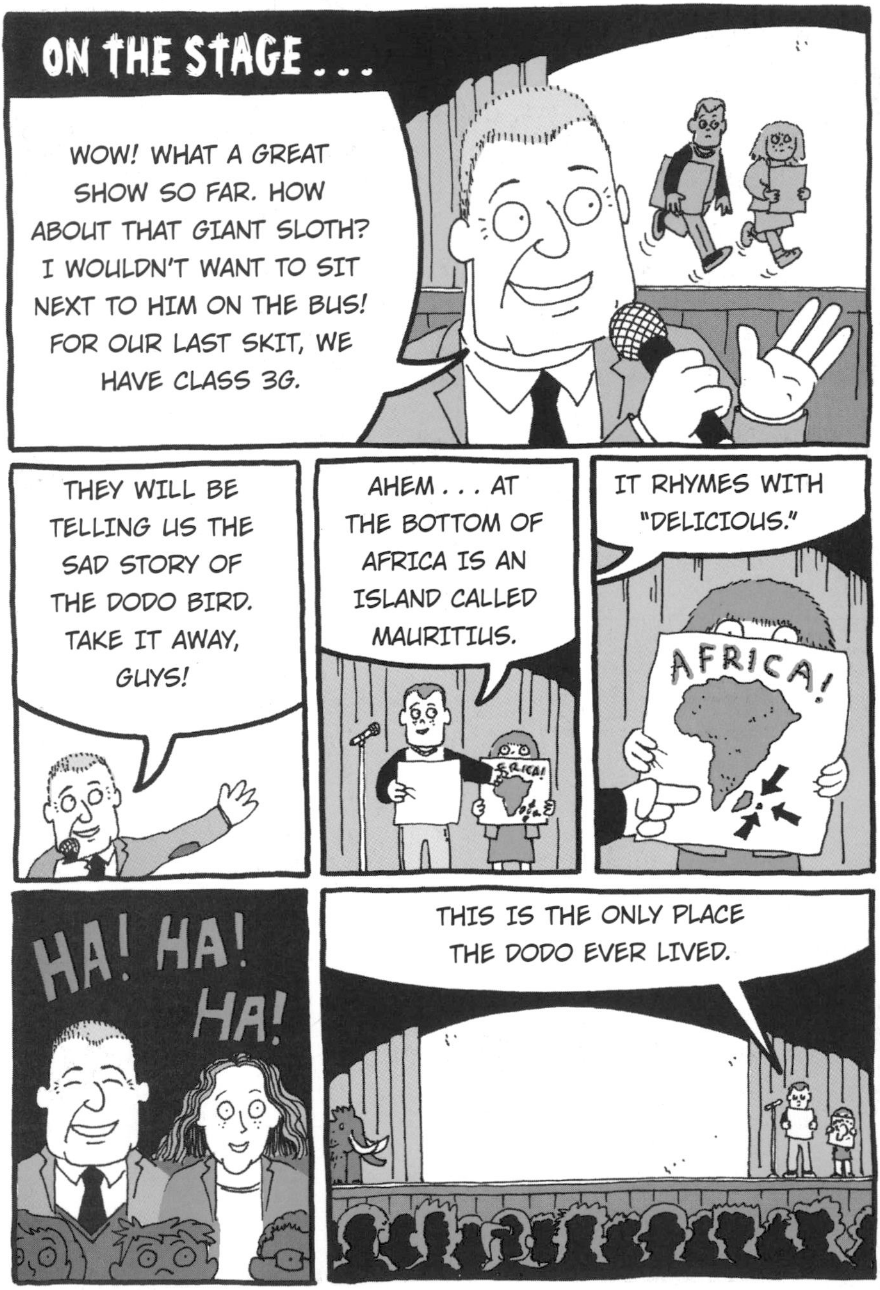
ON THE STAGE . . .
WOW! WHAT A GREAT SHOW SO FAR. HOW ABOUT THAT GIANT SLOTH? I WOULDN'T WANT TO SIT NEXT TO HIM ON THE BUS! FOR OUR LAST SKIT, WE HAVE CLASS 3G.
THEY WILL BE TELLING US THE SAD STORY OF THE DODO BIRD. TAKE IT AWAY, GUYS!
AHEM . . . AT THE BOTTOM OF AFRICA IS AN ISLAND CALLED MAURITIUS.
IT RHYMES WITH "DELICIOUS."
AFRICA!
HA! HA! HA!
THIS IS THE ONLY PLACE THE DODO EVER LIVED.

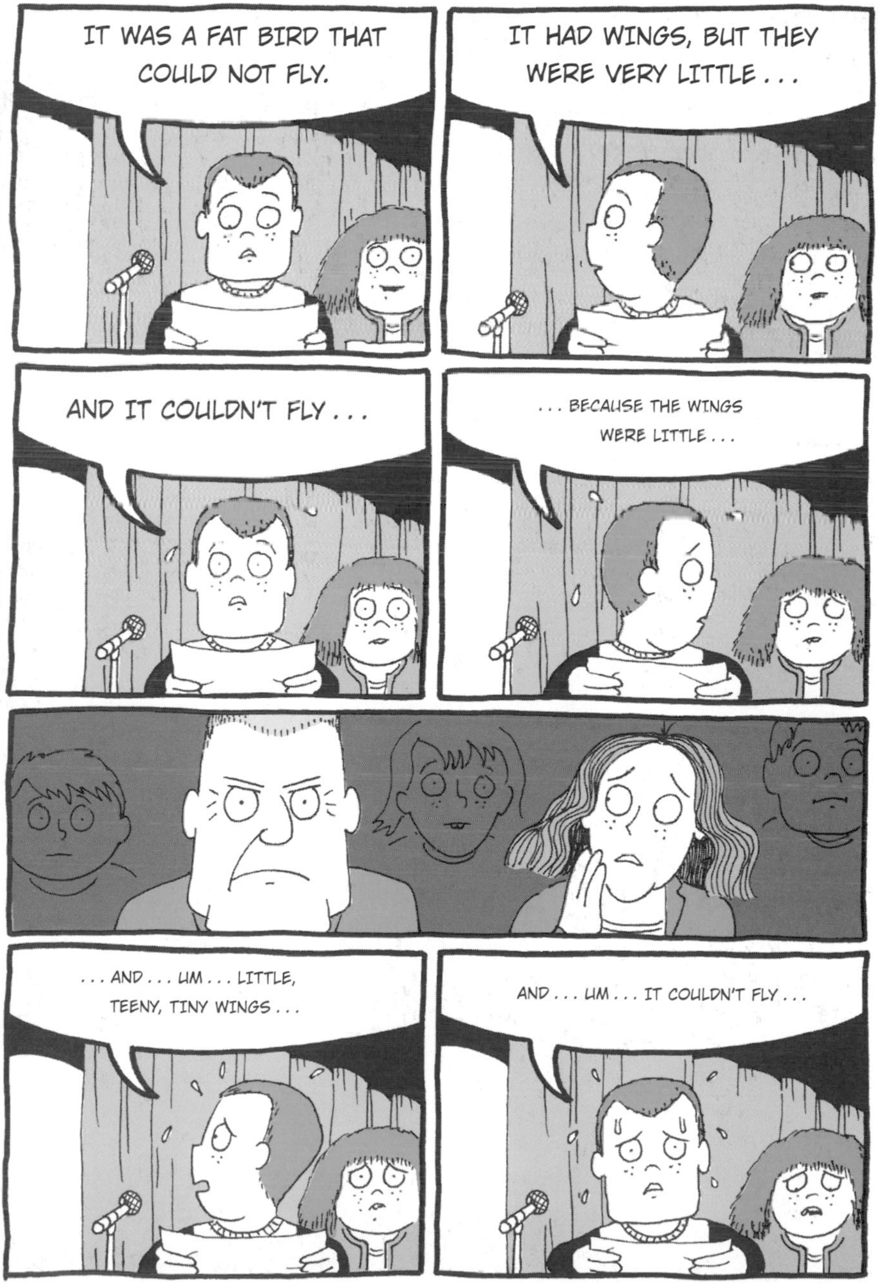
IT WAS A FAT BIRD THAT COULD NOT FLY.
IT HAD WINGS, BUT THEY WERE VERY LITTLE . . .
AND IT COULDN'T FLY . . .
. . . BECAUSE THE WINGS WERE LITTLE . . .
. . . AND . . . UM . . . LITTLE, TEENY, TINY WINGS . . .
AND . . . UM . . . IT COULDN'T FLY . . .

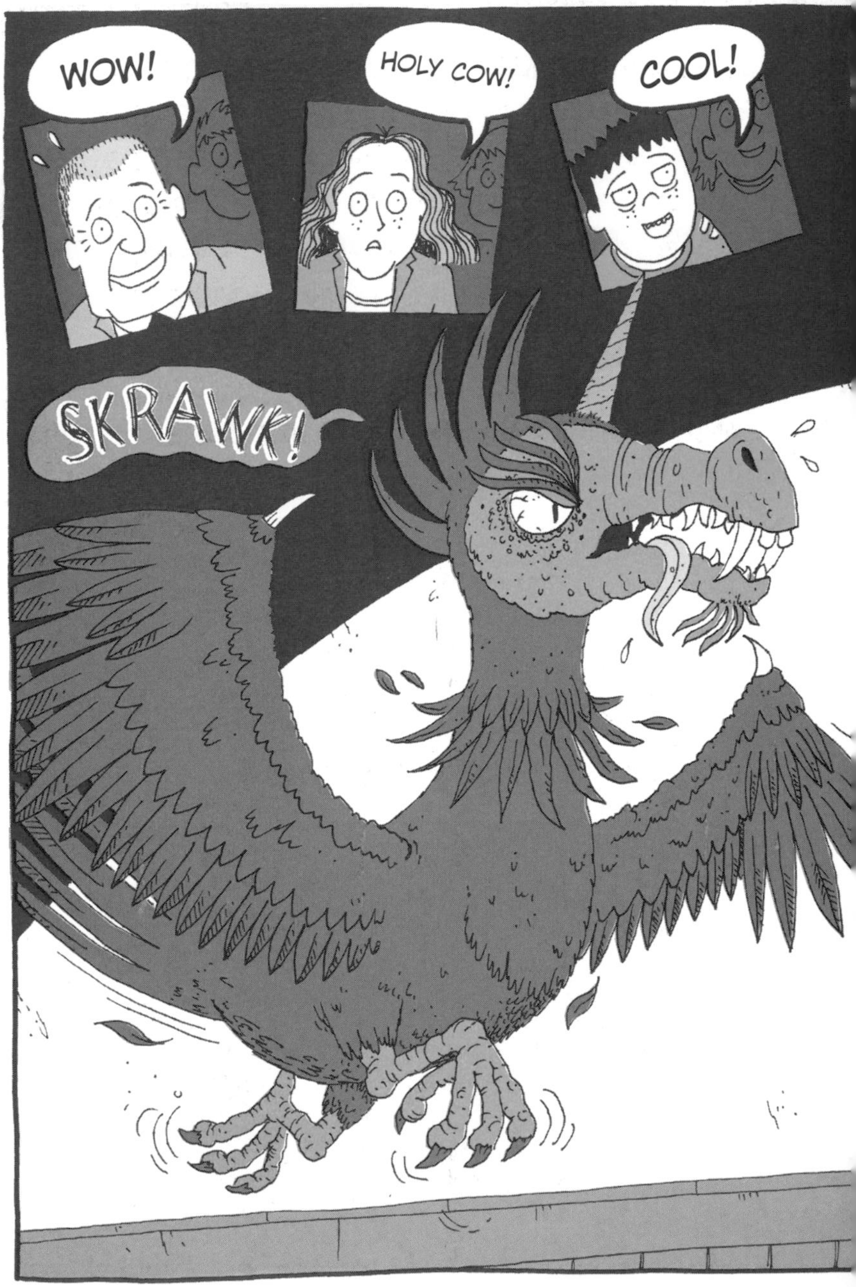
WOW!
HOLY COW!
COOL!
SKRAWK!

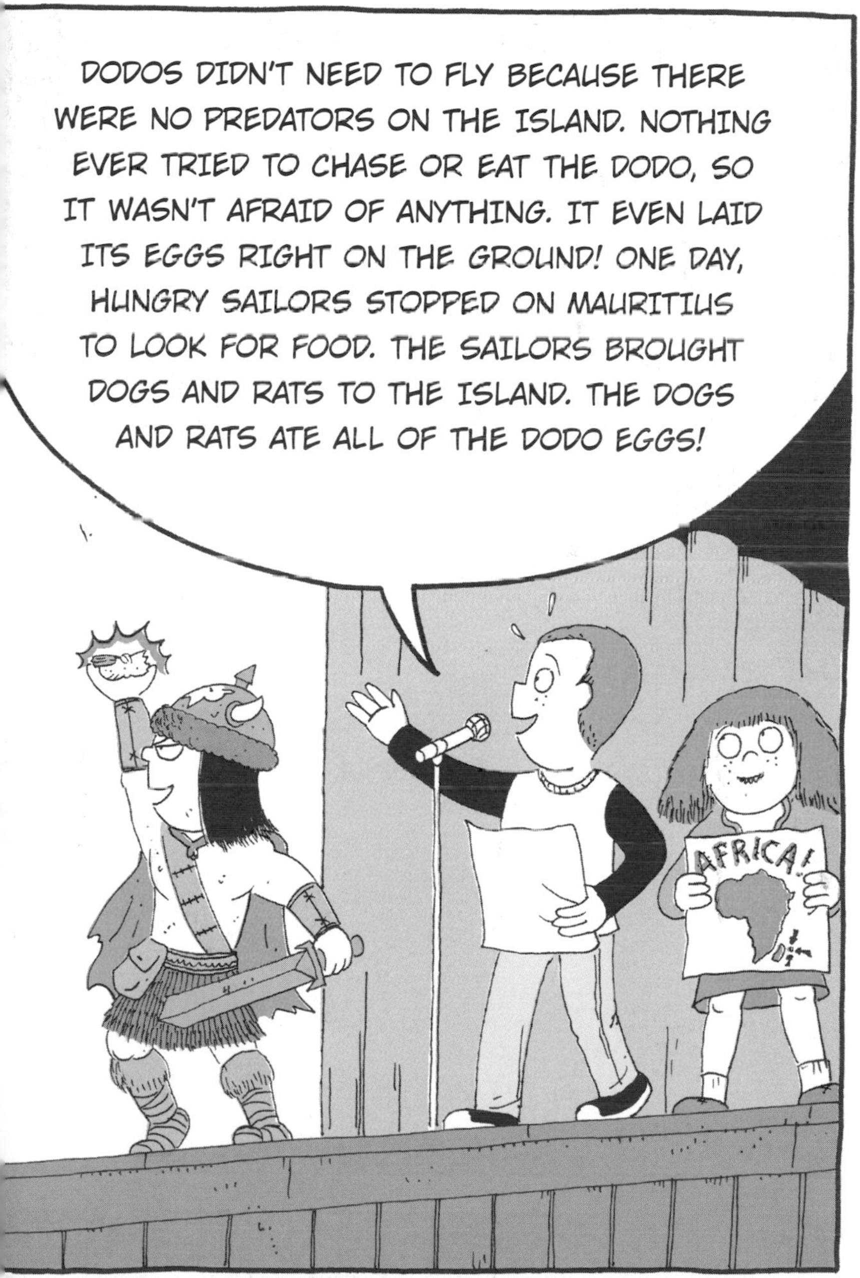
DODOS DIDN'T NEED TO FLY BECAUSE THERE WERE NO PREDATORS ON THE ISLAND. NOTHING EVER TRIED TO CHASE OR EAT THE DODO, SO IT WASN'T AFRAID OF ANYTHING. IT EVEN LAID ITS EGGS RIGHT ON THE GROUND! ONE DAY, HUNGRY SAILORS STOPPED ON MAURITIUS TO LOOK FOR FOOD. THE SAILORS BROUGHT DOGS AND RATS TO THE ISLAND. THE DOGS AND RATS ATE ALL OF THE DODO EGGS!
AFRICA!

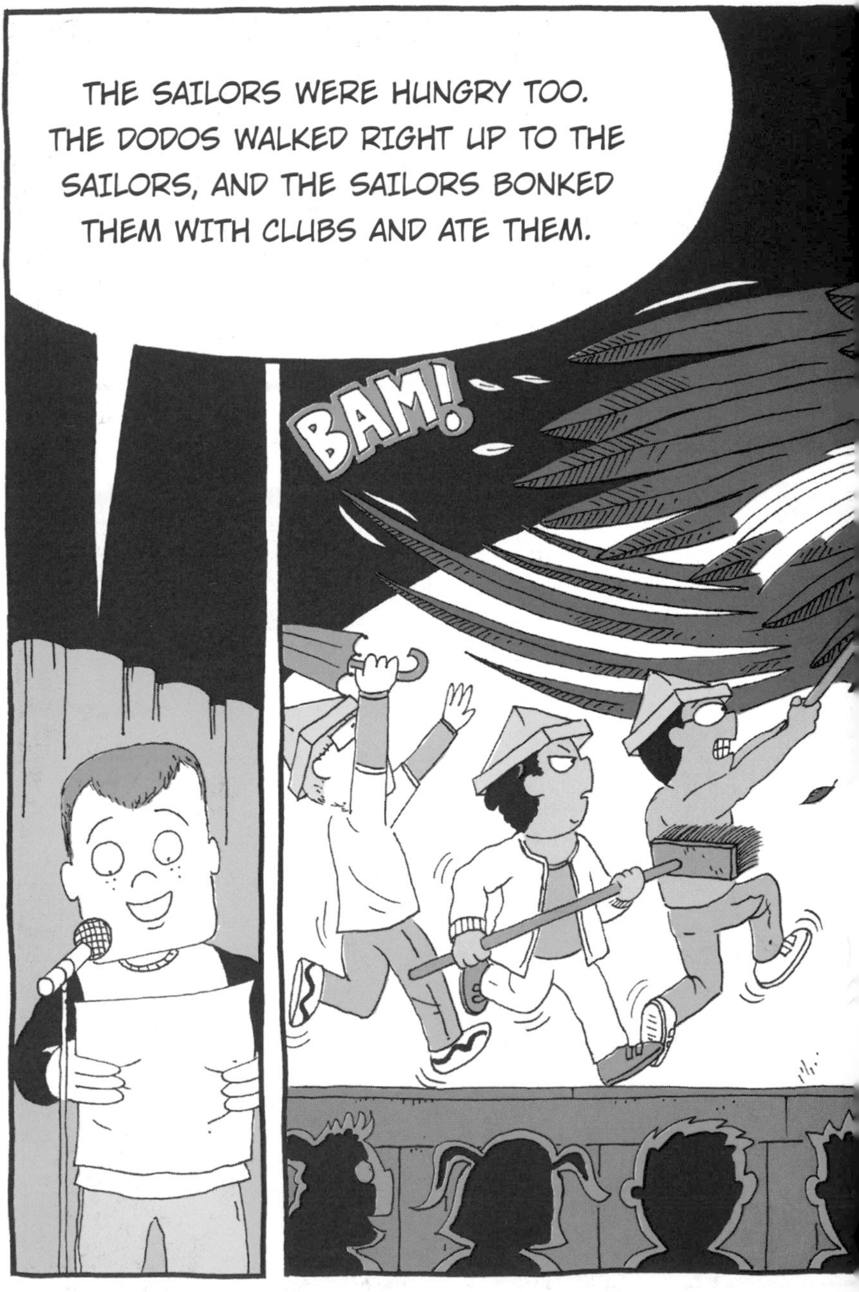
THE SAILORS WERE HUNGRY TOO. THE DODOS WALKED RIGHT UP TO THE SAILORS, AND THE SAILORS BONKED THEM WITH CLUBS AND ATE THEM.
BAM!

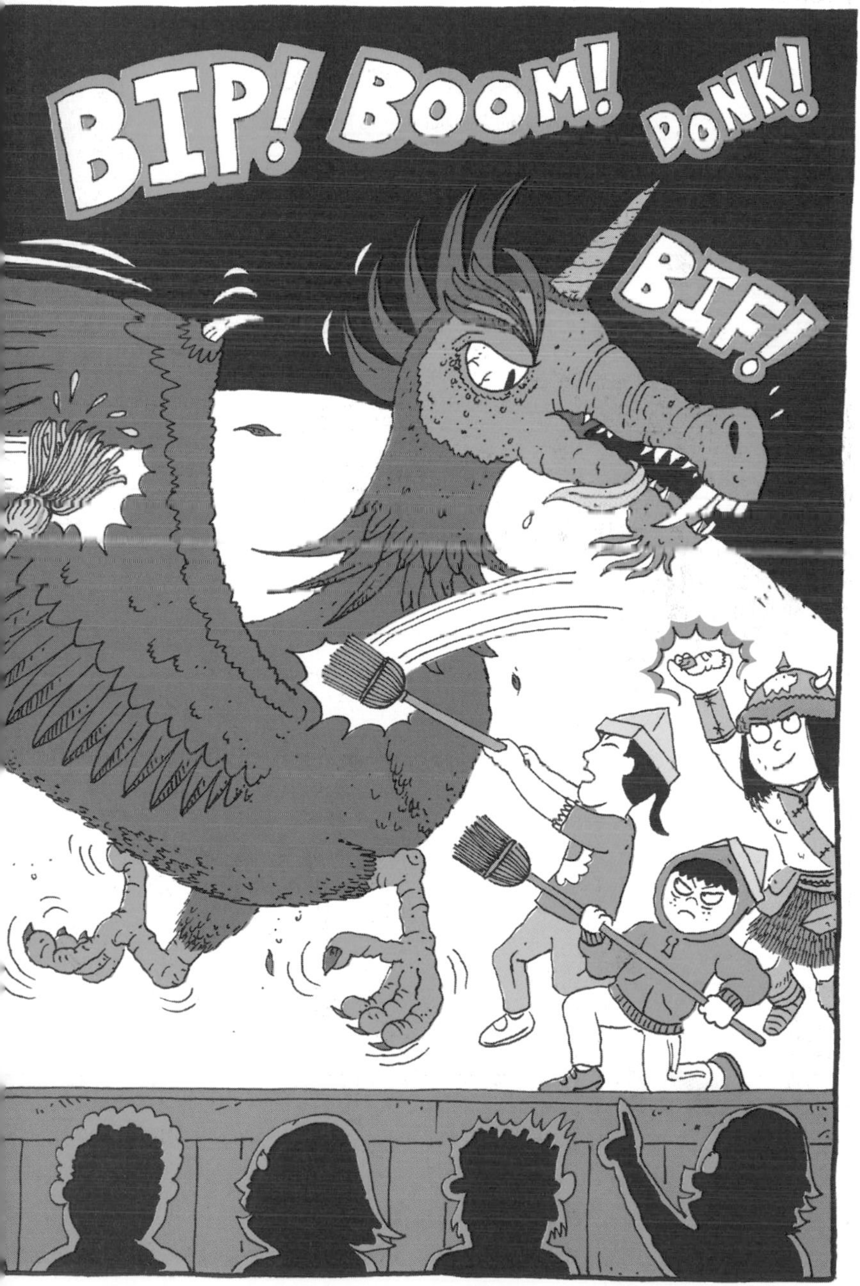
BIP! BOOM! DONK!
BIF!

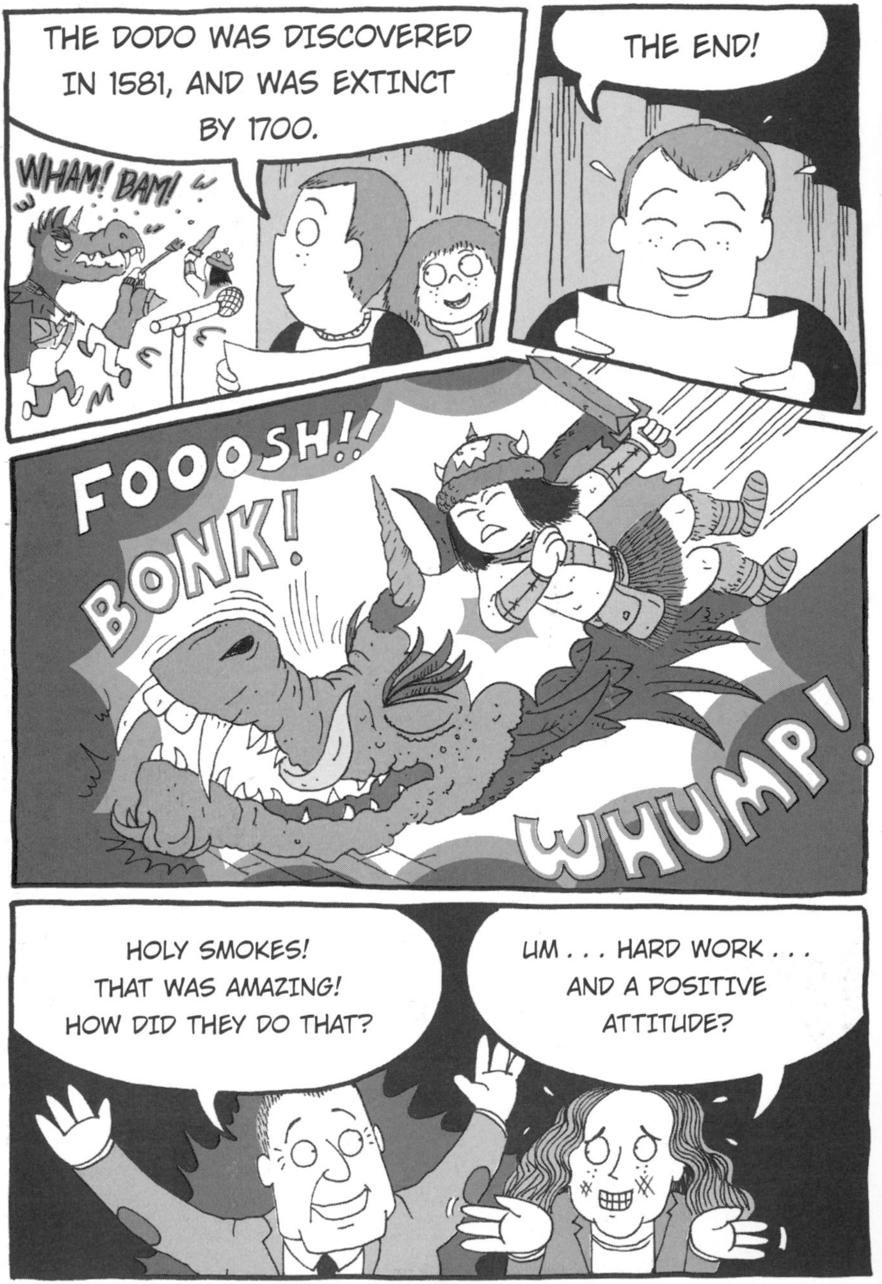
THE DODO WAS DISCOVERED IN 1581, AND WAS EXTINCT BY 1700.
WHAM! BAM!
THE END!
FOOOSH!!
BONK!
WHUMP!
HOLY SMOKES! THAT WAS AMAZING! HOW DID THEY DO THAT?
UM . . . HARD WORK . . . AND A POSITIVE ATTITUDE?

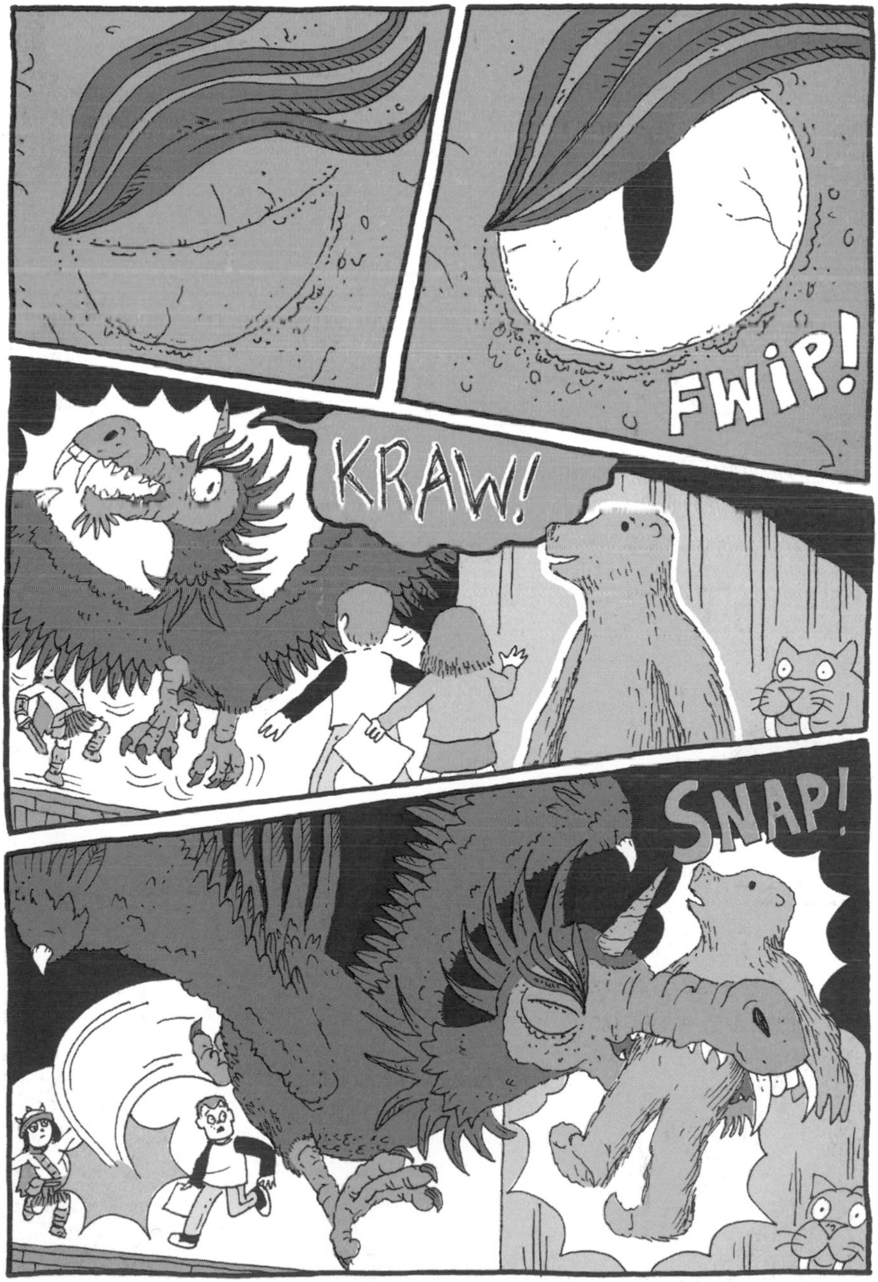
FWIP!
KRAW!
SNAP!

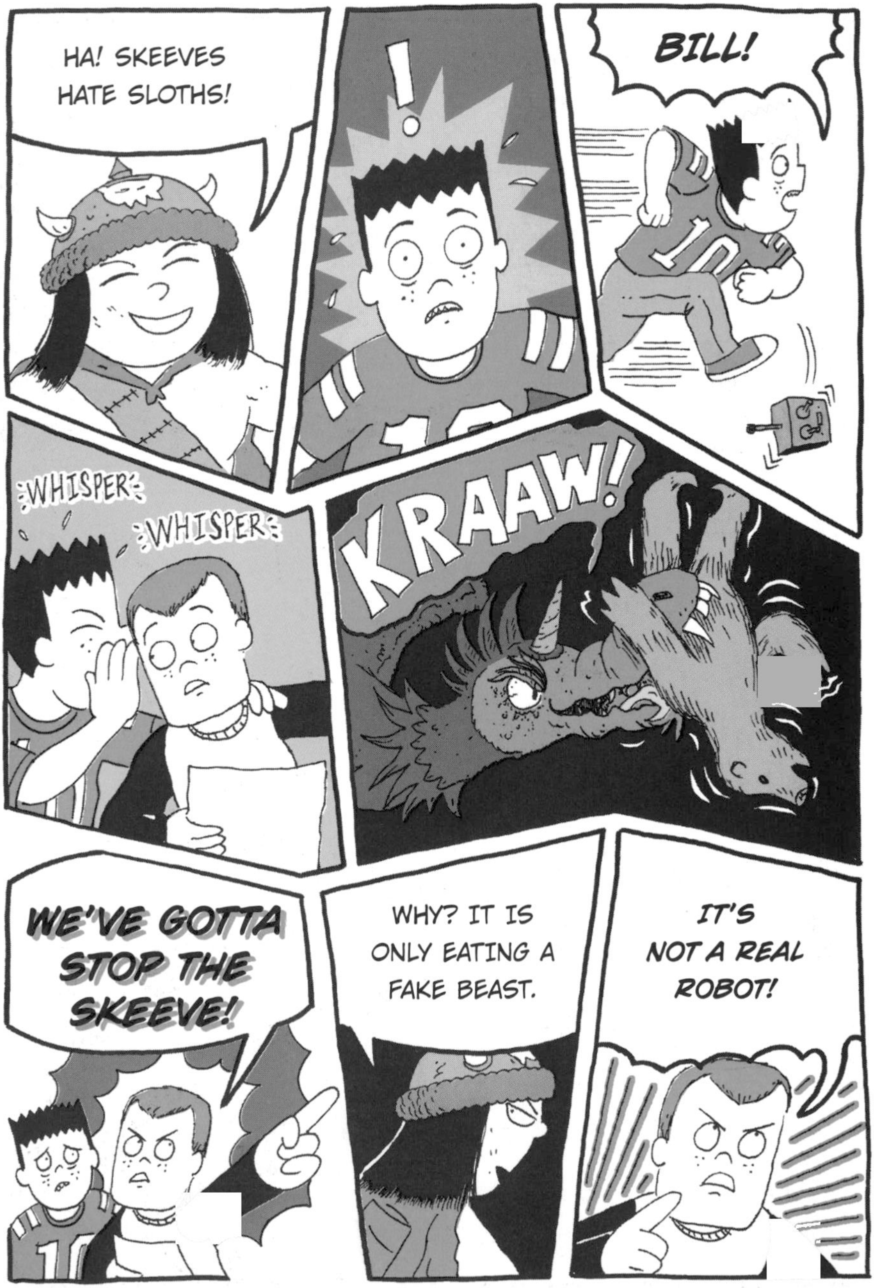
HA! SKEEVES HATE SLOTHS!
!
BILL!
WHISPER
WHISPER
KRAAW!
WE'VE GOTTA STOP THE SKEEVE!
WHY? IT IS ONLY EATING A FAKE BEAST.
IT'S NOT A REAL ROBOT!

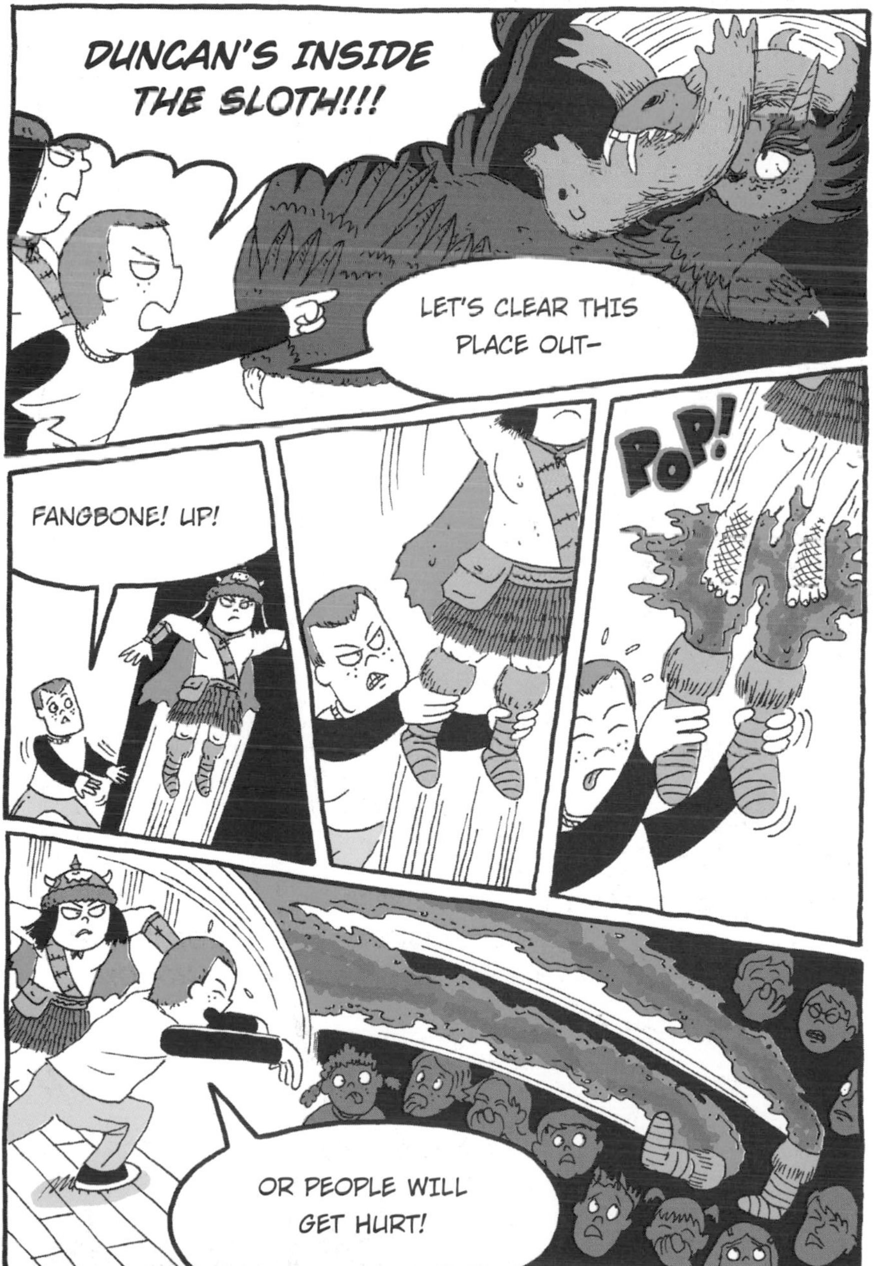
DUNCAN'S INSIDE THE SLOTH!!!
LET'S CLEAR THIS PLACE OUT–
FANGBONE! UP!
POP!
OR PEOPLE WILL GET HURT!

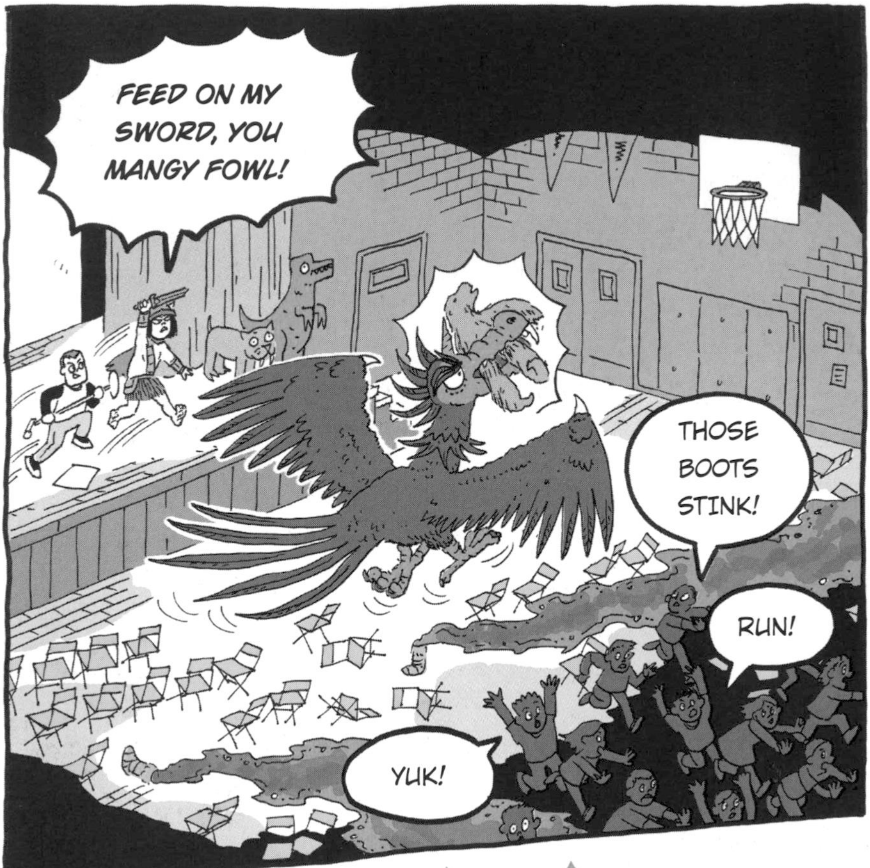
FEED ON MY SWORD, YOU MANGY FOWL!
THOSE BOOTS STINK!
RUN!
YUK!

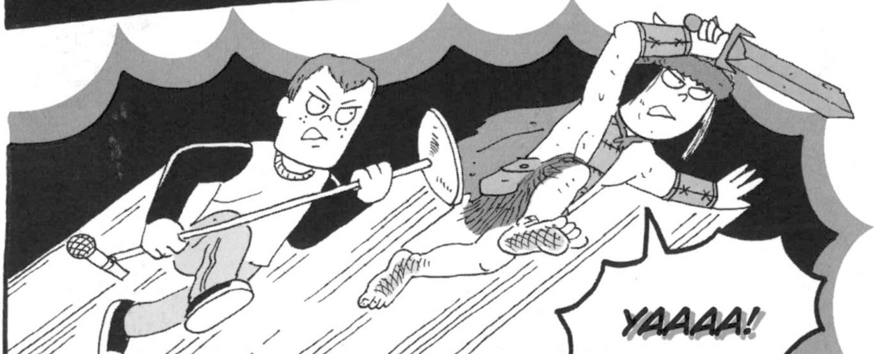
YAAAA!

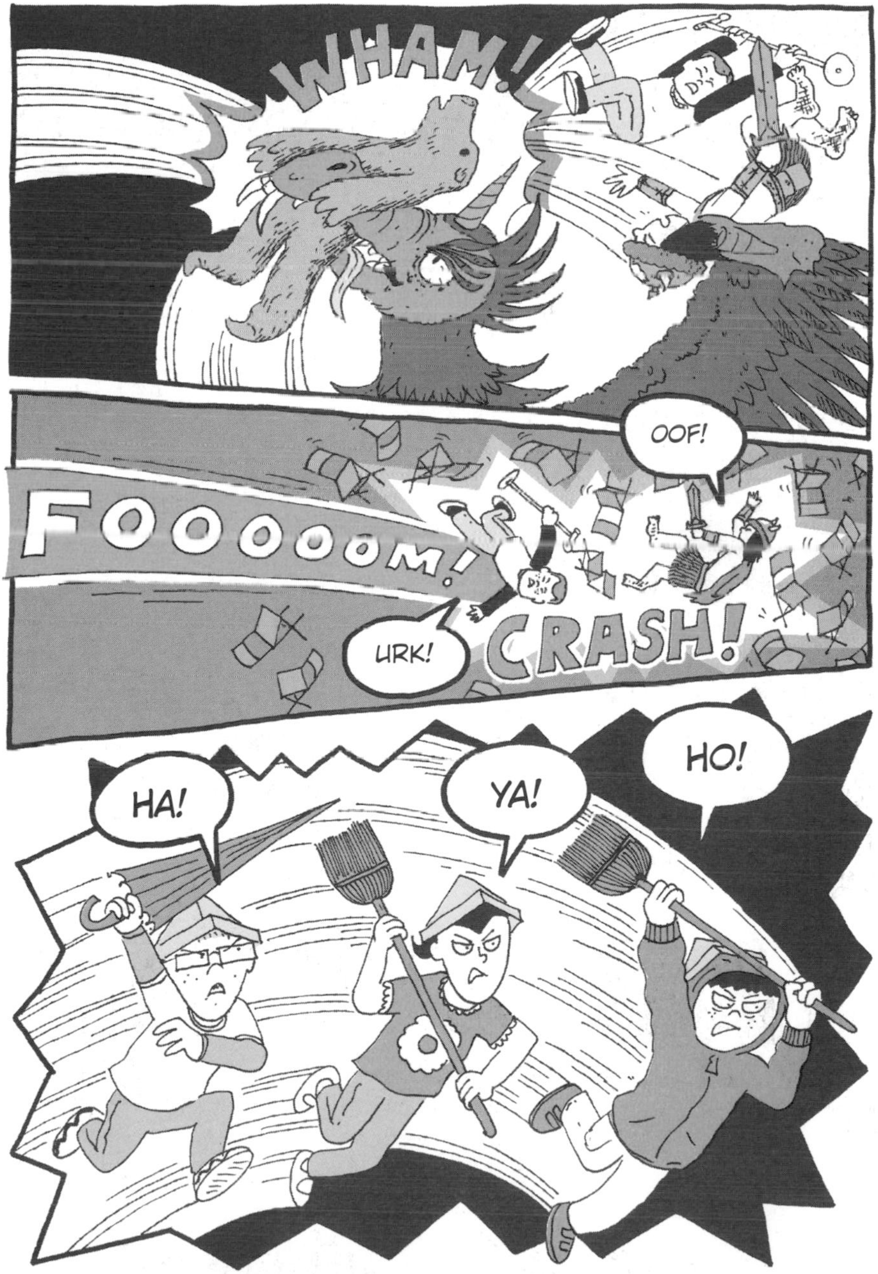
WHAM!
FOOOOOM!
OOF!
URK!
CRASH!
HA!
YA!
HO!

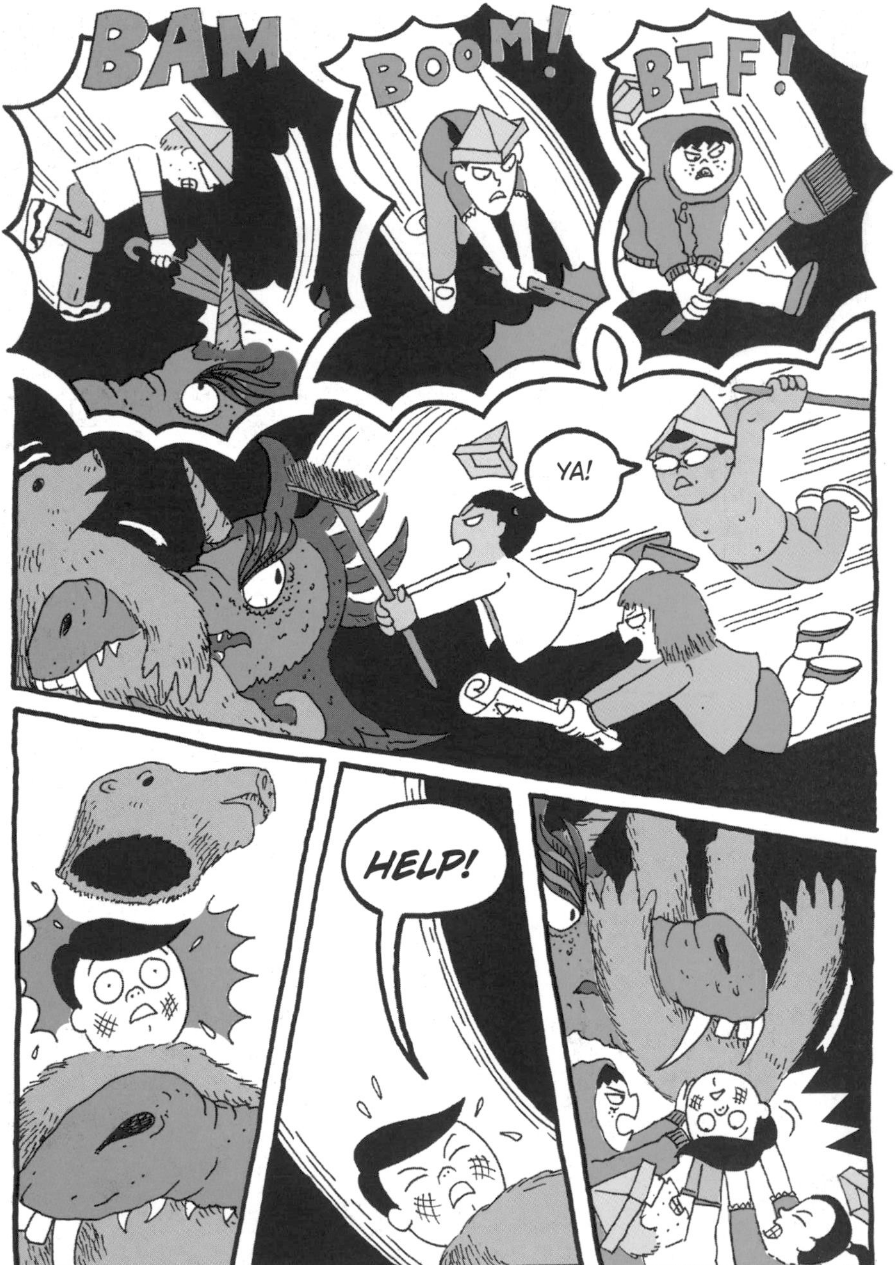
BAM
BOOM!
BIF!
YA!
HELP!

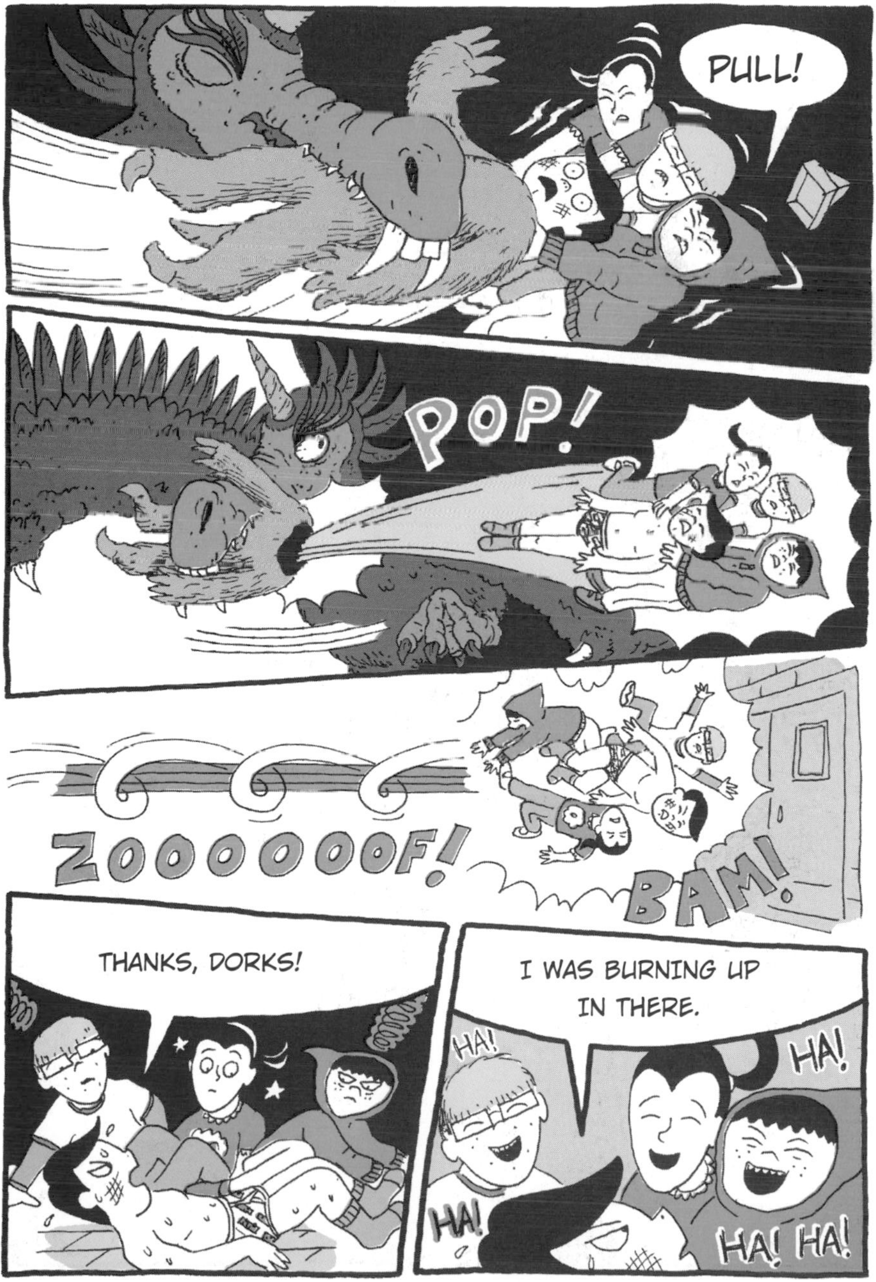
PULL!
POP!
ZOOOOOOF!
BAM!
THANKS, DORKS!
I WAS BURNING UP
IN THERE.
HA!
HA!
HA!
HA! HA!

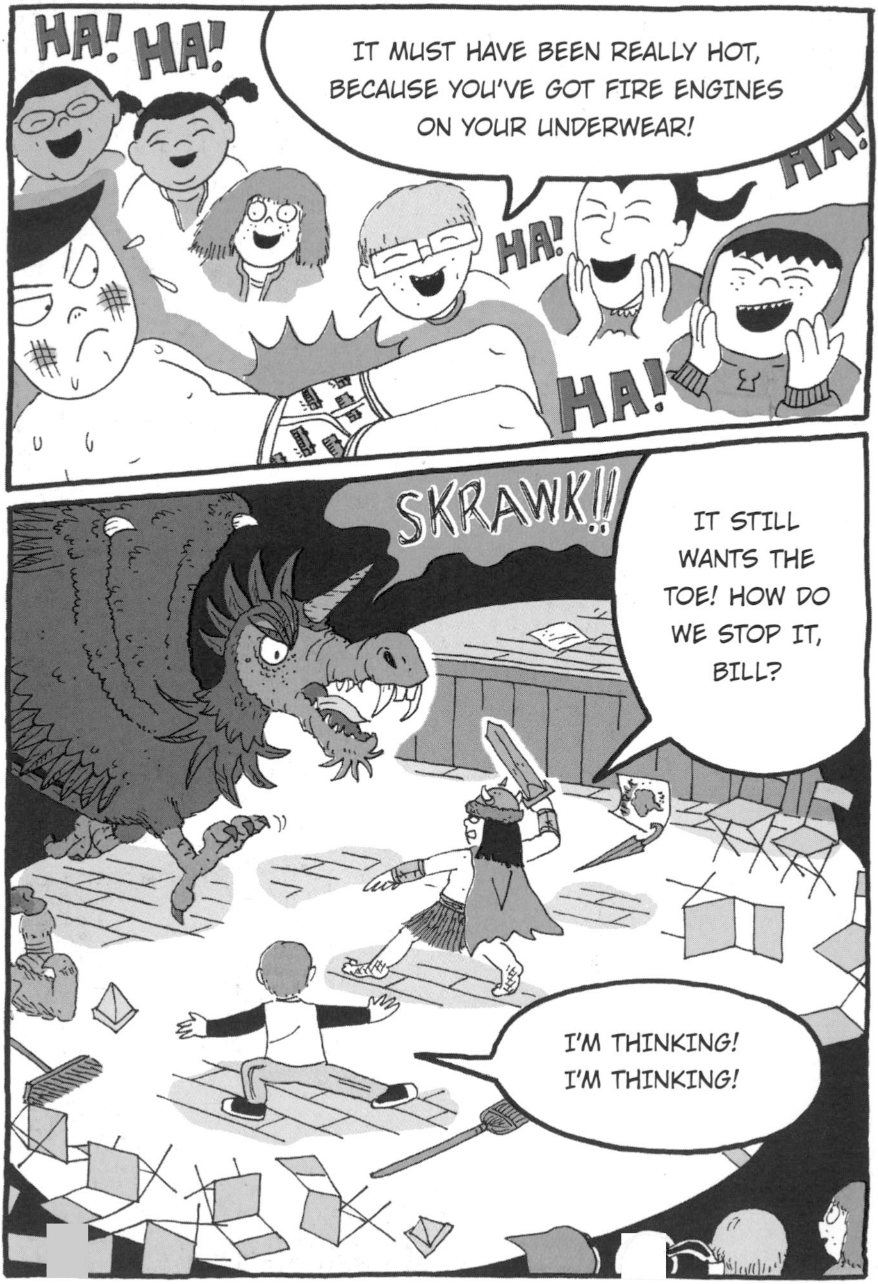
HA! HA!
IT MUST HAVE BEEN REALLY HOT, BECAUSE YOU'VE GOT FIRE ENGINES ON YOUR UNDERWEAR!
HA!
HA!
HA!
SKRAWK!!
IT STILL WANTS THE TOE! HOW DO WE STOP IT, BILL?
I'M THINKING! I'M THINKING!

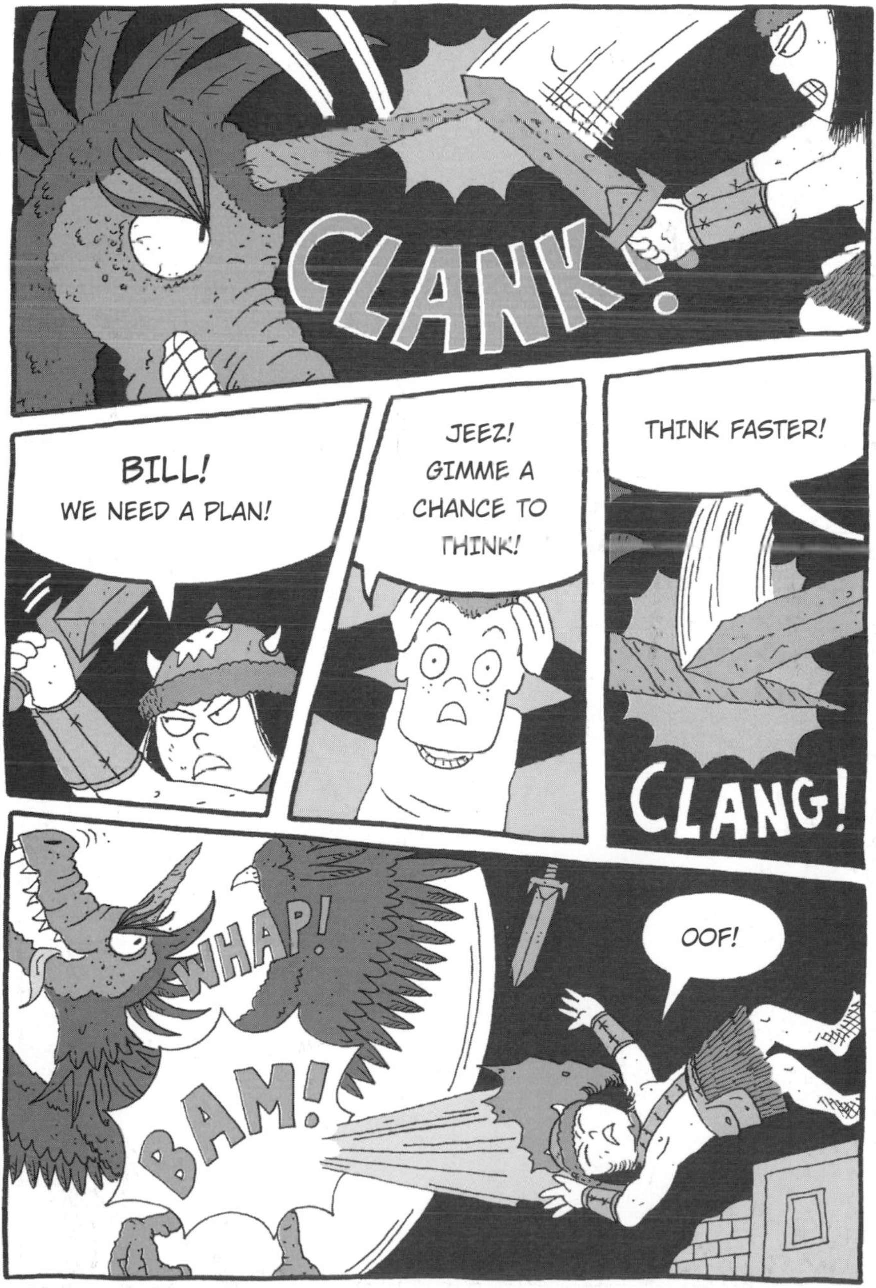
CLANK!
BILL!
WE NEED A PLAN!
JEEZ!
GIMME A
CHANCE TO
THINK!
THINK FASTER!
CLANG!
WHAP!
BAM!
OOF!

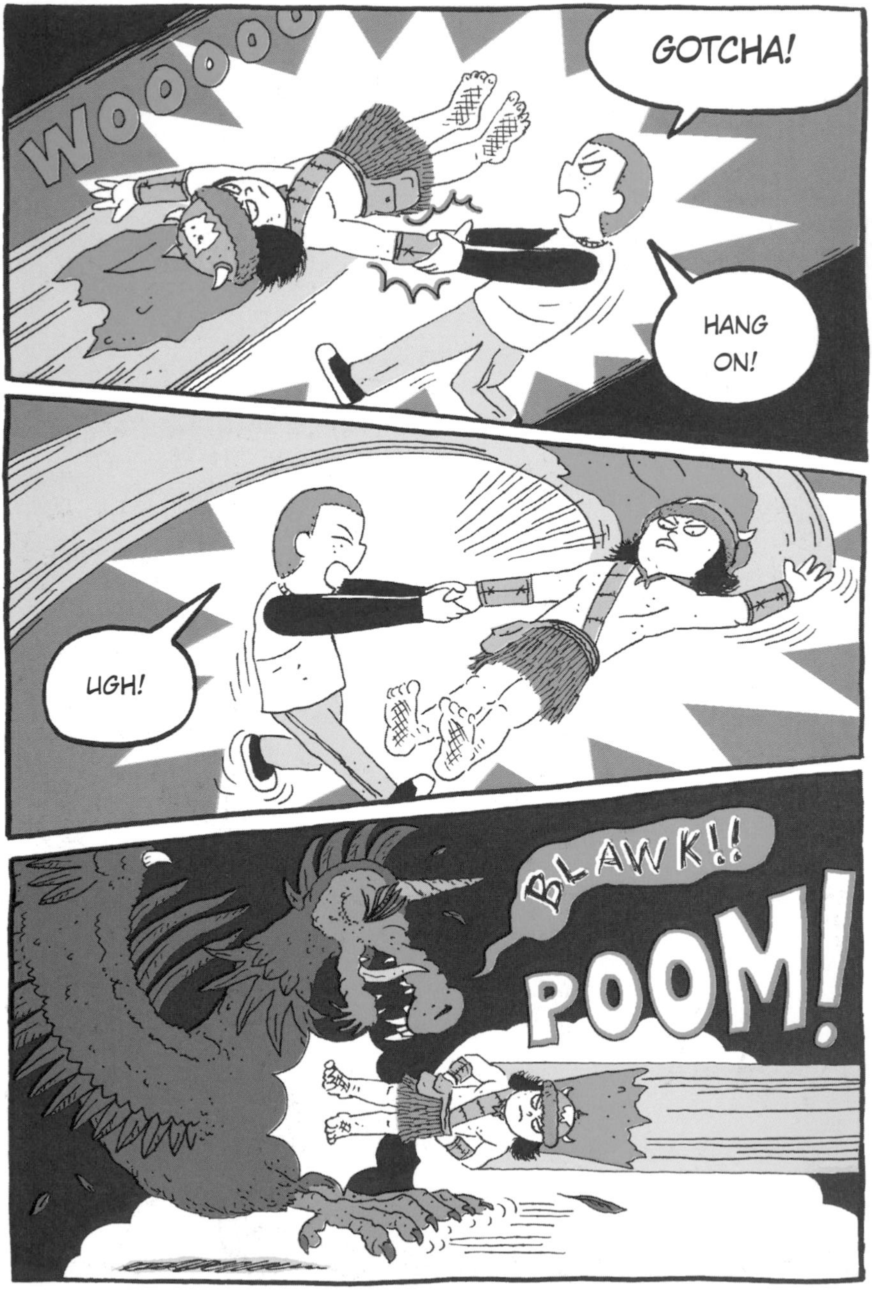
WOOOOO
GOTCHA!
HANG ON!
UGH!
BLAWK!!
POOM!

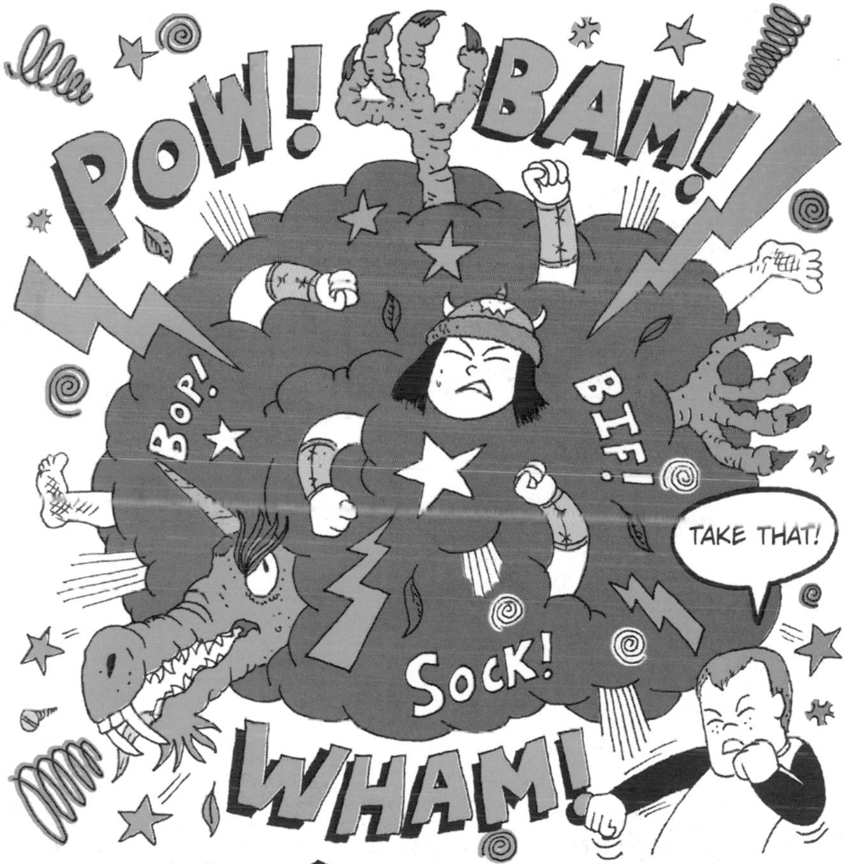
POW!
BAM!
BOP!
BIF!
TAKE THAT!
SOCK!
WHAM!

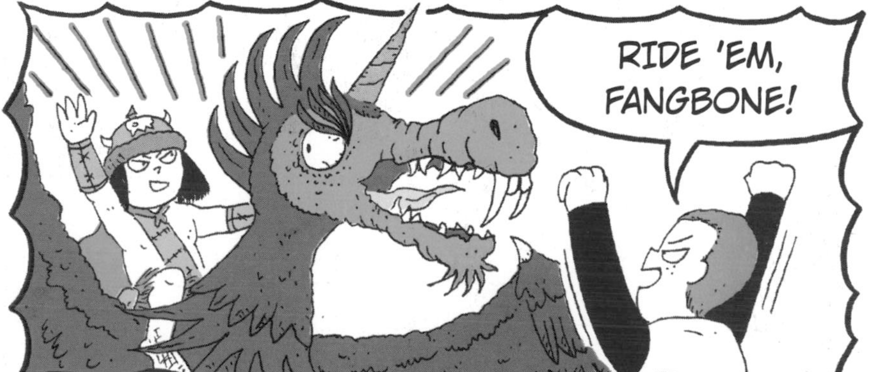
RIDE 'EM,
FANGBONE!

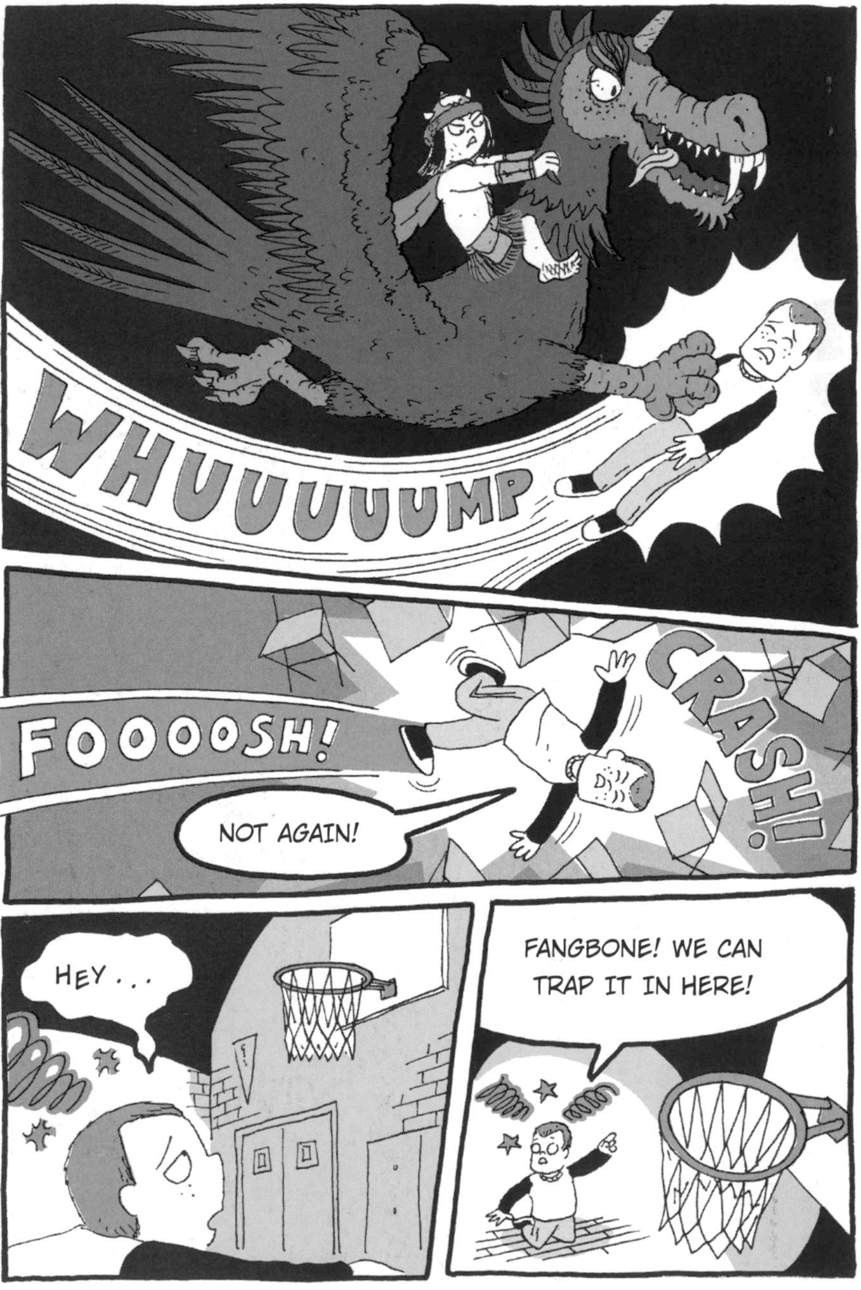
WHUUUUUUMP
FOOOOSH!
CRASH!
NOT AGAIN!
HEY . . .
FANGBONE! WE CAN TRAP IT IN HERE!

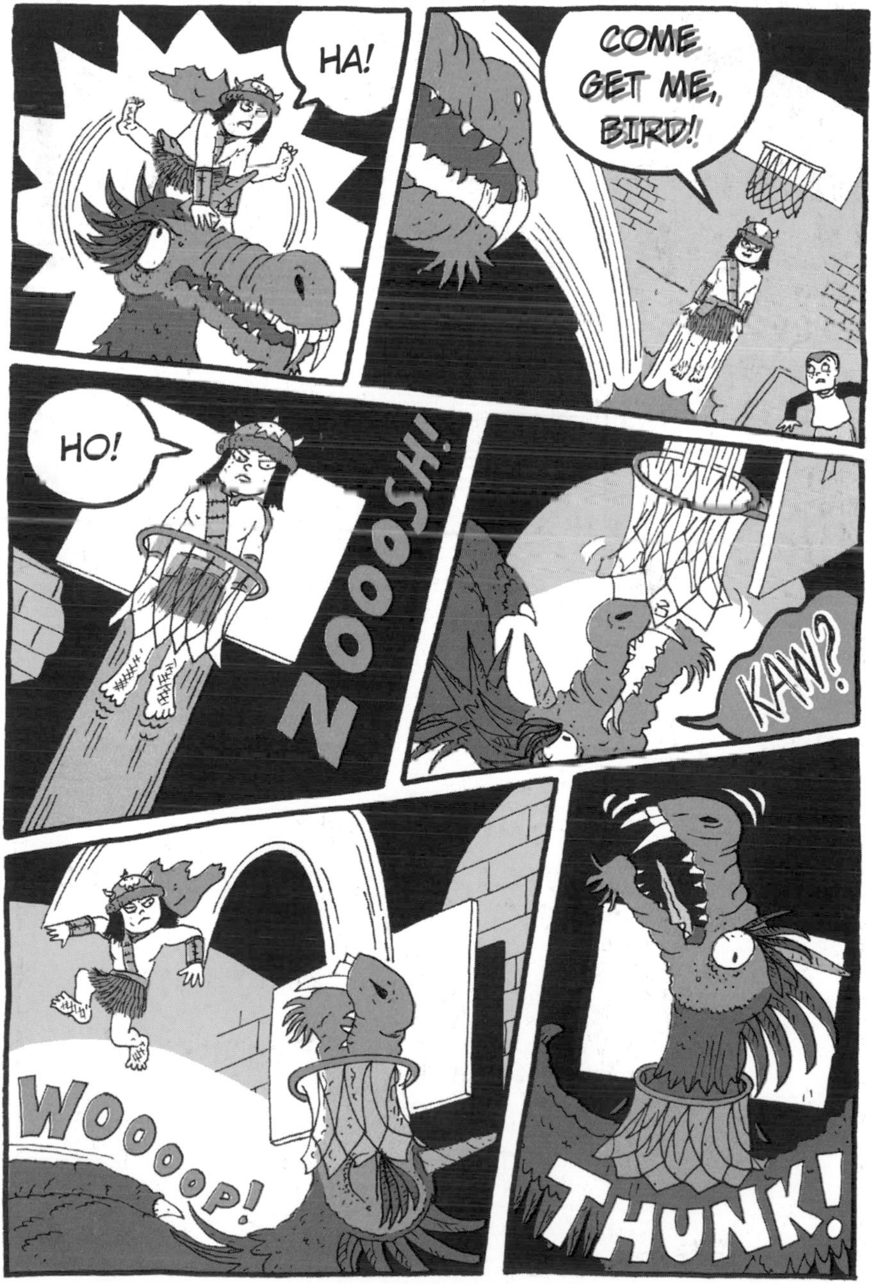
HA!
COME GET ME, BIRD!
HO!
ZOOOOSH!
KAW?
WOOOOOP!
THUNK!

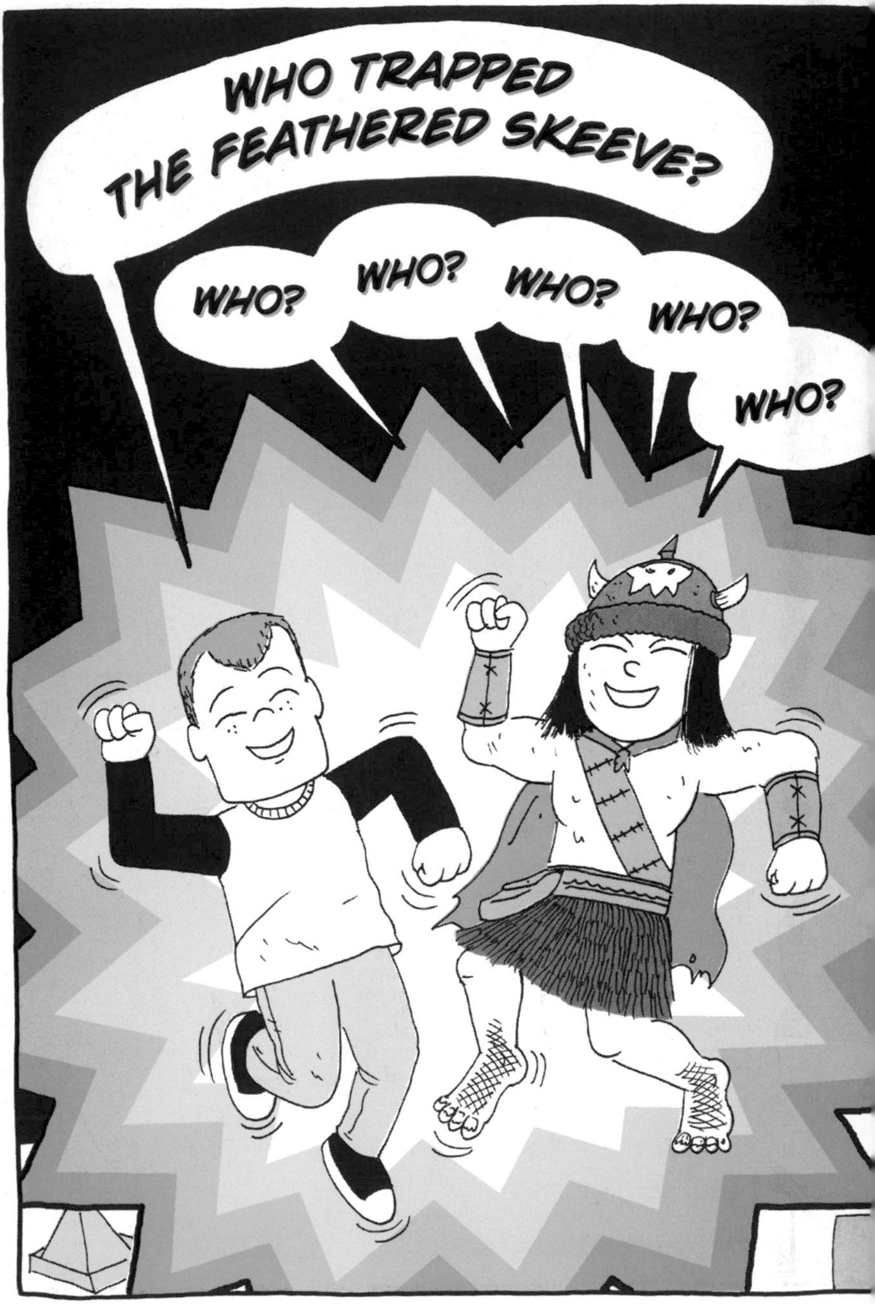
WHO TRAPPED THE FEATHERED SKEEVE?
WHO?
WHO?
WHO?
WHO?
WHO?

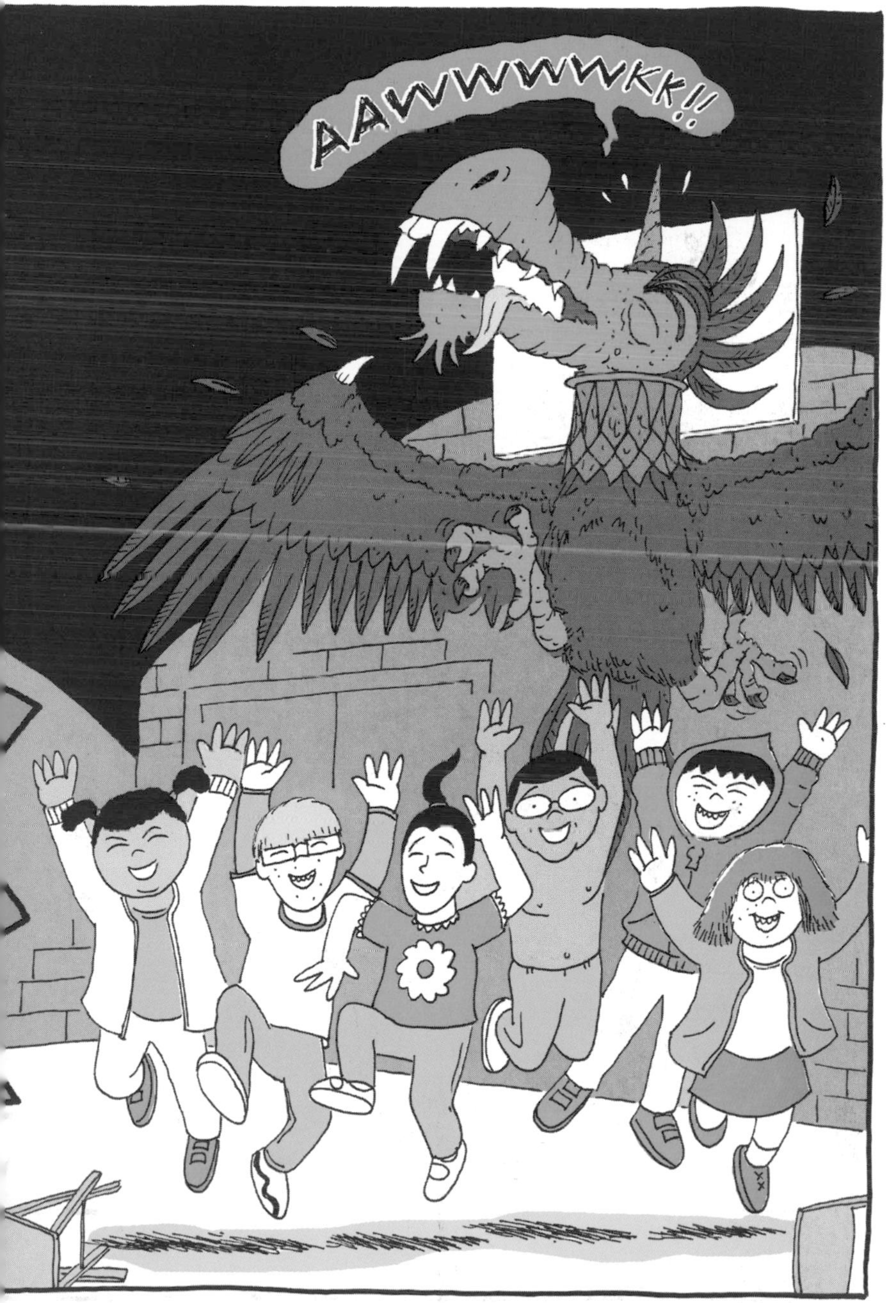
AAWWWWWKK!!

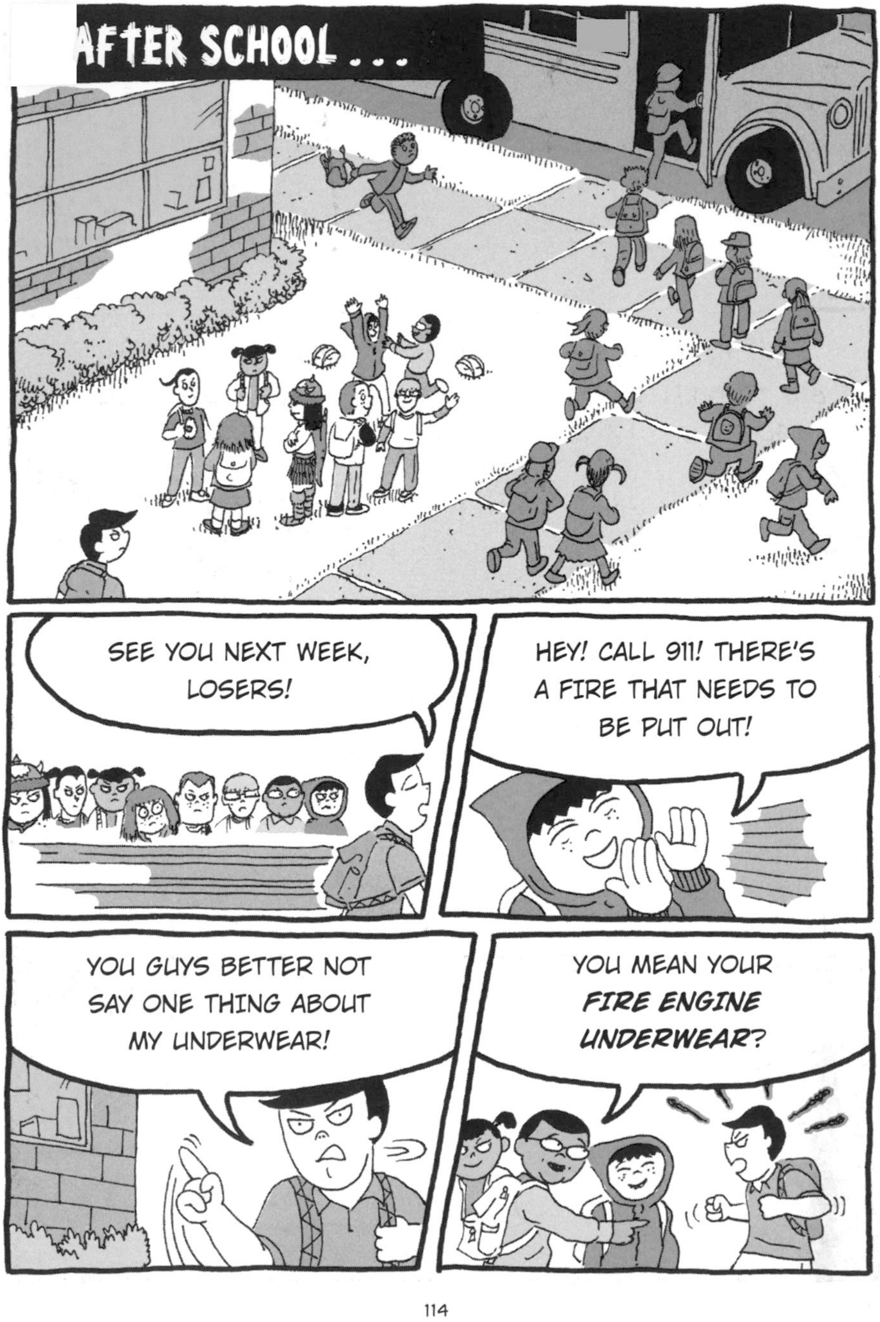
AFTER SCHOOL . . .
SEE YOU NEXT WEEK, LOSERS!
HEY! CALL 911! THERE'S A FIRE THAT NEEDS TO BE PUT OUT!
YOU GUYS BETTER NOT SAY ONE THING ABOUT MY UNDERWEAR!
YOU MEAN YOUR *FIRE ENGINE UNDERWEAR*?

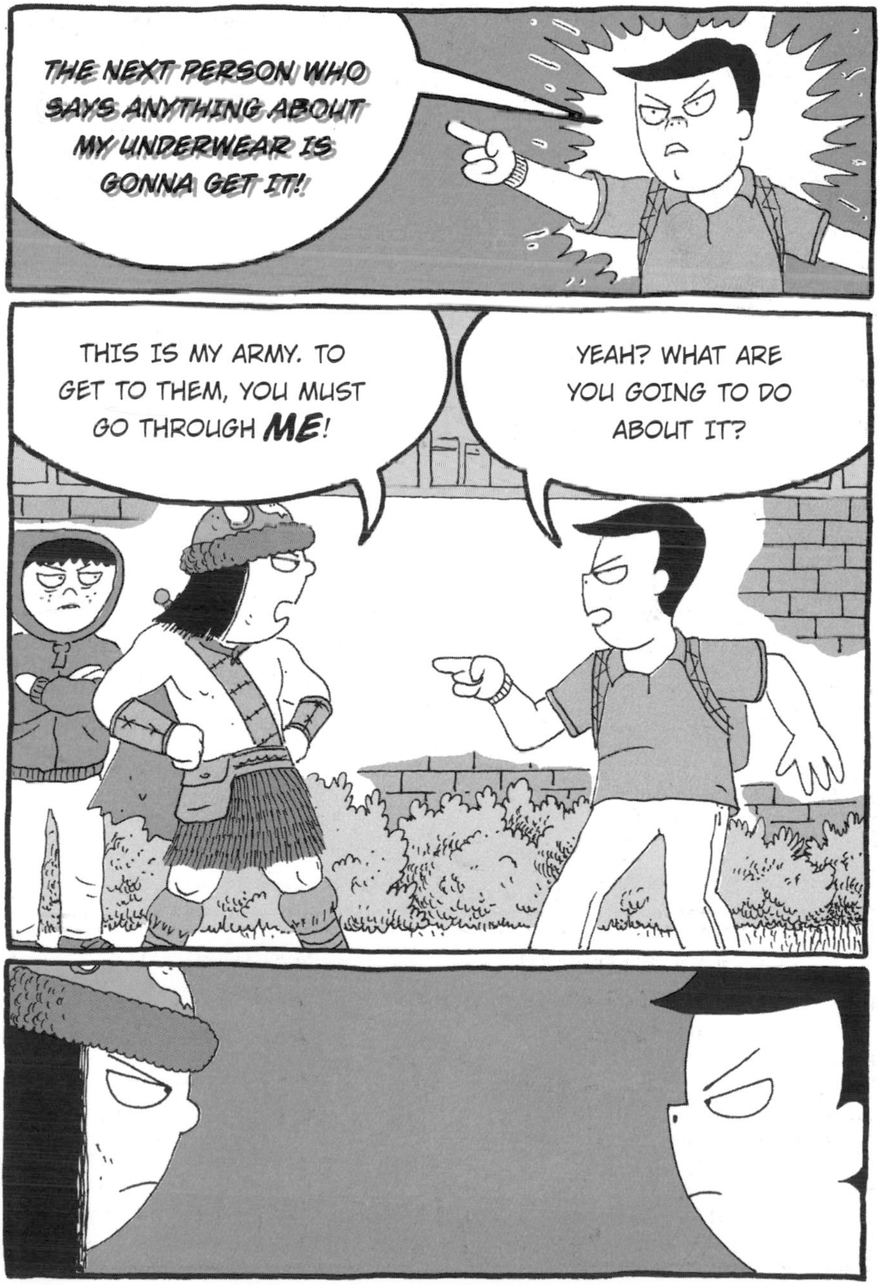
THE NEXT PERSON WHO SAYS ANYTHING ABOUT MY UNDERWEAR IS GONNA GET IT!
THIS IS MY ARMY. TO GET TO THEM, YOU MUST GO THROUGH **ME**!
YEAH? WHAT ARE YOU GOING TO DO ABOUT IT?

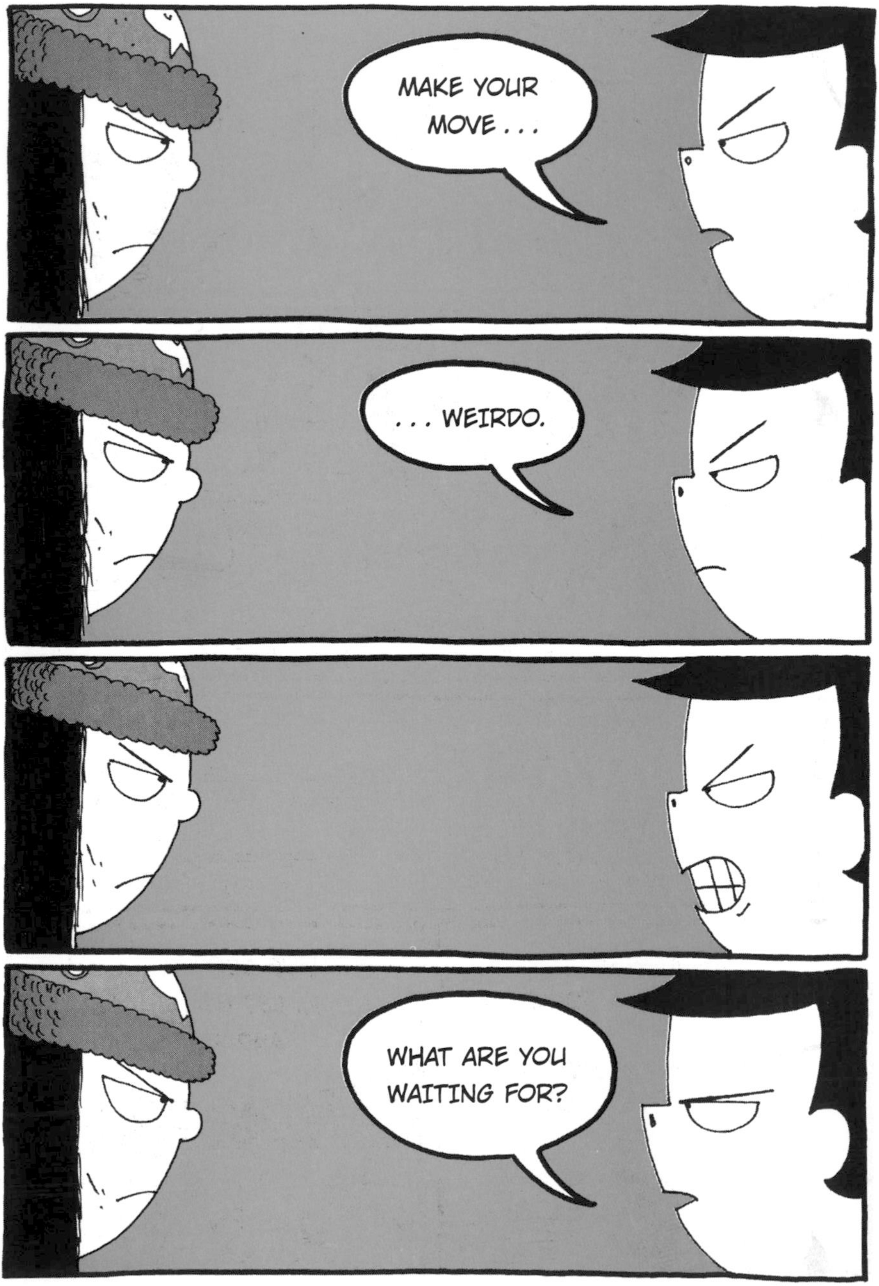
MAKE YOUR
MOVE . . .
. . . WEIRDO.
WHAT ARE YOU
WAITING FOR?

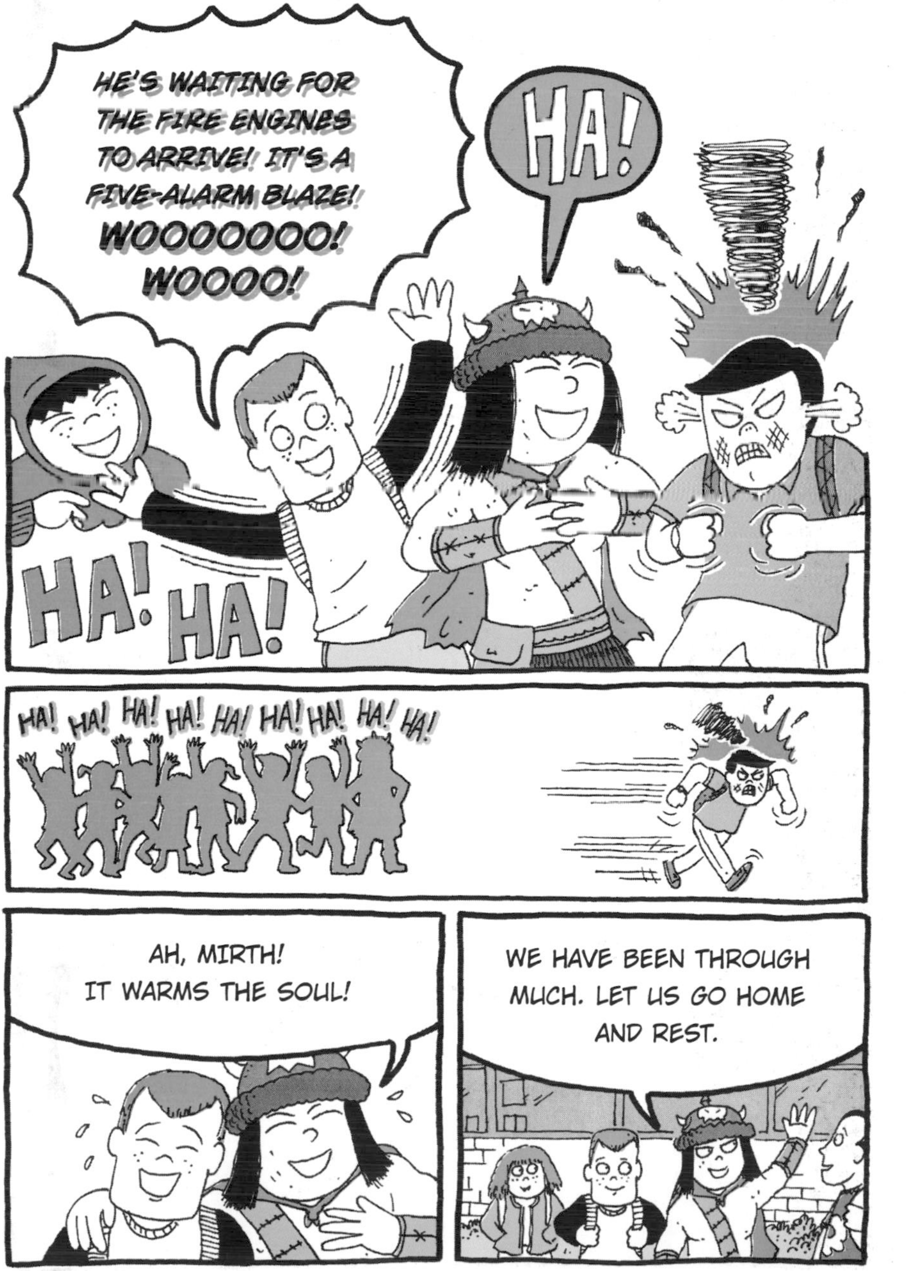
HE'S WAITING FOR THE FIRE ENGINES TO ARRIVE! IT'S A FIVE-ALARM BLAZE! WOOOOOOO! WOOOO!
HA!
HA! HA!
HA! HA! HA! HA! HA! HA! HA! HA! HA!
AH, MIRTH! IT WARMS THE SOUL!
WE HAVE BEEN THROUGH MUCH. LET US GO HOME AND REST.

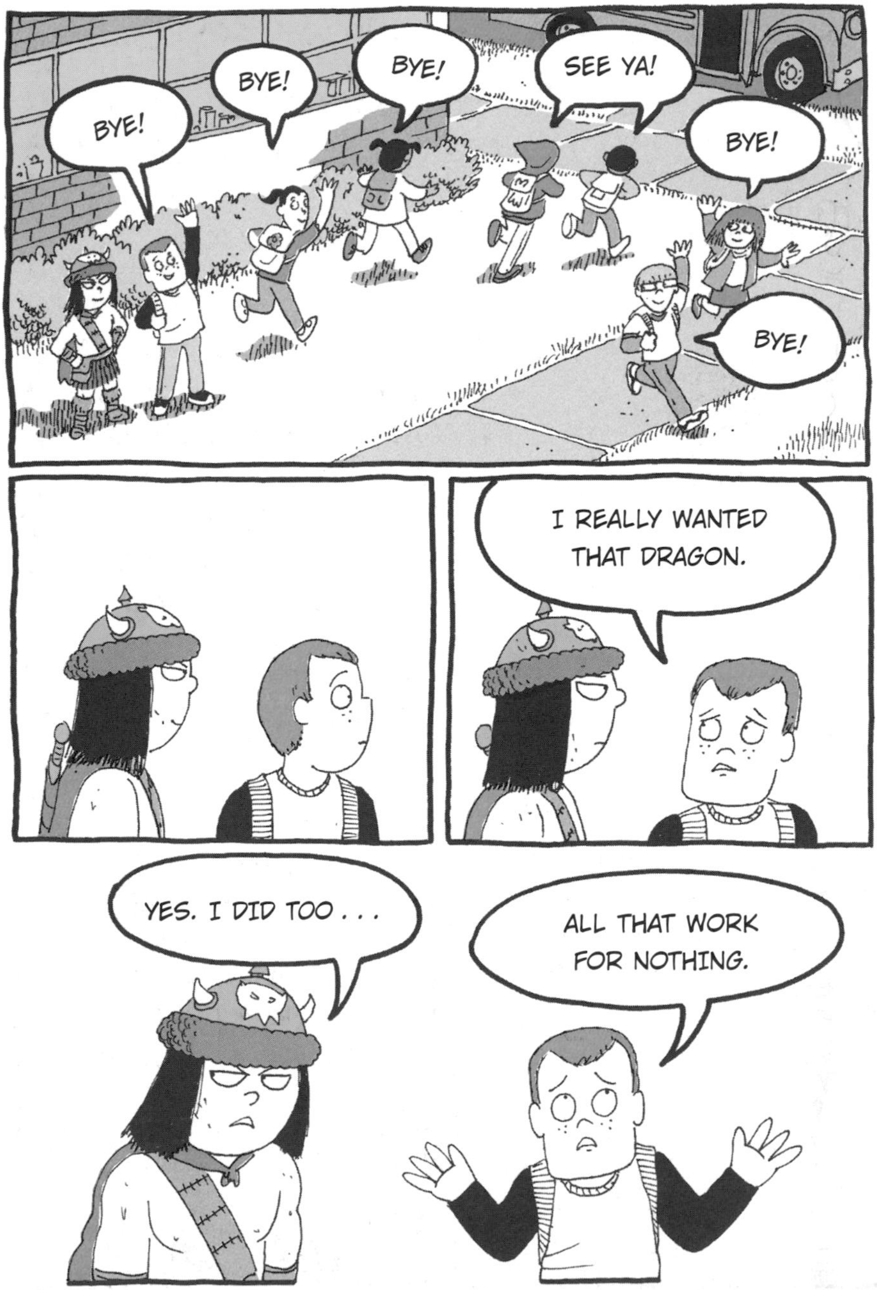
BYE!
BYE!
BYE!
SEE YA!
BYE!
BYE!
I REALLY WANTED THAT DRAGON.
YES. I DID TOO . . .
ALL THAT WORK FOR NOTHING.

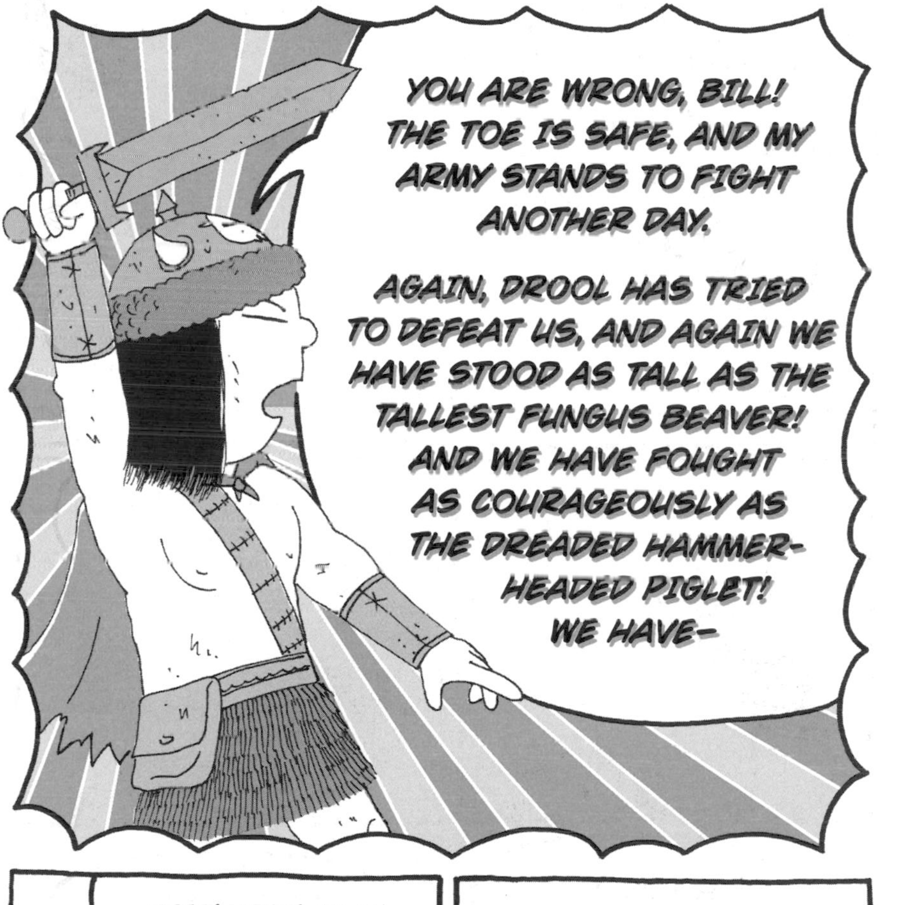
YOU ARE WRONG, BILL! THE TOE IS SAFE, AND MY ARMY STANDS TO FIGHT ANOTHER DAY.
AGAIN, DROOL HAS TRIED TO DEFEAT US, AND AGAIN WE HAVE STOOD AS TALL AS THE TALLEST FUNGUS BEAVER! AND WE HAVE FOUGHT AS COURAGEOUSLY AS THE DREADED HAMMER-HEADED PIGLET! WE HAVE-

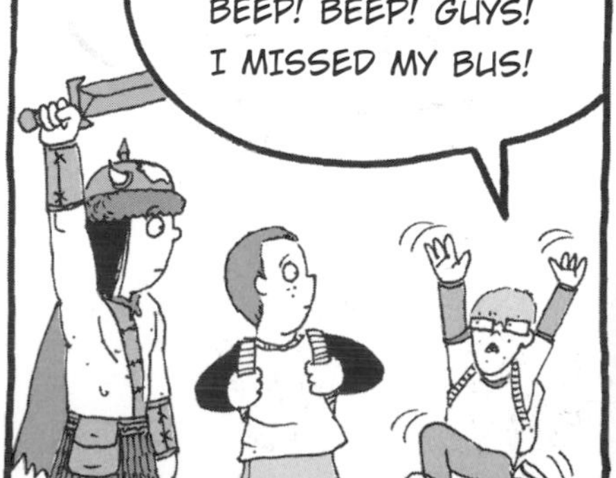
BEEP! BEEP! GUYS! I MISSED MY BUS!

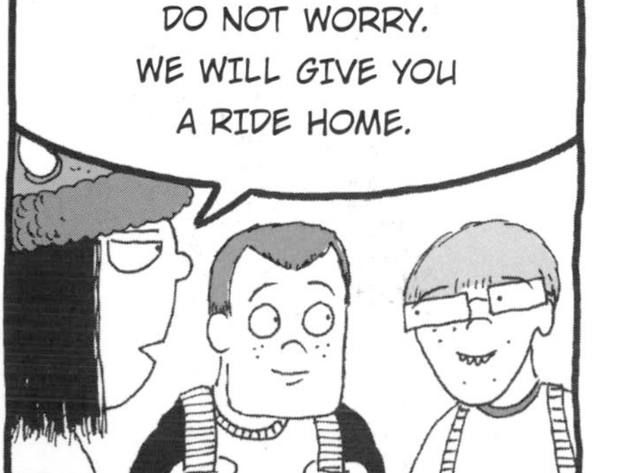
DO NOT WORRY. WE WILL GIVE YOU A RIDE HOME.

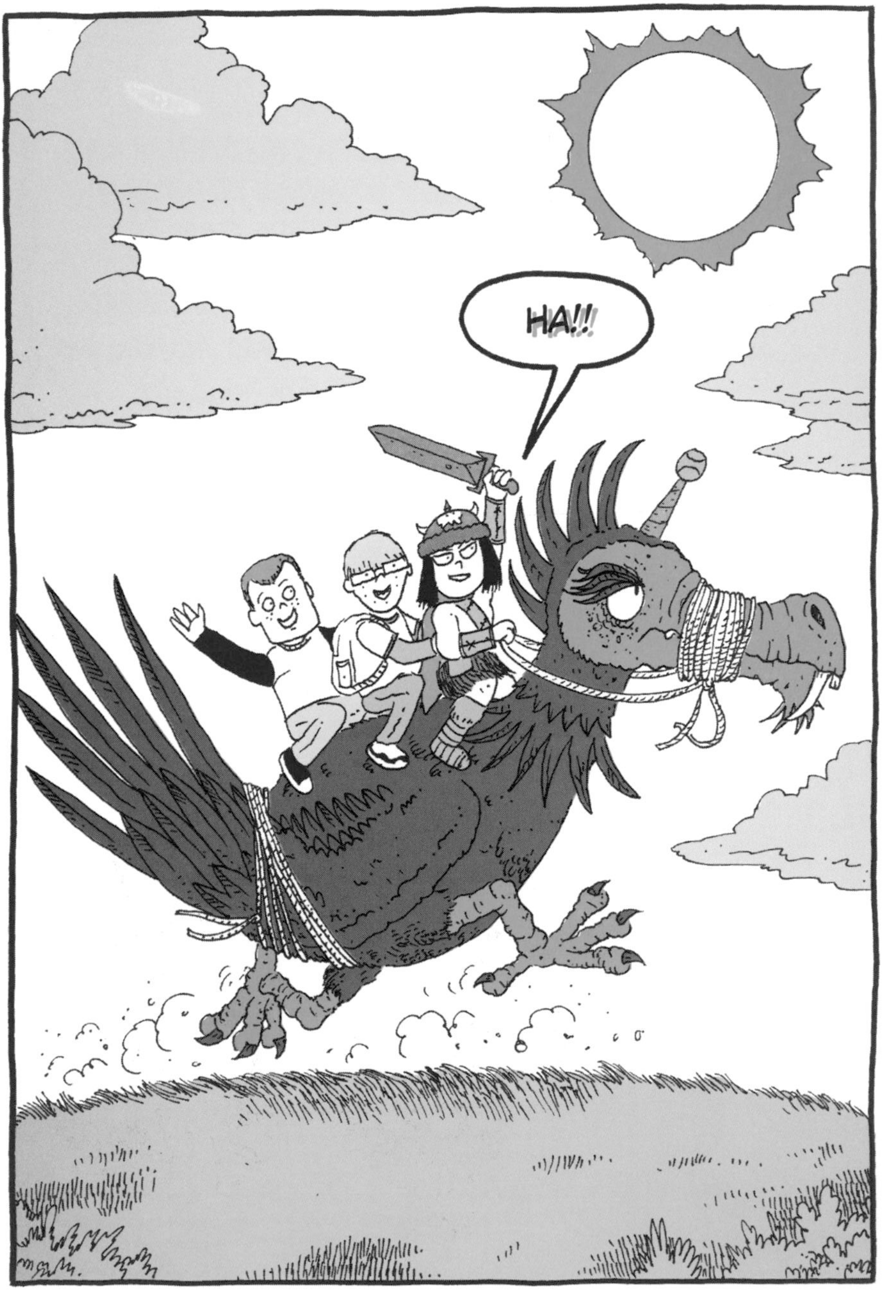
HA!!

THE END

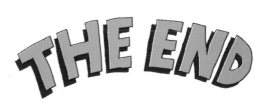

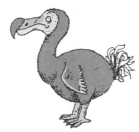

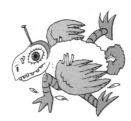

REAL DODO

3G'S DODO

MICHAEL REX IS THE AUTHOR AND
ILLUSTRATOR OF OVER TWENTY BOOKS FOR CHILDREN,
INCLUDING THE **NEW YORK TIMES** #1 BESTSELLER
GOODNIGHT GOON. MICHAEL HAS A MASTER'S DEGREE IN
VISUAL ARTS EDUCATION (K-12), AND WORKED AS A NEW
YORK CITY ART TEACHER FOR FOUR YEARS. HE VISITS
SCHOOLS ACROSS THE COUNTRY, AND HAS APPEARED ON
THE CELEBRITY APPRENTICE AS A GUEST ILLUSTRATOR.

MIKE LIVES IN THE BRONX WITH HIS WIFE AND THEIR
TWO BOYS.

BRACE YOURSELF FOR BOOK THREE OF
FANGBONE!
THIRD-GRADE BARBARIAN . . .

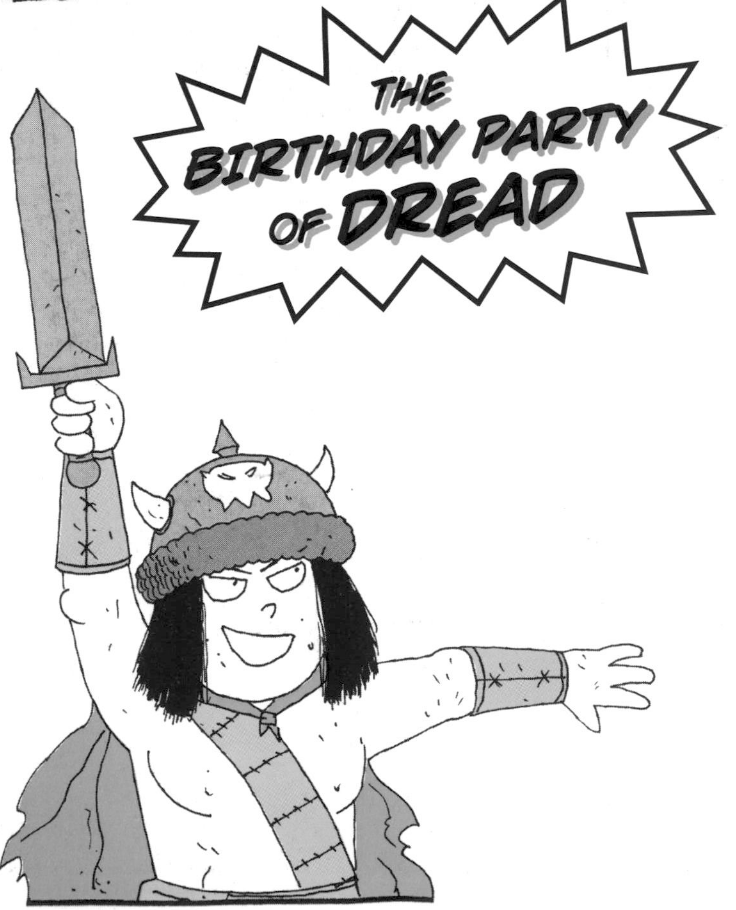
THE BIRTHDAY PARTY OF DREAD